GLITTER

Clydean O'Conner

Jacket Design by David Sadleir

Library of Congress - United States Copyright Office

DEDICATION

I retired from the casino industry after forty years of working for some of
the most power players responsible for the transition of Las Vegas from the
mob to Corporate America—the new mob. This is not a traditional thank
you to editors, publishers, and family members. Instead, I am grateful to all
the black-hearted pirates who rule the casino industry with an iron fist.
They provided enough material for fifty books.

ACKNOWLEDGEMENTS

This book would not have been possible without the help of friends and family members who came to my aid when I needed it most: Rachel Korfman, Julianna Russo-Tryde, David Sadleir, Mark and Sue Potes, Cheryl O'Gara and Jeffery Bissel, and a Rottweiler named Anubis who sat by my side and assured coffee was waiting in the kitchen.

PROLOGUE

A plume of oily black smoke spread an ugly stain across the cloudless sky over Las Vegas. A scream of protesting tires cleaved the air as they sought traction against asphalt turned soft by a blistering sun as three yellow fire trucks raced through the parking lot of Caesar's Palace. Guests are roused from their beds by uniformed security guards, who underwent hours of intensive training for just such an emergency: *fire*, the dreaded foe of all hotels.

Grainy eyed men and women, in various nightclothes, are ousted from their suites and herded onto a safe area in the parking lot—away from the high-rise tower and potential of an explosion which might rain shards of glass on the soft, coddled bodies of international high-stakes gamblers.

Racing away from the big yellow trucks, firemen assaulted the building still lit with hundreds of lights which gave off a soft glow. Ventilators strapped to their backs made an eerie, alien sound as firemen drew deep breaths of clean, life-giving oxygen. Captain Murphy, identified by the name stenciled on the back of his heavy rubber jacket, gave the thumbs up signal and a specialty unit entered the Fantasy Tower on the run; each man knew the marble statues of Roman gods and goddesses surrounding the entrance might end up as lavish embellishments on their final place of rest.

Frantic, a stocky hotel manager directed firemen toward the flight of stairs which would take the high-rise team to the "Rainman" suite, currently occupied by a high roller from Taiwan. When motioned to remain in the opulent lobby the relief filling the manager's face was almost comic to Captain Murphy and his boys.

Mounting fire escape stairs two and three at a time, fire-fighters checked ascending hallways for traces of smoke and tell-tale fingers of heat. Finally reaching the penthouse floor, the team fanned out across the stairwell, grateful for a chance to catch their breath and marshal the courage it would take to fight a raging fire. The Captain ran a probing hand along the surface of a metal door, which separated the fire escape stairs from the landing dedicated exclusively to the suite. Years of experience combating fires in mega hotels which hugged the Las Vegas Strip, like palm trees in a desert oasis, revealed old man fire did not occupy the hallway decorated with expensive cherry wood tables, plush carpet surrounded by deep green Carrera marble and original oil paintings in gilded frames. Halfway down the lavish hall, black, ugly smoke billowed from beneath the door of the suite made famous by Tom Cruise and Dustin Hoffman in the movie 'Rainman'. Dense, dark clouds sent obscuring streamers of smoke in every direction.

"Hose!" Murphy screamed into the two-way radio clutched in the trembling fingers of his gloved hand. "No one goes in that room without water!"

In a voice thick with emotion, the newest member of the unit croaked, "Jesus, Murf, what if those hi-rollers are in there?"

Previous duels with just such a killing fire tempered the Captain's iron determination. "Then they're already dead--and we've got a fire to kill before it takes the whole God-damned building!"

Vaulting the stairs, another fireman unrolled the hose coiled over his shoulder with the speed and accuracy developed during countless hours of training.

"Now!" The Captain shouted the command to send water coursing through the hose at his feet. Brass and oak double doors leading into the suite gave way under the impact of thousands of pounds of water pressure. Murphy was prepared for smoke and fire; he already had the plastic shield lowered over his face; the oxygen tank on his back filled his lungs with purified air. He'd been a battalion chief a long time and he braced himself against the blast which always came when fire discovered a new source of oxygen. But he wasn't prepared for the wall of flame which devoured thick carpet saturated with a flame-retardant chemical before it was installed in the luxurious casino.

The sight which met his eyes defied years of training. The water wasn't quenching the fire--it seemed to be feeding it! New, fresh flames leaped to consume the suite of rooms expensive enough to feed an entire third-world country as the hose shot water across the threshold. Murphy grabbed the hose away from the new man on his team and battled his way inside the room

CHAPTER ONE

Detective Danny Armstrong squatted on his haunches, fingering the residue which once was a mattress in an expensive circular bed--now turned to charcoal by the fire which obliterated the most exclusive suite in Caesar's Palace. Smoke streaked what was left of the blown-out glass bubble above the Jacuzzi overlooking a fountain lined entrance . . . which led curious tourists and high rollers from across the globe into the exotic world of gaming. Vegas took on an entirely different personality once the sun came up and the thousands of lights gave way to day light. A casual observer might be duped into believing it was like any other resort destination.

The raw, harsh sound of a body bag being zipped shut made Danny turn his head. One of the ambulance attendants was having a tough time suppressing an urge to vomit as he loaded charred remains on an awaiting gurney.

"Hooker, don't ya' think, Danny?" Words sort of eased through the snap, crackle and pop of gum being chewed unmercifully by the coroner's assistant, Jeff Cloudwalker. A Navajo by birth, Jeff was educated at a Seventh Day Adventist school on the reservation near Mexican Hat, Utah. Danny knew the harder Jeff worked his gum the more nervous he was.

"In Vegas?" A sardonic grin cut a wide swath through a young man's handsome features. Six feet two in his stocking feet, Detective Danny Armstrong was the kind of guy mothers dreamed of for their daughters. Tall and blond, he had a build which announced he spent time working out his frustrations with life in a gym instead of hoisting one tall cool one after another at some cheap topless bar a few blocks off the Strip, like a lot of other cops. Danny was lucky enough to possess a strong jaw line and a prominent slab of bone above his eyes--rugged good looks, yet boyishly charming, left no doubt about his natural masculinity. If he let his hair get a little long in back, it curled along the top of his collar. But curly hair, charm and good looks just got in a detective's way. Danny discovered this quickly after he got promoted. Better to have the kind of face people

1

never remembered—so you could slip in and out of bars, eavesdrop on other people's conversations, hang out in casinos a little too long and no one was ever the wiser.

Jeff's jaws worked his gum like a Sumo wrestler having trouble with an opponent. "Don't be a wise ass--Captain at 9 o'clock."

The Captain glanced around a once glamorous suite, now reduced to wet, black cinders. "Any make on the woman?" His scowl was as dark and foreboding as the room.

"None yet, Captain. It'll probably be up to Jeff and his mad scientist master to make a positive ID--there wasn't much left of her." Danny turned to stare through the shattered Plexiglas bubble which provided an incredible view of the Strip from the suite's marble Jacuzzi, now stained a dull, myopic shade of gray by smoke and ash. Brilliant sunshine streamed into the 'Rainman' suite set against a backdrop of scintillate blue, which seemed totally inconsistent with the interior of a now somber room.

Cloudwalker followed the direction of Detective Danny Armstrong's gaze, then his eyes traveled slowly to his friend's preoccupied expression. He'd seen this look before--it meant Danny was grappling with one of the philosophical issues which plagued mankind.

"Sort of like life, wouldn't you say, Captain?" Danny asked.

The Captain stripped off thin latex gloves with a resounding snap and threw them against what used to be an expensive teak dresser inlaid with wedges of mother-of-pearl. "What is?"

Cloudwalker rolled his eyes toward the sagging ceiling destroyed by water and fire. The Captain wasn't a spiritual man, he'd spent his whole life dealing with rape, murder, and the cast-offs of society. He had difficulty traversing the labyrinth of Danny's philosophical land mines.

"Out there," Danny's finger pointed at the sky beyond blackened glass, "everything's all sunshine and palm trees and well-tended roses. There's not a single scrap of paper littering the Strip. The lawn looks like it gets manicured every morning, fountains sparkle--you'd never know this was the desert if it wasn't so hot! On the surface, these hotels portray a perfection that's surrealistic--they're too flawless. What goes on inside causes people to get burned up! Like life--a lot of people spend all their time cultivating the outside and never stop to consider what's going on inside."

2

Brass clips, which held the coroner's medical bag shut, clacked loudly as Cloudwalker slammed the sides together. "Armstrong, you remind me of my grandfather. He sits in front of his hogan and rambles on for hours. Weird stuff. Like the earth being our mother and the trees and rivers our brothers and sisters." An involuntary shudder tracked the length of Jeff's spine. "That old man gives me the creeps sometimes."

"Sounds like a man I'd like to meet." Danny's eyes roved the blistered spiral staircase, scorched marble which housed the suite's private Jacuzzi and what was left of an elegant crystal chandelier, seeking something he'd over- looked, searching every crack and crevice, pursuing, penetrating--wondering. "He lives a day's ride out of Chinle. Right in the heart of the Navajo nation. You ever been on horseback, Danny?"

"A couple of times."

Jeff watched the detective from the corner of his eye. Although a curtain of cinders clung to his pants cuff, and the shine on his shoes was dimmed by a veil of fine gray ash, Danny Armstrong still looked like he'd be more at home in the board room of the Mirage than on a horse in Canyon de Chelly.

"You should respect people, Jeff, even if you don't understand what drives them." Danny continued to stare out the shattered Plexiglas bubble at the bright sunlit day.

"My grandfather can't even read and trying to explain how a computer works is impossible!" The shame he felt at his grandfather's technological ignorance stole across his wide round face.

"I'll bet he knows a lot more than you give him credit for, Jeff. You've got to respect your family and love them for their peculiarities. All we ever really have in life is our family. You've got to admit my Mom is weird, but she's earned a lot of respect over the years."

Captain Murphy's face leached of color; he'd dealt with Catherine Armstrong many times over the course of his thirty-year career at Metro. She was a driving force. Like a hurricane. Or a tornado. Catherine had a habit of sweeping into a situation, blowing down the status quo, then vanishing like a mist, leaving by-standers questioning their grip on reality! How on earth Detective Danny Armstrong developed along normal lines was one of the wonders of the modern world. Must've been the influence of television, the captain thought. He probably grew up watching Leave It To Beaver, The Donna Reed Show and Father Knows Best to have a grip on the real world even if it did seem a little tenuous at times. The Captain shot the Indian kid a warning glance.

Jeff knew the Captain well enough to realize he shouldn't provoke him, but his curiosity was tweaked. Curiosity about the white man's world got him out of Chinle, away from the deep cleft of sandstone which had been his family's home long before Cortez ravished the Southwest. Curiosity led him to forensics as certainly as a waiting lover. Curiosity held him in its vice-like grip just as surely as the ferocious traps his grandfather set to ward off marauding coyotes in spring, when lambs and kids were still vulnerable. He'd heard stories about the indomitable Catherine Armstrong, queen of the red- hand artists who pandered so-called psychic talents--like tarot card reading, palmistry and other Voodoo nonsense his grandfather believed in--to the weak and defenseless. And yet, Jeff had no way to explain the mysterious methods Catherine used to solve murders, robberies and other crimes of violence which failed to yield to traditional methods of police investigation. But solve them she did, time and time again. And the product of her unorthodox upbringing was turning out to be a brilliant detective. "You mean Catherine The Great? Hell, I'd love to meet the old broad!" An embarrassed silence fell like the final curtain on a play as Jeff realized he'd used the term he frequently heard bandied about the station house.

Danny snorted with amusement. "She's one hell of an old broad-- I'll gladly give you that!"

Phones were ringing off the hook. Janet, the beleaguered department secretary, rolled her eyes at Danny as he passed. She gripped the phone like she wished it were the caller's neck and her tone of voice conveyed irritation. "No, we cannot give out the identity at this time. We must notify immediate relatives before any information is released to the public. Of all the gall . . ." she spat at the phone as she slammed the receiver back into its restraining cradle.

"Get used to it, Jan," Danny said, a shy smile matched the concern in his eyes. "This story's so big press hounds are going to be dogging us day and night until the judge brings the gavel down on the murderer."

"Jeff's sure about the ID?"

"Yeah, 'fraid so. There was enough of a fingerprint left to match it with her Sheriff's Card. We tracked down her dentist through the Health and Welfare records over at the Culinary Union."

4

"Jesus, Danny, who'd want to kill the most beautiful show girl in Las Vegas?"

"I don't know, Jan, but I'm going to find out."

The phone rang a shrill alarm and Jan jumped, her thoughts about the murdered girl were so engrossing the business at hand was temporarily forgotten. "Danny," she threw the detective a warning glance, "it's the Governor."

"Jesus, Mary, Joseph--it's already started! I've got a bad feeling about this case." Danny straightened the knot in his tie as he reached to take the phone from the detective division secretary's outstretched hand.

"Hey, Ma! You home?" Danny and Cloudwalker entered the back door which opened into the kitchen.

The smell of freshly baked chocolate chip cookies hit Jeff like a fist. "She knew I was planning to stop by today."

From the backyard, the house looked like any another middle-class residence. The lawn was trimmed, flowers were pruned with loving care and the fence which protected the neighborhood from Catherine's monstrous Rottweiler boasted a fresh coat of pearl gray paint.

The front of the house, however, faced Charleston Boulevard. Black macadam was laid down to accommodate cars which waited while their owner's hoped Catherine The Great could give them a clue as to what the future held in store. The part of the stucco house facing the busy thoroughfare was painted a muted shade of violet. Gingerbread shutters framed alarmed windows in white, and Victorian cupolas, situated beneath sheltering branches of enormous Cottonwood trees, stood at oblique angles to the rest of the structure. The place had an appealing ambience--despite the neon hand on the curb which promised to reveal the mysteries of past, present, and future.

"Hey, Ma! I brought a friend." Danny helped himself to a hand full of cookies and passed the plate to Jeff, whose mouth watered.

"There's milk in the fridge." A haunting, melodious voice called out from the shadowy depths of another room.

Danny opened the refrigerator. "Where's the beast?" He turned at the sound of a strangled gasp which clawed its way up Jeff Cloudwalker's throat as a dog nearly as wide as the doorway marched into the room, dragging his paws along the tile.

The swaggering, dominating gait so characteristic of Rottweilers frightened Jeff and he wasn't afraid to admit it. A head as big and square as a black bear moved slowly from side to side as the dog surveyed the kitchen and its occupants. A line of saliva pooled and thickened at the corner of jaws so powerful they could pulverize bone. The advance on Cloudwalker was deliberate, premeditated. Slowly, his head down, massive shoulders swinging, the Rott traversed the floor. Jeff had no place to go. He was pressed into the corner, where the cabinets met; even if he jumped up on the countertop, it was an easy distance for such a big dog to follow.

Unperturbed, Danny retrieved two glasses from the cupboard and prepared to fill them with cold milk. "He wants your cookie."

Jeff willingly tossed it onto the floor--the cookie disappeared, and the head swung up again--eyes surveying, nose searching.

"Damascus! Leave Danny's friend alone!"

Jeff's eyes flew to an attractive woman in the doorway; his jaw dropped before he had the decency to cover his surprise. This must be the old broad's younger sister!

"Danny, for God's sake, why do you let Damascus intimidate all your friends?" Pale blue eyes swung toward Jeff, who was still pressed against the cupboards. She extended a lean, tanned hand in greeting. "Hi, I'm Catherine Armstrong, Danny's mother."

"It's his job, Ma. That's what your dog does best."

Catherine pulled several pieces of paper towel from a holder mounted beneath the cupboard and proceeded to wipe the accumulation of drool and cookie off the Rott's face. Like an unwilling child, the huge animal twisted and turned and chuffed with annoyance, but Catherine held his choke chain tight in one hand while she continued to clean his mouth with the other.

"Jesus, Ma, you treat that dog like a kid."

"I know, but if you'd get married and have children maybe I wouldn't have to . . . "

"Don't start, Ma!"

6

Her blue eyes sparkled; Jeff could never remember seeing a look of such unabashed adoration when Catherine passed the plate of cookies to her son.

"Hope springs eternal, dear."

Jeff recovered enough from his astonishment to study what, for all intents and purposes, appeared to be a completely normal, middle-aged woman. Barefoot, dressed in shorts and a tank top, Catherine was still shapely. Fresh from the shower, blond hair rested against her shoulders, pushed back from her face by a wide hair band. She wasn't what he expected at all!

As if divining his thoughts, Catherine turned her formidable powers of attention on Jeff. "I'll bet you thought a psychic would wave a magic wand rather than push a mower to cut the grass?"

Unable to suppress the amazement dominating his expression, Jeff acknowledged that was what he'd been thinking! "Ah, well, ah--you're not exactly what I thought I'd find."

"A lot of people tell me that. Professionally, you have to play a certain role."

When Jeff first encountered the psychic at the scene of a crime Catherine was called in on, she'd been wearing a black jump-suit, with her hair all wrapped up in a paisley turban. Enormous dark glasses hid most of her face. He was shocked when he found out the mysterious woman police turned to when all other means of technology failed was also the mother of the best homicide detective on the force!

"Have another cookie, Jeff." The tinkling voice cascaded through the sunny kitchen. "I'll make Damascus behave."

As if chastised for begging, the Rott laid his head on the floor, but his eyes continued to follow the movement of Jeff's hand from the cookie plate to his mouth and back again. A pool of saliva soon appeared beneath the dog's thick lips.

"What's up, honey?" Catherine shifted the focus of her gaze to her son again.

Danny stuffed the remainder of a cookie in his mouth, reached into his pocket and withdrew a badly tarnished bangle bracelet--a thin gold band with a row of diamonds set into a slotted channel. "I want you to read this for me."

Catherine didn't bother to examine the proffered bracelet. She pulled a chair away from the table and sat down in the bay window which created a cozy eating alcove in the kitchen. "Why don't you two get comfortable?" Leaning back, she closed her eyes and rolled the bracelet between her hands. Cocking her head as though listening to some internal voice, Catherine's face assumed an expression of struggle. "I don't like this. Hot--fire. Burning--flames are everywhere."

Jeff inched closer, fascinated by the obvious conflict in the psychic's emotions. The Rott rose to his feet, inserting his muscled body into the space in front of Catherine--just enough to warn Jeff not to move any closer.

With a furious flutter, Catherine opened her eyes. "Danny, this doesn't make sense."

"Mom," his tone was sensitive, soothing, "just tell me what you received. Sometimes things are clearer to me because I'm familiar with the case."

"I saw a brilliant, glittering light--then a dark, obeisant cloud eclipsed it. The two are related . . . somehow. Suddenly, the phrase came to mind, 'all that glitters is not gold'."

Jeff felt as though the deep brown eyes that were so much a part of his Indian heritage were going to burst from their sockets. "You told her, right?"

Ignoring his friend, Danny prodded Catherine to continue. "The light was bright?"

"Yes, on the surface everything is bright and sunny--but something ugly lurks just behind. You're dealing with a facade. Something ominous is behind the light. Danny, things are not what they seem to be. Don't be deceived."

"Keep digging?"

"Deep. Very, very deep. This one is going to take a lot of investigation, sweetheart. A lot."

"You told her, right? I won't believe it if you say you didn't tell her!" The scary tingle his grandfather called gooseflesh made the hair on the back of Jeff's neck stand erect.

"Told me what, Danny?"

"Ma, Jeff isn't used to you yet."

"Oh." Catherine turned the bright blue gaze on the Indian boy to whom she'd instantly taken a liking. "Jeff, what do you think Danny told me?"

"About the girl. Her name."

Catherine cocked her head again, listening intently to a sound audible only to her ear. "Bright. Shiny. Sparkling. No, that's not quite it. Glittery, no--glitter. Glitter? Her name was Glitter? Could that be right, Danny?"

His infectious grin refused to be repressed. "Yeah, Ma. That's right isn't it, Jeff?"

A long, low whistle extruded between the Navajo's puckered lips. "I've heard a lot about you, Mrs. Armstrong, but until this minute I thought the stories were all a lot of bunk!"

The dark black fringe of lashes fluttered downward, then lifted. She thrust the bracelet back at her son. "Be careful here, darling. Things are not what they seem. I've never heard of anyone naming a child Glitter."

"It was her stage name, Mom. Darla Corey went by the name of Glitter."

"I remember her now! She won the title of the Most Beautiful Showgirl in Vegas recently, didn't she?"

"That's the girl!" Almost as if caught in a slow-moving dream, Cloudwalker reached for another cookie but was brought sharply back to reality when the Rottweiler made a lunge for it.

"Damascus! Knock it off." Catherine waved an admonishing finger in the dog's direction. The dog reluctantly returned to the floor. "What about the flames, Danny? Why did I sense fire? Is that why this bracelet looks so awful?"

"We took it off her body. She was burned to death in that fire at Caesars."

"Dear God." Catherine pressed her hands against her eyes, as though trying to block out a tortured image. When she lowered them, a stricken look dominated her face. "There's an incredible amount of danger here. The black cloud behind the glitter is a horrific force. Like a tumor, it has spread to many places."

9

"Can you be more specific, Mom? What places?"

Catherine shook her head; long blond hair swirled around her shoulders. "No, honey, I can't. Maybe it will come to me later. Right now, the only thing I know for certain is whatever was behind the girl, whatever caused her to be murdered is big, far reaching, and very dangerous."

"Murdered?" The word hissed between Danny's clenched teeth, but he knew better than to interrupt his mother's reading with a volley of questions.

"She thought she could handle it, but something she never expected took her life. She was completely unprepared. That girl never knew death was coming until the moment it claimed her. Be careful, Danny. More than usual."

The chill that made the hair on the back of his neck stand up a moment ago, laid claim to his entire body. Superstition, Jeff thought. Superstitious nonsense. But he couldn't quell a feeling the ghosts of Geronimo, Crazy Horse and Chief Joseph were pounding out a warning on a ceremonial drum.

Early summer in Las Vegas was normally a pleasant time of year. Fierce heat was yet to come, and the bone chilling cold of winter nights were consigned to memory, not to be experienced for another year. The warmth and lack of humidity made the air seem brighter and cleaner than it really was, but a sense Danny couldn't explain announced the future was not going to be filled with sunshine--it was going to be dark and stormy.

CHAPTER TWO

Danny reached for the remote control which opened the garage door as he came down the street. Receiving a pre-programmed sequence, the metal door began to roll up well before he reached the house belonging to his roommate, Malcom "Forbes" Bennett. The door started to lower when the front bumper of the dark green Jeep Cherokee broke the laser beam Forbes aimed across the garage. As the interior darkened, Danny sat for a moment after pulling the keys out of the ignition to allow his eyes to adjust to the gloom. When the floodlight came on, Danny smiled. He'd forgotten about the motion detector Forbes just installed--the guy was an electronic junkie. Danny fully expected the maid to be replaced by a robot as soon as a unit which was programmed to clean the toilets came out on the market.

After deactivating the high-tech security system, the lock released on the metal door leading into the family room of the expensive four-bedroom house at Canyon Gate—one of the many the high rent districts in Vegas. Danny laid his keys on the sofa table, glanced around the empty room, and called out, "Forbes, you home, buddy?"

Forbes' bright red Camaro was parked in the three-car garage, so he had to be in one of a couple of places: playing Nintendo in the den, working on his latest computer program in the downstairs office or taking a nap. How his friend could sleep in the middle of the afternoon was beyond Danny; but Forbes maintained he needed to shut down his mental computer at least once a day or he suffered a mental overload. The guy was as strange as he was smart, but Danny liked the quiet, unassuming genius.

"Forbes?" No answer.

"Must be sleeping," Danny mumbled, but only the cat responded.

J.J. the feral cat who called at the door one winter morning and decided to take up residency, took over the lives of the two young men with whom he graciously shared a three thousand square-foot Mediterranean style mini- mansion. The ten-pound cat welcomed Danny home with a yowl.

"Hungry, buddy?"

J.J. rubbed his head against the kitchen cupboard, a sure sign Forbes' electronic world became so engrossing he forgot to feed the big tom.

"Okay, I'm coming. Hold your horses."

The cat kept up the racket, knowing Danny would hurry to stop the never-ending rumble.

After depositing an aluminum can in the recycling bin in the garage just outside the kitchen door, Danny returned to the comfortably furnished family room, flopped on the couch, kicked off his shoes and reached for the remote control. With his thumb pressed against the button, he flicked through the channels piped into the house via the satellite dish on the roof. He settled on a movie as background noise, but his thoughts were far too fragmented to focus on the plot.

It wasn't too many minutes before he was staring at the ceramic tile and the raw wool rug woven by some Inca Indians in the Andes, which Forbes discovered at a flea-bitten pawn shop downtown. The glass table, who's finely carved wooden legs rested against the rug, held a curious assortment of artifacts Forbes found irresistible. His roommate engaged in a running battle with the cat over the position in which the objects rested on the table. J.J. had a penchant for knocking arrow heads, Kachina dolls and assorted feathered mandalas onto the floor. Every morning Forbes would faithfully retrieve them off the rug and replace them on the table. Off and on. Off and on. The battle for supremacy raged. Secretly, Danny's sympathy was with the cat--Forbes' treasured possessions were dust collectors as far as he was concerned.

Hearing the refrigerator seal smack when it pulled away from the enameled metal, Danny turned. "Hey, guy--sleeping again? Man, computer geeks have the life!" Forbes' preoccupation with neatness was evident in his appearance. He was tall and lean. At thirty-five, he possessed an ascetic face made up of sharp angles which might have been handsome with a layer of fat to cushion the harshness. Jewel-bright green eyes conveyed a perpetual sheen of amazement behind thick glasses which enhanced the effect. Not a single strand of mousy blond hair was out of place; his crisp white shirt was fresh from the cleaners and the crease in his slacks was so sharp Forbes could pass military inspection.

"Stuff it, cop-man. If you had to think as hard as I do the blood vessels in your head would pop. Why don't you go back to work and beat up a disadvantaged citizen?"

Danny grinned at his friend's challenge. "Things not going well, I take it?"

Forbes flopped at the end of the couch, a package of string cheese in his hand. When the cat heard the cellophane rip, he leaped into Forbes lap and started meowing. Pinching off a bite for himself and then one for the cat, he absently fed the big orange and white feline while mulling over the problem with his program. "I'm stuck on the multiple player aspect of the random number generator. With slots, it was easy because only one person pushes the button. It's man against machine, so to speak. The scenario for blackjack is more complicated because there's more than one activator. I'll get it--eventually. It's just taking longer than I thought."

Danny tried to swallow his smile as Forbes fed another piece of cheese to the cat without realizing how easily he was being manipulated. The big house, expensive car, all the toys a grown man could ever hope for were paid for by the computer program used by almost every casino in the country, was created by Forbes. He also developed a method of charting a slot player's coin-in and time played with a magnetically coded square of plastic, just like ATM or credit cards carried by millions of Americans. His program revolutionized the slot industry, giving it precedence over table games, a threatening scenario to old-time pit bosses. If successful, Forbes' plan to computerize pit games would transform established complimentary procedures used by casinos. It was going to be a hard sell for dealers, floormen and shift managers in the pit. They were an uneducated breed who hadn't changed since the Roaring Twenties, when Al Capon and Bugsy Siegel bludgeoned non-paying customers with clubs. The entrenched mind-set of most casinos was not suited to the complexities of technology. Old-time casino men, the flinty-eyed bosses, who ruled dealers with a swift kick in the heels if the customer won too many hands, feared the computer invading their territory as much as an aging stallion feared a younger, stronger, swifter male intruding upon his paddock. But they couldn't hang on to their iron- clad grip forever; too many CPAs were calling the shots now. The green felt jungles were slowly giving way to corporate boardrooms. The slot program made him richer than Midas, and if he successfully computerized table games, Forbes would be playing in the same league with Bill Gates!

Forbes finally noticed Danny's silence. "Bad day?"

"We got a positive ID on the girl at Caesars."

Waiting, Forbes didn't like the scowl which took command of

Danny's normally pleasant features. As silence stole across the room like the approach of a storm, Forbes mustered the courage to inquire. "Who was it?"

"Glitter, Glitter Corey."

"No! God, Danny, she was my walking dream. Glitter was the prettiest girl I've ever laid eyes on. What a body! A couple of guys I know even talked to her. They said she was as nice as she was pretty. Not stuck up like a lot of beautiful women. I can't believe it. And burned to death-- Jesus!" An icy shiver made Forbes tremble; he couldn't imagine what it would be to die in a fire. It gave him the creeps to think about it. "Any clues?"

"No, Jeff only got positive confirmation on her dental records an hour ago. We're trying to find out if she had any family now."

"Has the press gotten wind of it yet?"

"A few guys know--the Captain's a good friend of Pep Andrews, the Director over at the Convention Authority. He must've leaked information about her identity to Andrews because I got a call from the Governor just before I left the station."

"The Governor?" Forbes moaned, "This case is going to have everyone looking over your shoulder."

"Yeah, 'fraid so."

Forbes selected this house because the glass doors which opened onto the patio faced west. He liked to sit on the couch and watch the sun go down. Bright red sandstone in Red Rock Canyon took on an entire pallet of color at twilight. As the light began to fade, Forbes thought about the girl who was embraced by Las Vegas residents as their bright and shining star. 'Glitter' was an appropriate name for the golden girl with a mane of golden hair. She was chosen to go on sales trips with Convention Authority officials, dazzling crowds around the world, displaying legs as long as the Colorado River, when she was all decked out in skimpy, beaded, and feathered costumes which were the trademark of a Las Vegas show girl. Smitten by the beautiful girl, Forbes could recite her bio by heart. Darla Corey earned a degree in hotel administration from the University of Nevada, Las Vegas. She spoke so eloquently about the gambling Mecca perched at the edge of the great Mojave Desert., she made an outstanding ambassador.

As the shadows lengthened, and tentacles of darkness wrapped around the range of mountains sheltering the barren valley, Forbes felt his spirit plummet.

Why would anyone want to turn another human being into a lump of charcoal? At the thought of the fire which snuffed out Darla's life, Forbes shuddered again. He glanced at Danny, who was staring into the darkness crouching at the edge of the patio, beyond the floodlights, like a monster out of a childhood nightmare. Forbes knew Danny didn't see the flickering lights in the swimming pool, nor did he hear the dry, rasping rustle of the palm fronds as their spiny fingers trailed along the cinderblock wall.

In the distance, a coyote emitted a plaintive howl at the huge, orange moon which rose above the horizon on the west side of the valley. More yipping barks followed as others of his kind took up the coyote's challenge. The mournful sound made Forbes cringe. Instinctively, he felt as though the lonely creatures inhabiting the wasteland of alkali formations and scrub brush were issuing a messianic warning.

Danny approached the aging Strip hotel the along a narrow ribbon of sidewalk. Although the Flamingo had undergone a recent facelift, there were still scaly age-marred pockets. No matter how many coats of paint were applied or how often new carpet was laid, nothing could be done to disguise an outdated layout.

Winding his way through slot machines and a crowd of hopeful gamblers, Danny avoided both with the ease of a running back headed for the goal line. The flash of his badge was all it took to gain entrance backstage and Danny tucked himself into a shadowy alcove beneath rigging which hoisted sets aloft, out of the way of hurried dancers. He watched the show for a minute, then headed down a dim hallway toward the dressing rooms. He knocked, waited, then knocked again. The twitter and cackle of twenty-four women abruptly ceased when he entered.

Some faces showed relief, others alarm, when he offered his police identification to the battered old crone in charge of the girls. A quick explanation of his purpose brought an explosion of sound as each dancer sought to be the first to express her grief and rage over their friend's grisly death.

"Ladies, ladies. Ladies!" Danny had to shout to make himself heard above the scrape of beads and sequins, swish of feathers, babble of high- pitched voices and noise of cosmetic jars brushed aside by elaborate costumes. "I'll speak with each of you after the show. I just wanted to let you know I'll be around to take statements."

A loud, gavel-like knock on the door announced it was time for the dancers to take their places for the next number; Danny was quickly swallowed by a swirl of beads, feathers, sequins, and breasts displaying various amounts of skin. He stood by the doorway trying to catch his breath, watching the girls disappear down a gloomy hallway.

As the wardrobe mistress returned to her colorful den, Danny felt a presence at his elbow. Turning, he found a uniformed security guard lurking behind a rack of dazzling costumes which a stagehand just rolled through the door. He reached for his badge again, but the officer held up a protesting hand.

"I know who you are--the sergeant said you're authorized to be backstage."

"Hi, Detective Danny Armstrong."

"Yeah. You're going to interview the dancers. I'm 'sposed to lend a hand in case any of those jumping jacks turn flaky on you." Although the guard didn't offer to introduce himself, the brass badge above the pocket of his uniform identified him as Kevin Cox.

"Flaky?"

"Yeah, flaky. Most of 'em are either strung out on drugs or sleeping with the same sex. Flaky." The pronouncement contained a note of authority, like an officer outlining the purpose of a mission to enlisted men.

"You ex-military, Kevin?" Danny couldn't help but notice the close-cropped hair, the squared-off set to the shoulders, the ram-rod straight spine, like a metal pole was permanently affixed to his skeletal structure.

"I work at the Test Site three days a week. This keeps me busy. They need somebody trustworthy to watch over these flakes on the weekend--see they don't cause no trouble."

"Test Site, huh? You must have a top security clearance."

"Enough."

Something shifted in the security guard's eyes, something dark and sinister assumed command of his expression. "You work around the clock for three shifts?" Danny asked politely.

"Yeah. I don't like hanging around my apartment for four days, so I work here part-time."

"You like it here, Kevin?" Danny examined the man's eyes. The obscuring veil did not lift.

"Like I said . . . keeps me busy."

"Did you know Glitter?"

"Everybody knew her. Is this an official line of questioning?"

"No, strictly off the record. A man with military experience would probably pick up on things that'd be lost on most people"

The fact Danny recognized the value of his training made the security guard's eyes narrow; this detective was obviously not just another dumb-ass kid. "You mean, do I know something about the girl?"

"Or . . . do you have any suspicions?"

"About who killed her?"

"Well, you might have noticed something unusual, like a new friend or frequent phone calls, or whether she was stressed out--things like that."

Kevin's statement was made so matter of fact it sounded like a pizza preference. "She was having an affair with the owner of this joint."

"Oh? You know that for a fact--or through deductive reasoning?"

"I know it." Kevin's eyes flew left, level with his ear; the two-way radio went off just then moment and he reached for it with his right hand. After a brief conversation with someone at the other end, Kevin returned his attention to Danny.

"Was it common knowledge?"

"No. They were real secretive--the guy's married." The door opened with a bang as the dancers rushed back to dressing room, some pulling off their costumes as they approached.

"You'll have to leave now. The girls have to change for their next number." The wardrobe hag was all too glad to shove Danny out the door; the security guard seemed reluctant to follow.

"Guess you have to get up early to catch the bus to the Test Site?" Danny studied the way the security guard fingered the volume control on the two-way radio dangling from his belt and how his eyes kept darting back and forth between dancers as he rattled on.

"Yeah. Sometimes I drive, but not often. It's easier to catch a few winks on the bus. I was on the bus the morning Glitter got torched . . . in case you were wonderin'." He withdrew a small pad of paper from the trouser pocket of his uniform, the pressure exerted on the ink stem made a resounding click, and he scratched out a few lines. "Here's my address and phone number if you want to talk to me some more. What I know probably won't help you out much though."

Danny watched the guard walk away, then he glanced at the address and directions. The seven was crossed, military fashion--to make certain it wasn't confused with a one. Precise, neat up and down strokes slashed across the paper. A handwriting expert would classify Cox as a man not given too much emotion. Every "t" was crossed at the top; Kevin Cox had a high opinion of himself, not like a lot of wanna-be cops who couldn't make it on the force so they opted for a job as a security guard to have some power over other people, wear a uniform and carry a gun. Danny made a mental note to pull Kevin's social security number from hotel personnel records. He'd also ask Forbes to go on a fishing expedition through the Department of Motor Vehicle computer files. Danny had a feeling about the security guard that something unusual would turn up. He'd learned to rely on the extra-sensory intuition which made his stomach churn--it was never, ever, wrong!

Thankfully, the sun was dropping behind the jagged line of mountains, which provided a modicum of shelter for the arid valley, and the temperature was starting to cool. Professor John Jenkins was teaching an evening class in the Hotel Administration building on the UNLV campus, where he agreed to meet with Danny before his other students arrived. As an evening breeze began to stir, Danny ambled down the steps in front of the Artemus Hamm building, passing beneath the shadow of a tall black sculpture which looked like a flashlight on his way to Professor Jenkins's classroom. It was still too hot to walk fast. The summer wind was like standing in front of a blast furnace, but as a native of Las Vegas, Danny appreciated any breath of air--no matter how hot or how feeble. It swept down the corridor between the tall buildings, pushing dried leaves and scraps of paper ahead of him.

The classroom was still empty when Danny opened the door. Professor Jenkins sat behind a desk facing rows of chairs with a wide arm on which more zealous students could take notes while flipping through pages of a textbook.

"Professor? I'm Detective Danny Armstrong."

"Oh, yes. Detective Armstrong. You're here to talk about Darla Corey. Terrible, just terrible, her dying that way. She was one of my brightest students, you know. I never did understand why she took up dancing in that horrible show. She could have had any management position she wanted, you know. Brilliant girl, simply brilliant. I never understood her decision." The professor studied Danny over the top of his half glasses; gray eyebrows lifted, and his expression melted into a classic portrait of confusion. Like many department chairmen, the world outside the university seemed strange, almost alien, as if all other life forms existed in a parallel universe--vaguely felt but seldom encountered.

"You were her academic advisor, right?

"Yes, yes. I arranged for an internship in Senator Hastings' casino in Ely for Darla. The Hastings family owns most of northern Nevada, you know."

"No, sir, I didn't."

"Oh yes, my goodness yes." The academic pallor retreated momentarily as his skin suffused with pride. "The Senator's family is one of the most politically prominent in the state. They own huge tracts of land. Cattle ranchers. Good men, strong family--since Nevada's infancy, really. Do you know the Senator?"

"No, sir, I'm sorry I can't say that I do."

"Well, I used my influence to get Darla the internship because I felt she had the potential to make it to the top. Never hurts to know the men at the top, career wise, you know."

"Yes sir, I believe that. Exactly what did Darla do at the Hastings casino?"

"She apprenticed in the pit--as a floorman, er, person, as I recall. Darla had a position in the casino, I remember that quite clearly."

"Do you know how long she was there?"

"Oh yes." He peered over the wire rim of glasses greasy with fingerprints and blinked, as if he were seeing the detective for the first time. "She worked there three summers."

"Do you suppose the Senator would remember her?"

"I'm sure he would. He set up a scholarship fund to pay for Darla's college tuition after her first summer there."

Like the cold finger of a dead man, a shiver tracked the path of Danny's spine. The chill of intuition made the hair on his arms stand erect despite the summer heat. "Was that a normal thing to do? Did the Senator sponsor many kids at UNLV?"

Pulling on a chin too long for the rest of his face, the professor stared out the window at shadows collected by twilight. "Well, I never had him do it for any of my other students. But you must understand, Detective, Darla was not just any student--she was at the top of her class. Brilliant, just brilliant. I never understood how someone with that kind of mind would participate in a review show--topless, no less! Never. Just never understood her reasoning." The professor lapsed into silence, as though retreating to an interior classroom where only he was allowed the privilege of lecturing. Danny slipped from the room quietly--the old man never heard him go.

The desk in the station house was ancient and battered. Its metal surface was the recipient of constant abuse and bore the scars of years of wear with shabby dignity, as if it were proud of its enduring service to the taxpayer. Danny sat at the desk, a cell phone cradled against his shoulder. At the coffee pot in the far corner of the room, his partner, Sonny Yi, poured a cup of bitter brew and slurped it so loudly Danny waved at him to keep quiet. Korean by gene pool, Las Vegan by birth, Sonny was a product of the garish world of gaming. He'd attended grade school, junior high and high school in the city beyond the Strip. After graduation from UNLV with a degree in Criminal Justice, Sonny worked his way off patrol into the detective unit with the grit and determination characteristic of his Oriental forefathers.

Returning to the desk opposite Danny's, Sonny sipped the hot liquid, made a face, and flipped through the file folder in front of him. "Damn, can you make sense of this personnel file?"

Danny loved his partner with the kind of enthusiasm that made one male team member slap the rump of another. His mother was certain the bond forged by testosterone demanded men cluster together in packs. Although it was no longer necessary to sneak up on a woolly mammoth for the preservation of the tribe, Catherine thought the ghosts of those early ancestors compelled men to participate in team sports, lounge around in bars together, and plot strategy in board rooms against other corporate tribes in the never-ending quest for territory.

"There's no next of kin listed as a beneficiary on the death benefit plan provided by the casino."

A high-pitched whistle trilled through teeth which were corrected to a precise uniformity by Sonny's childhood orthodontist. "That's weird. What the heck did she do for Christmas? The show is closed for two weeks in December."

"I asked that very question. Her friends said she usually spent the time roaming around the desert searching for ghost towns--with a camera."

"Weird, weird, weird."

"I've got a feeling about all this . . ."

Sonny put his fingers together and made the sign of the cross in front of his face, like he intended to ward off an evil spirit. "Here we go with the 'feeling' again. You spook me, Danny, you really do. Have you been talking to Catherine?"

"Nope. This hunch is all mine. I think Darla Corey is an assumed identity. Forbes ran a search of DMV and Social Security records. Seems she just showed up in town from out of nowhere--there's not even a high school transcript on record at UNLV! How did she get admitted? Darla never applied for a driver's license in another state, but her date of birth indicates she was eighteen when she enrolled at UNLV. Most kids've been driving a couple of years or have worked in a fast-food joint by that time. She's got a Nevada 530 prefix, so she never applied for a Social Security number until she got here."

"Christ, Danny, someday all the electronic snooping you have Forbes do is going to get you guys in trouble!" He took an exaggerated sip of coffee; the rude noise caused their secretary to look up. Sonny blew Jan a kiss and gave her a menacing wink--then returned his attention to Danny. "Has Jeff finished the autopsy? What if nothing unusual turns up? Where do we go from there?"

Danny twirled a pencil with a badly chewed eraser back and forth

21

between his fingers, the wooden shaft clicking against his class ring. Pensive, he stared at the desk blotter filled with all kinds of cartoon-like doodles. The faces of Mickey and Minnie Mouse, Pluto, Goofy and Donald all stared up at him as if waiting for a response. "I don't know. But I won't get desperate until Forbes has a chance to do more digging."

The telephone rang with the shrillness of an incoming mortar and Danny jumped. Reaching for the phone, he pulled it off the receiver with a yank, enforcing its silence. "Detective Armstrong."

"Danny?" Forbes' was tentative; he hardly recognized his roommate because of the stern tone of voice.

"Yeah. Forbes? Sorry, my mind was elsewhere, and the phone shattered my train of thought."

"Your famous sense of intuition was right on again, old buddy. The real Darla Corey died in an automobile accident in New Jersey when she was four."

"How'd you find that out?"

"I ran a computer search of the Bureau of Vital Statistics for all fifty states. New Jersey showed up. Some counties don't have the resources to cross reference births and deaths. She could have been born anywhere so finding a record of a live birth might take a lot of time--or prove virtually impossible. She had to have one though, or she couldn't have gotten a Social Security number."

"Maybe, but the birth certificate could have been a forgery."

Forbes was busy shredding the computer sheet into a thousand tiny pieces. "Yeah, with enough money, you can get one that looks really authentic. Maybe you should start searching police records for a forgery expert. Finding one that was in business over twenty years ago might prove tough." He disconnected the cell phone with the button beneath his thumb.

Danny stared at the lifeless instrument willing a clue to appear on the display which identified the caller. If the dancer wasn't Darla Corey, who was she and why was it necessary for her to assume a false identity?

His mother was right: nothing was what it seemed!

Jordan Grey was a distinguished looking man. Tall, tan, silver haired, still lean, and athletic despite his sixty plus years of existence. The owner of the Grey Company, of which his Las Vegas casino was just a link in the chain of casinos that included cruise ships, Caribbean islands, Indian reservations, and several riverboats on the Mississippi, moved with an animal grace reminding Danny of a lion, or maybe a panther. Lions hunted in the open, panthers stalked their prey under cover of night and brought their quarry down in unguarded moments. Rising from behind a desk as large as the deck of an aircraft carrier, Grey crossed the stadium-size office to greet Danny at the door.

"Detective Armstrong, I'm happy to meet you, even if it is under such unfortunate circumstances."

"Yes, well, I have a habit of meeting people that way. I wish the situation could be more favorable."

"I haven't been able to sleep since I got the news about Darla's death. Unfortunate, most unfortunate." Grey's tread was light as he glided across a wool carpet between the outer door and his executive desk. Once the exotic wood desk was between himself and the detective, Jordan Grey seemed to relax. With dignified grace, he rang for his secretary and requested coffee. The motion was worthy of a Hollywood actor. "So, Detective, what is it you want to know?"

"How long did Darla Corey work for your hotel?"

"I don't really know. Just a minute, I'll call Human Resources."

In a tone of voice which somehow maintained a balance between authoritative and friendly, Grey requested the information. He dropped the phone back into its cradle after listening intently for a few moments. "Darla came to work here when she was twenty-one."

"Do you know how she came to get a job as a show girl? I talked to Professor Jenkins, dean of the hotel school at UNLV. He indicated Darla was one of his brightest students. He felt certain she was destined for management."

"Yes, I remember the situation clearly. Pep Andrews, the Director over at the Convention Authority, asked me to give her a job. He spotted her in a group of students when he was giving a lecture. As I recall the circumstances, he was impressed with her questions about the future of gaming and the impact riverboats and casinos on Indian reservations would have on Nevada. Pep decided she would make a great spokesperson when the Convention Authority made sales trips around the country. I hired her as a favor to him. Surprisingly, she picked up dancing real fast and before long she claimed the lead in the show. Beauty and brains. A rare combination."

The phone rang again. Ignoring it, he depressed another button. A wall of oak paneling slid back to reveal a group of television monitors. Their glassy, glowing eyes reflected ever-changing positions of surveillance cameras above the pit. The impatient ring sounded again, and Jordan snatched the phone off the hook. Displaying impatience with another interruption.

A glimmer on the floor attracted Danny's attention from the corner of his eye. As unobtrusively as possible, he pushed his chair away from the conference table, which stretched in front of Jordan Grey's desk, to get a better look at the object. A gold band around the center of a Waterman pen caught and held the light from the recessed light fixture overhead. Jordan was busy depressing buttons controlling the angle of the camera above a blackjack dealer. Zooming in on the player's cards, Grey was absorbed by the scene being played out at the 21 table. Danny knew about rumors regarding the hotel owner's obsessive fear of being cheated. His surveillance system was one of the most elaborate in town. Although it was far from infallible, Grey thought the intimidation factor to both dealers and players off-set the exorbitant price.

While Jordan's attention was riveted on the wall of screens, Danny scooped up the pen. Discreetly putting it in his jacket pocket, he rose to leave. "Thanks a lot Mr. Grey . . . if anything comes up, I'll get back to you. Oh, just one more thing."

Grey's eyes never strayed from the monitors.

"You're a member of the Downtown Progress Association, right?"

"Yes, but I resigned as chairman a few weeks ago. I'm proud of my record," his eyes swung in Danny's direction for the first time in several minutes, apparently satisfied the player wasn't a card counter, "and I never missed a meeting. It was time to step down though--to let some younger shooters have a go at it. Fresh blood, innovative ideas."

"So, you were at last week's meeting?"

"Yes, it was a breakfast meeting, why do you ask?"

"Just curious."

"Well, call me if you need me, Detective. By the way, would you like to go to dinner and see the show? Give my secretary a call any time . . .

on the house. I'll be glad to comp you or any of your friends."

"Thanks a lot, Mr. Grey. I'll take advantage of your offer one of these days."

"Do that, Detective, you do that."

Darla Corey owned a real classy townhouse in a new development in Green Valley, which recently sprang up on the southeast side of Las Vegas. White stucco, tile roof, a nifty little courtyard all spruced up with wisteria vines. Wrought iron patio furniture made it look like the kind of place a beautiful woman would own. Femininity exuded from every dainty nook. Inside, Sonny rummaged around the kitchen while Danny sifted through the desk in an alcove below the stairs. A year's worth of bank statements was stacked in a drawer. You could tell a lot about people by where they spent their money. Darla had several different Master Cards and Visas, which reflected modest charges, along with an assortment of department store credit cards. There was a respectable balance in her checking account but certainly nothing to get killed over. He ambled into the front room and stood admiring the bookcase for a few minutes. Many current novels lined the shelves and a few oversized picture books extolling the splendors of the High Sierras. One shelf burgeoned with an accumulation of textbooks gathered throughout college. A chintz covered couch, ablaze with several shades of pink flowers dominated the center of the room in front of a fake fireplace, containing ceramic logs and a gas foot which imitated a real fire. Round end tables draped with ruffled cloths, matching one of the deep pink flowers in the couch fabric, supported white china lamps topped by pale pink pleated shades. It was a bright room. A woman's room, a nest delightfully feathered to suit any female of the species--although it was not as sophisticated as Danny thought it would be. Homey--comfortable and homey.

"Find anything interesting?" Sonny called out from the kitchen, his exhaustive search of pots and pans, spices and refrigerator having come to an inconclusive end.

"Maybe." Danny pocketed several canceled checks and climbed the stairs to the bedrooms. Darla's bedroom was a cloud of white eyelet. The four-poster bed was covered with a down quilt which was absolutely the last thing anyone would ever need in the desert, but it was fluffy and frilly and pleasing to the eye. Pillows trimmed with yards of lace and ribbon

25

were placed against the headboard with a practiced casualness too perfect to be random. The message light was blinking on her land-line phone and Danny depressed the play button. A deep, masculine voice boomed through the room.

"Hey, baby, meet me tonight. After the show. I'll be waiting--all primed and ready."

From the doorway, Sonny crooned. "Oooh, man! Sounds like the dude was already hot!"

"Yeah, I wonder who the voice belongs to? None of the men in her life I've interviewed so far. Seems like Darla might have gotten around."

Sonny slid back a mirrored wardrobe door. "Jeeesus Holy Christ!" He stood aside, allowing Danny to look at the fancy clothing. "Must be a million bucks worth of stuff in here."

Labels were from big name designers; expensive fabrics, lots of satins, silks, and lace. Danny's eye roved along the rows of dresses, suits, blouses, hats, and shoes. In a wardrobe as extensive as the one hanging in Darla's closet, Danny was surprised not to find an expensive fur coat or two!!"

In an exquisitely worked wooden box on the top shelf of a Louis XIV étagère, Sonny discovered a cache of jewelry which would make the Queen of England envious. "Get a load of this!"

Danny removed a gold nugget-style ring, with a shank worn thin in the middle. "Looks like she might have worn this one a lot. Sonny make a note of this piece on the inventory. I'm going to borrow it for a few days."

The slim plastic pen bearing the logo of the Gold Coast Hotel and Casino dipped and bobbed over a small spiral notebook Sonny habitually carried in the back pocket of his jeans. "Okay. Taking it to Catherine?"

"Yeah. I'm stopping by on the way home from work. Did you get those cookies I left on your desk the other day?"

A wide smile made the epicanthic fold, which protected the eyes of his ancestors from the harsh winds blowing down of Mongolia, lowered across irises as black as a moonless night. "Come and gone, my man, they've come and gone. Nobody makes cookies like Catherine!"

"I'll bring you more if she hasn't fed them all to her worthless dog."

"No reason to get mad at him, Danny. Damascus serves a purpose."

"What? Slobbering? Destroying my new Nikes? I don't know why she puts up with him!"

"She's safe, Danny. No one in their right mind would come through the front door when Damascus slams against it and barks loud enough to wake the dead."

"It is the dog's single redeeming factor, but an alarm system would be a lot less trouble."

"Undoubtedly. But who would keep her warm at night?"

Danny slid the closet door shut and turned out the lights in the feminine room. "I think my Mom needs to get married."

"No, you don't." Sonny lost his eyes to his smile again. "You're just as spoiled as that dog and if you had to share her attention with someone else you'd be even more jealous than you are of Damascus."

"I'm not jealous of stupid dog, Sonny."

"Yes, you are!" Chuckling, he slapped his best friend on the back as they headed down the stairs. "Are we all done here?"

Surveying the living room one last time, Danny let his eye rove along the walls. Ansel Adams prints hung above the stairs, along with various other black and white photographs of places in Nevada Danny recognized. Goldfield, Panacea, Silver City--all bore silent witness to the glory of Nevada's past. "Darla was a pretty good amateur photographer. I like these pictures."

When Sonny opened the door, the last rays of a setting sun struck the photo of a derelict building-- all that remained of the once proud mining town of Rhyolite. Home to thousands of miners, saloon keepers, prostitutes and merchants who pandered to the hardy souls living in a mining camp. When the silver ran out the people trickled away too. Danny stared at the photograph for a moment before closing the door on the house of a woman who was as much an enigma as Nevada's past.

One of the last territories in the continental United States to be admitted into the Union, Nevada was still a primitive frontier in everything from social graces to political acumen. From its granite spine snow-capped mountains to the monochromatic desert floors carpeted by sand and sagebrush, Nevada stretched forlornly for miles in every direction. It was a harsh land, despised by some, fiercely championed by others. That's the way it was, Danny mused, you either loved the stark, hard-edged ridges of bare, forbidding stone which ruptured from the earth--or you hated Nevada's vast plains. The Mojave Desert was populated with worthless scrub and patches of scorched bunch grass. The earth was scoured clean by a hot, volcanic wind. Love or hate. Maybe Nevada was a mirror of life itself. Love or hate. Who hated Glitter enough to kill her? Or, had someone loved the girl so much they refused to share her? Love or hate. Danny closed the door on the comfortable world the beautiful girl would never see again.

"Ma? You here?" Danny braced himself against the kitchen door--awaiting the inevitable. With a thrash and clatter, the Rottweiler slid along the tile as he sought purchase when he rounded the counter running at full tilt. Although he tried to be prepared, when the force of rock-hard muscle, taut sinew and heavy bone hit him in the center of the chest, Danny fell backward against the door. "No jumping! Damn it, Damascus, stay down!"

"Damascus! You know Danny doesn't like you to jump on him!" Catherine's voice floated into the kitchen from the depths of the room in which she conducted readings for half of Las Vegas' residents.

"Ma, that's why he does it!" Casting the dog a warning look, which was disdainfully ignored, Danny pulled a chair away from the kitchen table. "I brought a couple of things I want you to read."

"Okay, honey." Dressed in a caftan, Catherine stepped into the room. "My next client won't be here for an hour."

"I thought you were going to quit doing readings after dark, Mom. It's not smart to let people in the house at night. The town's not what it used to be."

"It's Judge LeMoye."

"Oh." Danny dipped into his pocket to remove Darla's gold ring and Jordan Grey's expensive pen. "Tell me what you pick up from these."

Settling into a chair across the table from Danny, Catherine reached for the enameled pen and rolled it back and forth between her hands. Eyes closed, her head cocked to the right--she breathed deeply several times as she mentally relaxed. It never ceased to amaze Danny how much his mother's physical appearance changed as she made the mental

28

shift to access information through a process completely foreign to most people. Her facial features seemed to soften and lines around her eyes and mouth disappeared. It was almost as if his mother became someone else when she accessed this heightened state of awareness, although Catherine never claimed to be a spiritual channel. A sudden exhalation of air announced information was beginning to seep through the porous surface of her mind.

Impressions came fast and furious, like a rapidly shifting kaleidoscope. "I'm seeing a connection. Links in a chain. But one is broken beyond repair." Muscles in her abdomen cramped with so much force Catherine had trouble breathing. Feelings. Impressions. Subtle, almost defying explanation. "The bond was thought to be very, very strong. Could never be broken . . . but somehow it was." She paused, still fingering the pen. Knitting her brows, Catherine struggled to make sense of shapes which loomed against the landscape of her inner mind. "Two men, now, I am seeing two men. One in his late fifties or early sixties, but still good looking. Silver hair. Tan. The other man is older still." A hiss, a sizzle, then a blinding force like the corona of the sun reached Catherine's senses. "Both men are powerful, they radiate power like a rock radiates heat from the sun. There is a connection between the old man and the one with silver hair. Money. They are connected by money." Her fingers clasped the pen as though it were the only piece of driftwood in a turbulent sea. Images shifted, separated, moved apart--distinct, yet together in form and substance. "There's more. Now I see five people. The silver haired man. Another is wearing a uniform. Three more are indistinct, they are consumed by shadow. Wait. Another image is coming." A frown creased her brow and she chewed at her lower lip without being aware of it. "A pentagram--with someone at each apex of a five- pointed star. The old man sits at the center like a spider in a web." Suddenly, Catherine's eyes flew open, and she looked at Danny with an out of focus stare. "A pentagram represents the forces of evil."

When Catherine's gaze returned to normal, the Rott padded across the kitchen floor, his leathery pads scraping the tile with a soft, muted shush- shush. He dropped his head into her lap and without thinking, she began to stroke the broad expanse between his ears. After a moment of ecstasy, the dog emitted a long, whimpering moan. She said, finally, "Who does this belong to?"

"Jordan Grey."

"The owner of the Grey Casinos?"

"One and the same."

She picked up the pen and began to toy with it again. "I don't know who the old man is, but I don't like him. His aura is dark and foreboding."

"Would you mind holding the ring?"

"For you, darling, anything."

As if divining her intention, the Rottweiler flopped against the sliding glass door, where he had a perfect view of the backyard and could stand guard against trespassers. The dog's deep brown eyes flicked from the lawn to Catherine's face, and he became unnaturally still. Like the sphinx, the Rott seemed to stand guard over his mistress' journey into the unknown. Although he'd never been trained to move away from Catherine when she began to psychically read an object, it was as though the beast sensed his presence might interfere with the tenuous connection to a world beyond. With a startled cry, Catherine dropped the ring and it clattered across the floor.

If the ring had suddenly coiled at his feet like a rattlesnake ready to strike, Danny would not have been more shocked than he was by his mother's reaction. "Mom! What is it? What did you see?"

"A death's head! Oh, Danny, you've got to be careful. There is so much danger here. I've got a terrible feeling this case could mean death for thousands--literally thousands of people!" Tears suddenly welled in Catherine's eyes, turning them a deep shade of aqua. The emotional trauma of being associated with desperate people at desperate times in their lives was a facet of the psychic world she'd learned to cope with years ago. Keeping a wall between her personal emotions and the suffering of her clients was an absolute necessity, but this feeling clawed its way into her world. Instinct warned it had the power to tear everything she loved apart. "I don't know why, it isn't clear, but there is a deep crevice in a field of red. Something awful, really awful, is seeping out of this open chasm. It's spreading like a cancer. And it has the power to wipe out entire cities! Danny, I'm frightened!"

CHAPTER THREE

J eff Cloudwalker released sigh of exasperation. Bands of gray churned out by a humming printer were interspersed with erratic striations of white and black. The lines contained a spectrographic analysis of trace elements in the samples taken by the guys in forensics at the scene of Darla Corey's death. When light passed through matter the spectrograph captured unique patterns. Nature imprinted upon each of her creations a fingerprint of sorts. Every molecule, atom, every part, and particle of matter had its own distinctive signature. A VGA monitor could display the breakdown of light into an electric rainbow of color. The graph being churned out by the printer contained far less impressive spikes in various shades of gray.

Hands, the rich brown color mandated by his Native American ancestry, swept over the computer keyboard. One screen after another appeared on the monitor as Jeff checked and rechecked current information. He could find no error in computation, no miskeyed data, nothing was overlooked. Forking his fingers through the thick thatch of jet-black hair, Jeff felt his frustration mounting.

A combination of elements, the likes of which he had never seen before, dominated the computer screen. The chemical composition was so alien Jeff was at a total loss for an explanation. He hated to ask Dr. Ralph Worthen, the chief pathologist, for help, but the old man had an uncanny ability to find information which might elude Jeff for hours. With a single glance the pathologist could put his finger on the most obtuse combination. Reluctantly, Jeff transferred the data onto a disc and headed for Dr. Worthen's office.

"Dr. Worthen? Could I trouble you for just a minute?" Jeff poked his head around the door.

Eyes, as wise and worldly as the dominant male in a wolf pack, lifted. A bush of heavy brows formed a shade over the predatory eyes Jeff found so unnerving. Even on his best days, Dr. Worthen's face resembled the slabbed features of Frankenstein in an old Boris Karloff movie. Tall, lanky, with heavy bones, the doctor seemed unfamiliar with a body which lacked athletic grace and muscular coordination. For all the limited appeal of his appearance, a remarkable brain was encased inside thick plates of bone which made him look like the missing link between an ape and Neanderthal man.

"Come in, Jeff, come in." A deep base voice rumbled upward from somewhere low in his abdomen with resonant tones for which an opera singer would have given his heart and soul.

"Ah, Dr. Worthen--I've got something here I need your expertise on. Can I put this disc in?"

"Just a minute, let me save what I've been working on." Long fingers, slightly swollen at the joints, covered with skin the same pallid color as the corpses over which he labored, jabbed at the computer keys with authority. "There, now let me have it."

Disc inserted, the doctor brought up the file, then leaned back in his ancient chair, whose worn springs emitted a groan of protest. "Hummm." He rubbed the nose which dominated his prehistoric face. A rasping sound filled the lab as he absently stroked his cheek because the most brilliant pathologist on the west coast had once again forgotten to shave.

Jeff settled back to watch Dr. Worthen ponder the spikes and bands of color on the screen. The forensic expert could have worked in any crime lab in the country, but his wife was frail, and her health demanded a dry, sunny climate--so they decided to move to Vegas nearly a quarter of a century ago. Crime busters from the big cities, like New York, LA, and Chicago, routinely called on Dr. Worthen for an expert opinion. It was one of the reasons Jeff took a job in a location he considered as barren and forsaken an outpost of civilization as his boyhood home on the Navajo reservation. But, several years under Dr. Worthen's tutelage would mean he could work anywhere he pleased, and the sunny beaches of California held a magnetic appeal to a kid who'd grown up amid monoliths of sandstone; earth comprised of red dust eroded from the cliffs by an abrasive wind; creosote bushes which clung to life with a tenaciousness known only in the desert.

"Ever seen anything like it, Doctor?"

"Hummm." The stroking hand continued to massage the stubble on his chin. "Strange, very strange indeed." Bony fingers tapped against a few keys, permeating the office with a hollow, plastic sound. "See this--

here?" His finger traced an erratic pattern of chrome yellow, electric blue, struck through with broad stripes of magenta which radiated downward into deep purple.

"That's hydro-carbon."

"Right. But here, where the blue begins--here we begin to see the signature of methyl, tertiary, butyl, and ether. That's what oil companies add to gasoline to help oxygenate fuel and make it burn more efficiently."

"So?"

"And here," he jabbed at the screen in the other corner, "is a mixture of the chemical compounds in detergent--to make a combustible engine run cleaner. I'd say what you're looking at is a premium grade of gasoline made in a Texaco petroleum plant. Probably one on the Gulf of Mexico. The general manager down there always goes a little heavy on ether."

"How do you know that?" Jeff's expression melted from one of studious intent to bewildered admiration.

"I was called in as an expert witness on a case in Houston a few years ago. Arson. I was able to identify where the suspect was getting his fuel and that gave the police an area to begin their search. Nothing to it really. You see, Jeff . . ."

The doctor leaned further back in the protesting chair as he began one of the informal discussions for which Jeff lived and breathed.

"Not only do elements leave behind a one-of-a-kind signature, but human beings do also so as well. Just as handwriting reveals clues about a person's character, so does everything else a human being touches. The refinery's general manager, the one I spoke about, has his own philosophy about the correct mixture of gasoline. The difference between the product which comes out of his plant and one in California may be minute, but it is the subtle differences in all things that make everything original. Like our fingerprints, or the retina of our eye--even our voice pattern. DNA, for god's sake! The Almighty, in His plan for the inhabitants of our earth, made every plant, mineral and human beings unique. Something we can call our own. The combination of atoms which make up every substance on earth decrees no two of anything is exactly alike."

Jeff nodded, even in identical twins there were pathological differences he'd been trained to detect. "There's a spike here I don't understand."

Keeping a finger depressed on the page-up key, the doctor moved the graph. "Ah! Yes, here it is." Lifting his glasses to rest on his forehead, Dr. Ralph Worthen brought the wrongly put-together face closer to the monitor, as if proximity could summon an answer. "Most unusual. I can't think what the combination of these elements would produce. Metallic sodium isn't readily available although calcium carbide can be purchased at most hobby stores. This band, here, looks like the gelatin preferred by most pharmaceutical companies for common medicine capsules. This is strange, Jeff, truly strange. Here is the signature of potassium nitrate and this band appears to be nothing more than an ordinary variety of wood." He traced the graph with his finger, following an erratic course of the color mixture up and down. Deep furrows brought graying eyebrows together in a taut line across his forehead. Rapacious, darting, eyes--blacker than deep space, swept across the computer screen repeatedly while he accessed the enormous memory data base of knowledge he'd amassed over the years for a comparable substance. "Don't know what it is for sure, Jeff. An old friend of mine used to be the head of forensics at the FBI. I'll email him this information--maybe he can give us some relevant input. All unofficial, of course. I don't want the lads in homicide to get wind of this until we know for certain what we're dealing with."

Offering an affectionate pat on the back, Dr. Worthen praised the most promising student he'd had in years. "Good work, son, somebody else would have missed this. You've got the mind of a modern-day Sherlock Holmes!"

Jeff was so filled with pride he felt as though his heart might pump blood out of his eye sockets. Dr. Worthen was never sparing with words of encouragement, it was more that Jeff was hard on himself. He tried zealously to be an exact replica of his mentor and when the intelligent old man complimented his work, Jeff knew the decision to leave behind his family, his tribe, the world of sandstone, flocks of sheep and goats, soaring temperatures and the ancient dwellings of the Anasazi was the right one.

"Only, Jeff--don't tell Danny just yet. Let me find out for sure what this is and then we'll call the boy."

A grin split the moon-round face. "Okay, I'll try to keep my mouth shut but you know how perceptive he is. Sometimes I think he can actually read my mind."

Dr. Worthen liked Detective Danny Armstrong as much as Jeff did. The doctor went out of his way to encourage their friendship and he was always willing to offer his expertise to students enraptured with a field of study most people considered abhorrent--the cause of death.

But Ralph Worthen had spent his life fighting death. He hated death and made a crusade of challenging the hold it had over humanity. Somehow, some way, he hoped by studying its causes, it's myriad and manifest methods--someday, he would cheat death of its ultimate victory!

Danny sat behind the wheel of an unmarked patrol car. On the passenger side, staring out the window, Sonny watched several dancers leave the hotel through the time office exit, his attention trained on a tall blond insiders said was Darla's closest friend. When a white Mercedes exploded from the employee parking lot, Danny jammed his patrol car in gear. "Here we go!"

They followed the sleek foreign car at a discreet distance, down Industrial Road, past the garish pink and white back entrance of Circus Circus, beneath the Sahara Avenue overpass. A quick jog down the Strip, in front of the Stratosphere Tower, and the dancer's car seemed to be headed toward brilliantly lit downtown casinos. An aura created by neon, a soft yellow haze, hovered over buildings backlit by electricity--Glitter Gulch.

"I'll bet she's headed for the Golden Gate."

"Only a buck and a half for prime rib after two in the morning." Danny grinned; his partner's voracious appetite was legendary at the station.

"Yep. Best deal in town. Can we eat too?"

"Why not!"

The coffee shop was filled as noisy diners jostled one another for an opportunity to eat plenty of good grub at low prices. They slid into a booth close to where the dancer joined a blowzy redhead, who was already seated in another worn, fake leather booth. Giving the waitress their order amid peals of raucous laughter from the women behind them, the plain clothes detectives settled down to eavesdrop on their conversation.

Sonny surveyed the room. Low, smoke-stained ceiling tiles were replicas of hand-worked tin ceiling tiles popular in the 1800s. Unfortunately, the effect only served to make the room seem dark and dingy; a layer of smoke, like a thick oily fog, hung in the air. "I can't believe how many people are eating at two o'clock in the morning!"

"Why not? We are."

Shaking his head at his partner and best friend's ability to cut straight to the heart of any matter, Sonny said, "Yeah, but we're different. We're still working."

"This is a twenty-four-hour town, my man, a city that never sleeps. Someone is always going to work in the middle of the night and someone else is just getting off at two in the morning. I think that's why a lot of people can't hack it here--a normal lifestyle is out of the question in Vegas . . . things like holidays, Saturday and Sunday off or a nine-to-five shift just isn't part of our way of life."

"You're right." A bone jarring alarm bell went off in the casino announcing a big slot jackpot. A carousel attendant called the amount over a loudspeaker which raised the noise level another decibel as friends of the winner shrieked their joy and suckers, who had faithfully dumped nickels, dimes, quarters and dollars into unfruitful machines for several hours, moaned a chorus of protest. "That 'n the gambling. Some people can't leave the slots and tables alone."

Danny watched the winner get pounded on the back by a tipsy brunette, who was probably his girlfriend or a date for the night, hoping to claim a share of the booty. "I can't imagine putting my whole paycheck into a slot machine."

"Yeah, especially after hanging out with Forbes. Damn, I used to think you stood a better-than-even chance of hitting a jackpot." Sonny watched an over-weight floorman reset the machine after the customer was escorted to the cage to sign a W-2 form and receive the remainder of his jackpot which couldn't be contained by an old-fashioned coin hopper inside the machine. Some downtown casinos resisted installing 'ticket-in/ticket-out' machines because they ruined the atmosphere created by a big jackpot winner.

"According to Forbes jackpots are random, purely random."

"It cracks me up to hear the guys at the station talk about their winning strategy for video poker. You can't make 'em believe there's a computer chip inside the machine that turns up the cards."

"A random number generator--a slice of pre-programmed silicone."

"Fortunes, fortunes are dropped down the chutes and some of them never wise up."

"How do you think Steve Wynn paid for the Mirage, his good

looks?"

"It's still beyond me ..."

Danny held up a silencing hand and Sonny stopped talking, his attention riveted on the exiting dancer's reflection in the mirror behind the bar. Slapping enough bills on the table to cover the tab and leave a tip far too generous for a cop, Danny and Sonny rushed to follow the girl onto the street. "Stay on her tail, I'll go get the car." Danny trotted off in the direction of the five-story parking garage.

Streets were as brilliantly lit as if it were broad daylight even though it was the middle of the night. Thousands of blinking-winking-pulsating incandescent bulbs and hundreds of miles of rainbow-hued neon made it easy to keep track of the dancer as she made her way beneath a canopy of lights over Fremont Street, headed for the Plaza. Milling crowds provided effective camouflage for the Korean, who looked like any other tourist in jeans, cowboy boots and a cotton tee-shirt emblazoned with an obscene message. Effortlessly, he dogged the girl, staying far enough back to blend in with other pedestrians crossing the street. From the corner of his eye, Sonny saw an unobtrusive, pale green Chevy roll into view. Without breaking his stride, he slid into the passenger seat and pointed to the dancer.

One of the things that made their relationship so unusual was the unspoken communication which flowed between the two partners as naturally as the uttered word. Danny eased the Chevy back into traffic and allowed the car to crawl down the street as if guided by a gawking tourist. At the Plaza, the girl took a hard left and headed toward the Nugget. "Shit, if she goes in there we'll lose her," Sonny groaned in protest.

"Naw, if she heads inside, jump out and tail her. I'll drive around the block until you come out again."

"She could easily spot the Korean Kurse."

"Let's change places." In a move well suited to a pack of clowns spilling out of a tiny car in a Ringling Brothers' circus act, Sonny slipped behind the wheel while Danny wiggled across his partner--the Chevy never slowed down but their antics attracted the attention of a few passing tourists. The two detectives learned through trial-and-error Sonny's Asian heritage was soon spotted in the predominantly Caucasian city if he pursued a suspect too long.

"There she goes."

Danny jumped out of the car at a dead run, sprinting through the cluster of people gathered on the street to watch another sucker playing an enormous slot machine called Big Bertha with the worst odds in every casino.

Cautious about threading his way through the press of tourists around turn-of-the-century antiques which lent a special elegance and charm to the Nugget, Danny kept a watchful eye on the graceful girl. She stopped, looked around as if seeking someone, then plopped down on a bar stool at the edge of the slot area. Danny flagged a change girl, purchased a roll of quarters, and ordered a beer from a passing cocktail waitress--then settled down to wait, trying hard to ignore the incessant clanging of a bell announcing another jackpot winner. His stationary position would allow him to overhear conversation if someone met the girl or if they remained at the bar. A video poker machine provided the perfect camouflage; he and fifty other frenzied gamblers pushed hold buttons with the inspired faith of a newly baptized Born Again.

The dancer was about halfway through her second drink when a guy slid onto the next stool. From the lack of surprise in her expression, the dancer knew this guy, who looked like he belonged in a bad B-movie. Black hair, tied in a ponytail, was slicked away from his face in hopes imitating Steven Segal would provide the intimidation factor he wanted to project. A deep olive complexion, rapacious black eyes and heavy bands of muscle added to the overall impression he was not a man with whom an ordinary person should mess. Danny had no trouble making a positive ID on the guy the department suspected was a courier for the east coast mob, Robbie Russo. He had a hard, handsome face which was easy to remember. The son of an aging Don, rumor had it Robbie was being groomed to take over his father's business interests in the west. When he spoke, Danny struggled to remain seated at the video poker machine. It was the voice on Darla Corey's answering machine! The couple left the bar, arms entwined around each other's waists. They were headed for the bank of elevators leading to guest rooms.

On the street, Sonny commandeered a parking space on a side street hugging the Nugget. The crazy Korean was leaning against the car, radio blasting, making lewd comments to every passing female. He snapped his fingers in time with the heavy metal music, popped his gum and presented thoroughly obnoxious characteristics to pedestrians.

Shaking his head, Danny got into the patrol car. "Man, you're impossible. What you're doing is considered sexual harassment these days."

Sonny grinned, losing his eyes to his humor. "Yeah, it sure is. But some of us ain't got no Anglo-Saxon beauty, you know. We got to beat the streets for our women!" He exploded with good natured laughter. "Find her?"

"Sure did." A queer feeling in the pit of his stomach welled up and took control of his emotions. "On the arm of Robbie Russo."

"Dooo tell!"

"That's not all." The feeling was stronger than ever now. It was a burning sensation, but it couldn't be compared to an acid stomach--it was purely emotional in nature. It was the sort of feeling you get when you took the first big plunge on a roller coaster, or when a plane hit a pocket of air and plummeted hundreds of feet in a matter of seconds. His throat was dry, and words got stuck halfway up his throat. "It was Russo's voice on Darla's recorder."

"The Senator can see you now." With cool efficiency and practiced ease, the secretary ushered Danny into an inner sanctum presided over by the distinguished Senator from Nevada.

"Ah, Detective Armstrong. Your timing is ideal--I've got a half-hour before I need to depart for Washington."

Danny looked the Senator up and down with a calculating eye. A familiar face stared back at him; he'd seen it countless times on television and in the newspaper. The Senator was if nothing else, excellent at public relations. A man of about average height stared back at him. Impeccably groomed, a blown-dry hairstyle, a suit from Saks, Bally's shoes, expensive gold cuff links, a heavy nugget style ring and Cartier watch with a face comprised of a million sapphire chips, conveyed wealth and good breeding. He exuded an aura of old money--at least as old as money could be in Nevada.

"Thanks for seeing me on such short notice, Senator. Your secretary told me you've got a heavy schedule."

"I've got to get back to Washington this afternoon. There's a committee hearing on the future of water rights for the Colorado River. With how fast Southern Nevada is growing, we can't afford to be cut out of our fair share anymore. Nevadans have just as much right to that water as anyone in California. I've got quite a fight on my hands, but fortunately I think I've worked out a deal with the boys from Colorado to trade them our gaming expertise for water shares. They don't have the population base to require the large water reserves allocated to the state."

"If gambling ever really takes off in their state it could be a lucrative trade."

"My secretary said you're here about Darla Corey. What is it you'd like to know?"

"Something about her past. Seems as though she's quite a mystery, we haven't been able to track down any family members. Since she worked for you several summers and you set up a scholarship fund for her at UNLV, I thought maybe you'd know more about her than the dancers she worked with."

Alarm reflected the Senator's discomfort. "Detective Armstrong, this is really embarrassing to admit when I've made myself out to be such a man of the people--I'm ashamed to say I don't know if Darla even had a family!"

"What about her personnel records?"

"Just a minute. I'll call Ely." Freshly manicured, his fingers kept missing the numbers on the keypad and he had to make three attempts before the call finally went through. A commanding, authoritative tone of voice spoke to the hotel operator. "This is Senator Hastings. Ring me through to my sister." In response to Danny's look of inquiry, he added. "My sister is general manager at our property in Ely. She can retrieve Darla's file for me. Kristin how are you?"

Danny made note of the change in the Senator's voice. Apparently, he had genuine affection for his sister, who was considered one of the State's most qualified gaming operators by many influential people.

"Listen, sweetheart, do me a favor. Remember Darla Corey? She interned with us about five--no, maybe eight years ago. We were so impressed with her ability we paid her tuition at UNLV. That's right! The pretty blond girl. I need you to get her personnel file and see if she had any beneficiaries listed. I'll wait." He put his hand over the receiver and spoke in Danny's direction. "It'll only take a minute. Kristin has everything on computer up there. Ely may be a backwater berg, but she insisted our entire operation use state-of-the-art technology. Kristin expanded our operation by marketing to the corporate environment. We get a lot of big corporations from back east who use our place as a management retreat. She had the runway at the airport enlarged to accommodate some big-assed jets. There's nothing to do in Ely except hold meetings and gamble! I didn't think it would work--but it has." His attention returned to the phone receiver. "What's there? Are you sure? Will you email a copy to me right now so Detective Armstrong can have it? Okay, thanks. Love you too."

He replaced the receiver, then accessed the interoffice communication software in his computer. In seconds a beeping sound came from a gray plastic box which revolutionized the transfer of information around the world; white paper protruded from the tray as the electronic message found its way via satellite to his computer.

"Here you are, Detective. I wanted you to see this. Darla listed herself as an orphan . . . with no next of kin."

Danny scanned the page. Date of birth was listed as August 28, 1979. Place of birth: Newark, New Jersey, in St. Anne's Hospital for Foundlings. An illegitimate birth? Put up for adoption?

"Thanks a lot, Senator. This really helps. No one else had any of this information."

"Well, Darla was barely nineteen when she interned her first summer at our place. Maybe she was ashamed of her origin but was too naive not to report the information on an application for employment. Now, if you'll excuse me, I've got to get to Hughes."

Hughes was the terminal for private jets and as far as Danny knew the Governor was the only one who traveled aboard the State-owned plane. "Do you fly, Senator?"

"No, but I find it a lot more convenient to take my family's corporate Lear back and forth to Washington. That way, I don't have to meet an airline schedule. Kristin doesn't need the plane too often and it doesn't cost the taxpayers anything."

"Senator, I've got just one last question."

"Sure, shoot." Placing file folders and stacks of paper in an eel skin briefcase, the Senator closed the locking mechanism and spun the dial fast--too fast.

"When did you learn about Darla's death?"

"Let me think." The ceiling came under his scrutiny as he tried to recall the circumstances. "Oh yes, I was on the plane. The pilot told me just before we touched down in Washington. I was called back for an emergency hearing on a bill to fund the nuclear waste site at Yucca Mountain."

"Yucca Mountain? That's a big issue these days."

"Unfortunately, people have been misinformed by a hostile press. The site would do a lot for the State."

"I don't know about that, Senator. Seems like having a mountain filled with radio-active waste in your back yard isn't such a great idea."

"You just proved my point, Detective. If you understood the first thing about how safely the product can be transported or how much income the State would receive by agreeing to become the recipient, you'd change your tune. Nevada doesn't have a whole lot going for it, you know. We don't have much to attract future growth--other than gaming."

"That's one of the reasons I like it here. I don't want to live in LA or New York, trapped with millions of other people. That's what makes the desert so special--it only appeals to a few! Senator, did you know when too many rats are put in a cage they turn into cannibals? That's what's wrong with big cities. Too many people, too little space. Me, I want to look out and see the horizon. I don't want a bunch of tall buildings blocking out the sun. I like the sound of coyotes yipping in the distance. In winter, we put hay on the other side of our fence because my roommate's property backs up onto a section of Federal land. You'd be surprised at how many wild burros and mustangs come out of the mountains to feed as soon as high passes get snow. We found an old bathtub at a thrift store, and we keep it filled with water for our little wild life menagerie--desert tortoises even pay us a call occasionally. I don't know, Senator, sometimes progress isn't all that it's cracked up to be. Thanks again for your time . . . and the information on Darla."

When Danny stepped out of the air-conditioned comfort of the Federal Building he felt like he'd walked into a blast furnace. He glanced up and down the street--heat generated waves made the air seem to shimmer. The financial center of Las Vegas sprouted several tall buildings, but it wasn't anything like New York--you could still see the turquoise sky which spread over the wastelands of Nevada. Danny said a silent prayer of thanksgiving for the blistering summers and taint of gambling. Those factors preserved the wonders of the desert; for just how long, Danny wasn't certain.

When Danny got home Forbes was out back, the garden hose snaked over the fence. For a city boy, he got a big kick out of feeding wildlife. He kept talking about running a plastic pipeline into the foothills to create a series of artificial ponds to provide water to endangered mountain sheep which still inhabited the area. He'd already turned the plot of land behind his fence into a Mecca for quail. The sight of a hen leading her little brood across the desert floor gave both bachelors an unexpected thrill.

It was such a beautiful evening, Danny brought a couple of cold beers and a bag of chips out onto the patio. "We got anything for dinner?"

"Sandra is going to bring Chinese on her way out."

"Is Elaine coming along?"

"I think so."

Forbes was unusually busy working the pool sweep back and forth Danny sensed the evening had probably been arranged for weeks. Sandra was a real nice girl, just the right type for Forbes. She never displayed any jealousy over his work--which could captivate his attention for hours. All the holiday dinners, birthdays, and other moments throughout a person's life which needed to be celebrated were organized by Sandra. The tall, lanky customer relations officer at Citibank had an annoying habit of trying to fix Danny up with the "right" woman. Due to the clerical nature of the banking industry, it appeared every female in Southern Nevada worked for Sandy at one time or another--and he felt like he'd met half of them. Only this time, it was different. He genuinely liked Elaine. She was as dark as he was blond, as tiny as he was tall. She was also as talkative as he was silent, so the attraction surprised him.

Popping the top off a beer can, Danny settled into one of the comfortable chaise lounges and prepared to watch the sun go down. He squinted against the bright orange disc steadily lowering behind the granite spines which sheltered the valley. "You get any info back on the real Darla Corey yet?"

"Ah, yeah, as a matter of fact I did." Putting the long-handled net used for scooping foreign objects out of the pool in its customary resting place on the block wall, Forbes headed for the den. When he reemerged, he had a piece of paper in his hand. "I got hold of the microfiche from the daily newspaper in Trenton and paid them to email a copy of the article about the accident."

Danny's gaze was fastened on the transformation taking place on the mountain. Dusk was painting canyons with ever deepening shades of magenta and gray. Before long indigo would steal across the sky, to be replaced by a midnight blue so dark it was almost black, against which a carpet of stars would soon emerge.

43

"The driver who caused the accident the real Darla Corey was killed in the crash. He was drunk."

"Look at this." Danny fished the email out of his pocket he'd obtained from Jordan Grey.

"Home for Foundlings? She listed her place of birth as an orphanage?" As twilight settled over the desert, photoelectric cells around the pool came on, casting circles of light on a manicured lawn in a pallet of assorted colors which Forbes seemed to be studying. "How could an orphan even think about going to college?"

"Something else interesting happened last night."

"Oh? What's that?" Forbes handed the email back to Danny without taking his eyes off the pool lights.

"I followed the girl that was supposed to be Darla's best friend after she got off work. She met Robbie Russo in a bar. While they were talking I realized it was Russo's voice on Darla's recorder."

"You're kidding!"

"Why would a known mob figure leave a message on Darla's phone in a tone of voice which conveyed familiarity--real familiarity? And how did an orphan get admitted to UNLV with no record of ever having graduated from high school? Did you get the information on Kevin Cox?"

"No. And now that you mention it, that's odd. Under the Freedom Information Act, I can usually obtain a full name, rank, gross salary, past and present duty assignments, with an office, or duty telephone number where the serviceman can be contacted. Awards, decorations and whether they ever attended a military school are part of their military file. Ordinary data usually comes back in a few hours." He glanced through the sliding glass door at his computer in the den. "The message light isn't on, nothing's been emailed to me yet."

Danny appeared to be studying red sandstone rocks which created the west wall of the valley. The desert landscape encouraged introspection and seemed to foster solitude. His eyes followed a dry wash, which was a river of dust in summer, from its origin at a higher elevation to where it spread out across the desert and disappeared into sand. "I think I know the identity of two men in the pentagram my Mom saw. I'll bet the silver-haired man is Jordan Grey and I'm almost sure the guy in uniform is a security guard at the Flamingo, Kevin Cox. Now Robbie Russo enters the picture, the youngest son of a mob king pin in the east. Seems to me all roads just might lead to Rome."

"Rome, New York?"

"It was a metaphor, Forbes, don't take me literally. This case is like a bullet. Trajectory is ruled by the laws of physics. The angle of the entrance wound tells you where the bullet came from and that's precisely what we need to know."

"You and Catherine and your feelings. Why can't you prove things like a normal detective? If I could figure out how Catherine performs her feats of magic, maybe I could put some faith in your mysterious emotions. But I can't, it doesn't make any sense. How can she hold something in her hand and extract valid information?"

"Catherine says the mind is the last great frontier. We know less about it than the vastness of the galaxy surrounding us."

"Danny . . ."

"Forbes, you've got to get rid of your notions about what constitutes reality. Maybe science will never get a handle on how Mom gathers information like she does, but it doesn't mean she's a lunatic. She's different, that's all. Like an Idiot Savant."

"What's that, Danny, another metaphor?"

"An Idiot Savant is a term for a person who has one brain function developed all out of proportion to the others."

"Catherine's got it together in other ways."

"She's probably the sanest person I know but she has a tough time fitting in. Ordinary people are afraid of her; they think she goes around reading their minds all the time."

Forbes studied the swimming pool, its floodlights refracting spheres of yellow, green, and red in ever widening circles. "Does she?"

"Nah! She's got too much integrity to poke around in other people's intimate thoughts. It's like throwing a switch. Catherine only tunes in when she wants to."

"I never wanted to be around her for too long because I thought she was going to uncover my inner most secrets."

"Yeah, I know. You and a lot of others. That's why she stays to herself most of the time."

"Maybe I have avoided her."

"One of her best traits is she understands other people and doesn't pass judgement on anyone about the circumstances they find themselves in."

"Danny," Forbes tone of voice was as reflective as the water in the swimming pool, "why would anyone want to kill such a beautiful, talented girl?"

"Everything happens for a reason, Forbes--even if we don't understand." It was Danny's turn to study the floodlights dancing beneath the water stirred by an evening breeze as the land began to cool. "I've got to find out who killed Glitter. I have a feeling this is tied to a lot more than one murder."

Danny shivered, aware of a cold emptiness inside, a hollow sense of loss he couldn't quite identify. He closed his fist--smashing the beer can. The metallic sound traveled up a ravine carved into the mountain by centuries of rain and wind. A hawk's cry seemed to mimic the sound and echoed up the narrow canyon--toward elusive mountain sheep living above the arid valley. It was an apocalyptic sound, a fear generating sound; it was the sound of death and destruction . . . and murder.

CHAPTER FOUR

Ron Mellon reached for the phone. His movement was slow, laconic. Like he didn't care whether he answered it or not; he just wanted the d thing to stop ringing. "You have reached the office of private detective Ron Mellon. When you hear the beep please leave a message and if private detective Mellon is so inclined, he'll call you back."

"I hope detective Mellon is monitoring this call because it's mighty important!"

When the voice on the other end of the line turned out to be his good friend, Homicide Detective Danny Armstrong, a wide grin claimed possession of his fleshy face. "Danny, buddy, how the hell you doin'?"

Ron was built like a bull, a huge square head appeared to sit on top of his shoulders due to the inappropriate girth of his neck; upper arms as big around as most men's legs; a barrel chest broad enough to disguise the beer belly, which expanded and contracted according to how much time he had to drink. Coarse, curly black hair capped his head and trailed down the side of his face to create a bushy mustache which reminded people of Zorba the Greek or Gene Shallot. If Ron didn't have neon-white teeth, no one would have known when the private investigator smiled.

"What's happenin' out in sin city? Hot enough to fry eggs on the sidewalk yet? The weatherman said it was going to be a hundred and fourteen fires of hell degrees tomorrow in Vegas! You horny toads and lizards can keep it! Me--hey, I'm out here in my porch swing, a cool breeze is blowin' in off the ocean, looks like we might even get a few showers this evening to kinda cool things off! You jealous yet, buddy?"

Danny visited Ron's beach house for a week last year. It was all he could stand. After living with Forbes, who was compulsively neat, Ron's castle was a living nightmare. The kitchen was cramped and dreary--it desperately needed a new coat of paint to replace the one which was applied nearly a decade ago. Most of the major appliances were scraped and dented and the refrigerator looked like a scientific laboratory for growing new species of mold. In the bathroom, the floor was chrome yellow from all the times Ron missed the pot when he was too drunk to aim, and the collection of cat hair stuck to the floor beneath the sink was more than Danny could stomach. There were newspapers and magazines stacked on the floor from six months ago. The carpet between a sagging couch and the television stand was threadbare; it did little to hide cracked and discolored linoleum beneath it. Danny loved the strapping detective with all his heart but hanging out with him in his habitat was out of the question. Next time, he'd stay in a hotel, bring pizza and beer out to the house, and sit on the porch, where he could enjoy the clean air and salt breeze. "I've got something I need you to look into, Ron."

"I'm between cases and all yours, pal. Shoot!" Ron swung his feet off the porch railing and sat up straight, focused on Danny's every word. Listening to his friend's story, with the phone compressed between his shoulder and jaw, Ron jotted down a few notes as Danny explained the bizarre coincidences in the showgirl's murder. "You're sure it was Robbie Russo?"

"No question about it."

"Damn, buddy, this could be rough. The Feds and boys at the State have tried to nail Russo for every crime in the book. Nobody's ever been able to get him into court for as much as a traffic violation."

Danny smiled as the finest investigator in the east registered a descriptive expletive, which expressed his frustration with the legal system. They'd met in Vegas when Ron was hot on the trail of a sixteen-year- old girl who ran away from her wealthy family. As a courtesy, Ron checked in at the station to let the local cops know he was in town to track down a stray kid. Like opposite ends of a magnet, the young men became friends at once--although their personalities were worlds apart. "I need you to find the real Darla Corey's family, if she had any."

"1966 was a hell of a long time ago, Danny."

"I know . . . but I'm desperate. I'm not about to go to the police because there's always the possibility informants might blow the case before I can make it."

"Sad but true, my man, sad but true. Why don't you email me a copy of the death certificate and the newspaper story about the accident? I'll check out the orphanage, but I seriously doubt if there was such a place. Sounds too hokey."

"Truth is stranger than fiction."

"Yeah, but my gut tells me this is too convenient. By the way, how is Catherine?"

"The same, as always. She sends her love."

"How's Damascus?"

"He farts, drools and pisses on everything--other than that he's fine."

"I just like to ask about him to get you all worked up, Danny. Gives me something amusing to think about when cable goes on the fritz."

"I don't find the dog amusing at all."

"I know--that's what's so funny!" Ron broke into a laugh so loud a flock of gulls took flight, squawking and screeching as though someone lobbed a rocket in their midst.

"Here's something else I want to pass on." A new note had taken up residency in Danny's voice; it conveyed anxiety, worry and more than a hint of apprehension.

Instantly alerted by the change in tone, Ron stopped laughing and gripped the phone so hard bronzed skin beneath the coal black hair on his knuckles looked like it might rupture. "Yeah? What's that?"

Danny related Catherine's vision about the pentagram with five men standing at the apex of each triangle. He described how upset Catherine became the minute she picked up the gold ring which belonged to the murdered showgirl.

The sun had set in the west long, long ago and wind coming off the ocean turned brisk. But Ron didn't notice the drop-in temperature, he was sweating. The hand clenching the phone was slippery and the tangy odor emanating from beneath his arms seemed to be fanned in his face by the nocturnal breeze. It was a nervous sweat, and it was acrid. He believed in Catherine, with good reason.

In the months it took to track down the runaway girl he'd been sent to find in Las Vegas, Ron became well acquainted with the psychic. Fascinated, he would tag along to the scene of a crime and watch her disseminate information from a realm he finally decided had to be cosmic. When he got back to Jersey, Ron made it a habit to hire Catherine as a consultant . . . only he kept their association a secret. Solving cases with the information Danny's mother obtained from a source that was both spooky and mesmerizing, Ron established a reputation for being the best private investigator around. Pretty soon people were coming to him from all up and down the seaboard. He had money in the bank for the first time in his life, although wealth and possessions were concepts which were foreign to the man of Armenian descent; he was only interested in being comfortable--and happy. Catherine's mysterious talents allowed him to pick and choose the cases he was interested in, but he already had a feeling about this one! He wasn't going to like it.

"What happened then?"

"She saw something red, a lot of it, and felt it represented death. Then a black tar-looking substance began to ooze out of a crack in the red and this stuff had the power to kill thousands of people. She was really frightened, and it scared me because she never reacts emotionally to a reading."

"... And she was holding the dead girl's ring?"

"It was only in her hand a few seconds because she threw it across the kitchen, like it suddenly turned red-hot. She was so agitated there were tears in her eyes and, Ron, I've never seen that kind of thing happen before. Not once in my life--and I've probably watched her do a million readings."

Fog began to curl in over the ocean. It crept up the beach, lingering along the sand. Like the killer fog Moses called down from heaven to punish Pharaoh for not letting the Hebrews leave Egypt. The mist advanced toward him like a predator stalking prey. Ron shivered, trying to keep his attention trained on the voice at the other end of the line. He'd sat on this porch, in this chair, and watched the fog roll in for years. It never seemed treacherous before. Now it contained menace as it crested the dunes and swallowed up strands of long grass, consumed by its monstrous advance. His attention was drawn back to the conversation, abruptly.

"Catherine said for both of us to be more careful than we've ever been before because there's something lurking just below the surface--and its evil."

Evil. It occurred to Ron he equated the advance of the fog to a story from the Bible he hadn't thought about since childhood--before he got old enough to leave home and escape the claustrophobic morals of his Pentecostal parents. Yet he was hearing it--hearing it from a source he deeply respected--Catherine Armstrong.

Ron stared at the obscuring fog which was only a few feet from his porch. A sudden fear of the dark, of bogeymen, of a devil waiting to pull sinners from the path of righteousness into the burning fires of hell made him jump out of the deck chair and head for the door. Sweat poured down the side of his face in wide rivulets and the ugly black stain beneath his arms spread across the back of his shirt. He slammed the door and shoved the dead bolt lock in place with the hand that wasn't clutching his cell phone. His heart pounded against his rib cage with the furious roll of a timpani drum. He shook his head and tried to concentrate on what Danny was saying. He was a grown man; a grown man being ridiculous! He hadn't experienced this kind of fear since he was a kid--waking up from a bad dream inspired by his minister father.

The image of red and blackened magma boiled up through the resisting layers of his subconscious. Instinct admonished Ron--he was connected to Catherine and somehow the picture displayed against the inner screen of his mind was being transmitted directly from the psychic to him.

Fear closed the passages to his lungs as surely as if he were having an asthma attack. Red did mean death, he could feel it. Ron Mellon could feel death in every bone in his body!

When the phone rang at seven o'clock in the morning, just before he stepped into the shower, Danny knew it was his mother. He didn't know how he always knew--but he knew just the same.

"Hi, Ma. What's up?"

Nonplused, Catherine seemed to expect him to know she was calling, even though it was an unusual hour for her to reach out to him. "Honey, I just got a strong feeling you should send Ron a color picture of Glitter."

"A color picture?"

"Yes, I'm sure the LVCVA must have a million publicity photos. They used her in their ad campaigns all the time."

"Gotta feeling for why I need to send him one?"

"No, dear, I don't. I only know you need to Fed Ex it out today." She glanced into the warm brown eyes of the Rottweiler who was patiently waiting for the last few bites of her toast. "Don't forget, Danny, it has to be color. Black and white won't be right."

51

Danny learned a long time ago simply to act on random bits of information that were as commonplace to his mother as the morning news was to others.

"You'll do that today, won't you, dear?"

"I'll get on it as soon as I get to the station, Ma."

"Okay, call me if you need me. I'll be home all day."

"Maybe I'll pick up a sandwich from Subway and Sonny and I'll drop by for lunch."

"Oh, that'd be great!"

"Make sure Damascus is locked outside when we come."

"Danny . . . "

"Just kidding Ma, I know you love him more than you do me."

"Danny . . . "

"I'll see you around one!"

Forbes and Sandy were standing in the kitchen when Danny entered through the door to the garage. Sandy was tearing lettuce leaves into a bowl and his roommate was deeply involved in chopping a tomato into precise pieces with the new knife he'd ordered off a late-night television commercial.

"Hi, guys." Danny glanced around the family room, trying not to be too obvious as he looked to see if Elaine accompanied Sandy. "What's for dinner?"

"Steak and salad," Sandy's tone of voice was neutral but she responded to his inquiring glance. "Elaine's out back, tending the grill."

"Women were not meant to cook over an open fire--that's purely a man's prerogative." Danny headed for the sliding glass door.

A breeze blew smoke from the grill beneath the patio overhang, and it lingered there a moment before dissipating with another gust. Acting as though he were fighting his way through a raging inferno, Danny took the tongs from Elaine's hand and motioned her away. "Here, let a man do it."

"Gladly," Elaine said with a sweet smile, "after all, cooking over a fire is a man's territorial domain."

"You sound like my mother."

"That's where I got it."

"Oh?" Danny sprayed water over the glowing embers to cool the fire and placed the steaks on strips of hot metal--a satisfying sizzle rewarded his efforts. "I didn't know you'd met her."

"I haven't. Forbes was telling Sandy and me about some of her theories."

"She's not crazy—just idiosyncratic." Danny watched the slender young woman out of the corner of his eye, trying to judge her reaction to his mother.

"Forbes had us take your mother's psychographic test today."

"And?"

"It was a lot to learn about yourself in one afternoon, but I confess, it seemed accurate. Where did your mother find out about all this stuff?"

"Catherine's goal in life is to determine how the mind works so she can better understand her own abilities."

The wind shifted, and smoke generated by fat dripping from steaks onto the coals began to blow into her eyes. It provided just the excuse she'd been looking for and Elaine rose, coming to stand near Danny. "Forbes said he created a program to track test results from your Mom's human subjects."

"Yeah, it's been a lot of help to her."

Her closeness made Danny nervous, Elaine could tell. If she kept him talking about a subject he was at ease with--maybe a sense of comfort would rub off on her. He was so cute, and shy. She found those traits endearing--he seemed to be everything her father and brother were not. "Do you think we'll ever understand what makes us tick?"

"Catherine thinks so. She says the brain is a big computer and human beings are programmed just like software."

"From my experience, I've found working with a computer pretty complicated."

"People generally follow the way they were programmed to behave as kids." He reached to turn off the gas flame; the steaks could finish cooking with ambient heat from lumps of lava rock beneath the grill. "We're all products of what we've learned." Glancing at shimmering water in the pool, he asked. "Do you swim?"

"Not very well."

"Are you afraid of water?"

Elaine shook her head, dark curls eddying around her shoulders as she replied. "No, not at all. It's just that I grew up in Kansas and didn't get to go swimming very often."

"Well, what if you'd nearly drowned as a child?"

"Then I'd probably be afraid of water." Deep brown eyes engaged him sincerely; living with a father who believed a leather strap insured good behavior made her appreciate Danny's gentleness.

Genuinely flattered by her attention, Danny felt a surge of confidence. "According to Catherine, if someone had a couple of bad experiences with water they'll try to avoid repeating the situation. She says the same principles apply to every aspect of our lives. Things we don't like usually stem from a negative experience."

"Including relationships?"

"Sure!"

"Then--why do people seem to make the same mistakes over and over?" She leaned forward; pressing her body into the space between them; why did her mother waste her entire life hoping things would get better?

"Because they only know how to behave one way."

Sandy appeared on the patio with a bowl of tossed salad in her hands. "Mind helping me set the table, Elaine?"

"I'll go get everything!" She disappeared into the house in search of napkins, a tablecloth, plates, and silverware.

"Sandy, I like Elaine. Thanks for bringing her along."

"She's a great girl, one of the best supervisors we've ever had at Citibank. Other women trust her--and that's important when you've got an office full of females."

Forbes had a long-neck bottle of beer dangling from each hand, "Want one?"

Taking a beer, Danny asked. "Forbes, did you get any info back on Kevin Cox?"

"My email light is flashing. Maybe I got a response." Forgetting about the steaks, Forbes headed into his office. When he emerged, he had a piece of computer paper clenched in his hand. "Danny . . . "

He reached for the sheet of paper Forbes thrust toward him, the beer left on the edge of the grill. A brief glance at the printed information made him cringe. "Kevin Cox's records are sealed?"

"That's what it says." Forbes examined the paper again, as if he couldn't believe what he read the first time. "The Military Locator Service will normally supply anyone with a current unit number and the installation a person on active duty is assigned to. Both the Department of Veterans Affairs and Paternity and Child Support Locator Service reported access to Cox's file was denied. Even his passport application is protected."

"Cox must be hip-deep into some pretty heavy stuff. Can you get around the protection code?"

"Boy, that'd be tough. Pentagon files are notoriously difficult to crack--for obvious reasons."

"So, what do we do now?" Danny's expression turned sour. He'd been counting on the information in Cox's file more heavily than he realized.

Elaine returned, her arms filled with eating utensils. "Did you know the Great Wall of China was never breached but the country was invaded by the Mongols four separate times?"

Three pairs of eyes turned to stare at her, incredulousness the common denominator in all their facial expressions.

"I went on a trip to China last year sponsored by the university. Our guide said the watch towers along the Great Wall were supplied with a mixture of saltpetre and wolf dung to create a long-burning fire. If the Mongols approached, a fire was lit, and a warning reached Peking within hours."

Forbes couldn't suppress his irritation with such a seemingly irrelevant comment. "Yeah, so?"

"So, if the wall was impregnable, how did the barbarians manage to invade China?"

Shaking her head, Sandy served up the salad and waved at Danny to take the steaks off the grill. "Beats me, how'd they do it?"

"They bribed the gate keepers."

A dawn of awakening came fast for Forbes, as if a bolt of lightning stair-stepped down from a bank of sodden clouds and the sudden crack of illumination made him feel as if a battering ram burst through the barrier which placed his brain in gridlock. "I don't know why I didn't think of that myself!"

Bewildered, Sandy looked to Danny, who seemed just as confused. "Got any idea what this lunatic is raving about?"

"Absolutely none, but I'm starved, and the steaks are ready."

"You can't be serious about eating at a time like this! Danny, get on the phone to that cretin friend of yours. The crummy guy in Jersey."

"Ron Mellon?"

"Yeah. Have him do a little skullduggery around the Pentagon."

"I hate to sound stupid, but why?"

"Because Elaine just gave us the answer to solving the mystery of Kevin Cox."

Elaine's expression was serene as she handed Danny steak sauce he hadn't asked for yet, but somehow knew he wanted.

"Have Mellon find out who would know the computer passwords for a file sealed in the main frame at the Pentagon--like the one belonging to Kevin Cox."

"That shouldn't take too much digging--but why do you want to know?"

"Because then we'll be able to find out the security password," Forbes decided he was hungry after all when the smell of steaks which had been marinating in Mesquite sauce all afternoon reached his nostrils, "and then we'll bribe the person who knows the code!"

Elaine blushed but was thrilled Forbes grasped the implication so quickly. Her eyes were huge and dark. Clear, direct eyes. Eyes that had witnessed more than her share of misery but managed to remain free of bitterness.

Each time Danny met her gaze, his breath caught somewhere in his throat for just an instant.

Danny stood with his feet apart, a shooter's stance, as he aimed at the target at the far end of the gallery. Both he and Sonny were due for weapons qualification, and they were spending a few hours of practice at the American Gun Club, just off Spring Mountain Road.

Slamming the clip up the butt of the Smith and Wesson 9mm with the heel of his hand, Sonny slipped on large lens glasses which were tinted bright yellow, adjusted his hearing protectors, and squeezed off a few rounds. With the push of a button, Sonny drew the target along heavy gauge wire toward him.

The front door opened, momentarily flooding the foyer with light. Danny squinted against the sudden brightness. Silhouetted against a setting sun were the broad shoulders of a powerfully built man, but his features were obscured by the penumbra of bright light.

As Danny turned back to the target, something at the edge of his peripheral vision aroused his curiosity. The image in the doorway plucked at the cord of memory. Danny pointed his service revolver at the target, but kept his torso angled at the foyer so the guy at the entrance would remain in sight. Oblivious to everything but aim and accuracy, Sonny hadn't noticed of the man waiting in the lobby.

After retrieving bills tossed on the counter, the weapons attendant handed a Heckler and Koch PM-5A1, the weapon of choice for most SWAT teams around the country, and four fully loaded clips.

The target clattered up the track and Sonny tallied his score. He would qualify again this year with ease. In fact, his scores were good enough to make the division marksmanship team which was just getting organized. Finally noticing his partner's concentration was on something other than target practice, Sonny shifted the direction of his gaze although he was careful not to turn and stare. Whispering, Sonny asked. "Who is it?"

"Kevin Cox." Danny watched with a mixture of admiration and

dread as the part-time security officer fired an entire clip into the paper bull's eye at the furthest distance in the range. Even from where he was standing, Danny could tell each shot was within a millimeter's radius of the center. With the confident motions of someone well acquainted with sophisticated weaponry, Cox swiftly withdrew the empty cartridge holder and rammed home another clip.

"Come on, let's get in the car before he notices us."

If Cox happened to glance at the door as they made a hasty exit, Danny was confident the setting sun would occlude any identifying details.

"Do you know which car is his?"

"No. Let's park across the street and wait for him to leave." Danny slid behind the wheel and headed for the bar on the other side of the street which catered to the country-western crowd. He slid the green, unmarked Chevy between two other cars, but maintained a direct line of sight to the building with the red and blue bull's eye and a cartoon of an older man teaching a young boy to shoot painted on the exterior wall.

When Cox finally exited the building and slid behind the wheel of a fancy Camaro, the deep purple color of a new bruise, Danny nosed his car into traffic and maneuvered in behind the security guard.

"You see the way he handled that Heckler and Koch?"

"Yeah, I did."

"He dumped a whole clip dead center into the target."

"Cox is obviously accustomed to handling some heavy-duty fire power."

They turned on to I-15 and headed north. Traffic was light, so it wasn't hard to keep track of the Camaro, although Danny allowed the sporty car to maintain a good lead as it shot through the interchange onto Highway 95. The Las Vegas valley was growing at such a rapid pace they almost reached the Mt. Charleston turn-off before houses started to thin out. A mileage marker on the highway indicated Reno was only four hundred miles away. When the Camaro didn't turn left, toward the mountain resort which provided welcome relief from the blistering temperatures on the desert floor, Sonny moaned. "Are we going to follow him all the way to Reno?"

"I don't think that's where Cox is headed."

58

There was a lengthy pause while Sonny stared at the Camaro darting in and out of other cars on the highway. "You think he's on his way to the Test Site, don't you?"

"Another twenty-five miles and we'll find out."

"Ease back, traffic's light, so we can keep his tail-lights in sight for quite a distance."

The two detectives concentrated on glowing red orbs floating above the road ahead as dusk deepened into twilight. When the entrance to the largest military reserve in the United States loomed closer, Danny sped up. A guard at the gate must have recognized both the purple car and its lone occupant because the sporty vehicle sped through the barrier with no appreciable signs of slowing.

When the line of faded umber hills bearded with scrub brush thrust between the unmarked patrol car and the guard house, Danny pulled off onto the shoulder, spun the car around and headed back to the broad valley. Las Vegas shimmered as darkness claimed the desert. Millions of lights made the city seem bigger than it really was. Even from twenty miles, it was easy to pick out the Strip and cluster of gaudy hotels on Fremont Street. Those areas were ablaze with the greatest concentration of lights. Residential areas, which spread from Sunrise Mountain to Mt. Charleston, from Hoover Dam to Boulder City disappear into the west so far it seemed like Las Vegas would merge with LA someday. An unusual silence fell between two men concentrating on the same objective; when Danny finally spoke, Sonny jumped.

"I wonder if Forbes can find out Kevin's area of assignment at the Test Site. I've got a funny feeling it might be Area 51."

Lights behind the dash cast a sickly green pallor over the Korean's face. "You're kidding--aren't you? You're trying to spook me, right?"

As the lights of the gaudiest city in existence grew brighter, Danny gave into the feeling that had been nagging at him all night. Rumors about Area 51 surfaced every now and again. The Stealth bomber was developed under a complete cloak of secrecy in the remote area accessible only to highly classified personnel. A couple of years back, a local newsman conducted an expose on a supposed government cover-up regarding Extra Terrestrial activity on earth. According to some reliable sources there was a real UFO in one of the huge hangers constructed in the middle of the most God-forsaken stretch of desert in Nevada. Unfortunately, before the uproar of the local citizenry could generate momentum, the newsman disappeared. No one ever knew what happened to Harold Kennedy, but he never anchored another prime-time news program in Las Vegas.

The chill of intuition which guided Danny all his life made gooseflesh rise on his arms. Fear rose and fell in him ever since he'd first thought about the Test Site--at the moment it was running at high tide although he tried to swim against it. "The stuff the military does out there is so secret even the Pentagon doesn't know about it."

"There've been rumors about Area 51 for as long as I can remember, Danny, and I don't think anything has ever been proven."

"You're right, nothing's been proven."

They both stared out the windshield at the encroaching glow of lights as bright as the Aurora Borealis. Finally, Danny summoned the courage to give voice to thoughts which plagued him. "All those people who got cancer in Utah were down wind of the atomic bomb detonations the government conducted above ground in the '50s. They can't prove anything either. But a lot of people died. Now it's a matter of public record over a thousand nuclear bombs were exploded at Frenchman's Flat right up until 1992. Over nine hundred were exploded underground, some directly into the Great Basin Aquifer."

Sonny turned toward Danny. The eerie glow of dashboard lights made it seem like the flesh had melted off his best friend's head. For one brief, awful moment, Sonny felt as though he were staring at the bones of a skeleton; primordial fear took command as logic evaporated. "Doesn't the aquifer under Nevada contain more fresh water than the Great Lakes?"

Danny's voice ricocheted through the interior of the Chevy like a ball bearing rattling around in a tin can. "Yeah. The government hasn't been exactly square with us on a lot of matters. There's more going on out there than we know. My mother's right--nothing is what it seems."

Fear assumed a strangle hold on Sonny's emotions. His throat constricted, and his eyes began to water, an involuntary reaction to the debilitating sense something awful was going to happen. A morbid recognition that Death was lurking close--too close--to his home. Although reluctant to accept it, Sonny realized his friend spoke with the clarity and vision of an Old-Testament prophet!

Lights from the black and white unit threw splashes of red and blue across pavement hot enough to fry an egg. Sonny pulled his car into the parking lot behind the Wholesome Bakery, out of the way of traffic hurrying beneath the railroad overpass on Charleston. An older woman leaned against the concrete wall, a puddle of fresh vomit pooled around her feet. The boys from the squad car were being heavy-handed with the old gal because she'd splashed their shoes when she puked.

"Hi, guys. What's the haps?" Sonny sized up a woman, about sixty, whose looks were claimed by alcohol long ago. She was wearing an oversized pink sweater and a pair of white stretch pants, which emphasized the ripples and valleys of cellulite in the back of her legs. Over-processed hair was bunched in unattractive clumps, like she'd just rolled out of bed and hadn't bothered to run a brush through her tattered locks.

"Got a complaint from the owner of the bar on the corner. She was causing quite a ruckus. Taxpayers were almost relieved of another burden though, she damned near stumbled out into traffic."

"Gonna take her in?"

A look of disdain passed between the two patrolmen. Sonny knew they were dreading the possibility she might toss her cookies inside the squad car on the way to the drunk tank downtown. "How about if I take her over to the women's shelter at Salvation Army?"

With relief so pronounced it was almost visible, the two officers nodded in agreement. "Yeah--go ahead."

Sonny opened the front door of his Toyota as if he were about to usher the future Queen of England inside a limousine. "Here you go." He placed her purse on her lap with care and closed the door softly.

The smell of alcohol was overpowering but Sonny refused to open the window. Instead, he directed the air conditioning vent at his face with as much discretion as possible. He needn't have worried though, the woman had leaned back against the headrest and her eyes were closed.

When he pulled into the shelter, the director met him at the doorway almost before the car came to a complete stop. "Hi, Sonny, got a guest for us tonight?"

"Sure do, Sam. I think the lady could also use a sandwich and a cup of coffee. Got anything left from dinner?"

Supported between the two men, the aging cocktail waitress made her way into the community dining room with as much dignity as she could muster. They found an empty table as the shelter director scuttled toward the kitchen. When he returned, Sam Levenkowski carried a tray heaped with crustless chicken sandwiches cut in fancy shapes and two steaming mugs of coffee. "You were responsible for the chicken, my friend, so I thought you might as well enjoy the benefits."

"South Point came across, I take it."

"Your talk with the Food and Beverage Director helped us out a lot these past few weeks."

"Well, hell, they might as well give the shelter the banquet left-overs rather than sell them to the hog farmer in Pahrump."

"Still--I appreciate your efforts in our behalf. Yell if you need more coffee."

Sonny watched Sam amble through the dormitory which housed upward of five hundred men. Even though it had been twenty-five years, the man who spearheaded the Salvation Army shelter still walked with a pronounced limp earned in the shelling of Da Nang. Pushing a sandwich in the woman's direction, Sonny took one for himself. After a bite he nodded approvingly. "It's good, try one."

The woman wolfed her way through chopped poultry layered between four slices of whole wheat bread as though she'd never had a meal before. By the time the tray was empty, a more natural glow blossomed on her cheeks, and she sat up a little straighter, less tipsy than when she'd entered the large room filled with beat-up picnic tables.

"I can make arrangements for you to stay here a couple of nights-- if you don't have any place else to go. My name's Sonny Yi, Detective Sonny Yi."

"Thanks for not lettin' the cops haul me off to the tank. They're hard on women down there. I've got a little place of my own over on Fifth Street. It's not much, but the price ain't ritzy either."

"Okay, I'll be glad to take you home--if you'd like me to."

"That'd be nice. Cabs are kinda out of my price range right now. I lost my job the other day. By the way, the name's Rita. Rita Brown."

Sonny extended his hand across the table. "Glad to meet you Rita Brown." The smile eclipsing his eyes was warm and genuine.

The shelter was his pet project and Sonny made a habit of calling on high school chums, who made the hotels and casinos a career, asking them for donations in the form of used blankets, furniture too worn out for guest rooms and food not consumed by revelers at a banquet or convention. "Where did you work?"

"I was a change girl at Sassy Sally's. They said my bank was short once too often. Maybe it was. I don't remember. It's going to be a couple of weeks before my unemployment kicks in. The bastards down at the Culinary Union said they think they'll have trouble placing me because of my age." A vigilant glint rose in the woman's blood shot eyes.

"Rita, it's illegal to discriminate because of age. Let me know where the union sends you, I might know somebody in HR who can help out." Sonny withdrew a business card from the wallet in his hip pocket and handed one across the table to the alcohol battered woman.

"Thanks." The hand which reached for the card belonged to a woman who once took pride in her looks. Her motions were still feminine, and long fingernails testified to a recent coat of polish. "Why are you bein' so nice to me? I ain't got nothin' you'd want."

Shifting his weight against the cheap redwood bench, it squealed. With a shy smile, which seemed out of character in the normally brash detective, and a hesitant tone of voice, Sonny offered, "I want to be a writer someday--stories! You never know when the people you meet will provide you with material for a novel. You've got an interesting face, Rita Brown. I'll bet you could tell me a thing or two about the early days of Vegas!"

An expression tinged with delight claimed the woman's haggard features; it seemed to come from a sunny chamber which had been covered over for so long it surprised Rita to discover it was still there. "Sonny Yi, I could tell you stories about some of the big wigs in this town that'd make your hair stand on end!" She laughed, a deep throaty laugh, a laugh of genuine assurance.

"Why don't I take you home now? But first, Ms. Brown, I'd like to make a date for dinner tomorrow night. We can go anywhere you'd like and talk the night away."

"Anywhere in town?"

"You name the place and I'll pay the price."

"Kiddo, that's the best offer I've had in years!"

Catherine Armstrong opened the back door of the home she also used as a business before the Judge could knock. After ten years of friendship, it still came as a surprise that she could sense his quietest approach. "Hi! Ready for dinner?"

"Just a minute, I need to lock the front door. Come on in."

"Where's that dog of yours?"

As though summoned, the Rottweiler stepped from the shadows of a darkened living room. A woman's dog, the Rott sized up the person in the doorway carefully--then crossed the tiled kitchen floor in a predatory gait. From somewhere deep within the broad expanse of chest cavity, a low rumble sounded like distant thunder.

"Catherine, do you think this dog is ever going to accept me? How old is he now?"

"Five." Dressed in a short black dress, black stockings and high heels, long hair resting against her shoulders, a casual observer would never have guessed Catherine was close to fifty. "He likes you well enough, Carrington, it's just that we're alone a lot and he's as spoiled as an only child. He resents it when I leave the house."

"Catherine, he's a dog."

A web of lines around her eyes gave personality to her expression when she laughed. "Not to me! Where are we going for dinner?" She bent over, to kiss the Rott's massive head, leaving a faint lipstick stain on the glossy coat. "I'll be back soon, Damascus. Don't worry."

The Judge opened the Mercedes passenger door for a woman he would have been delighted to marry--but repeatedly refused him. "The Bacchanal Room."

"Caesars!"

"Tonight, lovely lady, we're on a comp. I called in a marker from the Senior VP of Operations."

"For the Casino Host you kept from being placed in the black book?"

Judge Carrington LeMoye shook his head as he navigated around the hood of the expensive German auto. His thoughts were as clear to Catherine Armstrong as a well written legal brief was to him. He'd quit trying to keep anything from her a long time ago.

The Gaming Control Board maintained a list of undesirables who were banned from entering casinos throughout the State if their name appeared in the government agency's "black book": Card counters, known mob cronies and other disreputable characters. Charlie Covington had questionable affiliations, of that there was no doubt, but the Judge managed to keep the guy from being locked out of the gaming industry.

The big Mercedes rolled up beneath the porte cochere which welcomed visitors to the posh resort. A uniformed valet attendant reached the car quickly, recognizing the distinguished figure emerging from an interior darkened by black tint on the windows. "Evening, Judge." After escorting Catherine to the curb, the young man returned, handed the Judge a claim ticket, slid behind the wheel and flew toward the valet parking area-- tires squealing in loud protest.

Catherine Armstrong had been in Caesar's Palace many times. She was familiar with the layout of its sprawling casino, Cleopatra's Barge, the promenade of shops, restaurants and the Forum--Caesar's answer to competition inspired by the Venetian and the threat posed by the opening of all new properties springing up around town. But this evening, the glitz and glamour was different. A nacreous haze seemed to hang over a glittering world of crystal chandeliers, velvet, white satin togas on gorgeous cocktail waitresses, marble, polished brass, the click of dice and shush of cards on green felt tables. The noise generated by two thousand slot machines almost drowned out a rock band grinding out the latest top forty tunes in the casino lounge. Catherine felt tense, as if a feral kind of danger lay in wait somewhere between banks of slot machines and rows of Blackjack tables. When they passed the elegant elevators, which led to the Fantasy Tower, the psychic felt a magnetic pull which demanded action. "Carrington, do you know the Hotel Manager on duty?"

The Judge scanned the registration desk, looking for a familiar face. "Why yes, I do. Matt O'Brien is the son of one of the Assemblymen in your district, why?"

"I'd like to see the 'Rainman' suite, if possible."

Carrington LeMoye witnessed the expression change on Catherine Armstrong's face often enough to know she was responding to an inner urging. "Our dinner reservation is for 8:30."

"Couldn't you call the Maître d' and tell him we've been detained?"

The pleading look accessed his heartstrings so completely he could not have refused Catherine if she'd asked him to fly to the moon by flapping his arms. "Wait here."

After placing a call on the closest house phone to the Hotel Manager, a young man quickly appeared with a slim plastic card in hand; technology replaced old-fashioned metal keys with an encoded magnetic strip on a small plastic rectangle.

"Good evening, Judge. I'm afraid there's not much to see in the 'Rainman' suite--it's still being refurbished."

"That's all-right son, we'd just like to look around a minute before we go to dinner."

Catherine clutched the evening bag so tightly her knuckles were sharp and white as they entered the opulent elevator. Their footsteps echoed eerily on a polished marble floor. When Matt O'Brien opened the door, Catherine reacted with terror.

"Dear God," she whispered as she tried to stave off the panic which threatened to engulf her. Silence in the suite was sepulchral and somehow threatening. Its air was dank and warmer than in the casino. A huge living room was as dark as a basement although Catherine knew her imagination was painting shadows blacker than they really were.

"What is it?" Judge LeMoye was alarmed by the tremor in her voice, it held a quavering note which instantly put him on the defensive.

"Carrington, let's get out of here--right now! Please."

"Of course. Son, will you get Valet on the phone? Tell them to bring my car around immediately. Also, call the Maître d' in the Bacchanal Room and tell him we won't be having dinner. I've got to take the lady home."

A thick, heavy red cloud poured in on Catherine from all directions. She felt like the temperature on the elevator landing had risen a thousand degrees. Red. Then black. A sticky substance rolled down the hall to engulf them. It made her head spin, Catherine fisted her hands and turned directly toward the encroaching fog, determined to understand, determined to face the horror. Death. Death was all around her. She sought the Judge's arm, desperation overriding logic, making her feel as though she had to escape--would do anything, absolutely anything, to avoid the feeling something as awful as Bubonic plague was about to be unleashed in Nevada. Suddenly, she could no longer fool herself. She realized her confused, disoriented state was the result of mind-numbing fear. She tried to deny what was coming, tried not to think about it; she struggled against the impressions which poured into the elevator, but in her heart, she knew. *She knew.*

CHAPTER FIVE

Harold Kennedy stared out the window at a rain-grayed landscape. Blustery wind was huffing outside, punishing the desert floor with its turgid breath. Daylight was melting into darkness. It seemed as if all color had been washed out of the mountains surrounding Las Vegas. Gusting at a steady twenty to thirty miles an hour, it seemed more like fifty when it blasted his shabby office building broadside. If Harold had to give the wind a personality he would have called it a banshee because it shrieked across the parking lot, shaking spindly pine trees with unabated fury until they dropped their needles.

While the wind moaned beneath badly weathered eaves as rain began to hiss at dirty panes of glass, Harold pondered his bleak destiny. It was a word and a concept to which he'd given little thought--until now. If anyone questioned him about his belief in destiny a year ago he would have laughed and said he was the captain of his own ship of fate. Now, it seemed a cold, hard, irrefutable fact that all men and women bowed beneath Destiny's implacable hand. No matter how hard you tried, no matter how talented or dedicated or filled with ambition and enthusiasm-- ultimately Destiny decided the course of your life.

It was monsoon season in the dry, dusty desert and the sky outside was darkening. Although still early, stormy, weak light made it feel like evening. If he were to be totally honest with himself it felt later than that-- it felt like the end of the world was waiting on his doorstep.

Harold decided he'd better get into his office, fill his coffee cup, and go to the bathroom. Anything to stop the downward cadence of thoughts which threatened to turn into a full-blown depression--with the potential to end up in an all-night bender. In the lavatory, he poured cold coffee down the drain and glanced into the mirror. What he saw shocked him!

Bloodshot eyes stared back. His eye sockets appeared to collapse into his skull, like supporting bone and network of tissue caved in under the weight of his recent experiences. His face was gaunt and shockingly pale.

All the blood in his lips apparently took up residence in the whites of his eyes. Harold thought of himself as being a square man in every respect; a thick, blocky body; stubby forearms covered with sandy hair; a heavy face he'd once considered charming; a mouth too thin to be in harmony with his other features; a nose ending in a lump; and eyes just wide enough to make him appear as though he were in a perpetual state of wonder.

At one time, Harold thought his plain, average, unthreatening features were what endeared him to the viewing audience of Las Vegas. Ratings on his six o'clock television news show consistently blew the competition out of the water for several consecutive years. He thought for certain one of the brass in to attend the National Association of Broadcasters convention would tap him for bigger and better things than a community with a relatively small population could offer.

But that was before Destiny stepped in and snatched success from his grasp. It all started innocuously enough; on a dark and stormy day--like today. Maybe the wind and rain were what tripped the switch on his mental treadmill. The endless loop of thought which demanded he analyze what went wrong, over and over again. The investigative work he'd done on the Test Site was an outstanding piece of journalism. Some of the news magazine format shows expressed serious interest in running at least a version of the story. When one of the major network VPs called about airing it during prime-time network news--Harold felt certain he'd made the leap to the big time.

It seemed like everything was within his grasp. While he hadn't signed a contract with anyone to air the piece nationwide, there was so damned much interest he hadn't even thought twice when the plum of a job was dangled in front of him. He should have known, damn it, he should have known!

Within six months of quitting the station, not a single network offer panned out. All the months of demanding work uncovering secret military hardware developed at the Test Site vanished like a wisp of smoke. And the high paying job at the Nuclear Energy Commission, with all its cushy government perks and connections to important people--dried up like a mud flat in the Mojave Desert. Here he was, working nine to five in a squalid ad agency with barely enough business to eke out a meager living for him and his partner.

Spring brought an exorbitant amount of rain. The Colorado River Basin Authority was considering letting the water run over the spillways at Hoover Dam for the first time in years. Maybe he'd drive out to the dam tonight. The tall concrete horseshoe enclosed on both sides by towering canyon walls seemed like a place in a dream when the floodlights threw pools of color along sheer rock walls and smooth surface of tons of concrete holding back the Colorado River. Hell, maybe it wasn't such a promising idea, it would be too tempting to throw himself off the dam--to end his torment once and for all.

Back in his office, the phone shattered the silence with a discordant buzz. "Yeah." His tone of voice was unnaturally harsh, but his mood matched the steady drizzle which continued to slide down dirty windows. "Okay, put him on." Sweat turned his shirt collar sodden when he heard the Senator's over-friendly tone of voice.

"Harold? Harold Kennedy?" Senator Mathias Hasting addressed him as warmly as a long-lost friend.

"Yes, Senator, this is Harold Kennedy."

"I had a tough time tracking you down, Harold. No one at the station or NEC seemed to know where you were working these days."

"Well, Senator, the government and I didn't exactly part on the best of terms."

"I'm sorry to hear that. You know how stuffy the boys in Washington can be at times. Their way of doing things back east is foreign to those of us from Nevada. I've had to learn to keep my holster in the leather, so to speak. One thing my tenure in the Senate has taught me is to keep my temper in check. Anyway, enough about me. I've missed your sagacious news reports, Harold. How have you been?"

Harold was pleasantly surprised at the note of concern in the Senator's voice. "I'm getting by. The action isn't what I'm used to, but maybe I won't die of a heart attack at fifty-two."

The Senator glanced at his watch. He needed to leave for the airport in fifteen minutes if he was going to make it to Nevada in time for the fundraising dinner at Bally's. He didn't have a lot of time for schmoozing with this loser; better to make his pitch and get off the line. He'd let Harold mull the offer over for a few days. The CEO at First Interstate Bank owed him some favors. Mathias called in his markers to learn Kennedy's ad agency was barely hanging on. A big client with a lot of advertising and public relations needs was just what the ex-newsman needed to stay afloat.

"Harold," the Senator cleared his throat, as if the next words dried up somewhere along the esophageal tract and he was having trouble, sincere trouble, getting them out, "I, ah, I don't know quite how to put this. Oh, what the hell, I'm just going to come right out and say what I've got to say and then get off the phone. No point in wasting your time. Harold, I consider you one of the most honest men I know. That's what got you in such big trouble, son. Few people appreciate that quality anymore, especially in the political arena. But I'm different from the rest of the pack, Harold, and I can't stand to see a good man go down. Particularly when you did the right thing. I want you to take over the advertising and public relations for the Hastings family casinos. We're not in the same league with the guys on the Strip, but I'm sure you'd find the account sizeable. We could use your expertise and you'll find my sister a dream to work with. She's got a lot of innovative ideas, but she can't translate them into good advertising messages. I'll give you some time to mull it over. Hey, maybe you could spare a few days to run up to Ely and do a needs assessment on our place. We've also got a hole in the wall over in Hawthorne, but if you're driving it's a nice break on the trip along Highway 93. Now, just because we're small, I don't want you to turn us down sight unseen. Please, Harold, talk to my sister, Kristin, then give me a call."

The phone line went dead, and Harold Kennedy stared at it like the handset had become an oracle who just predicted a future beyond imagining. Was he dreaming? Had he finally gone around the bend? Was he hallucinating about salvation? Glancing at the digital display indicating the phone number of an incoming call, Harold reached for an old, dog-eared phone directory. The area code was for Washington, D.C. He *had* been talking to Senator Hastings!

Too small! Good God, a local Taco Bell would be a welcome addition to his roster of clients. Maybe there was a benevolent God in heaven after all. Harold Kennedy shot through the door of his office calling his partner's name as he exploded down the hall!

The heat and humidity of Newark was oppressive now that Robbie had grown accustomed to desert dryness. He couldn't seem to stop sweating and it irritated him the brand-new Armani shirt was sticking to his ribs like a layer of BBQ sauce. There was one thing he did like about the east coast though. Women seemed to appreciate his dark hair and olive-tinged skin more than they did out west. Even though Vegas was a five-hour drive from the sunny beaches of California, blond hair, blue eyes, and a golden tan attained by Anglo-Saxon pigment drew women like a magnet. He returned appreciative glances cast at him with a suggestive leer of his own as he approached a minibus which would take him to the rental car agency at the far side of the Newark Airport.

After bestowing an inviting wink on the desk clerk, Robbie scooped up keys to a Lincoln Town Car and, with reluctance, left the air-conditioned comfort in the building for the street outside. Congestion was crushing. Robbie was surprised at how much he'd grown accustomed to the wide valley with its broad streets lined with buildings which were seldom more than a couple of stories high. Unless you were in the lengthy shadows cast by one of the four or five thousand room mega-hotels which peppered the desert floor like buildings on a Monopoly board, the sun was always shining down on you.

Nosing the big black car into traffic, he headed for the wooded estate his father owned a few miles from Millburn. Robbie cursed the clog of honking cars impeding his progress. A tough guy persona he adopted always faded when he got anywhere near his father, Jake Russo. The old man was a rough bastard. Robbie gave him credit for fighting his way to the top of the mob food chain. He'd given up trying to love his father years ago; he respected the Don, and envied his power, position, and cunning. Jake's intelligence was legendary. Robbie admitted his sharpness of mind, the ability to sum up a situation in the blink of an eye, an almost sponge-like capacity for soaking up information was not genetically passed on to him.

Robbie was a lot more like his mother, a one-time opera hopeful. He wore his emotions on his sleeve; the macho image was like a suit of armor he donned whenever he felt threatened.

After Jake staked a claim on his mother, it would have been unseemly for a good Italian girl to devote time or energy to anything but her husband and children. God forbid she develop a career! When Maria DiBenedetto married a no-account kid off the streets, her parents were frantic. An immigrant's ambitious dreams for the first child to be born on American shores vanished like mist before the summer sun. Grandmama DiBenedetto never forgave Jake for ruining her daughter's chance at becoming a world- class diva. Robbie loved his mother and grandmother with whatever heart he had--other women were for indulging his animal passions. Almost all other women.

Sweat began to pour down the side of his face and he tried to tug his thoughts away from Darla Corey. He loved the nickname, Glitter, it suited her sparkling personality. Robbie tried not to think about the golden girl anymore. Whenever he did, a deep, dark gloom lasted for days. He forced his thoughts to remain focused on the coming encounter with his father. Why did the old man demand he come east? Everything was going smoothly in Vegas; he'd followed the Don's instructions to the letter. As far as Robbie could tell every "t" was crossed and every damned "i" got dotted. That much he had inherited from his father!

Braking to a choppy stop in front of the fancy iron-work gate which separated the secluded estate from a quiet street, Robbie smiled bravely into the camera lens. With a rapid blur of his hand, which attested to numbers committed to memory, he punched in the proper sequence on a numeric pad inside in a brick pillar. A fortune, a literal fortune, was spent on the electronic surveillance system, which protected his father from would be rivals and unexpected visits from the police. The gate slid back slowly, another built-in protection feature. From the den in the enormous castle-like structure, sheathed with slabs of thick gray slate brought all the way from the mountains of Wales, his father could override the mechanism if he decided the occupant of the car was not welcome. Robbie witnessed the gate demonstration. It was really a battering ram overlaid with twining leaves and clusters of grapes cut from half-inch thick iron plate. The velocity was controlled by a button at his father's desk. When traveling at full speed, the gate could ram an average automobile into the reinforced concrete wall on the opposite side with the force and impact of an onrushing locomotive.

Maria Russo met her son on the porch. Jet black hair was now streaked through with silver and a figure which was once the talk of all Jersey in the '50s and '60s had swollen and sagged with time. Snapping black eyes missed nothing, although his mother learned to keep her suspicions to herself at the very beginning of her marriage. When Robbie stepped out of the Lincoln, she rushed down the steps to embrace him.

Maria Russo's children were the light of her life and Robbie was the only one of her large, animated flock separated from her by such an enormous distance. It was a grudge she still bore against Jake for sending her precious baby son to a God forsaken wilderness! Where her children were concerned, Maria challenged Jake with the ferociousness of a lioness protecting her cubs. But Robbie wanted to go, desperate to prove his worth to a man the poor boy was incapable of pleasing. No matter, Robbie was her favorite child and had a way of pleasing her that was beyond explaining! She was enchanted by his winning smile, the tall, muscular body, his plum-dark eyes which were the perfect mirror of her own--this last child was truly her child, and Maria knew in her heart of hearts it was the reason Jake was so hard on the Robbie. Her husband resented the bond between them which only strengthened as the years went by. It infuriated Jake and he refused to accept there was something in this world he couldn't control, couldn't manipulate to suit his ends. Jake had the last laugh after all and dealt her a punishing blow by sending her beloved son into the cruel Nevada desert.

"Mama! You're more beautiful than the last time I saw you!"

"I can't remember that far back! And lying will get you nothing with me, my darling--only the sun, moon and stars." Maria clutched her son and buried her face in his chest. "Robbie, Robbie, life is not the same without you."

Robbie pulled her away and held her at arm's length. "Mama, he can't last forever. Then things will change, you'll see." He kissed her tenderly on the forehead and led her into the house. "Where is he?"

"Where is he ever? In his office. Don't be too long, I've got lasagna cooking--just the way you like it! I want to spend the whole afternoon out on the patio. We'll look at my roses and drink coffee, just like the old days--before you went away."

The expression which pinched her face was so pleading, so vulnerable, Robbie felt as though he were watching his mother age before his eyes. "We'll do that, Mama. I won't be with Jake long and then we'll be able to enjoy the rest of the afternoon together. I won't go back to Vegas until tomorrow, after you've fixed me some breakfast."

"Ah, Vegas! A despicable place! Nothing grows in the desert. I've been there, Robbie. Not a blade of grass, not a tree, God punished that land!"

"Yeah, Mama, I know." Robbie smiled, his mother's love of gardening was probably the only reason she'd been able to keep her sanity living with Jake Russo for fifty years.

As he headed down the long hall toward his father's office, Robbie's feet turned leaden. As though the weight of the millennia was suddenly pressed upon him, his spine seemed to lose its rigidity. Robbie felt his personality metastasizing, changing from the important man he was in Vegas to a repentant child headed for another whipping.

The Don was at his desk, his chair turned to look out French doors framing the rose garden. Banks of white roses, his favorites, lined two sides of a brick patio onto which the many paned glass doors opened. If a casual observer were not aware of the Don's true occupation, the den would have looked like the private retreat of an English country squire. Tall bookcases stretched from floor to ceiling and were filled with hundreds of leather-bound volumes which had never been opened; graceful furniture fashioned from expensive hardwood, cushions covered in antique tapestry, were positioned in front of the fireplace. A wall unit, that when opened revealed state-of-the- art security technology rivaled only by the CIA, was behind his desk.

"Ah, Robbie, my boy!" Recent surgery on his throat left his words garbled and gravely. The plastic surgeon did a masterful job of reconstructing his larynx and jaw. Only a fine red line of scar tissue was visible above the silk cravat. "How are things in the west?"

"Fine, Dad, fine."

"I'm glad to see you've tied up loose ends with the Grey properties. Our control was a little 'iffy' when the Grey Group hotels first changed hands. I feel better now that we have a firmer grip on the reins."

"I'm confident of our bank connection. It would take more than an internal auditor to uncover a direct tie from us to Grey. The dummy corporations in the Cayman Islands and Ireland, along with our cache of friends on the Board of Directors, should keep our identity from the Gaming Control Board."

Radiant green eyes regarded Robbie with interest. The Don's eyes were his best feature, clear, direct, but a violent aspect seemed to simmer just below the veil of familiarity he used with his son. Despite radiation on his head and neck, the Don still had a full head of wavy hair. Illness streaked the earth brown locks with wisps of gray and there was a sulfurous yellow cast to his skin, but power and authority still emanated from the man who controlled an empire far larger than most modern-day kings.

"You haven't called your mother lately, she's been worried about you. She thinks I've exiled you to Siberia."

"I like Vegas, Dad."

"Yes, it seems the desert agrees with you." There was a new air of confidence about his son. Robbie looked him directly in the eye for longer periods of time, but perhaps the most revealing characteristic was not his posture or eye contact, it was the new note of manliness in his voice. The quavering, cowering tone the Don found impossible to tolerate had vanished.

Jake knew he needed to prepare Robbie to take over the family interest because his time was close at hand. If lines of authority were not firmly in place, the whole infrastructure would collapse in a scramble for

75

power and territory between the lesser families. Robbie was likable, a quality which was important now days. Men didn't respond with blind obedience anymore--they had to be motivated! Jake was almost glad he wasn't going to be around a whole lot longer. Change always took its toll and he knew the well of energy which had always sustained him, even in the most trying times, was drying up fast.

"I've been busy Dad, with the time difference and all, sometimes it's hard to keep in touch with her."

"She's your mother, Robbie, and she's getting older. Call her, it would make her happy."

"Is that why you wanted me to come home?"

Vegas' soaring temperatures must be cultivating a whole new awareness; either that or running his own operation with an enormous degree of success was giving Robbie the courage of expression. "I have a letter that's too important to entrust to an ignorant courier. You're my right hand now, Robbie. I want you to find a way to deliver this to Senator Hasting--in person."

"Jesus, Dad, I don't know if I should get that close to the Senator. What if somebody sees us?"

"Be creative. It's important the Senator to know you by sight."

"Yeah, well, I hope this isn't the kind of news over which he'd kill the messenger like Caesar did!"

"A comedian! Vegas has turned you into a comedian! I should applaud humor like that? This is important!" A hand flecked with liver-colored spots and striated with punctured veins scabbed over from repeated intravenous injections pushed a sealed envelope across the desk.

Robbie picked up the cream-colored envelope and snapped open the locks on the briefcase at his feet. Twirling the tumblers, he sealed the case against invasion. He glanced up at the man he scarcely recognized as his father anymore. Fleshy parts of his face had dissolved into sharp edges and angles. Closely cropped graying hair seemed to bristle with stoic tension. His ferocious green eyes, which peered onto the world from beneath a deep, bony brow, seemed more prominent than ever. Illness sharpened his father's nose until it looked like a hatchet had been driven into the center of his face. His mouth had deteriorated into a thin slash, and his jaw seemed as prominent as those of predators which could snap their quarry in half with a single bite.

The raspy voice struck Robbie as being tinged with fear and it surprised him to realize his father finally found something to be afraid of— death-- and it was approaching fast.

"Go visit with your mother. She misses you." Jake turned toward the row of television monitors displaying the view of cameras surrounding the property. Sighing deeply, the old man settled deeper into his chair and closed his eyes.

Shock waves continued to surge over Robbie, claiming him, challenging the only world he knew. He felt a little like Christopher Columbus, Lewis and Clark, even Marco Polo, when he realized his father was dying. A completely unfamiliar world was going to open soon. Boundaries he considered firm and fixed were going to blur, he could feel it! A lightning-like strike of intuition fluttered up from his subconscious and laid hold of his entire body with a powerful chill. The thought was too awesome to contemplate; it had to be a momentary flight of imagination. It couldn't possibly be true! Yet on a primeval level he couldn't explain, Robbie suddenly realized his father was preparing him to take over when he was gone!

Jordan Grey sat facing the wall of television monitors, a look of horror frozen on his face. All but five eye-in-the-sky cameras zeroed in on the frenetic winner of the 'Lots A Bucks' five-dollar slot carousel. Some lucky son of a bitch just hit a big progressive worth a million--in cold, hard cash. You could count on one hand the number of times a customer put all five coins in before pushing the spin button. Twenty-five dollars a spin was a bunch of money to throw down the chute for customers who frequented his joint. You could count on it! God damn it, he had counted on it! The theory proved infallible, until today.

The winner of the 'Lots A Bucks' jackpot was large--over two hundred pounds, six-three, muscular--and he was so filled with excitement it looked as though he might burst wide open at any moment. Only the winner's broad face was tranquil; his normal expression was probably as placid as that of Jersey cow, to which he looked like he was related. His wife, or girlfriend, or sister, or whatever the hell their relationship was, jumped up and down, clapped her hands, screaming with delight at the top of her lungs, and pounded the winner on the back until he looked like he just might cough up a lung on the newly installed carpet.

Slot floormen and slot club hostesses converged on the winner from all over the casino. Cocktail waitresses moved in for the kill with the cunning and avarice of a hungry lioness. A couple of drinks, along with a toothy smile and a peek at a pair of boobs straight off the silicone assembly line, and the "tip" would be a whole lot bigger--if the million-dollar winner was plied with enough free booze to float a battleship. The 'Lots A Bucks' carousel was the scene of general pandemonium while the slot shift manager on duty tried to take down all the pertinent information. It was his job to shepherd the winner to the casino cage, where cashiers would require him to sign a W-2 form--to make certain the Feds got their cut first out of the million-dollar jackpot before the winner got his money.

No one on the casino floor knew there wasn't enough money in the reserve fund to pay out an entire million dollars! Only a few thousand dollars remained in a jackpot account. If anyone found out, the Gaming Control Board would lock his joint up tighter than a God-damned drum. Jordan was beginning to feel the first stirring of panic. A carefully manicured hand reached for a special phone mounted on the console beside his desk. He was shaking like a drunk coming off a two-week binge.

Grey decided he required something to fortify his courage before he placed the dreaded call. He couldn't wait too long though; the lucky bastard would be clamoring for a check within the hour. The slot staff was well trained, they knew just what to do. The assistant manager called the Westward Ho, next door, requesting the lucky bastard's luggage. Then a member of the bell staff would hot foot it across the expanse of black macadam to collect the son of a bitch's suitcase and the rest of his personal effects. His room would be "on the house" from now on, food in all the restaurants, including the gourmet room, would be complimentary. The slot management team would leave no stone unturned in their quest to have another crack at the cash the lucky bastard might walk out the door with at any moment. Corks popped, and champagne flowed as the casino manager presented an enormous fake check made out for a million dollars to the asshole winner. Press news sources would have a love affair with this bovine fool for about twenty-four hours. The winner's picture, holding a gigantic PR check made out for a million dollars, would be flashed around the world via the miracle of electronic communication and the Grey Group Resort Hotel and Casino would get a million bucks worth of free publicity-- but that was no consolation right now.

Grey tossed back a shot of Crown Royal and filled his glass again. Some of the gawkers were starting to walk away, hopefully they'd spend a lot of time at the tables and slots tonight. He was certainly going to need every God damn dollar he could get his hands on in the next twenty-four hours. At least payroll wasn't due for a few days! There was no point in delaying the inevitable any longer. Jordan depressed the only button on the hidden phone.

The voice which answered was so garbled he didn't know who he was speaking to at first, but it could only be one man. "Jake?"

"Yeah, Jordy. Long time no hear. Things been going good, huh?"

"Until today Jake, until today. I've got a problem, a big one and I need your help immediately or run the risk of being shut down."

"Jordy, Jordy, what the hell's happening now?"

"The million-dollar jackpot just hit."

"So?"

"I can't cover it. If the GCB finds out the account is empty, I'm outta business. They'll seal the doors and count down the rest of the cash in the cage."

"What do you mean . . . you can't cover it?"

"Damn it, Jake, just what I said! I don't have enough funds in the reserve account to pay off the winner."

"I thought you arranged to pay them a specified amount for the rest of their life."

"Our jackpot wasn't set up that way. I thought more people would play the machines if they knew they had a shot at getting a million dollars in one lump sum."

"And your reserve is empty?"

"Almost."

It had been a long time since Jake Russo exploded on another human being. Radiation drained him or mellowed him--who knew the real reason. But Jordan Grey's stupidity was more than he could tolerate. All the fancy clothes, all the time in Ivy League schools, all the boards and civic organizations of which he was a member hadn't done a damn thing to improve his competence. "Jesus, Mary, Joseph . . . Jordy! Where did you put your fucking brains, up your ass? Of all the stupid things I ever heard! Didn't our accountant tell you to keep the million in the bank drawing interest? Didn't he give you specific step-by-step instructions on how to pay the winner out of the interest dividend? Haven't you had it explained to you enough times that you never, ever, touch the fucking principle? What did you do with it, smoke it up, piss it off on some God damned hooker, drink it away? What, Jordy, what?" Anger shot the barge of adrenaline through weakened veins and arteries; it had been months since he'd felt like getting up and walking. Now Jake stormed around the elaborate office, waving his arms in the air, breathing hard and fast, his face purple with rage, the veins on his neck standing out so far, they were in danger of bursting.

"I wish to Christ your old man was still alive, Jordy! First, he'd make hamburger out of your face and then he'd get things straight at the bank! Unfortunately, times have changed, and I can't get on a plane and come out there to clean up your fucking mess anymore! If your joint wasn't so important to our working capital I'd let the Board hang you by the balls, I swear to Christ I would."

A spasm of coughing made Jake double over and he hurriedly retraced his steps to his tall leather chair behind the desk. Leaning his head back, he tried to slow his breathing. Always alert, Marie hurried through the French doors, withdrawing a bottle of morphine from the pocket of her sweater as she approached. A single swallow returned some of the color to his cheeks, another and the coughing settled to an irregular hack. With the phone still cupped against his shoulder, Jake waved his son into the room. "Marie, thank you. I feel much better now. Robbie and I have business to discuss. It's better you don't hear the words I'm about to speak to the jackass at the other end of this line," he shouted.

Marie patted her husband's sweaty forehead, took the pain killer from his hand, and slipped out of the room, leaving the men in her family to conduct their sordid business.

"Jordy, this is your lucky day. Robbie's here. I'll put him on the next plane out of Newark--better yet, he can charter a jet and head back to Vegas within the hour. You think you can handle things by yourself just a little while? Try real hard Jordy, real hard. Try to be half the man your old man was, will you--for just a couple of hours?"

Jake slammed the receiver down so hard the crash reverberated throughout the room. Fury left him spent, helpless. He motioned for Robbie to help him operate the surveillance equipment. One of the television monitors displayed no picture and after punching in several numbers on what looked like a remote control, the face plate swung aside, revealing a vault filled with money. "Count out a million, Robbie. Take a hundred thousand for yourself to cover expenses. Then get your ass out to Vegas as fast as you can. I'll call our pal at the bank and tell him you're on the way with the money in case the shit-head who won the jackpot shows up with a Grey Group check before funds can be deposited."

"Yeah, Dad, don't worry. I'll take care of everything. Maybe you ought to go to bed now. I'll call you when I get to Vegas--to confirm when the transaction is complete."

Glittery green eyes, which reminded Robbie so much of a snake when he was a kid, regarded his son with new respect. The boy seemed taller, as if his frame had suddenly filled out but Jake was smart enough to realize pride swelled his son's chest and straightened his spine. Laying a shaking, withered hand on Robbie's arm, Jake hobbled toward the door. "Yeah--call me."

It took Robbie a full five minutes before he realized his father left the room without closing the vault. Robbie had never seen so much money in one place in his entire life. The vault at Caesar's Palace didn't contain as much cash, even when they were expecting a bunch of black check baccarat players in from Singapore. Carefully counting out the stacks of bills, Robbie took the exact amount his father authorized--not a dollar more, then closed the safe and spun the dial. Glancing around the room to make certain nothing was out of place, Robbie called to his mother.

As he kissed her goodbye on the porch steps, Robbie promised to call every night. A pair of handcuffs was in the pocket of the sports jacket slung over the seat of the car, an item he habitually carried. Extracting them hurriedly, he fastened one end over the handle of the briefcase, the other he locked securely around his wrist. On the limo ride back to the airport, Robbie reviewed the events which just transpired at a much slower pace. He still couldn't believe his father walked away from an open safe.

A BAC 1-11 was warming up on the runway when the limo braked to a sudden stop near the hanger. Taking the steps two at a time, Robbie patted the cockpit as he rushed past, shouting at the pilot to take off before he was safely belted in. As the lights of Newark grew smaller, Robbie allowed himself to relax. A slow smile stole across his face. Today, for the very first time in his life, Robbie Russo felt like a real man.

Sonny held the oak and stained-glass door to the Redwood Bar and Grill open for Rita. With a cheerful wink, he informed the hostess, whom he had known since high school, he and his date had arrived for dinner. The smiling hostess might have seen stranger sights in her twenty-five years than most females of a comparable age in Cleveland, Ohio, but shock froze her smile into an imitation of a grimace when Sonny stood aside and allowed Rita to proceed him into the fashionable gourmet room.

There was a running joke around the station that if Sonny Yi didn't know someone wherever he went, it wasn't worth the trip. What most cops on the force didn't realize was Sonny made it a habit to get to know busboys, waitresses, dealers, used car salesmen, retail salesclerks, bank tellers--little people, doing little jobs. Las Vegas's backbone, as Sonny thought of them. He waved at the bar-back, said hi to one of the cocktail waitresses and pumped the hand of the waiter he'd requested serve them dinner when he called for a reservation.

The Redwood Bar and Grill was in a nice little joint several blocks off Fremont Street, on the far edge of downtown. Rita glanced around appreciatively at forest green upholstery on the booth, the warm redwood paneling and fake fireplace which crackled with the cozy effect of a fire in a mountain lodge.

"Since you didn't specify where you wanted to go. This happens to be my favorite restaurant." Sonny handed the menu board across the table to Rita. "Anything special you'd like to eat? I whole heartedly recommend the crab legs."

"Crab, huh? Boy, you are the last of the big spenders!"

"Tonight, fair lady, the world is yours for the asking. I know the GM and we're on a comp!"

"Then crab legs it is for me, bucky boy! That, and a spinach salad and I'm even going to have dessert!"

"You've got to try the apple dumpling, Rita. It's fit for the gods." Sonny drew his fingers to his lips and kissed them with a smack so loud it drew the attention of several other diners. The California Hotel and Casino catered to the Hawaiian market, but this restaurant was a favorite with locals too, which filled the room with an equal mixture of Asian, Hawaiian, and Caucasian faces. Sonny and Rita blended in like Southern Baptists at a Pentecostal revival.

On Monday night the room emptied out early. As soon as the meal was cleared away, after-dinner drinks were served, and coffee poured in the china cups, Sonny leaned against the padded booth and rubbed his stomach. "I'm so full I could pop!"

"Yeah, it was good. Now I'll bet you want me to pay the piper!

"Rita, you're a cynical broad."

"I sure am, bucky boy, with damn good reason!"

"Tell me about it. How old were you when you came to Vegas?"

"My old man threw me outta the house when I was fourteen. Ma got sick and died about then and I quit coming across for him, so I wasn't worth the price of my keep anymore. I drifted around LA for a while, then caught a ride with a real swell hunk of man, who promised he'd take care of me."

"Did he?"

"Yeah, for about forty-eight hours. After that I was on my own. The bastard wouldn't even let me ride back with him. Didn't leave me with bus fare either."

Sipping his coffee, it was a story he'd heard a thousand times. Kids on their own, abused kids, abandoned to the streets, and subjected to the whims of predators who roamed them. "How did you get along?"

"Well, back in the '50s casino owners didn't much care how old you were if you looked good. So, I got a job slinging drinks at the Horseshoe. Made more money than I ever knew existed--there was a lot of action downtown in those days. Fact of the matter was work wasn't always so good out on the Strip back then." Rita withdrew a pack of cigarettes from a worn leather purse and held them up to Sonny, "Mind if I smoke?"

"Not at all. Other diners have cleared out for the night and the manager won't mind this time in the morning." Fishing through his pockets, Sonny came up with a cheap Bic lighter and leaned across the table to offer her a light.

"That's right sweet of you, bucky boy. You treat me like a real lady." Lines around her mouth and eyes deepened as she sucked on the cigarette, then squinted as she exhaled its smoke.

"Your mannerisms tell me you were once a high-class chick!"

"Yeah, once. Before I lost my looks. Sonny, when a woman loses her looks, she might as well pack it in 'cause there ain't no one going to step up to bat for her anymore." With a quick downward flutter, Rita lowered her eyes and appeared to study the glowing ember of her cigarette so the tears gathering in her eyes wouldn't be apparent.

"I stood up for you the other night, Rita. If I hadn't you'd be sitting in the drunk tank at Metro rather than in a booth at the Redwood Bar and Grill." Sonny couldn't help himself, he felt sorry for the woman and for the life of him he couldn't explain why he felt compelled to help her.

"You're right, Sonny, you did. And I'm grateful . . . so I'm going to tell you a story you probably won't believe. It doesn't matter much what anyone believes anymore. I know it's true and I'm the only one that's got to live with myself."

The waiter refilled their cups with coffee. Rita watched him walk away, "It's pretty long and involved, they going to throw us out of here soon?" Sonny stretched his arms across the back of the booth in both directions. "Nah, they might send the piano player home, but they won't care if we stay awhile. You've got my curiosity aroused now and wild horses couldn't drag me out of here until I hear every word of what you've got to say."

Flattered by the sincere attention, Rita settled in comfortably, put her elbows on the table and leaned forward, so she didn't have to speak too loudly. "The Stardust used to be owned by the mob until a couple of years ago."

"Rita, that's not news! Everybody in town knows that's why the Gaming Control Board shut them down."

Suddenly coy, Rita fluttered her lashes. "Yeah, but I know for a fact all they did was change the window dressing! It's still in the hands of the mob!"

"Jordan Grey is one of the most respected casino operators in town. His family goes back a long way, Rita. His Dad was a pillar of society in Vegas, for God's sake!"

"I know but once upon a time, when I was young and beautiful, I was sort of engaged to the bag man for the Grey operation. He used to take their money back to Jersey."

Atavistic fear--and the reliance on the instinct it invoked--made Sonny decide to press the woman to continue. It was the primordial instinct for survival which drove him into action without thinking about the ramifications of what might follow. Sonny did not know how he knew the boozy old woman was telling the truth, he just knew that he did. "Sort of engaged?"

"I like to think so. I like to think he meant every word he said--but

I ain't totally stupid. More than likely, I was just another skirt to him, but we lasted nearly ten years."

A haunting mist rose in her eyes; it made Sonny think of pictures he'd seen of concentration camp victims peering from behind barbed wire fences; it was a pleading look, one that begged him to convince her someone truly loved her--at one point in her life. "Rita, ten years is hardly a one-night stand! Skirts are one-night stands. Ten years means he must have had genuine feelings for you, or he wouldn't have kept coming back."

"Yeah--maybe. I think Jake Russo told him to get rid of me--I was hitting the sauce heavy then. The old man probably figured I'd get drunk and blab. But I never did," a single tear rolled unchecked through the mascara, powder and blush, "I never did."

The warning knell of intuition Catherine Armstrong taught him to listen to without passing judgement, pealed like the bells of Notre Dame inside Sonny's head. Outside, in the switch yard across Main Street, a train whistle played a one-note dirge. It was a hollow, cold, mournful sound and it reminded Sonny of music played on drums and flutes during a traditional Korean funeral. "Why are you telling me this now?"

"Cause Benny's been dead for years and I just heard the old man has terminal cancer. Maybe I want to get in one last lick before he croaks-- just to let him know he ruined my life and I counted for something, long ago."

"How do you know the Grey family is connected to the mob?"

"When Benny 'n me was runnin' together, he'd pick me up and tell me we were takin' a little ride--to pack a suitcase because we'd be gone several days. Back then, there was a back door out of the Stardust cage which opened right into the parking lot. Benny'd leave me in the car with the engine running and he'd knock on the door. In a matter of seconds, a hand would shoot out with a briefcase. I never saw no faces, so I couldn't testify, and Benny knew I'd die before I'd take the stand against him--if it ever came to that. So, Benny, he'd grab the case and we'd high tail it to Reno. Then we'd hang around a joint up there Jordan Grey's Dad had an interest in. Before long, Benny, he'd come in and say to get ready we were headed for San Fran. Most of the time we'd fly in a prop job that could only hold four people. The pilot and Benny'd be up front, talking away and I'd be jammed in the back with a bunch of suitcases--just like we were honeymooners or somethin'. Then, big as life, we'd be off for Niagara Falls. Only when we headed out west again, we didn't have no suitcases. We did that a lot. Then Benny, he got religion or something. He dumped

85

me, married a local girl, and became a pit boss for Hugo Grey's operation downtown. Benny ran the joint for a long, long time. There was quite a lot of talk for a while about how Hugo got the money to open his own operation. I know it came from Jake Russo, directly or indirectly, or Hugo wouldn't've hired Benny. I figure he was put there to keep an eye on Russo's investment."

"So, how does all this tie the Stardust to the mob?" Sonny's heart was beating fast, his palms were moist with perspiration, and he felt the icy snake of fear uncoil in his belly.

"Well, Hugo put Jordan through one of them fancy colleges back east--got the boy all dandified, while he was going around donatin' money to the college and founding local civic groups--stuff like that. Years pass, and the boys at the Stardust got so damned open about their skimming operation the Gaming Control Board decided they'd better shut them down. Then, lo and behold, the State invites the Grey family to step in and run the operation because they're such honest, above-board folks. A credit to the gaming industry, if I remember the words right!"

It was the emotional snake again, it had uncoiled and was crawling up his spine. Sonny felt like needles of ice were pricking his scalp and the sensation made hair on the back of his neck stand erect. If half of what Rita said was true, this could turn out to be Nevada's equivalent of Watergate. It would mean the agency designed to govern gaming, to keep it clean and respectable, was infiltrated by the mob! Jesus! If picked up, where would this thread end? Was his partner right? Did everything point to Jersey? And if it did, would it involve a man with so much power he'd never been arrested for any sort of crime? Jake Russo was a major league player and Sonny knew he and Danny were far from heavy hitters.

Like a wisp of smoke trailing from a campfire, the memory of Catherine's vision floated up from some obscure synapse in Sonny Yi's cerebral cortex. He saw the image of a five-pointed star as clearly as if he were having a vision himself. Five men, one in each apex, a hideous, evil being at the center. With a certainty Sonny felt verged on the point of clairvoyance, he was certain Jake Russo was the old man in the center!

It was fight night and Matt O'Brien felt like a star-struck teenager, but he couldn't help himself. In one hour, he'd checked in Sylvester Stallone, Arnold Schwarzenegger, Maria Shriver, Bruce Willis, Tom Cruise and Kidd Rock. Big stars, fading stars, stars on the rise, it seemed like half of Hollywood was staying at Caesar's Palace on the night of the heavyweight championship bout. The outdoor arena was a sell-out, scalpers were hawking tickets for twice and three times what the casino was charging. Most of the movie stars were complimentary anyway, their presence was like icing on the cake to high rollers flying in on private jets from all over the country. His company cell phone went off and Matt grabbed it with annoyance.

"Matt?"

"Yeah, what's the matter, Vinnie?"

"We got the limos stacked up out here like cord wood. For some stupid reason the tower's not letting the jets land. You want some of us to come back? It might be more than an hour before the first private lands."

Matt surveyed the lobby, it was jam packed with arriving guests. Front desk clerks couldn't process credit cards fast enough, and the lines were already ten and twelve deep. If he ordered the limos back to take care of customers arriving on commercial flights it might mean a delay for some of the stars and premium credit line players. "Vinnie, stay where you are. I'll call Bell Trans and see if we can order some back-up. The last thing I need is a Platinum card asshole screaming his lungs out to the Casino Manager we weren't there to pick him up. Stay tight. If it's going to be longer than an hour, call me back."

Body heat generated by stress made Matt long to take off his jacket, a capital offence at Caesars. He might as well run around the lobby in his underwear as be caught in shirt sleeves. Protocol was everything and Assistant Hotel Managers had to dress the part of a junior executive whether they were melting like wax dipping down a candle or not!

At that moment both Jennifer Lawrence and Julia Roberts whirled into the lobby, followed by a gaggle of photographers. They smiled, preening graciously for the camera, becoming more radiant and bubblier by the moment. Well, Matt thought, they were on stage just as surely as if the ladies were witches stirring the pot in a production of Macbeth.

His cell phone shrieked again. Matt glanced at his watch. Five more hours until the main event. It was going to be a long, hard night.

The far corner of the stage was as dark as a sealed grave. No light

87

penetrated a network of cables which lifted sets aloft. Nothing pierced the velvety black-out curtain separating the stage from closely packed rows of tables topped by upended chairs. Silence hung over the footlights like a finely woven shroud. Dancers and crew had long since departed and abandoned the stage for spouses and families over an hour ago.

Soft and muted, footfalls padded across the highly polished hardwood stage floor. Worn smooth by years of leaps and pirouettes, constant refurbishing and more dancers fleet of foot, the boards reflected the glassy patina of years of use and maintenance. A gloved hand probed the curtain wall, searching. Although the searcher had a general idea of what he sought, the exact location needed to be determined by touch. Fingertips poised, the palm of his hand parallel to the wall, he sought an irregular surface.

Many minutes passed before his hand stopped, poised over a crack in the drywall. To anyone else, even a hotel engineer, it would look like a careless job of patching. Drywall mud was applied too generously and had cracked along the tape line as it dried, or so it seemed. With the touch of an index finger, a small door opened, revealing a yawing cavity inside the wall.

The searcher put his briefcase on the floor, then muffled brass locks with a gloved hand so they would open without a clack. As the clasp released the searcher paused, waiting for footsteps from a security guard, a late-night stagehand, an errant member of the crew. When no one appeared, he lifted his briefcase lid.

Quickly, the searcher stuffed banded bundles of bills into the hollow between metal studs. When the briefcase was empty, he tapped a spring-loaded latch to seal the camouflaged vault. On impulse, the searcher pushed against the door again; this time it didn't release--and that meant someone was watching. Someone, somewhere, was flipping a switch which sent an electric current through the lock. Someone knew he was here and someone else would monitor his silent retreat, to make certain all the bundles remained in the safe. What did they take him for, an utter fool?

Keeping to the shadows, the searcher silently departed.

CHAPTER SIX

Elaine Kullberg sat staring out her office window. As a supervisor in the customer relations department at Citibank, she earned a workstation by one of the tall windows overlooking a wide expanse of lawn which terminated at an artificial waterfall created by a pile of massive sandstone boulders. It was late and traffic from the Strip was beginning to thicken as casino executives and dealers, who earned as much as the president of a lot of corporations, made their way home to The Lakes. She watched a chain of cars pass by, unable to keep her mind on the end of the month report which charted how many calls were handled by each of the girls in her section. It needed to be completed today, but Elaine's thoughts kept wandering to Detective Danny Armstrong. She was irresistibly drawn to the phone, like the compelling force of gravity which sucked all matter into a black hole. She reached for the receiver at least a dozen times, only to pull back. Hesitation and vacillation were not a normal part of her make-up; only she couldn't decide whether to call Danny at the station. Staring at the clock, Elaine knew he'd be there now. If she was going to call, now was the time--before he began to patrol the streets.

"Good grief!" Elaine exclaimed so loudly several of the clerks swung in her direction because an irritated tone of voice from their supervisor was a rarity.

Disgusted by the tremor that took control of her hand, Elaine jabbed at the keypad as though she intended to poke the eyes of an imagined offender--maddened by the indecisiveness which thoroughly dominated her courage. "Damn it, summon up a little nerve." Where was the old Elaine who used nerves of steel to wrestle car keys away from a drunken father; where was the girl who raced away from Barstow, put herself through college and landed a job at one of the largest banking institutions in the country--without ever looking back, always keeping her eyes firmly fixed on the future. The phone fell silent as the operator transferred her call to the detective division; the silence festered like a week-old sore. Her pulse quickened, and her heart raced as she waited for an answer.

"Detective Armstrong."

"Hi, Danny?" Elaine's words were soft, tentative and at the same time compelling.

"Elaine? I didn't expect to hear from you!"

"Have I interrupted you? Maybe I shouldn't have bothered you at work. I'm sorry . . ."

"No! It's okay, really. So--how are you?"

The sun cast gold and copper streamers all over Clark County, there was not a cloud in the sky to diminish its rays by a single degree, but a premonitory tingle followed the path of Danny's spine and gave him a chill. A feeling, a sense of knowing, owned his emotions and he knew to pay strict attention to that intuitive sense. Change was occurring at a rate of speed incomprehensible to the average human being, and when someone got a glimpse of what might be in store for them--as Danny had just now--it was both impelling and intimidating, enlivening, and frightening. Danny knew he had to act, and he had to act immediately or the opportunity within his grasp might slip away, never to come again.

"Elaine, ah, a guy over at the Stardust has been offering to comp me to dinner and the show. Would you be interested in going some night?" Danny felt the words turn to dust in his mouth, his tongue was dry and powdery, like his saliva producing glands were eliminated by a sudden, powerful dose of radiation.

"How about Friday? I've got a day coming and that's your regular day off, isn't it?" Elaine knew the answer before she asked the question. If Danny finally worked up enough courage to ask her out--she wasn't going allow him time to reconsider.

"That'd be great." Fate was not a foreign concept because he'd grown up listening to his mother discuss the ramifications of karma. While he didn't think God was looking down on him through some sort of cosmic keyhole, Danny couldn't help but wonder about what kind of miracle lay just around the corner. For a shy, quiet guy to find a bubbly girl, who took all the pain and embarrassment out of personal encounters, was as much a miracle to him as the parting of the Red Sea was to Moses. "What time?"

"Why don't I meet you at Forbes? About seven?"

"Okay! I'll see you then!" Danny put the phone down feeling like a million bucks. Asking Elaine out to dinner hadn't proven difficult after all! Self-indulgent pride burst like a balloon pricked by a pin when he glanced at Sonny, who was nearly doubled over with laughter.

"Man, I haven't seen you this proud of yourself since the time you caught the winning touchdown pass in our Homecoming game against Rancho! Elaine is one smooth operator. She reeled you in hook, line and sinker and made you think you were the one with your hand on the tiller!"

Danny wadded a sheet of paper and threw it at Sonny as hard as he could. "Knock it off, will you?"

Although laughter filled his eyes with tears, Sonny managed to deflect the incoming projectile. "Aw, come on, Danny! How often do I get to make fun of you about a girl? On the other hand, partner, how many times have you taunted me about all the rotten encounters I've had with wily females-- the kind I'm so susceptible to?"

"Get out of here. I've got to call Jordan Grey to take him up on his offer. I can't do it with your Korean face grinning at me like I'm about to be Kublai Khan's next victim!"

"Okay, okay, I'll go to the john, but make it snappy. Dr. Worthen is expecting us in half an hour."

After flipping through his dog-eared rolodex, Danny punched the direct line to Jordan Grey's office. A sugary voiced secretary answered, and he explained the nature of his call. She put him on hold while she checked with the owner of the Stardust about the arrangements. When Jordan Grey came on the line Danny was taken by surprise.

"Detective Armstrong, I'm delighted you've decided to take me up on dinner and the show."

"Mr. Grey, I'd like to bring a date . . . if it isn't too much trouble."

"I would be seriously disappointed if you didn't. When do you want to come?"

Danny indicated the date and time. Fervently wishing he had the knack of engaging in social pleasantries, he sensed an underlying hesitation in Grey's voice he couldn't quite label. If the casino executive kept talking he might be able to decipher the strangeness.

Fortunately, Grey seemed reluctant to terminate the conversation and asked, "Do you have any leads as to who might have killed Darla Corey?"

There it was again--a tone which conveyed anxiety and strain. "As a matter of fact, I'm on my way over to the Coroner's office now. Dr. Worthen discovered something unusual in the results of the Spectroanalysis on the samples gathered in the "Rainman" suite."

"Spectroanalysis--what's that?" Jordan had endured far too much stress in the past forty-eight hours. He stared out the window at the pollutant-heavy haze trapped beneath an inversion layer, which blanketed the suffocating valley. An unpleasant mixture of sulphur and carbon dioxide added to the misery of one-hundred-and-ten-degree heat. A bile-yellow afternoon matched his sulfurous mood. As the sun rolled down the western sky, reaching toward the mountains which boxed in Las Vegas, Jordan felt wrongness in the air. The hot, blast furnace wind might have been tolerable on any other day but now it seemed as sinister as the fires of Hell. On this afternoon, menace clotted the air and he subconsciously reacted with the preternatural surety of the hunted that a hunter had suddenly arrived on the scene.

"Spectroanalysis is a method of breaking down the chemical elements in all matter. If there was anything out of the ordinary in the room Darla Corey was killed in, Dr. Worthen could detect it."

Despite super-heated air outside, Jordan Gray felt a coldness in his belly. "What do you mean, out of the ordinary?"

"Well, the fire didn't start on its own. It had help, and Dr. Worthen is the man to tell us how that happened."

Jordan Grey's fear was broadcast to Danny as surely as if he were a disc jockey on the radio. It was intense fear, irrational fear, the kind of fear which made men go mad and jump off tall buildings.

The stentorian two-part thudding of his heart boomed like a kettle drum; sweat sliding down the side of his face was almost audible; the sound of a gavel coming down on his future rang as clear as the bells of Notre Dame. "I'll make all the arrangements for your evening, Detective. And--if you hear anything about Glitter, Darla, be sure to call me. As her employer, I have a vested interest in finding out what happened to a very sweet, likable girl. I'd like to have the opportunity to share it with the other dancers first, you know, so they don't read about it in the paper."

"Sure, Mr. Grey, I'll do that." Danny hung up the phone and sat staring at it as if it were a rune which could translate feelings coming at him from every direction. He sensed a presence. The way a person can sense when someone is staring at them from behind; the way you feel a storm coming on a humid day. Someone was out there, waiting. With clairvoyant certainty, Danny knew there was more death yet to come.

Carrington LeMoye reached for the phone. The voice on the other end was familiar, he'd spent enough time with Charlie Covington over the past few months to recognize the flat, nasal tones ladled upon the English language by the inhabitants of the eastern United States.

"Judge, I gotta problem."

"Charlie, Charlie, there's only so much I can do for you."

"Really, Judge, this'll be the last time. I'm in a lot of hot water. The Gaming Control Board is shaking me like a gopher in a Rat Terrier's mouth. They've been keeping track of all my calls and now they've subpoenaed my monthly profit and loss statement--for the last five years."

Carrington LeMoye studied his reflection in the windows of the den. With nightfall, the breeze became a hot, gusting wind; it was parched and dehydrating. It blew dry leaves from the big Mulberry trees in the front yard along the sidewalk and harried little clouds of dust out of the flower bed. He wasn't sure he wanted to help Charlie, but the obnoxious casino host had a lot of connections to people with whom he'd been friends for nearly thirty years. People who put him in office in the first place; people who contributed to his campaign fund year after year. Not substantial amounts, nothing that wouldn't hold up under scrutiny, but the moral support of important community leaders was even more important than monetary consideration. "What profit and loss statements?"

"Casino accounting generates a report listing the gaming activity of all customers who're coded to me. You know--table players who come to town throughout the month. The GCB is busy trying to dig up dirt on anybody remotely connected with me. Hell, Judge, I take care of a lot of friends of friends. They're my bread and butter. If they think calling me for a room is going to put them under a microscope, they'll quit calling all together. Judge, that's how I earn my living! I need you to do something-- call 'em off, will ya?"

Sighing deeply, LeMoye forked his fingers through rapidly graying hair. He was still a good-looking man, the reflection in the blackened window confirmed it. His status in the community was stable and solid; he was both well-liked and respected. Defending the antics of a third-rate hoodlum with questionable ethics was not exactly the reason he'd chosen to become a judge. "Charlie, as an attorney, I can assure you the law is not chiseled in stone. Its very flexibility is what allowed this country to withstand some rigorous social shocks. Like a coil of wire, it can be stretched and curved. Short of blatant theft or outright murder, it's pretty easy to stay on the right side of a constantly shifting line if you're getting good advice from the right people."

"Does that mean you know a way to get 'em off my back?"

Outside, night pressed against the window and the wind wrestled with one of the low-lying branches on the Mulberry. Carrington had been meaning to tell the gardener to trim the tree, so more sunlight could reach the grass. Leaves slapped against the side of the house and branches scratched noisily along the brick. The scrape reminded the Judge of fingernails being raked down a blackboard and it made his blood run cold.

"Charlie, I might be able to get an injunction, but if you don't keep your nose clean the boys at the Board will find a way to get rid of you. It's an election year and it'd look mighty good on an aspiring District Attorney's score board if he made an example of you."

Sitting on his patio, Charlie watched a storm rolling up from the Gulf of Mexico over Sunrise Mountain. The temperature dropped at least ten degrees in a matter of minutes. An evening calm was ravaged by an ever-increasing wind and skinny Cypress trees around his pool shivered. There was something ominous about the way their spiny branches pawed at the air. An oily nausea ripped through Charlie as he contemplated a dust devil boiling across the narrow strip of desert behind his house, unchecked. In the squall following the storm front, the sound of rain striking his patio cover was mournful, like the steady beat of an Asian temple drum. Cold sweat broke out on his upper lip, and he shuddered, as if the dread he felt was a powerful electric charge generated by turbulent weather. Charlie decided the weather reminded him of his drug running days in Cambodia. He'd been young then, too damn young. The Khmer Rouge shaped the still moist clay of his personality and gradually fashioned him into a mere shell of a man who would sell his own mother if the price was right. He established such effective supply routes for opium-resin from blood red poppies to reach a product hungry American market they were still in use today.

"Judge, there's some things I ain't got no control over. The people who know me is one of 'em. I do all kinds of favors for all kinds of people. That's what a casino host is supposed to do, and I don't get paid to run a background check on everybody who's got my number. If I quit answering

94

the God damn phone then I'm either gonna be out of a job or end up in the desert somewhere with a bullet in my brain. Years from now some motorcyclist or off-roader will find my bones and if the cops'r lucky, they'll identify me. More'n likely, I'll just be relegated to the John Doe file, and nobody'll even remember I existed."

The ugly sound of desperation in Charlie's voice was unmistakable, it wasn't merely hopelessness, it was darker, stranger and more terrifying than anything Carrington LeMoye had heard in all his years on the bench.

Denise McKinsey glanced fretfully at her cheap Timex watch. She crossed the parking lot in hurried strides, anxious to reach a faded Mazda parked in the next-to-last row. Her supervisor gave her a batch of files to code before she left the office, which meant she'd have to hit all the traffic lights just right or she'd be late at the day-care center again. The last thing she needed right now was an additional charge for extra time the kids spent at preschool. There was no one else to call, Denise had no family, and it was times like this that made her wish she wasn't so damned alone.

As she gunned the worn-out auto through the yellow light, a car slid into traffic from the shadows of the gloom-mantled alley nearby. Denise was far too concerned with making it to the day care center on time to notice other cars which branched off at the same expressway exit. With only seconds to spare, she sprinted into the cubbyhole office. Her kids were in the back room, glumly watching television. There wasn't another soul in the place but the close-of-day sitter and the three McKinsey children.

"Hi, Danielle, sorry I'm late."

"I'll get the children's coats. I was just about to go on over-time."

"I know, I'm lucky I didn't get a ticket trying to get here. I think I just broke the land speed record!"

Bustling the boys into the car, Denise made sure their seat belts were cinched tight before she started the engine. "We've got to stop at the grocery store on the way home and I want your solemn promise you'll behave. Mommy's had an exhausting day, and I don't feel like being a referee tonight, okay?"

Sullen looks and pensive pouts met Denise's glare in return, but she clung to a forlorn hope the boys would behave while she grabbed a few things for dinner. Given her low energy level and the boys' unbridled enthusiasm, there was no way she could maintain control if they decided to act up once inside the store. She did the best she could, trying not to yell at them, struggling to keep from swatting Timothy on the bottom, but when Jeff ran the grocery cart into a display and broke a jar of jam, Denise felt her frazzled nerves give way. "Now look what you've done! Damn it, Jeff, I don't have the money to pay for that!"

A man bigger than a mountain sauntered around the corner at that very moment Roger shoved his shoulder into the side of the cart, which ricocheted into the display again, threatening to knock fifty more jars of red raspberry preserves onto the floor. With movements as quick and athletic as a trapeze artist in a high wire act, the man's strapping, beefy hands steadied the precarious glass containers and eased them safely back in line. "Whoa, there buddy. What wild Indian tribe did you escape from?"

Roger was a shy little kid, he didn't warm up to strangers easily but the infectious grin peeping from beneath a bushy black mustache had a miraculous effect on him. He retreated behind his mother's skirts, but kept a friendly eye trained on the thundering stranger.

"Thanks. I couldn't face another disaster today."

"That's okay, glad I came around the corner when I did. Maybe I should follow you to the check-out stand to make sure you don't lose any strays."

"If I did, it would be the *'Ransom of Red Chief'* for any one of these three Indians."

"Red Chief, huh? I didn't know anybody read O. Henry anymore."

"It's been a long time, but with three boys just four years apart, I think about that story every day!" Denise smiled a little wistfully; the boys had settled down in the presence of such a powerful man. They probably needed a lot more male influence in their lives, but their father called it quits when Jeff was barely a year old. Too much responsibility for him; Jesus, what did he think he was leaving her with--a life of luxury, fun and games?

A generous smile framed by an equally generous mustache was positively dazzling. "Looking back on it, I'm sure I was quite a handful for my parents. Healthy boys seem to attract trouble."

The checker rang up a total for the scant supply of groceries in the bottom of Denise's cart. She was going to have to figure out a way to make a pound of hamburger and gallon of milk stretch for several days. There was enough gas in the car to last until payday and she could go without lunch for the rest of the week. Hopefully, the boys wouldn't hit a growing cycle that left them ravenous all the time for the next six days. When an aging woman, whose application of iridescent blue eye shadow made her look like a Galapagos lizard, called out the total, Denise's face drained of color. She didn't have to dig through her purse, Denise knew she was almost five dollars short and there was no spare change rolling around in the bottom of her badly worn shoulder bag. Quickly scanning the contents, she began to tally up what to take off the bill.

When the thick arm, covered with curling dark hair thrust a bill toward the checker, it took her a moment to realize the man, who saved the jelly display, was paying for her groceries.

"Oh, please, I can't let you do that."

The cash drawer opened with a ring and the checker counted the change into Ron Mellon's outstretched palm, which seemed to radiate authority. "It's already done." He glanced out rain-streaked windows toward the McDonald's across the street. "You boys feel like eating over there?" His thumb hooked toward the yellow glow of the neon arches.

A chorus of joyful shrieks drew annoyed stares from other customers anxious to get home before the rain began in earnest. Denise was embarrassed by the ruckus, and she rushed the kids outside into the car.

Ron didn't let up. He leaned through the open window, egging the boys on. "Say, when was the last time you fellows had a fruit pie and a milk shake? Who likes chocolate?" The din grew to the thunderous level of canons firing on Fort Sumner. Ron grinned at Denise. "Drive your car over there and I'll meet you inside. There's nothing in the trunk that won't keep for an hour and these boys are hungry. Fill 'em full enough and they might let you get a decent night's sleep. Come on, how about it? On my word of honor, I won't do anything but feed these kids. You look like you could use a passel of calories yourself."

You could tell a lot by looking someone in the eye. Some people couldn't maintain eye contact for more than a few seconds, but this guy didn't blink. He had warm eyes, kind, and loving eyes. The kind of eyes she used to dream about when she was young and immature, and still believed in happy endings. "Okay, but don't say I didn't warn you. These boys are a lot to handle."

Ron stuck his hand through the window, past her shoulder, and displayed a wide-open palm. The size and implied power was intimidating, and the boys immediately settled down to await the outcome of what the stranger intended to do to them. "See this?" He moved his hand back and forth, tantalizingly slow, as if he were charming a cobra out of its basket. "This hand is directly descended from Tucomsa, the mightiest warrior in the Mohawk nation! This hand can throw a tomahawk into the center of a tree at fifty paces. This hand has wrestled a mighty Grizzly bear to the ground and carried many a deer into camp after the hunt. You will respect this hand. When it tells you to be quiet and not aggravate your mother, you must obey, or there will be no chocolate milk shakes because this is the hand that will pay for them."

The boys glanced at each other beneath lowered lashes, mesmerized by the low, rumbling voice and their incredibly good fortune-- both for the prospect of a meal at McDonalds and meeting up with the entertaining stranger. They remained unnaturally quiet all the way across the highway and slid onto the benches in the restaurant as silently as if they had been bound and gagged.

For over an hour Ron Mellon amazed the boys with unlikely stories about Indians and cowboys and buffalo hunts. By the time Jeff finished his hamburger he was sitting on one of Ron's huge thighs, hanging on every word, spellbound, as the floppy mustache moved up and down while the entertaining man talked. They ate their French fries and pelted the stranger with questions. When Denise protested the time and announced they had to head for home and bed, cries of anguish filled the nearly empty room.

"I mean it! I've got to go to work early tomorrow, and you guys have school. Get your jackets and stop fussing! Mr. Mellon has been very kind, and I won't have you ruin a delightful evening!"

Sullen, the boys slid into their badly worn winter coats. Ron helped Timmy zipper the jacket which had been repaired several times. Standing at the side of the car, Ron waited for Denise to start it. The whine of a nearly dead battery brought tears to Denise's eyes. "Oh shit!"

With a reassuring pat on the shoulder, Ron motioned for her to unlatch the hood. He hovered over the engine a few minutes, tinkered around with a couple of wires, then opened the trunk of his car. From where she sat, Denise could see the back was filled with all sorts of equipment. With a wrench in his hand and a rag in his hip pocket, Ron disappeared beneath the hood again. "Now try it."

Denise turned the key and to her complete amazement, the car kicked over right away.

"A battery cable was loose. It's nothing serious, but the distributor is cracked, and it looks like the spark plug wires haven't been changed for at least fifty-thousand miles. Denise," his infectious grin and friendly brown eyes diluted the frightening image conveyed by such a massive body, "listen, I don't want to be forward, or scare you, but I've got a place on the shore. It's sure not much, but the boys would have fun and if you'd drive out early Saturday morning I can tune up your car while they run around on the beach."

"Oh, I couldn't ask you to do that. You've already paid for my groceries and bought us all dinner!"

"I've got everything I need on hand. I sort of make a habit of collecting things. My place usually looks like a cyclone hit it because I've got so much crap shoved everywhere. Please, Denise, the kids deserve fresh air and sunshine--some place they can discharge a little pent-up energy and not have the neighbor's yelling at them all the time."

The pleading expression on all three faces met her inquiring glance in the rear-view mirror. They melted Denise's heart and destroyed her normally flinty resolve. Ron Mellon was a nice man, a good man, the inner voice of intuition assured her she had nothing to fear. "All right, but I insist on bringing a picnic lunch."

Beaming, Ron thrust a business card through the window. "Here's my number. Call me on Friday and I'll tell you how to get there. If I don't hear from you I'll track you down . . . I mean that!"

"You'll hear from me, but you'll probably be sorry after a day with these boys." Suddenly, Denise felt flustered, and a slow blush suffused her complexion with a flattering shade of pink.

"I like kids, I was a boy myself once. Maybe I remember my childhood just a little too vividly." Something in his expression seemed to harden and his face was suddenly scored with deep lines of misery and anger. The big, fearsome man melted away. In his place came a hurt little boy, one who experienced far too much of the suffering life always seemed to dish out to the young and defenseless. Denise sensed Ron was kicked around by life as much as she was.

"I'll call you on Friday."

She only glanced back once, Ron was still standing in the parking lot watching their departure. His presence was comforting, it made her feel as though he was watching to make sure the car didn't die again; that she made a successful maneuver onto the expressway; that one of the boys wasn't hanging out the window or her groceries were spilling out the trunk. Despite the logic which deemed it impossible because they had only just met, Denise felt protected for the first time in years. The glow in her cheeks never diminished and she felt at peace. A sensation she didn't feel often and humming along softly with the tune on the radio, Denise found herself looking forward to the remaining three days of work at the Pentagon.

An alert expression in the Rottweiler's eyes changed. Like the bits of glass in a kaleidoscope sliding into a different pattern, the round, light brown circles above the dog's eyes lifted, then dropped, only to lift again. Rising, Damascus padded across the office and jumped onto the window seat, a habit Catherine tried to discourage with absolutely no success. He surveyed the street--watchful, peering into the night.

The asphalt on Charleston was silvered by the sudden summer shower. A strobe-like flash of light, the first of the storm, pulsed at the window and thunder cracked, shaking the glass. The sky seemed to be torn apart by the percussive blast, and rain poured down in one tremendous outburst. Halos of light from streetlamps wavered, their incandescent aura casting a sodium-yellow glow on water rushing along the gutter.

Catherine noticed the Rott's tenseness and suddenly the hair on his spine stood erect. As she watched him, her throat tightened, and she found it difficult to draw breath. Demanding her thoughts still, she could feel the icy gaze of someone standing on the other side of the street as surely as she would have felt a clammy, fondling hand. Determined to control the growing fear threatening to gallop away with her emotions, Catherine knew she had to keep a tight rein on panic.

The dog's ancestors mandated he protect his mistress as surely as his genetic code determined the size of his head and the girth of his chest. The rumble which came from deep inside his huge rib cage inspired even more fear in Catherine than the sensation of being watched. She'd never heard such a fierce warning emanate from the dog before. Someone was watching, watching, and waiting, just across the street.

The sky exploded with a blast of thunder so powerful it shook the entire house. Thunderheads hurled across the valley--dark, knotted, malignant masses moved with fantastic speed out of California; chain lightning stair stepped down from clouds so low they seemed to brush the treetops. In a split second of illumination, Damascus caught sight of a stranger hovering in the shadows because he threw himself off the window seat and lunged against the door. With a mad frenzy of barking, he whirled back to the window. Saliva flew in all directions as his rage built. Furious barks challenged the supremacy of booming thunder which added to the roaring din. Common sense warned Catherine not to try to calm the dog; let the Peeping Tom know the strength of the brute within the house.

Suddenly, the extrasensory method of gathering information employed by Catherine's brain warned her this was no ordinary Peeping Tom. She was being stalked. *Show no fear*, the functioning portion of her brain demanded. *Remain at your desk, keep your eyes trained on the shadows where the assailant is hiding. Show no fear. Casually reach for the phone.*

The dog paced back and forth on the window seat, then froze as movement in the shadows drew his attention. Spine straight, tail rigid, legs locked and braced for action, he surveyed a rain-slicked street with a level of concentration considered unique to man.

An ectoplasmic thought announced the stranger was working his way closer to the house. What if he shot Damascus? Fear galvanized Catherine into action. The Rottweiler filled a vacancy left by the departure of her only child and as she dialed Danny's office, Catherine prayed for a quick response. At the sound of her son's voice, Catherine felt an almost devastating relief sweep through her body.

"Danny," her words ominous, not conducive to debate, "someone is outside."

The sentence was lost to the racket caused by the dog as he barked with rage and thrashed at the windowpane with frantic paws. Damascus' reaction filled Danny with panicky alarm; for the first time since his mother brought the dog home, he was grateful for the brute and his unflinching loyalty. "Mom, get under your desk! Call Damascus to you and don't let go of his chain. A squad car will be there in seconds . . . hang on, I'm on my way!"

Without bothering to cradle the receiver, Danny sprinted for the door, yelling at the dispatcher to get a squad car to 1304 E. Charleston on a code silent. The dispatcher knew it was Catherine's residence; the girl was a frequent patron of the psychic, and it was impossible to keep the tension from her voice as she sounded an alarm.

The entire Metropolitan police force knew the address of 'Catherine The Great' and squad cars from all over the city began to converge on a row of modest houses, most of which were turned into businesses because they faced a street which was now one of the city's primary commercial arteries.

Catherine responded to Danny's orders, sliding inside the hollow square at the center of her heavy oak desk. Losing sight of his mistress, Damascus lunged off the window seat in a frantic search for Catherine. When he got close enough, she grabbed his collar. "Damascus," she screamed above the roar which shattered the window where her dog had been only an instant before. "Down!"

The Rott dropped, forcing her further under the desk with his massive body, sheltering her from another projectile--prepared to protect her at all costs. Plaster showered the desk and floor as a spray of bullets slammed into the wall. The frenzied barking and furious growls were as threatening as the shots fired in her direction.

A commotion in the yard announced the arrival of the patrol car and within seconds Catherine heard her son's voice, twisted by fear, above the howl of a worsening storm. "Mom! Mom!" Without thinking, Danny shoved his revolver against the lock and blew it apart--the key to the front door in his pocket, forgotten.

Lightning sizzled across swollen black clouds, but when a sharp scalpel of electricity severed the underbelly of the storm, rain began to fall in torrents. Danny was drenched by the time he forced the door away from the splintered frame. Damascus would give no ground, although he recognized the tenebrous voice, he kept Catherine pinned until Danny reached them and stroked his head with reassurance. "Its okay boy, she's safe now."

Danny helped Catherine from beneath the desk, a quick glance assuring him she was unharmed. His heartbeat was as loud as the storm outside when another flash of lightning illuminated the menacing pattern of holes in the wall--where his mother's head would have been had she remained sitting at the desk one moment longer. Damascus was unnerved by the number of squad cars and police officers milling around outside. His flanks quivered, and his nose flared, sensing they meant no harm but still alert to danger. "Mom, let's go in the kitchen. We'll all feel better in there."

Away from the rain and wind howling through the shattered window, away from bullet holes which represented such imminent danger, Catherine sagged onto a kitchen chair. The prolonged flow of adrenaline

102

had taken a toll; she was physically depleted. Damascus leaned against her leg, his body positioned between Catherine and anyone who came through the kitchen door.

Sonny's face was as pale as any Caucasian's when he entered the kitchen after an exhaustive search of the yard and detached garage. "I don't think he ever got close, Danny. Looks like he fired from across the street." Sonny met his partner's astonished gaze with the same measure of dread. From that distance, in a worsening thunderstorm, the shooter had to be one hell of a marksman!

Danny threw the towel with which he had been drying off at the television set in anger. Damn! Damn! When would people listen? He stomped across the bedroom and turned up the volume. An early morning newscaster was interviewing the distinguished looking Senator from the State of Nevada, Mathias Hastings.

Using the well-oiled tones of a polished diplomat, Senator Hastings was pontificating about legislation which would make Yucca Mountain the repository for all nuclear waste in the country, if the measure passed with a majority congressional vote. Hastings droned on about the repository's incredible safety features, quoting several scientists hired to study the mountainous area within the 1,350 square mile Department of Energy reservation.

"For God's sake," Danny fumed. These scientists were being paid by the government! What did people expect their findings to be? Researchers receiving grants were not going to bite the hand that fed them by filing a negative report! Anger poured bile into his stomach and nausea twisted his belly, hard. "Stupid! Stupid! Stupid!" he yelled at the television set in the corner.

There was absolutely no danger in placing tons of nuclear waste which would remain radio-active for a million years at the center of a fault line. No danger at all! Hell, any fool knew an earthquake couldn't destroy tons of reinforced concrete! Why look at all the freeways in L.A. that never collapsed and buildings which never sustained any damage when the earth shifted a couple of feet! Everyone knew earthquakes never, ever jolted Nevada. The trembler which hit 6.1 on the Richter scale just outside of Beatty proved the government sponsored scientific theory quite conclusively! And why worry about tons of nuclear waste which would

103

pass through Las Vegas by train or tractor trailer rigs to a nuclear dump just one hundred miles north of the city!

Yeah, Yucca Mountain could survive any natural disaster, scientists were positive! Well, Danny wondered, what about the consequences that couldn't be foreseen today, or tomorrow, or fifty years from now? What about the future generations of children who would grow up in Nevada? Were they all to be consigned to birth defects, abnormal levels of cancer, or the millions of other things which could go wrong with the human body when it was exposed to radiation? Jesus, he wanted his kids to grow up strong and healthy!

His kids. The thought was sobering. Someday he would have kids. He wanted them, a whole houseful; so, his mother would have the enjoyment of a lot of grandchildren. Why should his kids have to live with the potential hazards of a nuclear dump site in their back yard? What about kids growing up in Missouri, or New York, or Washington, D.C.? Were the kids in Nevada less special than other places?

The warning knell of intuition was so strong it forced Danny to lean against the bed because he was afraid his knees were going to crumble. The television camera zoomed in on the Senator's face. His smile was a formidable weapon too. Too wide. Too full of unbelievably straight teeth, utterly devoid of compassion and his eyes conveyed an icy reptilian stare.

Danny never imagined one of the major insights of his life would come while sitting stark naked in front of a television set, watching the early morning news. Understanding came to him in a split second, while he was groping for a towel, as if the flow of time had been sliced apart by a quirk of reality. This man, the man who was elected to represent an entire state full of trusting people, represented only one interest. Politics, power, and money were as intertwined as the serpentine head of Medusa. Politics meant power and power was gained and protected by money. Were there no honest men on Capitol Hill anymore? Was there a single man with a shred of integrity left in the entire government of the United States of America?

Forbes was at his computer desk, which took up one entire wall of the bedroom he converted into an office. More for recreation than business purposes, the quirky genius put together a main frame with enough capacity to launch the space shuttle and guide it back to earth again.

He gathered electronic components from all over the world as one country after another dismantled hardware made obsolete by the end of the Cold War.

It didn't take a degree from the Harvard School of Business to create a dummy corporation and Forbes had enough financial reserves to make him an attractive buyer to countries desperately in need of cash. As his electronic equipment list amassed, so too did his ability to tip-toe through information encoded on magnetic tapes stored in the cavernous electronic warehouses of the IRS, CIA, FBI, Department of Homeland Security, and all segments of the armed forces. Forbes was confident he'd be able to mine access codes to hundreds of Pentagon files before long.

At this moment, he was perusing a list of electronic surveillance paraphernalia Interpol was selling off. What he would do with some of the high-tech instruments designed for eavesdropping, wiretapping and image enhancement wasn't important. As a man with a gadget fixation and enough money to indulge his whim, Forbes was giddy as he sent a purchase order over the FAX for a rife mike so powerful it could pick-up conversations five miles away, an image enhancement scanner which could discern print in a newspaper from a picture taken by a satellite orbiting the earth, and a teeny, tiny computer chip inserted into a telephone cable at a junction box which could monitor conversations throughout an entire house. Every phone would act as a receiver/transmitter and according to the Interpol evaluation of the bug, Forbes was certain he could hear a mouse fart once the chip was in place.

As a red light on the FAX indicated his PO was received in Switzerland, Forbes leaned back in the expensive leather recliner with a smile. A carpenter friend of Danny's fabricated a stand, which tilted and revolved, to hold his computer keyboard. His entire system was completely wireless, so he could wheel the stand anywhere and continue to type into the computer. Although it was just about the last straw for Sandra, there were times he continued to work on his programs while sitting on the toilet. Forbes had learned to capture formulas and ideas on the spot before fleeting ideas were lost.

Catherine convinced him his brain was at its creative best when he was relaxed and comfortable and Forbes soon realized he did his best work in the big leather recliner. Danny's mother was the only person who didn't find his methods eccentric, but Forbes discovered through trial and error how well the psychic's advice worked! If the business world ever discovered the standard office environment was as conducive to creative thought as a guillotine, Forbes was certain he'd face stiff competition in the future.

Soon, Catherine Armstrong was confident, assembly lines and workstations would be considered as archaic to the creative process as leeches were to medicine today. Over Sandra's continued protest, Forbes planned to keep taking his keyboard into the bathroom until he mastered a program to track table games players as effectively as the one he developed for slots.

Only the palest gray glow still illuminated the sky in the west. Ghostly formations of alkali cast skeletal shadows along the sunbaked desert floor as a full moon began to ease over Sunrise Mountain. Hills bearded with denuded sage bore evidence of a scorching summer uneased by rain. The last ashen light was fading from the western sky and night was coming on fast. The desert could get as cold at night as it was hot during the day. Kevin Cox shut off the air conditioner as he rocketed through the sweltering summer night. An enveloping blackness was grave deep and just as oppressive because there were no artificial light sources to cordon off his gloom. Kevin felt as if all the oxygen in the atmosphere turned as viscid and unbreathable as honey.

He had a queer, unshakable feeling. Like his fate was already sealed, like there was something out there, and it was coming to meet him. For a single moment, the pounding of his own heart filled his eardrums, and he was rendered deaf to the hum of the Camaro's tires on asphalt, whipping wind around its aerodynamic windshield, and the blare of Kenny Rogers whining about a woman who left him from his favorite satellite radio station. The forlorn landscape penetrated him, its vastness demanded soul-penetrating introspection, and it drove an intuitive chill so deep into his bones Kevin shuddered.

The road divided and he took the fork to the northeast. There were no sentries posted because there was no need. Area 51 had only one way in and one way out. Entry to the thousand-mile square compound was gained by inserting a magnetically encoded card into a box mounted on the gate, which scanned both fingerprints and retinas. The ten-foot fence surrounding Area 51 crackled with the buzz of high voltage electricity. Even the wildlife, lizards, snakes, random coyotes, and the population of jackrabbits which roamed the area had learned to stay clear. A high-pitched whine meant instant death. But that was only the first phase of the surveillance system considered fool-proof by the wizards of mayhem at the

Pentagon.

Kevin didn't like Area 51. It gave him the creeps every time he reported to the blade-thin project commander, who never left the network of tunnels augured out of bedrock. Like an ugly troll guarding a bridge, the wacked out ex-commando was so pale the dark circles beneath his eyes looked like ink spilled on white paper. Sam Sampson possessed an unbelievably long face, which because of its gauntness, reminded Kevin of the worn-out horses which ferried tourists through the streets of New Orleans in buggies. Where the black rings diminished, his skin faded into a bluish cast, and the watery redness of his eyes betrayed a man who spent many sleepless nights worrying about one bogeyman after another. Sampson even seemed like something that might have arrived from outer space. Kevin wondered if the Colonel absorbed so much information about alien craft he lost any human qualities he might once have possessed!

After parking his car beneath camouflage nets strung above the desert floor, Kevin slowly made his way toward the entrance to a subterranean vault. Pressing his face against the glass, Kevin tried not to blink when the ruby red beam of the laser scanner crossed his eyeball--searching a lace-like tapestry of blood vessels for a match. When the electronic hum of another panel being shifted into place by massive Kray computers sequestered ten stories beneath the mountain of granite, dissipated into the cool night air, Kevin placed both palms against what looked like an ordinary square of Plexiglas. The thin blood red line passed over his hands as a scanner searched the design of whorls, lines, and ridges unique to him.

A toothless hag in a Saigon market, who predicted the fate of American GIs for pennies, pointed out five intersecting lines which created a star beneath the ring finger of his left hand. She said he was born with second sight. Kevin didn't believe in that kind of nonsense. The only thing he ever excelled at was swift reaction to unexpected events and the cunning honed by surviving situations in which lesser men might have perished.

Once the computer was satisfied the genuine Kevin Cox stood outside a gate more difficult to open than the vault at Fort Knox, a metallic hum signaled an electronic welcome. For the life of him, Kevin couldn't figure out why taxpayers had to cough up the dough for all this high-tech surveillance equipment when a couple of guards with their wits about them could have done a better job of recognizing faces and voices!

A long corridor was harshly lit by a few incandescent bulbs strung across the ceiling like a drift net. The glare created by the refraction of light off miles of white ceramic tile made Kevin think of a research hospital, the kind that performed ungodly experiments in the name of science. Only this wasn't a place you came to get well. People disappeared in here; there were never any bodies to bury, no evidence left behind to tell tales. People just seemed to vanish; their relatives made to believe their remains would turn up in the desert years from now. Kevin shivered; he'd rather go back to being a tunnel rat chasing down Viet Cong soldiers rather than have another meeting with Sam Sampson. Hell, he'd probably agree to open heart surgery with no anesthetic if he never had to meet Sam Sampson again!

There were times Jeff Cloudwalker was so glad he left the Navajo nation behind his delight was rapturous. He liked the bright lights of Vegas; loved the glamour of famous entertainers' names on gigantic marquees; he thrived on the constant bustle of a twenty-four hour a day town. It never ceased to amaze him he could get a full five-course dinner throughout the city at four o'clock in the morning! He wasn't a drinker; he couldn't be. The genetic code of his ancestors decreed an intolerance for alcohol which allowed no violation. Still, it was nice to know you could get a six pack of beer at the local convenience store any time you wanted. Nothing special ever happened on the reservation. In Vegas, something crazy happened every day! If Steve Wynn wasn't announcing his plans for a new resort, Circus was busy erecting a huge roller coaster in the middle of a water park entirely covered by a roof of pink plastic glazed to protect tourists from the sun! The five-thousand room green MGM Grand with its nine-story tall golden lion at the entrance drew tourists through the front door into the themed casino like a magnet but it scared all the Asian high-rollers who thought the lion was bad luck. So, they took a magnificent statue covered with gold leaf and threw it in the trash. And the giant Sphinx in front of the pyramid-shaped Luxor right between the castle motif of Excalibur and the Singapore themed Mandalay Bay just blew his mind every time he traveled the Strip. Only in Las Vegas! Mammoth hotels were being built with the frenzy of sharks on the trail of blood.

Then there were other days, like today, when he missed the towering monoliths of Monument Valley with his whole heart. Red sand covering the valley floor called to him. Fluffy white cumulus clouds foraged across a sapphire blue sky were a mirror image of his grandfather's sheep grazing below in deep canyons. The beauty of the Navajo nation thrust a knife of longing deep into his heart. He knew why.

That damned old man walked better than ten miles to get to the telephone at the trading post. Knowing his grandfather as well as he did, Jeff was certain Broken Blue Feather didn't even bother to saddle his old paint pony. He'd probably reached for his walking stick to ward off snakes, whistled for his half-coyote, half-mongrel dog and headed for Chinle. Jeff was equally confident his cousin, Alice Spring-In-Summer, insisted their grandfather spend the night in Chinle before returning to his hogan deep in the left arm of the canyon. Damn him! Damn that old man! He was like a flu you couldn't shake. Frigid chills of warning racked Jeff's body and kept coming at him in waves.

Trying to disregard his grandfather's warning was impossible; Broken Blue Feather dredged up ghosts of his Native American past. Although Jeff wanted to believe in hard science and the logic contained in textbooks, computers, and periodic tables, when his grandfather walked ten miles across scorching sands to relate the warning of a vision which came during an ancient tribal ceremony performed in his medicine lodge--Jeff responded out of pure instinct. It made things a little easier to call Danny knowing the detective wouldn't dismiss his grandfather's message because it came in the form of a vision. Just the same, he hated relating information from a realm which refused to yield its secrets to scientific instruments. But he had to, damn it, he had to!

"Hey, Danny! I haven't seen you for a couple of weeks." Jeff struggled to keep his tone of voice light, bantering.

"I figured if I called before you had the Spectroanalysis report you'd think I was snooping. I know how Dr. Worthen likes to play his cards close to his chest when he's on to something."

Jeff went pale beneath the warm brown skin bequeathed to him by his ancestors. Danny always seemed to know what was going on without being told. "Yeah--well, he plans to call you in the morning--but the report isn't why I'm on the phone." Despite his determination, in spite all the mental rehearsing, Jeff felt his throat constrict and his voice raised a squeaky octave, like he was on the threshold of puberty again.

Instantly, Danny shed social pleasantries. He was well acquainted with the Navajo's nuances of mood. "What's up?"

"I heard about your mother."

"First time in my life I've been glad she owns that stupid dog. Even with the racket he was making, a Rottweiler is no match for an automatic weapon. We dug the slugs out of the wall behind her desk--a Koch and Heckler put them there."

"I'll bet it scared the daylights out of her."

"I think she was more worried about that crazy dog than she was about herself."

Jeff snorted with amusement. He couldn't imagine a human being getting the best of a confrontation with Catherine's dog.

"Catherine's more angry than scared right now. She can't figure out why she didn't know it was coming."

"You mean--like a premonition."

"She's usually damned good at that sort of thing," Danny said, frowning.

"Do you believe in premonitions, Danny?"

"Sure. I've had plenty of my own. I follow my feelings regardless of how bizarre they seem at the time. Catherine says logic is man-made, so it can be distorted. On the other hand, we don't have control over our feelings so they're almost impossible to misconstrue."

"You think that is really true?"

"Yeah, I do." Danny hesitated; he sensed Jeff was searching for a way to bring up what was really on his mind.

"My grandfather called me a few hours ago."

"No kidding? I thought he lived in the middle of nowhere."

"He does. He walked a long way to get to a phone. He had a feeling about something and wanted me to pass it along. It concerns you, at least I think it's you."

Instantly alert, Danny swam against the tide of excitement threatening to claim his voice. "Jeff, I'm really interested in what your grandfather has to say."

Relief took up residence in Jeff's tone; he was grateful Danny wasn't going to make fun of Broken Blue Feather--because he loved that crazy old man despite his alarm inspiring ways. "He said his message was for the man who sought the gold. Broken Blue Feather didn't know your name or anything, but he felt the person was a close friend of mine--one whose mother is a medicine woman. He had to be referring to you and Catherine, Danny, I don't know anyone else who might fit his description."

"What else did the Chief say?" Exhilaration slammed the blood through Danny's arteries, making his ears ring.

Jeff was pleased Danny used a title which conveyed enormous respect for his grandfather. Although Broken Blue Feather was not a tribal chief in the Navajo sense, Jeff knew his friend was being sincere. "He said there were many conspiring against you. Because you love our land. That's why he walked miles to get to a phone. He knew you respected the desert, like our forefathers. He said to tell you the medicine woman is strong. Her visions are powerful. You are to study the message of her visions, then you'll know what happened to the gold and what's about to happen to the desert. Broken Blue Feather is casting a sand painting every day at dawn, so his medicine will join with your mother's--to help her save our land."

Pensive, Danny's voice sounded like the soft sough of wind through tall Cottonwood trees, which drew sustaining moisture from rocky stream beds veining the desert. "Help her save the land. Jeff, I don't know what that means. Do you have any idea?"

"That old Navajo communicates with coyotes and lizards better than he does with me!"

Danny chuckled, sympathetic with Jeff's plight. There were times when he was young he thought his mother was born on Mars. She always talked about weird things--like neurolinguistic programming and altered states, and beta endorphin highs and subconscious programming--things no self-respecting linebacker had any interest in at all! "Jeff, do you have any time off coming?"

"As a matter of fact, I've got a week of vacation I've got to use before the end of the month or I'm going to lose it. Dr. Worthen's been after me to go to Chinle and visit with my family."

"Would you mind if I tagged along?"

"To Chinle? That's the other side of the world!"

"I've always wanted to visit Canyon de Chelly. Maybe if I talked to your grandfather I might get a better understanding of his vision."

"Are you sure you want to drive all the way to Chinle?"

"Yes, and I want to meet your grandfather at his hogan. If you think he'd let us, I'd like to spend the night. We could bring along some camping gear. Frankly, I can't think of anything I'd rather do than sleep under the stars in the heart of the Navajo nation!"

The phone was ringing off the hook by the time Ralph Worthen finished got his fly zipped up. Although it was well past five o'clock, he thought one of his assistants would still be in the lab. Irritated, he grabbed for the phone. "Hello! Worthen here."

"Ralph?"

"Yes, Jenkins, yes! Did you get the report?"

"You sitting down?"

"Should I be?"

"If you've got any sense left in that big ugly head of yours!"

"No need to turn nasty, Jenkins, I only asked you to do a little undercover work for me, that's all."

"Ralph, you and I go back over thirty years and we've investigated all kinds of murder and mayhem. I wasn't prepared for this, and I don't think you're going to be either."

"Okay, I'm sitting down now. Tell me what you found."

"Do you know anything about the Special Forces division of the Army?"

"No more than what you gather from newspaper reports."

"Well--back in the '50s, the CIA supplied those guys with a lot of unusual weapons and techniques to use when conducting covert operations. Then sometime during the '60s. The Agency started to phase itself out of active political endeavors because the press was bringing a lot of heat to bear on them. The Tactical Special Division of the Agency was supposed to get rid of huge stockpiles of weapons and sabotage devices by burning them in large magnesium lined pits out at Test Site--Area 51. Because they could no longer rely on the boys at T.S.D. to come up with their nasty little war toys, Special Forces units had to develop some of their own. Frankford Arsenal served as the Research and Development Center for the Special Forces division until the '80s. During that time, the unit experimented with all kinds of weapons and sabotage devices, which could be easily assembled by field personnel in a hostile environment."

Ralph Worthen couldn't help it; he felt as though his head had been placed in a big vice and a ruthless fiend was mercilessly cranking the handle. He couldn't catch his breath and a big, pasty hand fumbled with the tie which felt like it was strangling him. A river of sweat poured down the side of his face and his shirt stuck to his back and sides despite the air-conditioned chill in the morgue.

Jenkins Monroe droned on; he'd overcome his initial shock and rushed to relate all the evidence on the legal pad beneath his hand. "A special segment of the development team was designated to create improvised munitions. They were responsible for finding ways to make explosives and incendiary devices from ordinary materials. The boys did a fantastic job of coming up with techniques which could be applied to any unconventional warfare situation. After Vietnam, their funding dried up so most of the juicy discoveries were never published in military handbooks. They just got shoved to the back of a filing cabinet somewhere."

Ralph Worthen knew what was coming next. He knew it as surely as he knew his days on earth were numbered. "You've uncovered something unpleasant, haven't you?"

"Yes, Ralph, I'm afraid I have. There are only a few people in the United States with enough know how to put together the kind of incendiary that burned up your showgirl. A simple, hot flame was created by mixing sawdust and bee's wax to make a long burning candle. Then the home-made candle was placed inside an ordinary paper bag. To achieve a long delay, a small vial with a tight-fitting cap was filled with concentrated sulfuric acid. Several capsules of potassium chlorate and sugar were added to the acid as igniters. When the acid ate through the capsule's gelatin walls, a molecular reaction caused heat to generate, which set fire to the wax and sawdust. The paper bag filled with this deadly combination was placed beneath a piece of wood furniture, like the dresser, so a good blaze would start. Here's the tricky part. The carpet, bedspread, drapes, even the girl's clothing, were saturated with a mixture of zinc dust and ammonium nitrate."

The band around Worthen's head was getting tighter and his lungs felt as though he were standing in a furnace--the air suddenly searing hot, depriving him of oxygen. Dr. Worthen headed for the water cooler, but he knew no amount of liquid was going to slake the dryness which turned his throat as parched as a stream bed in Death Valley. "Go on."

"Ammonium nitrate is a fertilizer you can get at any feed and grain supply and zinc dust is readily obtainable at most paint stores. What few people know is together they're harmless--unless the mixture comes in contact with water! The minute the fire hose sprayed water into the room it went up like a torch."

"That's why Captain Murphy said as soon as water shot across the threshold the whole room seemed to explode."

"That's exactly what it did, my friend, that's exactly what it did. This stuff's extremely volatile--it can't be stored for more than a couple of days and God forbid the weather should turn rainy because even a few drops of humidity can set it off. Only an expert could handle the combination with any degree of safety."

"Then the killer was an expert."

"Probably no more than a dozen people would know how to use it and get out of the room alive."

"You said something about wax and sawdust being a slow burning mixture?"

"The killer would probably have had three, maybe four hours between the time he left the room and when the blaze actually started."

"That could explain the cocaine."

"Cocaine?"

"There was enough in Darla Corey to keep her in a coma for several days. Only--her friends swore she never used drugs."

"The smell of smoke wouldn't have been enough to rouse her."

"She had so much junk in her system a hurricane passing through Las Vegas wouldn't have awakened her."

"Murder is an ugly business, Ralph. You want me to have one of my friends at the Bureau run a search on the known locations of all Frankford Arsenal personnel?"

"Yes, and if possible, will you also search for anyone in the CIA or Special Forces who might have had that kind of training? It couldn't take more than a few weeks to develop a list."

"It shouldn't, but I'd be willing to bet you won't find your killer on that list."

"No?"

"No. Men with this kind of background are too easily traced. My guess is someone with a high-level security clearance probably found the right person, then deleted all trace of his records."

CHAPTER SEVEN

Danny ushered Elaine through the brass and glass doors of the Grey Group hotel on the Strip. Lit up brighter than a Christmas tree, the entrance cast a pinkish hue over Elaine's hair and shoulders. She looked stunning in a green silk dress and Danny was as proud as an Olympic gold medalist when he escorted her through the casino to the posh restaurant.

After ordering steak and lobster, the two of them sat back to enjoy the elegant ambience of a gourmet room patterned after an English gentleman's club. Thick carpet, rich warm-toned woods, leather upholstery, crystal water glasses, sterling silver tableware placed on a cloth so white it refracted light cast by the chandeliers, created the ambience high rollers felt they deserved. After handing the menu back to the tuxedoed waiter, Danny mumbled a prayer of thanksgiving he only had to pay the tip--which was probably going to amount to several weeks' worth of recreational spending on a detective's salary. But tonight, he didn't care. He was in the company of a gorgeous girl, in a luxurious restaurant, and they were going to see a great show. Danny couldn't help but feel everything was right in his universe.

Staring across the table, he admired Elaine again. She was wearing a tight fitting, off-the-shoulder dress. Long dark hair nestled against creamy white shoulders and Danny was certain he'd never laid eyes on a more attractive woman. Conversation with Elaine was effortless, she kept him chatting about various cases, growing up with Catherine, his friends on the force, and one hilarious incident after another about his ribald partner and friend from childhood, Sonny Yi. Danny couldn't remember when he'd had a better time.

Over dessert and coffee, Elaine reached for Danny's hand. "Dinner was wonderful, Danny, and I've heard nothing but fabulous stories about the show."

"Boobs and feathers! What Vegas is all about! The image this city conveys to the rest of the world makes me cringe. Nobody seems to realize

116

we have schools and churches and Boy Scouts and the YMCA and everything else--just like the rest of America."

Wine suffused her skin with a warm glow and flickering candlelight reflected in Elaine's exotic eyes. "When I told my college roommate I accepted a management position with Citibank in Las Vegas--I thought she was going to faint. She couldn't imagine living here. She thought everyone stayed in hotels! Karen didn't know there was a whole city away from the Strip filled with all kinds of people. Now that I've been here for two years, her fears seem ridiculous!"

"Growing up in Vegas, the Strip was a place to stay away from because it was always clogged with tourists. The town's grown so much I hardly recognize it anymore. There used to be nothing but barren land from Eastern all the way to Sunrise Mountain--now its solid residential tracts. Northwest of town, you're nearly to the Test Site before houses stop. I'm afraid we're going to get nearly as big as L.A. in the next few decades. When it gets that bad, it might be time for me to move on."

With a gaze as soft as the candlelight, Elaine studied the shy young man at the other side of the table. "Where would you go--all things considered?"

"Too many places in the west are getting as crowded as the east coast. One of the things I like about the desert is the isolation."

"I never thought I'd get used to the heat, but I acclimatized rather quickly. If anyone ever told me I'd be swimming in a pool at midnight or would think nothing of going outside when it was a hundred and ten degrees in the shade, I would have said they were crazy! Now, look at me. I've become a true desert rat. She nested her chin in the palm of her hand and looked wistful. "I think it's the mountains that laid claim to my heart. Karen said she didn't understand how I could live in such a stark environment. She was horrified by the lack of trees and grass when she came to visit last fall."

"I suppose it takes some getting used to, but too much vegetation makes me feel claustrophobic. In San Diego, I'm okay at the beach, but when I turn back to land I feel closed in by all the trees and bushes hanging over freeways."

"You feel all out of sorts when you can't see the horizon."

"Yeah, how did you know?"

Elaine smiled and her whole face seemed as electrically charged as the lights illuminating the Strip. "I guessed." Anticipation was a skill she honed to razor sharpness in her youth. Keeping one step ahead of an abusive father was necessary to survival.

Danny felt his heart dissolve as though a hot knife passed through butter. He was glad they had another fifteen minutes before the curtain went up because the brilliance of Elaine's smile made his knees weak. Clearing his throat, the new silk tie he'd purchased for the occasion suddenly got as tight as a hangman's noose and shyness seemed to choke off the flow of words.

Her glance was drawn to the entrance by the attractive man standing in the doorway. Elaine nudged Danny. "Isn't that Jordan Grey? He seems to be looking for someone. Maybe he wants to speak with you."

"Me? Nah, he's probably got a big Baccarat player in from Taiwan."

"He's headed in this direction."

Jordan Grey thrust a friendly hand toward Danny. "Everything all right here, Detective?"

"Wonderful, Mr. Grey. Dinner was delightful. Thank you for inviting us. This is Elaine Kullberg, my date."

Swooping up Elaine's hand, Grey bowed low and kissed the back of her wrist in a display of continental charm. With a personable wink, he complimented Danny. "When you have a companion as lovely as this, I should think your evening would be perfect, Detective Armstrong. I stopped by the showroom and requested they put you in my booth." He flicked an admiring glance in Elaine's direction and winked again. "Ownership means the best seats in the house are yours tonight." When he turned back to Danny, his expression had altered. Charming manners and cosmopolitan, courtly gestures gave way to strain. "How's your investigation coming? Everyone around here keeps asking what happened to Glitter."

"Mr. Grey, the minute I know anything I'll give you a call."

"Good enough, I appreciate your concern for my people, Detective. I'll wait for your call." He bowed to Elaine again, "Have an enjoyable time at the show, Miss Kullberg. Detective, thank you for the introduction."

Danny studied the owner of one of the finest hotels on the Strip as he sauntered back through the restaurant, greeting customers, making comments to waiters, surveying the room like a king securing the boundaries of his domain. His back was straight, a little too straight, to Danny's way of thinking. His poise and charm were thicker than the occasion warranted, and the intuitive side of his nature warned Danny the casino operator wasn't the slightest bit interested in their opinion of the cuisine. Grey was fishing for something. His interest in the cause of Darla's death was too consistent for such a busy man.

"I wonder if that man owns stock in Crisco."

"What?" Danny flicked an inquisitive glance in Elaine's direction. "Mr. Grey is so polished he's downright greasy. All that charm is as phony as imitation perfume. Danny, he wasn't interested in us at all, he was pumping you for information about the case."

Surprised at how fast she saw through Jordan Grey, Danny couldn't restrain his admiration. "Was it obvious?"

Elaine rolled her eyes with disgust. "Like a shaky deal looking for a naive loan officer."

With a sudden burst of laughter, Danny tossed some bills on the table. "Come on, let's go to the show--after all, we've got the best seats in the house, compliments of the owner!"

Like a honeymoon couple, the two left the gourmet room arm in arm, with eyes only for one another.

Ron Mellon uncovered the brand-new rife mike with caution. Slowly peeling back a protective layer of bubble wrap, he emitted an exclamation of surprise. "Sweet balls of Jesus!"

When Forbes called to say he was sending a few gadgets he'd recently picked up at a government auction, which might come in handy with his investigation work on the Darla Corey case, he neglected to mention it was the kind of espionage equipment guys on the street could never obtain. Association with the eccentric computer genius taught Ron never to question Forbes' methods of procurement. It seemed like nothing was impossible for the electronic wizard. How he managed probably flirted at the chasm's edge of the law, but this mike would pick up conversations in the next county if weather conditions were right.

A brisk wind was coming in off the ocean and Ron stared at the line of clouds hugging metallic gray water. Hopefully, the weather would be fair over the weekend, so Denise's boys could run around outside. Ron made a mental note to stash his guns, along with any other potentially dangerous objects in the attic before they arrived. Boys would be boys--at any age--and it was better to avoid temptation than to have one of the kids get in trouble with their mother. If it were up to Ron, he'd have the boys out on the sand dunes and make them weapons qualified immediately. The best way to avoid an accident was to teach kids how to handle guns and ammunition so they respected their destructive force. No kid was ever too young to learn, but Ron sensed Denise would object and he wasn't about to do anything to upset the apple cart at this tentative stage in their budding relationship. Better to earn her respect, and trust. Once she got to know him she'd get comfortable with his influence over the kids. Suddenly, Ron realized he wanted to play a big part in shaping and molding these three energetic boys.

With a slam, he closed the trunk. He nosed the car onto the narrow road which led to the highway. There was no hesitancy about the choice of routes, he'd canvassed the countryside around old man Russo's estate several times and located a secluded spot well within the range of the espionage-grade directional microphone. One of his buddies at the phone company was going to install the logic-chip telemonitor in the junction box, through which the phone lines in the Russo house were connected to the main trunk line down the street. Due to its sophisticated design, an electronic sweep would fail to detect the chip because it drew no power from the telephone line and didn't depend on house line voltage changes to activate the recorder located in Ron Mellon's office--fifty miles away. In a couple of days, every phone in the house would become a transmitter, broadcasting the slightest sounds within its range.

Nothing was going to take place in the Russo home to which private detective Mellon was not privy. Nothing. Too bad electronic eavesdropping was inadmissible in court. Otherwise, the racketeer might end up spending time in jail.

Ron eased his car deep into a thicket of willows along the edge of a shallow stream bed which probably over ran its banks as soon as snow began to melt. Pointing the foam-covered head toward the house, Ron made sure it was secure on the dashboard, then placed headphones over his ears and settled back to wait. Because the equipment was new, and Ron hadn't bothered to read the extensive manual which came with the suitcase size recorder. When Russo came out of his bathroom hacking and coughing, the racket almost blew out his ear drums. With a quick yank, Ron snatched off the headphones, pawing at dials and flipping switches on

120

the control panel. Flustered, he mistakenly raised the volume to about twenty decibels. If any neighbors within a mile happened to be out in the yard, he was no longer operating under cover. It made Ron furious to have to be damned near an electronic engineer to deal with any sort of equipment now days! As far as he was concerned, the timer on a video recorder was Japan's way of getting back at Americans for beating them to a pulp in World War II! Who the hell could figure out how to record a movie when the directions were so difficult the average person needed a Rosetta Stone to translate them?

Finally getting the equipment under control, Ron relaxed, notepad in hand, ready to keep track of any information which might prove important. The sun began to sink over a line of pine trees providing a natural sound barrier between the highway leading back to civilization and the Russo estate. Ron's stomach was beginning to rumble, and his blood sugar was starting to drop, which always made him cranky. The afternoon proved fruitless, but Ron reminded himself stakeouts were seldom as productive as they seemed in the movies. The face of his boot camp drill sergeant came fluttering through a cobweb haze of memory. As if the crusty old bastard were standing at his elbow again, Ron heard the sergeant's favorite saying as clearly as if he were reliving the experience. "Son, life in the military consists of hours of excruciating boredom punctuated by moments of stark terror." That statement pretty much summed up what it was like to be in the detective business too.

With a few more lucrative cases under his belt, he could retire to a more respectable line of work. Maybe a dry-cleaning business. Nah, that'd be too boring when the boys got older. They needed their old man to work in a more exciting environment, somewhere they'd want to come and hang out after school. Like an arcade, or a car wash, hell--maybe a used car lot specializing in racy sports cars or off-road vehicles. When Ron realized the direction of his thoughts, he sat bolt upright, shaking his furry head as though motion would rattle loose a little common sense. Still, he couldn't keep from thinking about Denise, and the boys, and this coming Saturday. It had been years since he'd been attracted, sincerely attracted, to a woman.

A door slam pulled Ron away from such a pleasant interlude. Lights flicked on in the study; Ron leaned over the steering wheel, pressing forward, wishing something exciting would happen, hoping it wouldn't at the same time. A shrill ring blasted away the lingering state of bliss which was clouding rational thought and Ron forced himself to concentrate on the window.

He couldn't wait for the computer chip to be installed. It would eliminate hours of sitting cramped up in a cold car, scarfing down colder food and swilling bitter coffee. Besides being far more comfortable monitoring conversations from his porch, Ron was anxious to hear the other end of Russo's conversation.

"Yeah!" The gravelly voice was strained, it had been a difficult day for Jake, and he'd taken more of the pain killing opiate than usual. "So, you saved Jordy again? Good boy, Robbie, good boy."

The old man was obviously talking to his son because the name and relationship were on the list of people Danny provided. Russo was listening intently; the directional microphone amplified a raspy intake of breath and wheezy exhalation.

"You trust Covington? Can you find someone else to pay off the clowns in Security? I know, Robbie, I know. It's not as easy as it used to be. You gotta be discrete now days--it ain't like it was in the '50s."

Covington. Ron ran a thick finger down the list. Charlie Covington was a casino host who'd been in and out of trouble so many times his rap sheet could provide ample shade for the vast Nevada desert.

"Covington is getting too much heat from the new crop of bastards at the State. Either find a way to get to the guys on the Gaming Control Board or find a better bag man. Charlie's weak--always has been. If he gets too much pressure he'll bust wide open."

Ron began to sweat. The smell was the odiferous equivalent of a toxic spill: fear, rage, impotence, vulnerability, the poisons produced in times of stress flooded to the surface of his skin. Covington was a bag man for the mob! Holy Christ, if only the recorded conversation was admissible in court!

"What about that Judge LeMoye? Can we buy him off? Robbie, no man is that clean. Put some feelers out on him, he's gotta have a weak spot. Find a way to encourage the Judge to cooperate."

Hacking up phlegm produced by radiation, Jake was so breathless he was forced to stop speaking. He was afraid he was going to drown in his own mucus long before cancer claimed him. "Yeah, yeah, I'm okay. Tell me what you found out about the woman." The long pause was so absent of sound Russo's study might as well have been a vacuum. "You believe in that shit, Robbie? We can't afford to take any chances; the Grey's operation is too important to us. Don't hesitate to get rid of her."

In the silence which followed Ron found the beating of his own heart a soul-numbing slam. Like tiny metal slivers drawn to a magnet, shadows piled beneath trees and pooled along edges of the undergrowth. A threatening atmosphere clouded the air; Ron felt the skin on his arms pucker with gooseflesh, and an icy current quivered up the back of his neck, taking possession of his scalp, it slithered down his face and inexplicably Ron found tears scalding his eyes. A dismay borne of fatalism claimed his soul--the woman to whom Russo referred was Catherine, he could feel it in every nerve ending in his body.

Denise decided there really was a God in heaven because Saturday dawned bright and sunny. The breeze coming off the ocean was brisk, but the boys were expending so much energy they were too hot to wear their sweaters. It was wonderful to watch them run up and down sand dunes with such wild abandon. There was no need to tell them to be quiet, to watch out for cars, to quit running, jumping, spinning, and cavorting. Out here, without another soul in sight for miles, her three overactive boys could do anything they pleased and not get yelled at for one social infraction or another by a hostile neighbor.

The water was too cold for swimming, but waves were seductive to boys accustomed to asphalt and concrete. Timmy's pants were wet to the knees, but Ron shucked off the little boy's shoes and socks and put them on the porch to dry after rolling up his pants. Afraid he would catch the flu, Denise uttered a futile protest. Ron let Jeff run into the water a few times, knowing the boy would stay out when he got too cold.

Spreading an old wool blanket on the sand, Denise laid out sandwiches, cans of soda, the homemade potato salad she'd fixed late last night, and store-bought cream puffs, which were a real luxury on her limited budget. Like a pack of hungry wolves, the boys descended on the food; their appetites turned ravenous by a morning spent in the sun and sand. Ron attacked the salad like it was the last meal he'd ever enjoy and complimented Denise on her culinary skills with exuberance. Sheltered by a tall dune, the sunshine was warm, and Roger was soon fast asleep in his mother's lap.

Ron couldn't remember being more satisfied in his entire life; the real reason for his invitation seemed vague and far away.

"It's been a lovely day, it'll be hard to get back into the swing of things on Monday," Denise ran her fingers through Roger's soft brown hair. The fringe around his temples was damp because the sun's warmth and the heat generated by his mother's body caused the little boy to perspire. He stirred, and Denise stopped the gentle stroking, afraid he might wake up and be cranky the rest of the afternoon. Her soft laugh was carried away by the breeze, "My job is hardly the kind you can generate a lot of enthusiasm for anyway, but it keeps a roof over our heads."

Denise smiled, and Ron felt the cement of his resolve melt as though hit by a nuclear blast. "Oh, come on. You're not the type of person to be stuck at a boring job--you're too smart!"

"Clerks at the Pentagon don't get paid to be brilliant, they get paid for speed, dexterity and accuracy."

"And you're at the top of your classification, right?"

"As a matter of fact, I am. How did you know?"

"After dinner the other night I questioned a friend of mine in the personnel department about you. I wanted to hedge my bet, I guess. My heart's been broken before, and I couldn't endure a whole week of wondering if you'd show up today with the boys."

There it was again. The little boy aspect of Ron Mellon's personality Denise found so appealing. This hulking man of Armenian descent stared at tall stalks of grass waving in the wind, refusing to make eye contact with Denise, but an emotional shadow lingering in his expression conveyed more than words. Although he tried to keep his tone of voice light, Denise sensed every word laid bare unpleasant memories of childhood. Rejection left an indelible stain on Ron Mellon's soul and yet he still wore his heart on the edge of his sleeve. Anyone who bothered to look beyond the rough facade could see a badly bruised ego. "So, what did you learn about me?"

"You're single, that's important--I don't like people who bust up established relationships. You've been at the Pentagon nearly seven years and you've zipped to the top of your classification every time you moved to a new section. You're considered one of the brightest women in your department and your supervisor constantly overloads you with work because you always get things done. Everyone likes you a lot, partly because you refuse to be the object of pity. Your life is hard, real hard, but you don't complain, and you keep your troubles to yourself--more than you need to. Denise, you've got friends who'd be glad to help you advance, if you'd let them."

"I won't be considered a charity case."

"Pride goeth before the fall."

"In my case, pride is all I've got. If I didn't have that my boys would be in a cold-water flat and I'd be collecting a welfare check instead of going to work at a dead-end job every day. Sometimes I think I'd be better off on welfare, but I don't want my kids to grow up with that kind of mentality. I want them to know they have to work for what they get out of life."

Ron felt the knife of guilt twist between his ribs, but he knew what he had to do. Trying to sound casual, he asked. "So, what is it about your work you find so dull?"

"Coding. I'm in charge of making up access codes for all the different departments. Then I log them into the computer, link them up with authorized passwords and generally keep track of the information flow between departments. It's very, very routine."

"How the heck can you make up codes for thousands of files? Sounds complicated to me."

"It's not--once you devise a system." Denise pushed a lock of hair from her eyes and shaded them with the back of her hand as she searched the sand dunes for Timmy.

"You made up your own system?"

"It's based on an alpha-numeric rotation which changes every month. I pre-code files by year, month, and day. Once that information is in place, it's a matter of accessing authorized passwords and linking them with the code."

"If it's that simple, why do you have such a high priority clearance classification?"

"Because I handle a lot of sensitive information, service records and stuff like that."

"How do you keep it straight? You must deal with thousands of records every day."

"I do, but I've reduced the codes to something simple--that way I don't screw things up too often."

"Is that why your supervisor likes you so much?"

Her chuckle was more bitter than amused, "He likes me because I'm so damned poor I'm willing to work through my lunch hour just to get

125

an hour of overtime whenever I can."

"I find it hard to believe the Pentagon would be amenable to a simple system. It seems like they go out of their way to make things difficult--even with low priority matters."

"I probably shouldn't tell you this--but I don't see how it can hurt. After all, a backyard mechanic would have very little reason to rummage through sensitive Pentagon files."

Ron felt as though his liver was in the last stage of cirrhosis; the pang which sliced through the lower part of his abdomen was brutal. "You don't have to divulge information which might be considered privileged, Denise. You never know for sure what a guy like me could do with it!"

"Everyone sitting within fifteen feet of my desk knows about my system and we've never had a security leak. I just use the letters in the kids' names and plug them into a program that rearranges the alphabet, sort of like a random number generator in a computer. No two files are ever the same, at least there haven't been any glitches so far."

A bright sunshiny day grew dark and ugly for Ron--as if the door to Hell had been unsealed and swallowed up all the joy and laughter there was left in the world. He felt cheap and dirty and tawdry, as though he were nothing more than a common, ordinary street walker selling her body for a syringe full of heroine. This girl trusted him, he could see it in her eyes, feel it in the way she allowed her hand to linger on his just a fraction of a second longer than necessary--and he was going to betray her. Maybe the ravings of his minister father were right after all--maybe he would end up rotting in an everlasting, eternal Hell!

"Ah, Detective Armstrong. I see my favorite assistant was able to reach you." Dr. Worthen slid his horn-rimmed glasses above the slab of bone protruding over his eyes like a promontory of rock. "Sit down, Danny, sit down. Can I offer you a cup of coffee? Jeff says he doesn't like it, but my wife has a friend who sells a special brand of raspberry-chocolate flavored coffee. It's a treat for me because growing up on the south side of Chicago didn't afford my family luxuries quite so frivolous. We were the kind of poor people comedians make jokes about on TV these days."

"Thanks, Dr. Worthen, I'll try a cup--just to see what it tastes like!"

Ralph Worthen went to the sink, rinsed out a couple of chipped ceramic mugs, which looked like they'd been used to soak old auto parts in for weeks on end, filled the cup to the brim and handed it across the desk.

Danny tried not to look at the mug. It reminded him of the one Sonny gave him for his last birthday as a joke. A big plastic cockroach was glued to the bottom of the cup and its long, spiny feelers waved around in the coffee. As hard as he tried, the insect was so lifelike Danny couldn't force himself to use the mug, which Sonny found amusing. After a sip of the steaming brew, Danny grinned. "This is better than I thought. Catherine would like it a lot."

"How is your mother, Danny? Did you find out who shot at her?"

"Catherine's disciplined. She doesn't dwell on any unpleasant situations for long, but I know she is still shaken. The shell casing is untraceable and there were no witnesses because of the storm."

"Odd, very odd. A lot of curious things seem to be turning up just now. We got the report on the cause of the fire at Caesars."

Danny leaned closer. Despite radiant heat generated by the coffee cup, his hands grew cold and clammy. Outside, the sun touched the horizon and began to melt into a line of mountains on the west side of the valley. A golden aura of late afternoon sun was swiftly turning from orange to bloody red above the antediluvian ridge, which formed a rugged wedge between Las Vegas and the rest of the Mojave Desert. He felt pressed into the cheap plastic chair by the weight of fear; a terrible pressure for what he sensed was coming.

"A friend of mine, a retired Bureau Chief, did a bit of unauthorized snooping for me on this, Danny. The technical information will be a matter of record, of course, but the background surrounding where it came from must remain confidential. You'll have to do some digging to come up with names, places--facts to be admissible in court. What I'm about to relate is only a starting place, but it's a point of departure for your investigation."

"Okay, Dr. Worthen, I understand the ground rules. You're going to give me a theory and I've got to prove it."

"No wonder you're considered one of the brightest lads on the force. I can't help but harbor a suspicion you and your mother team up on the department's more baffling cases."

Danny knew the old man was stalling, trying to buy a few precious moments of time. The conversation was too forced; like he didn't want to convey what he knew; like he didn't trust himself to remain impartial and scientific; like he was afraid of the portent the news would convey. "Catherine's methods are unorthodox and wouldn't hold up in court--even with a lenient judge."

"Danny, I'm going to tell you what my friend, Jenkins Monroe, discovered and leave you to make sense of it."

The preternatural chill which was the alarm bell of intuition uncoiled at the base of Danny's spine. Although the day was stifling hot, the morgue was kept at a chilly fifty degrees to deter the natural deterioration process of a body. But the atmosphere turned oppressive because the weight of Danny's fear was as real as the drop in barometric pressure before a tropical storm. It was hard to catch his breath; he felt as though his lungs were frozen by the unit beneath the window churning out waves of arctic air.

"Jenkins is certain the room was torched by someone who trained with a Special Forces unit headquartered at the Frankford Arsenal. They experimented with some sophisticated methods of sabotage, including improvised munitions. The incendiary concoction which killed the girl was ingenious. A mixture of bee's wax and sawdust was used to create a long burning candle, then a plastic vial of concentrated sulfuric acid was placed beside the candle in a brown paper bag. Several capsules of potassium chlorate and sulfuric acid were used as an igniter. When acid ate through plastic, the chemical reaction between potassium and sulfuric acid created a blaze, which was fueled by sawdust and wax. Placed beneath a chest of drawers, that alone could have started a pretty good fire, but everything in the room had been saturated with a mixture of zinc dust and ammonium nitrate."

Danny stared at the pathologist, unable to pinpoint why Dr. Worthen seemed so nervous. Although his knowledge of chemistry was rudimentary, Danny knew ammonium nitrate was a common fertilizer and both sulfuric acid and potassium nitrate could be purchased in a variety of places. "Why would it take an expert to put together a shopping list of ordinary chemicals?"

"Zinc dust and ammonium nitrate are harmless--unless they come in contact with moisture."

"So that's why the suite was engulfed with flames as soon as the door opened, and the firemen went in!"

"The flame from the home-made candle would have set fire to the furniture, but it could have been quickly extinguished when a smoke alarm went off. Both curtains and couch cushions are treated with a flame retardant, and they created so much smoke Captain Murphy thought the whole room was ablaze. Quite correctly, he wouldn't let his men into the suite without the protection provided by a fire hose."

"When water hit the carpet, Captain Murphy said the whole room seemed to explode!" Danny blinked fast and hard, the situation suddenly took on a new meaning.

"The Captain went on record as saying he'd never experienced anything like it. In all his years of fighting fires, he'd never seen flames spring up as the result of being sprayed with water. Everywhere he turned the hose, he was met by a wall of flame. Nothing about his report made sense--until now. Jenkins also said the mixture is so volatile even a few drops of humidity could set it off prematurely."

Danny exhaled deeply, trying to repress the sudden flash of anger. "Whoever set the fire would certainly know rainstorms are few and far between in Vegas. Our arsonist is not an ordinary, garden variety fire bug . . . he's an expert."

"Jenkins thinks there are only a handful of people who would know how to safely use such an unstable combination. Obviously, the arsonist wanted a long delay between the time he departed the suite and when the room actually ignited."

"Enough time to create an alibi?" A coldness crept up his arm; the word alibi repeated through his brain on an endless memory loop. The security guard, Kevin Cox, had an alibi--he'd been on the government bus to the Test Site when the room went up. Jordan Grey was at a meeting of the Downtown Progress Association, a breakfast meeting attended by some of the most respectable men in Las Vegas. Senator Mathias Hastings was aboard the family jet, headed to Washington for a meeting on Colorado River water rights. Robbie Russo was beating the sheets with the blond dancer from the Stardust; the girl was willing to testify about the time because she'd gotten up to go to the bathroom and said she distinctly remembered looking at the clock. Four men--complete with iron clad alibis and a string of perjury proof witnesses. But a pentagram had five points and Catherine envisioned five people when she held the dead girl's bracelet. Someone else was out there--and that person was the missing piece of the equation.

"Jenkins is running a computer search of the Frankford Arsenal personnel records. Once I get it, your computer wizard can have a go at Social Security. He can check their master death list to see if these people

129

are still alive. If they are, he can find out where they're currently employed." The smile confined to the pathologist's lips did nothing to chase concern from his troubled eyes. "Danny, this kind of thing was never meant to use against civilians. Special Forces units were trained to go out of their way to avoid casualties in the private sector. Someone must have gone bad, really bad, to have used it on that girl."

The city morgue was a small building a block away from Valley Hospital. It had been remodeled in recent years, providing more space for an abundance of fatalities. The morgue also accommodated a recent influx of people flocking to a city which attracted more than its share of hoodlums, drug dealers, social misfits, and the cast-off flotsam of society upon which human predators fed. As he stared out a window toward the setting sun, the iron bars which provided steely security for the morgue cast bands of shadow across the floor.

Hunters and the hunted. Prey and predator. Life and death. Was man just another animal savagely defending a territorial boundary carved out by an instinct as old as life itself? Danny shook his head; he wanted to believe a higher faculty separated mankind from the blind, primeval urge to kill an invader. Yet a human predator killed Darla Corey for encroaching on someone's territory. But whose lair did she threaten--and why? An almost magical sixth sense which determined whether a cop was good or not, shouted at Danny--the answer lay buried in New Jersey.

Danny could not believe the desert was so green. Winter and early spring were wetter than normal, with storm after storm depositing an unusual amount of moisture on the high plateaus which made up land inhabited by the ancient ones, the Anasazi. After skirting the north rim and tall pines of the Grand Canyon, they'd crossed the Colorado River at its narrowest point, Lee's Ferry; the only place early pioneers were able to ford the awesome chasm which divided the entire southwest. Considered one of the engineering marvels of the modern world, Glen Canyon Dam tamed the Colorado, the wildest river in the West, holding it back to create the miles of shoreline for Lake Powell. They spent the night in a comfortable motel at the water's edge in Page, Arizona, then headed for Chinle at the crack of dawn. A blazing disc rose over the lake's sapphire blue waters through a pristine sky so clear Danny felt as if he were watching the dawn of creation.

He'd heard countless stories about Canyon de Chelly, home to the Anasazi and then early Navajo tribes; the deep cleft of sandstone was

Fernando De Soto's ultimate destination as he pursued a fabled City of Gold. Danny searched the library for books on the history of the Southwest and the fascinating culture of tribes who inhabited such a bleak, inhospitable terrain. The Hopi religion was old by the time the Pharaoh's built the pyramids; the Zuni had been crafting jewelry with a precision and delicateness which rivaled any Minoan creation, and the Navajo had been herding sheep and looming blankets long before Jesus learned his carpenter craft.

Millions of tiny white and yellow daises bearded a red sand carpet spread across the hills which stretched to the horizon. Tall stalks of bright red Indian paintbrush hugged a thin ribbon of asphalt that disappeared into the future. Stark white Sago lily petals were pierced by brilliant yellow heads of its stamen; the beautiful blossoms of the hardy plant were supported by a bush of dark, lustrous green. Overhead, clouds which looked like the puffed-out sails of galleons scudded across a turquoise sky. Danny felt as though an ancient longing was being relived as he leaned his head out the car window, sucking in clean, crystalline air, feeling intense sun scald his face, loving the landscape meeting his eyes with a fierceness which had no basis in logic or experience.

They had been driving for hours when Jeff finally swung off the main highway. The primary artery in the Navajo nation's heart consisted of two narrow lanes of asphalt which disappeared in either direction--with no other vehicles in sight. After negotiating a series of sharp turns, Danny was surprised when the highway dropped away from a high, flat plateau toward a small town, which camouflaged the mouth of Canyon de Chelly.

"There." Jeff pointed through a dusty windshield toward a stand of enormous Cottonwood trees hugging the banks of a sandy wash.

The canyon opening was shallow, but from where Jeff parked the Jeep, Danny could make out crimson walls which rose majestically above the creek.

"Stay here, I'll get Rosita to call my sister--to let her know we're going to spend the night in the canyon."

Danny nodded, speechless. There was no way to absorb the beauty of the canyon quickly. It was as though a piece of heaven descended to earth to remind human beings of their lowly place in Nature's order. Because of heavy winter rains the creek was running a foot deep and filled the wash to its sandstone borders. Willows, the color of bright spring grass, peppered wet red sand. Russian Olive trees thrust above willow thickets, their silvery blue-green leaves shimmering in a faint breeze. The setting sun gilded the Cottonwood's rough bark with a russet glow. Sunlight refracting off the water looked like a thousand gold coins had been scattered across the wash by a careless hand. Danny suddenly understood the illusion which lured Spanish Conquistadors into the uncharted wilderness of the Southwest was based on this kind of golden scene. The slam of metal was such an alien sound in this natural sanctuary it made Danny jump when Jeff closed the Jeep door.

"Pretty, isn't it?"

"I had no idea there was a place like this anywhere on earth."

"It gets better. My grandfather lives way back in the canyon. It's so quiet up there you can hear hawks drift on a current of air."

"No wonder he communicates with spirits."

Jeff slipped on his sunglasses. "Don't you get spooky on me too. My grandfather is bad enough." The transformation in Jeff was eerie. Like a step back in time, a wisp of dark hair fluttering against his high, prominent cheek bone, the lean brown arm that extended toward the gear shift created a subtle transformation which claimed his entire body the moment they entered the Navajo nation. It made Danny feel as though he were riding with Geronimo, Chief Red Cloud and Sitting Bull all rolled into one.

"Has your grandfather lived in the canyon all his life?"

"You can't hardly get him to go into Chinle for supplies in winter. He says it makes him nervous when he can't hear the earth breathe."

Danny pressed against the windshield, staring at mammoth sandstone walls as Jeff headed the Jeep into the stream. He couldn't begin to imagine what it must be like to live your whole life surrounded by such a vast force of nature. An indefinable feeling was taking shape in the bottom of his stomach. It bubbled up from somewhere deep within; it was a feeling he didn't recognize; it was a force like lava boiling up from a super-heated crater. Something was coming. Something which would change his life forever. "I can hardly wait to meet him."

"Mrs. Armstrong? You home?" Sonny shouted a greeting from the car, before he slammed the door, before he put the toe of his tennis shoe near the edge of her well-tended grass. "Mrs. Armstrong?" A

132

tentative footfall, followed by a cautious entrance into the backyard, accompanied by a tone of voice conveying tremendous respect for a powerful dog he expected to come storming through the back door at any moment. "Mrs. Armstrong, it's me-- Sonny!"

Sonny knew friends walked into the kitchen unannounced; acquaintances knocked; strangers rang the doorbell. A curious Rottweiler greeted friends, acquaintances were met with serious inspection, but woe to the stranger unprepared for a frenzied attack on the door, which always accompanied the sound of the doorbell. Even though he was familiar with the dog's behavior, Sonny still found it unnerving to walk into the kitchen without knocking. He learned to call out a greeting to his best friend's mother which made both dog and human aware of his approach.

Opening the door tentatively, Sonny stuck his head around the corner and called out again. "Mrs. Armstrong? Danny asked me to check on you about five o'clock. He said you'd be finished with your readings about now." Damascus was big for a Rott, he weighed in at one hundred and thirty pounds: One hundred and thirty pounds of muscle, backed by the speed of a striking snake and aggression mandated by an abundant supply of testosterone. The dog had a habit of dragging his paws along the tile floor, which generated a faint shushing sound. With the swaggering gait of a tiger or lion, the dog's shoulder blades heaved beneath a slick coat of black hair, and the muscles along his heavy rib cage rippled with a sinewy grace. Shush, shush, shush, heralded the dog's approach from the living room.

In the land of his forefathers only the wealthy had enough food to maintain a pet. Big dogs were kept as a means of defense. Sonny felt as though his parents behaved like they were still poor peasants, tilling rice paddies to eke out a meager subsistence, and they'd done an excellent job of passing along their traditional prejudices to their American-born son.

"Hey, Damascus, how ya' doin' boy?" Sonny extended one hand, so the dog could take an identifying sniff and quickly offered the Big Mac he purchased for the encounter with the other. Although Danny claimed the dog could identify the sound of his car six blocks away, Sonny preferred to think the huge animal was more inclined to recognize him by smell. Damascus was content with the hamburger until Catherine appeared at the door--then he blockaded the path to his mistress.

"Hi, sweetheart. Danny said you'd probably drop by while he and Jeff were in Chinle. Thanks for coming, but you don't have to ruin your weekend on my account."

"Really Mrs. Armstrong, it's no trouble at all. I always look forward to coming over here--especially without Danny, which means I get to eat all the cookies!"

An amused smile animated Catherine's expression as she headed for the refrigerator. "Sonny, you and Jeff, and the other boys on the force, help fill the requirements of an over-abundant maternal instinct."

"I don't think there's a cop in town who doesn't know when you light the oven. You're almost as famous for your chocolate chip cookies as you are for being a psychic." Sonny wanted to take advantage of the opportunity to be with Catherine all alone. "Mrs. Armstrong, I'd like to ask a couple of questions--if you have time."

"I have all the time in the world for you, dear." Catherine extracted a gallon of milk and reached into the cupboard for a glass. The Rott padded along behind her, looking pathetic, doing his best to con her out of a few cookies.

"I've been thinking a lot about your vision."

"About the pentagram?"

No matter how many years he'd known Danny's mother, Sonny was still caught off guard when she verbalized the thoughts which entered his head a fraction of a second before she spoke the words. "And--the five men. I know Danny feels Senator Hastings, Jordan Grey, Kevin Cox, and Robbie Russo are somehow involved in Glitter's death, and he thinks Robbie Russo's dad, Jake Russo, is the man in the center. So far, he hasn't come up with a clue as to who the fifth person is and I'm acting on a wild hunch. I wondered if you'd do another reading."

"Do you have some physical evidence Danny doesn't know about yet?"

A tide of crimson seeped up Sonny's face and faded into his hairline. Catherine already sensed there was something he'd come across after Danny left for Chinle. "I have a piece of fabric from the drapes which were doused with a strange incendiary substance. It got shuffled to the bottom of the evidence box."

"A what?"

"Dr. Worthen discovered the "Rainman" suite was doused with a mixture which bursts into flame when it meets water. Apparently, very few people know how to handle the combination because of its extreme volatility. I hoped if you held this scrap of material you might come up with something." Sonny extracted the cloth from a plastic sack, then changing his mind, resealed the zip-lock top and returned the bag to his pocket. "Forget it. It was probably a stupid idea."

Catherine extended her hand, demanding the bag. She ironed out the wrinkles with her fingertips. Eyes closed, her lips barely moved, her voice a faint whisper as she cocked her head toward the range of mountains in the north, drawn by an invisible, magnetic current. "Five, one. The number fifty-one keeps coming. It's as though the numbers are being hurled at me by a furious pitcher. For some odd reason--I seem to be a target."

She grew unnaturally silent. The dog froze, ears perked forward, the muscles in his shoulders bunched--ready to spring at an unseen assailant should his mistress suddenly cry out.

"Fertilizer. Dust. Acid. Nitrate." She shook her head, confused. "I keep hearing those words in my ear." Her face clouded, "Now I'm seeing three men. Only three people know the mixture because a combination lock keeps fluttering through my thoughts. One in California. Another north somewhere. Not Utah. Not Montana. Not Idaho. Wait. Tall pines and deep blue water. Maybe somewhere in the area around Lake Tahoe, somewhere in Northern Nevada. Now I see the image of a man in a hospital --no, a nursing home--an institution, where they put people with no place else to go. Florida, or maybe Georgia. By water, it's hot and humid. Heat and humidity are making this man miserable. No one seems to care about the hole in the window screen. He's being tortured by mosquitoes."

Catherine lifted her head abruptly; the Rott leaped to her side, his snout lifted, his eyes surveying the area above her head as though he were watching a messenger whisper in her ear.

Sonny shivered; he was trying to scribble a few notes, but logical activity was impossible because Danny's mother and her eerie dog shook him to the bottom of his superstitious Korean soul. A chill made thin hairs on the back of his arm stand at attention. Intuition announced an answer: Forbes could find the former members of the Frankford Arsenal munitions team somewhere in Northern Nevada, another in Florida--and he was willing to bet the last can of Budweiser in his refrigerator just one person would turn up in the densely populated State of California!

Easing the Jeep into gear after turning scarred Warren hubs to engage the four-wheel drive, Jeff jammed the gearshift into low. Slowly, wide tires sought traction against the soft stream bed, churning sand until the water turned red. Terrain in the canyon was so familiar to Jeff he had little trouble maneuvering the Jeep around gullies, where the creek was deepest, to forge across shallower areas the vehicle was tall enough to ford. There were several times Danny thought he was going to be ejected from the seat as Jeff maneuvered the battered vehicle up steep ravines, rumbling down the other side as they pressed deep into the left fork of the canyon. Clouds crowded the rim. Dark under-bellies of the tall, billowing cumulous clouds foretold the shower which would soon thunder across the mesa.

Overhead, an on-rushing roar startled Danny. Searching for the source of the awe-inspiring sound, he swiveled in his seat. Decibels mounting, the rumble sounded feral, hungry. With a crash which shook the ground and rattled low-lying branches of the Cottonwood trees next to the Jeep, a plume of water exploded over the rim of the canyon. It danced through the air, pulsating with an independent life. Lace-fine mist lingered as the frenzied jet of water raced down the sandstone wall, stained black by centuries of mineral deposits. A nearby Russian Olive tree shivered beneath a current of air and the soft, susurrating sound of rain falling from wet leaves was punctuated by the hard whack of tree branches disturbed by an increasing wind.

Ceasing as abruptly as it began, the storm galloped toward the horizon, but another front was close behind. The brief shower scrubbed the air clean of coal dust pumped into the atmosphere by a coal-fueled station at on the Navajo reservation. The plant generated electricity required to keep the white man's air conditioning units running at full capacity. The fiery sunset cast streamers of gold along receding clouds.

With a final protesting scream from the gear box, the Jeep surged over the last ridge. In the distance, tucked beneath the lip of a shallow sandstone cave, an old man squatted beneath a shelter of branches and brush. Roughhewn poles were poked into sandy soil. Small cedar branches formed the cross beams for a roof shingled with scrubby pine. If he felt rain dripping through the network of branches, the old Indian gave no sign.

Jeff braked to a slow stop, motioning Danny to head toward the hogan. Tradition demanded the doorway of a Navajo dwelling face east--to honor the rising sun. Clinging to the old ways, Broken Blue Feather constructed his eight-sided dwelling from brush and red clay wattle from the stream bed. A weak finger of smoke poked through the small opening in the center of a bough covered roof. The hogan floor was scooped into the earth several feet, an ancient design in perfect harmony with the elements--offering warmth in winter and cool relief from a sweltering summer sun. As they trudged up the hill to the hogan, the old man studied both young men with a cryptic stare. Once dark and lustrous, time-thinned, graying hair was held in place by a faded bandanna.

Broken Blue Feather gave a shallow nod of acknowledgement as Danny and Jeff approached but he never stopped outlining the mystical pattern which formed the boundaries of a sand painting detailed on damp earth beneath the meager shelter. A streamer of fine, coral colored sand spilled from Broken Blue Feather's palm with such precision and accuracy, it looked as though the line was created with a straight-edge ruler.

The old man's concentration was absolute, his movements precise. He radiated authority as he studied the link to the gods of his people. Finally, the painting satisfied his artist's scrutiny and he rose to greet the boys; smiling at his grandson; analyzing the white man who made the journey into the depths of the canyon. "I have been waiting."

Danny glanced at Jeff, who seemed ready to voice a protest. Undoubtedly, the chief's uncanny dreams announced their coming with as much clarity as a phone call.

Picking up a dried gourd, the ancient wise man of the canyon shook it in Danny's direction. Seeds clattered against a squash's sun-dried shell with a raucous blast which frightened off a flock of curious crows gathered in a nearby stand of brush. "Yes." His eyes narrowed, swallowed by leathery folds of nut-brown skin. "You are the one. The Ancient Ones said you'd come."

"The Ancient Ones?" Danny couldn't harness his curiosity about the old man's culture.

"Yes, Holy Ones, who walked our land in distant times, are angry. Men, cruel men, deposit evil in our earth and you must stop them!"

"Chief, your spirits are foreign to me. I am a stranger to your ways."

Broken Blue Feather extended his hand above the sand painting. Gnarled knuckles, twisted by the inexorable advance of arthritis, hovered over the mysterious glyphs of his ancestors. A faint tremor seized the old man; whether it was inspired by the energy transmitted through an inexplicable force or the handiwork of time, Danny couldn't tell. With eyes closed, weather-defined details in his face became so immobile it looked like Death reached out for the Chief and sucked him through the hole in

137

the floor of the kiva.

"My people have honored the power of sand paintings since the days the Navajo first claimed this land. These pictures tell the Earth Mother of our problems. Drought. Sickness. Enemies. Earth Mother listens to our grievances with patience. Soon a breeze begins to blow, or rain comes down from the sky as the shaman's hand brushes colored grains of sand to the four corners of the earth. Earth Mother takes our troubles to her bosom and the gains of sand return to crevices in the mountains, to gullies and washes which seam our land. Everything in nature returns to the great Earth Mother sooner or later. White men do not respect our Earth Mother. He pollutes rivers, blackens our air, strips our forest of its trees--this must be stopped, or Earth Mother will no longer be able to absorb our sand paintings and troubled times will fall upon our desert home."

The silence of the canyon provided a counterpoint of harmony to the plucking pizzicato of wind caressing the cracks and crevices in sandstone walls.

"There are five."

Five, five, five--echoed down the long corridor of stone.

The bolt of adrenaline which surged along arteries and veins jerked Danny into an extreme state of alert.

"Five conspire to destroy the home of my ancestors."

The flock of crows which settled back into the brush seemed to chorus the number; their shrieks giving sinister power to what should have been flat, lifeless, abstract.

Five--five--five--the echo inspired uneasiness.

Broken Blue Feather's body appeared to shrivel and dry; Danny watched the transformation with a mixture of awe and dread. The inner sense he followed so faithfully announced this holy man was using his last physical reserves to exhort information from a far-off realm.

"There is a symbol sacred to my people. It is a star with five points. It represents the sun, moon, stars, earth, and man himself. The intersecting lines bind the forces of the universe together. A medicine woman in your village, your mother--she has seen this star. Her vision is powerful. She has seen the five within. Her knowledge of four is clear." As though anchored on a current of wind, Broken Blue Father spread his arms above the sand painting. With closed eyes, he called upon ghosts of

138

his shaman forefathers to part the gossamer veil separating mankind from the spirit world. A deep sigh rattled somewhere deep inside the old man's thin chest. When he finally spoke, the words rasped between labored breaths. "The unknown person is powerful, both in spirit and in body. This person will unravel the fabric of lies the men in the star have woven so tightly."

Broken Blue Feather smiled as he separated from the nether world. Slowly opening his eyes, recognition of the present time and place claimed his expression. "In the days my ancestors walked the earth, we paid homage to Earth Mother. It was Earth Mother who blessed our crops and permitted our children to have children. We respected her powers and celebrated her in dance and song. Then the white man came with his selfish ways. They told us our Earth Mother was not important. We forgot her songs and paid her no tribute. Because we hardened our hearts against our Earth Mother the land withered, and our children moved away." Broken Blue Feather skewered his grandson with a penetrating glance.

In the distance, another low rumble trumpeted like an on-coming train and sheet lightning outlined barren hills on the eastern horizon. Intermittent, a distant fusillade grew louder, and a percussive blast rent the sky. Lightning flashed so white it charged the gathering twilight with the brightness of day. More rain would soon drench the canyon; it was coming down hard only a few miles away. To Danny, this deep gouge in the earth became hallowed territory where ghostly shamans rode astride spotted ponies, beating out a mournful dirge on animal skin drums. Danny couldn't hold his fear at bay, and fear fed the beasts the shamans were trying to drive away.

Broken Blue Feather's face darkened, and he curled his hands into fists. In a voice as flat as the mesa above the canyon, he issued a warning to Danny. "The medicine woman, your earthly mother, will have to confront this person with a terrible truth. Tell your mother the ancient ones walk at her side, they whisper in her ear. She has only to heed their silent counsel. They, and they alone, can help her find the one it is her duty to seek." With a mouth as dry as the desert in which he dwelled, the old man choked out the warning. "Tell your mother to be careful--nothing is what it seems."

Churning black-gray clouds finally unleashed their pent-up fury building at the mesa's edge. Rain scoured canyon walls, pounding trees and Broken Blue Feather's sturdy hogan. Danny could not dispel the ache which claimed his heart. Like a toxic chemical, despair settled into his bones, leaching strength from his body, robbing him of all emotional sunshine. Eternally lost. The phrase took flight through his mind like a house of cards flatted by a flurry of wind. A thin, involuntary wail crept up the back of his throat; it wasn't a human sound, it was more like the muted sigh of a wind instrument exhaling the last plaintive note of a haunting melody.

"Nothing is what it seems." Catherine's words when she held Darla Corey's charred bracelet.

Danny had faith in his mother, she would find the person who held the key to unlock the mystery of the pentagram!

Somehow.

Someway.

She had to.

Or all was lost.

CHAPTER EIGHT

Red and blue lights cast broad swaths of color along the access road to the freeway. A tall pine tree struggled for existence in a triangular plot of ground which funneled traffic toward I-15 or forced cars to go straight east on Sahara. Recent summer rains gave new life to a hardy species of desert pine, its boughs had more spring and softer, green needles were washed free of an accumulation of dust and exhaust.

Two police officers patted down a gaunt man standing beneath the tree. They descended on the drifter, another hapless victim of the indifferent society in which he dwelled, in response to an anxious call from a service station manager who reported the vagrant was shouting at passing cars. The manager said he was concerned the guy might cause an accident because people were slowing down to stare. Both officers knew he was more afraid the wigged-out panhandler would scare off potential business.

Even though the sun dropped behind Mt. Charleston over an hour ago, it was still nearly ninety-five degrees. Despite the cruel heat, the homeless man was wearing a flannel shirt with long sleeves and a dirty quilted vest from which loose threads flapped in all directions. Suspended from one tattered belt loop were two plastic jugs. Through another loop, a length of twine wrapped around a bundle of clothing from which several woolen socks protruded. What few possessions the fellow managed to collect were roped to his body. From his crazed expression, both officers assumed he was afraid to part with any clothing long enough to wash for fear one imagined villain or another would make off with them when his back was turned.

"We gonna take him in?" The rookie asked his partner with severity. Inside, he felt sorry for the poor fellow. Who knew what circumstance led him to this deplorable state? He stared at torn sneakers and grime encrusted fingernails which hadn't enjoyed the luxury of soap and water for weeks. The rookie silently thanked God for the road which led him to be an up-standing citizen with a good paying job and for a wife with a child on the way.

"Nah, jail's full. He'd probably sit in the drunk tank for a couple of hours, then he'd be right back on the street." The senior officer managed to retain some compassion for his fellow man--even after twelve years on the force. He'd heard bums speak as eloquently as a candidate for political office. And he learned a long time ago the high and mighty, who ruled the gaming kingdom in the desert, could be as depraved as any unhinged vagrant cast adrift in the ocean of unforgiving humanity. "Let's see if Sam can take him. I don't know what he's on, but he isn't drunk and he's too poor to be strung out on meth. If it's crack, I've never seen anyone act quite like this."

Heat and grime produced a body odor so powerful it quickly permeated the squad car; it seemed to be blowing through the AC vents and the rookie suggested rolling down their windows before they suffocated. Quick to agree, his partner wound the crank so furiously the rookie was amazed the knob didn't fly off.

Holding their breath for what seemed like an hour, both officers exploded from the patrol car before Sam reached the glass door separating the city's undesirables from a productive, tax-paying populace.

"Got one for you, Sam--a real humdinger." The rookie stood far away from the cruiser, letting a freshening breeze waft through the cruiser's open doors. "He's weird, but I don't think he's on drugs--at least none I know about."

"Not drunk?"

"Don't think so."

Both patrolmen stood back to allow a guy who should've been nominated for sainthood help the drifter from the squad car.

"Thanks for not takin' him downtown, boys. I'll look after him a couple of days. If he doesn't straighten out a bit, I'll call you. From the looks of him, he might need a few days in the hospital."

Relieved of their burden, both Metro officers retreated to their patrol car. "Yeah, Sam, call us if you need us. We can take him over to University Medical Center if he doesn't snap out of it pretty soon."

Sam waved. Supporting the dazed man beneath his arm, Sam helped him inside the shelter. "I gotta lot of fresh clothes I can give you. How about if you take a shower while I clean these duds up a bit? Then I'll get you something to eat. How long since you last ate anything?"

Something about the shelter manager's tone of voice conveyed

142

respect and sincerity. The fog shrouding his brain seemed to part a little. Kindness shed a weak ray of light on the vagrant's interior world. "Don't know. A coupla days, maybe. Had a donut right here just the other day. Some coffee too. It was good. Hit the spot."

"Great!" Sam patted the man on the back; the gesture conveyed sincere warmth and tentative friendship. "How about that shower now? I promise to return your clothes after they've been washed. Won't nothin' happen to 'em."

Unnaturally gray eyes regarded Sam Levenkowski with marked intelligence. Once, back in the good years, he'd been able to sum up another human by their body language and tone of voice. It'd rescued him from more than one scrape and saved him from a whole lot of trouble. This was a good man, maybe the last unselfish person left in America.

The vagrant let Sam lead him to a shower stall. With unbegrudging patience, Sam waited for the remnants of clothing to be passed through a sheet of cheap plastic which provided some self-respect accorded by privacy. "I've laid out clean clothes on the bench and I'll take yours to the laundry. By the time you eat supper, they'll be waiting for you. Shall I tell the maid to hold the starch?" Sam asked with humor.

A wide grin folded sunbaked skin in furrows as deep as an Iowa corn farmer's field. Too much work and too much worry kept the shelter operator from the luxury of excess weight. When he pulled the shower curtain back to evaluate him, the vagrant decided his rescuer was as lean as a share-cropper's mule and just as tough.

"We're not very fancy here, but if you're willin' to work, we got plenty of food and clean sheets. You won't be roasted by the sun, and you won't go hungry. And I'll do my best to find you a job. By the way, my name's Sam--Sam Levenkowski."

"Jared, Jared Pierce."

If he was reluctant to grip the soap-lathered hand which extended from the shower stall so tentatively, Sam never let it show. He looked Jared Pierce straight in the eye with respect and a degree of determination which broadcast Sam Levenkowski was also a damned fine judge of character.

After a mug of barley and beef soup, Jared felt his blood sugar begin to stabilize and the mysterious cloud, which befouled rational thought until there were times nothing made any sense, began to dissipate. Wolfing down several hunks of home-made bread restored a degree of calm to his troubled thoughts. Like sediment settling to the bottom of a bucket, he felt mentally clearer than he had in days. "Good grub, Sam."

"Yeah, the cook used to work in one of the big hotels till booze got the better of him. What's your story, Jared? You don't seem like the kind of guy to get tangled up in drugs."

"Not the illegal kind anyway."

Sam's eyebrows lifted above a large, lumpy nose which had been broken more than once. He pushed a lock of lank brown hair away from his forehead. "What do you mean, not the illegal kind?"

"How old are you, Sam?"

"Fifty, why?"

"You in 'Nam?"

"Served two tours, '64 and '66."

"What was your classification?"

"Supply sergeant, first class."

"Where?"

"Da Nang, mostly."

"You ever out in the bush?" His memory of the war years was darker than the sky at midnight. A relentless enemy: Fear's implacable clutch never seemed to leave him; his mouth hung open and labored breath rattled up in his throat. Pierce chewed his lip so hard it looked as if he might draw blood. He raised spastic hands again and again, working them through empty air as if he could wring an answer to his emotional dilemma out of the atmosphere.

"Once or twice, not very far. I was in a lot more danger in the streets of Saigon than I ever was in the bush." Sam studied the reed-thin man on the other side of the table. There was a violent aspect to his eyes and the tight-lipped, cruel mouth hinted at a raging torrent of anger lurking below the flash point of sanity. "What'd you do?"

"Airborne Ranger. Went behind the lines--a lot. Spent more time in Cambodia than I ever did in 'Nam. 'Course, we weren't officially there." Tapping the side of his head with a pasty finger, the ex-soldier fisted his other hand and seemed prepared to bang the table. He began to breathe faster; his anxiety announced by the hunch of his shoulders and the cork-screw tight knot of muscles at the base of his jaw. Tremors shook his spine

144

like the San Andrea fault jolting California. "Half my problems are because I tramped through miles of jungle that'd been sprayed with Agent Orange. Hell, I used to fill my canteen in streams running red with the God damned shit. Screwed up my body and messed up my brain--bad. 'Course the government, shit, they won't admit to anything, and I'll die before I go back to some God damned VA hospital. Guys in there'r treated worsen than if they were in an insane asylum."

Sam didn't like the expression staking an exclusive claim on Jared Pierce's face. The man could become monstrous, a hideous creature with the power to run rough shod over the innocent. There was a chilling quality to his tone of voice--it was whispery yet guttural, savage but tortured.

"The government sure got its money outta me, Sam. First, they discovered I had certain--aptitudes--natural abilities they honed and perfected. Eventually, I became as deadly a soldier as training could craft. I know how to use weapons, any weapon. Even empty handed I could kill you so quick you'd never know I was on you till you heard your own back break."

This guy was clearly in deep psychological trouble. Sam had done a lot of reading on the insidious manifestations of Post-Traumatic Stress. And Agent Orange, for God's sake! Researchers were still trying to unravel the pernicious effects the defoliant had on a human body. Fear's cold sweat trickled down Sam's rib cage. He felt a tightness in his chest, and a thickening in the back of his throat made it hard to swallow. "Say, how about getting a good night's sleep between some clean sheets? I'll bet it's been a long time since you had that luxury, huh, Jared?"

Jared Pierce swung his head in Sam's direction, but his gaze was fastened upon an interior landscape invisible to others. "I loved her. I really loved her." His fist hit the table so hard heavy ceramic mugs jumped and clattered against a cigarette burned Formica tabletop. "That crap, Agent Orange, it does things to a fellow, Sam. It messed me up. I'd wig out and say stupid things. She said I was becoming an embarrassment, hell, maybe I was. I sorta hit the skids after that. Been driftin' for several months now. It got so cold up north I decided I'd better head for a warmer country if I was gonna last the winter. I can't remember how long I'd been standin' on the corner before the cops brought me here. Things get kinda cloudy when I don't eat regular."

Sam clapped the man on the shoulder and said kindly, "Well, why don't you hang out at the shelter for a week or two? I gotta buddy over at the VA. He's taken on the plight of Viet Nam Vets as a personal crusade.

His dad died before Perez ever got a chance to know him. He's a real good lawyer and he's gotten benefits where others have failed. Maybe he could help you out too. Get a disability check or something."

"I don't want somethin' for nothin', Sam. I ain't never been on welfare."

"Jared, I kinda figure we owe it to you. You served your country, and you got messed up doin' it. VA benefits aren't like welfare, Jared, you can't think of it that way. You did your part--now it's time for everybody else to ante up."

A memory floated up from nowhere and Jared recalled wading into a ferocious fire fight. He remembered looking through a high-powered scope, the kind favored by assassins and marksmen, and remembered feeling as though he was looking beyond reality into hell itself. Wild eyes strained from the faces of his enemy; distorted with hatred and rage. Blinded with the blood lust of kill or be killed. A unit of North Vietnamese soldiers kicked fallen Marines, jerked them to their feet, then rammed them with bayonets. One gook slammed the butt of his rifle against an American kid's skull until it cracked open, and his brains spilled out like pieces of ripe red watermelon. Jared blinked, and the memory faded, but fear, horror and degradation was never more than a membrane thickness away. Maybe the citizens of the United States owed him something after all.

"Carrington, should I bring a hat? How hot do you think it's going to be out there today?"

"At least one hundred, Catherine. The viewing stand will have shade--but you'd better take a visor along, just in case."

Catherine entered a living room decorated to withstand the impact of living with a Rottweiler, straw hat in hand. A broad brim was banded by a patterned silk scarf, which matched her green silk jumpsuit. "Do you think this is suitable?"

"You'll turn everyone's head--including the Governor. It might be difficult to keep soldiers in formation once they get a glimpse of you in the stands."

"Flattery will get you everywhere."

"Were that true, you'd be Mrs. LeMoye."

146

"Don't start."

"We'd better hurry. It's a long drive out to the Test Site and I don't want to be late. The Stealth unit is only going to do two fly-byes and I don't want to miss either one."

Gathering up a large canvas bag into which she'd stuffed a bottle of sunscreen, dark glasses and a light sweater, for when it cooled down after dark, Catherine smiled. "You can take the boy out of the Air Force, but you can't take the Air Force out of the boy?"

Placing his hand in the hollow of her back as he escorted her through the kitchen door toward the big white Mercedes, Carrington refused to be goaded about his passion for airplanes. "The Stealth is seldom on public display and I'm not about to miss it. Someday, I might describe it to one of Danny's sons."

"Now there's a wonderful concept!"

After sealing Catherine inside the luxurious auto, the Judge quickly made his way around his car to the other side. Turning the ignition, a satisfied smile wreathed his face when the engine responded. "You mentioned Danny's been seeing the same girl for several weeks. Have you met her?"

"I think Danny's afraid I might appear too hopeful, so he hasn't brought her by to meet me, but I do get a good feeling about this one."

"See, maybe you'll have grandchildren yet."

"I hope so, Carrington, I really hope so."

As they passed the Mt. Charleston turn-off, Judge LeMoye switched on the cruise control. There were few cars out on such a desolate stretch of highway this early in the morning. "I always thought Danny's friends fulfilled your maternal instincts."

Catherine smiled, remembering pizza parties and late-night snacks after the football game which took place around her kitchen table. "There were times I felt like a surrogate for the Mogambo bird."

"What in God's name is a Mogambo bird?"

"It's a big ugly bird which lays its eggs in another bird's nest, then flies off to leave the adopted parent to hatch the egg and feed the chick. The Mogambo is usually stronger and more aggressive than other babies in the nest, so it gets more food and attention from its adopted parents.

Sometimes, a Mogambo even pushes rightful chicks out of the nest."

"And you were the adoptive parent to a lot of troubled boys?"

"Occasionally, I feel guilty about the attention I lavished on Danny's friends. I spent so much time and energy resolving the problems of other teenagers I wonder if I neglected my own son."

Carrington gave Catherine's hand an affectionate squeeze. "Danny is as well-adjusted as any kid alive. If he hadn't wanted you to get involved with his friends, he wouldn't have brought them home in the first place. That boy knows he has a secure place in your heart, Catherine." Carrington winked in her direction. "The only real competition he's ever had is your dog."

"Well, who else would sleep with me?"

"Is the position available?"

Laughter filled the Mercedes as Judge Carrington LeMoye and Catherine Armstrong sped toward a military checkpoint at the Test Site entrance. They chatted about local events, several hearings over which the Judge was presiding, and an interesting past-life regression case Catherine was pursuing, as they drove through parched alkali flats.

A small cinder block guard house had been erected at the left side of the road leading to the Test Site. On each side of the tiny structure, for miles in either direction, an electrified chain-link fence stretched toward the Sheep Mountains in the north and the gunnery range at Nellis Air Force Base on the south. When the Judge depressed the electric window control button, it was like opening a door to Hell. Inferno-like heat boiled into the car, conquering its air-conditioned coolness. Withdrawing his entry pass from the glove compartment, LeMoye handed it to the sentry.

Dressed in drab khakis, a once sharp crease in trousers and sleeves was reduced to a soggy line by perspiration. A band inside the bilious green helmet was designed to hold it securely in place, to provide protection from percussion blasts. In Nevada's summer months, the web of nylon functioned more like a sweat band. Despite continuous efforts of a small AC unit, no amount of equipment could sufficiently cool the thirty-square foot building dominated by four large windows.

"May I see your companion's identification?"

"Catherine, let me have your driver's license."

Rummaging through her purse, Catherine extracted the laminated plastic from her wallet and handed it to the Judge. The sentry's crisp, military movements pressed on Catherine like a heavy weight. There was nothing out of the ordinary about the guard's appearance, but there was a stiffness in his body language which couldn't be accounted for by military protocol. After comparing her signature with names on an authorized list of invitees, the sentry handed her license back through the window. Catherine reached across the Judge to claim the plastic-coated card.

"You're clear. Check your odometer reading--the turn-off is six-point-five miles. Stay on this road. The trail to the viewing stand is marked by a piece of rebar tied with a strip of yellow plastic. Travel south for another five miles." The sentry saluted as Judge LeMoye eased the Mercedes in gear.

Catherine watched the small building shrink as the car sped down a thin ribbon of asphalt laid atop the desert floor. Askew in the seat, she finally turned around and settled deep into the plush Corinthian leather, clasping her driver's license as though she were afraid it might escape.

Alert to every nuance of his companion's moods, Carrington turned down the volume on the CD player churning out the haunting vibrato of Barbra Streisand at her best. Like an occluding cloud, a frown obliterated the sunny mood stolen by the sentry. As her concentration deepened, arteries at either side of the psychic's neck stopped pulsing. Blood vessels which carried the spirit of a vibrant woman seemed to retreat. It was as though her arteries turned to stone and her ventricles packed were with ice to staunch the flow of blood. But Carrington had witnessed enough transformations in Catherine, which accompanied her inner voyages, to know he need not be concerned. With one eye on the woman at his side and the other on the road ahead, he maintained a silent vigil.

Although aware of where she was, another aspect of Catherine's personality split off and drifted away like a spirit abandoning the body. The sentry's face floated up from somewhere--nowhere. There was something familiar, something reached deep into Catherine's subconscious and stirred a mythic whisper. A soft, susurrate sound, the whisper. It breathed in her ear. Experience taught her to pay close attention to the whisper, because information came from the wellspring of consciousness seldom tapped by other living beings.

Brief.

Succinct.

Taciturn.

Words came in fragments, like piercing strobes of light.

Sentry. Danger. Pentacle. Glitter--linked by an unknown person. Four you know. The fifth will soon be revealed. Danger. Grave danger.

A corona of intense light, a phenomenon she could only liken to a solar flare flashed along Catherine's inner landscape. Flames roared and crackled. A chimera slithered across the blank, black window of her mind to hang suspended like heat waves in a mirage. An image, a many headed Hydra, was outlined against a great, orange ball of flame. Standing in the fifth apex of the pentagram, behind an unknown person, was a landscape so desolate it might have been the surface of the moon. Beyond--a ridge of snowcapped mountains.

Beware.

Catherine's head jerked up with a snap. Although her eyes were wide open and fixed on the road which stretched to its vanishing point, images poured in from every corner of her mind. A narrow valley dropped down through shadows of gray and blue and purple, finally to disappear as all softening colors leeched from the landscape. Far up the mountain, trees became thicker and bigger and bushier. Snow in the passes looked wet, cold, and forbidding.

Beware these four. Nothing is what it seems.

The whispery voice repeated the phrase as though it were an incantation to ward off evil.

Beware these four. Nothing is what it seems.

Catherine was overcome by an emotion so strong it made her nauseous. She was startled because Carrington had stopped the car and was opening the passenger door. An aching, incapacitating weakness claimed her legs when she stepped on to the gooey asphalt surface. White-hot sunshine dazzled her eyes and forced her to squint, and the skin on her arms and face instantly began to bake. Despite the sun and soaring temperature, she felt a cold shiver pass through her. Catherine glanced up at the sun, it seemed like the radiant orb was her talisman. If she remained in the desert, clinging to its thorny scrub brush, sharp, denuded ridges, and rugged spines of alkali, she would be protected by elements others thought cruel and harsh.

"Should we go back?" All thought of the Stealth Squadron vanished as Carrington studied the panorama of conflicting emotions chase

150

across Catherine's delicate face.

Swooping down to gather a handful of pebbles, sand and powder-dry earth, Catherine let the desert soil trickle between her fingers--its dusty granules quickly carried away by a steady breeze. She stared at a landscape so forlorn it had been avoided by Indians and settlers alike. When the glaciers which shaped the west retreated, salty mineral deposits left behind rendered the desert's thin soil lifeless and barren. Brushing the dust from her hands, Catherine squinted into the sun again. "No, we don't need to go back." She glanced at her trusted friend, smiling with the effort to reassure him she was anxious to see the big, black metal birds--military carrion with the power to destroy entire civilizations.

They drove in silence until they reached the turn-off marker, then Carrington reached to stroke the side of her cheek with tender concern. "Are you sure you want to go on?"

Radiant blue eyes regarded the Judge with dispassionate interest. He was a good man, a kind man, a deeply loving man, but marriage to a well-known psychic would ruin his political career. "I was trying to put the impressions I picked up from the sentry in some kind of order--to make sense of random scraps of information."

Drawing her body across the console, the Judge placed a protective arm over her shoulders; as if size alone could shield her from the world's hostility; hoping strength of character could protect her from those who would do her harm. "Explain your impressions to me," he said with such a note of tenderness it melted all reluctance.

Nervously chewing the cuticle on the left side of her thumb, Catherine's voice was distant. "The sentry is really keeping people in--rather than out. He's guarding an awful, awful secret."

"Catherine, as a Federal Court Judge, I can assure you rumors about the Test Site are concocted by people with too much imagination and time on their hands."

"The root word of imagination is *image*, Carrington. Sometimes people sense things they have no way to logically explain."

There were many facets to Catherine's personality Carrington admired. Few people could completely disarm him with their intelligence and powers of observation the way she did. Fewer still cared so deeply about the fate of their fellow man.

When she spoke, Catherine's mind was far away and the

hollowness in her words made it sound as though she didn't realize she was speaking. "Everyone involved in Darla Corey's death is hiding something. Nothing is what it seems. I can't shake the feeling that sentry is guarding something sinister--and its hidden deep underground." Suddenly, she relaxed, becoming calm and curiously serene, as if the interior of the car was the eye of a hurricane--and they drove between the storm just passing and the tempest to come.

"You received information just now, didn't you?"

"I caught an image of a forlorn valley rimmed by mountains. There were big pines and snow in the passes. I get the impression the person who can unlock the mystery of the pentagram lives in this kind of setting. When I scooped up the sand . . ." she stopped, examining her hands as if the lines and swirls contained a decoding system as complicated as that of Intrepid." I don't know quite how to describe what I felt."

A coldness claimed him. A gelid fear. He shivered beneath the cool caress of air blowing from the vent and the inner cold which refused to relinquish its hold on his body. "Try."

"For some reason, I feel as though I'm responsible for the desert." She paused to study the impoverished landscape. Some people never grew accustomed to the desert's monochromatic hues, but to Catherine they resonated with the same haunting interplay of light and shadow contained in Rembrandt's portrait of Jesus as a young man. "Five people are plotting to ruin Nevada's future. Four are motivated by greed. Our unknown person has an emotional bond with the man in the center of the pentagram, but it is a dark, ugly, love/hate relationship. None of them comprehend the unintended consequences which will plague the future because of their actions."

Judge Carrington LeMoye was a man who dealt with the harsh realities of life. He believed in action and reaction, cause and effect. Catherine's methods earned his begrudging respect because she was right so many times, it was like gambling with the house--the odds were simply in her favor. Still, the intuitive flash commanding his thoughts was met with utter disbelief. It rumbled up from his subconscious like molten metal, obliterating all the rational thought in its path. "Catherine, that's why most people don't want to know what the future contains for them! If they realized the consequences of their actions--they would be far more cautious." Another thought challenged boundaries of conventional wisdom which provided the foundation for laws over which he presided. With the dawn of awakening came an even greater respect for the woman who sat so quietly beside him. "If all of us could see into the future, we'd be self-governing. Judges, courts, lawyers, policemen--for that matter, priests and churches would have no reason to exist! Until this moment, I never realized why other people find you so intimidating. You pry the door to the future open so the rest of us see what we, and we alone, have created!"

"Perhaps you're right, Carrington, I never thought about myself that way before. I only know I've got to uncover the identity of all five people in the pentagram, or this desert will never bloom for my grandchildren."

Blond hair, blue eyes. Ron Mellon stared at the publicity picture of Darla Corey all decked out in a costume spangled with sequins and frosted with feathers. Sky blue eyes. Startling blue. Paul Newman or Mel Gibson kind of blue. Unforgettable blue. And pale blond hair like movie stars of the past. Harlow, Dietrich, Grable, Monroe. The silver blond of moonlight, almost iridescent.

Ron didn't know why he found Darla Corey's features so arresting. He'd seen plenty of blondes before. The girl was shapely too. Her breasts and hips swelled nicely--none of the anorexic look for him. He liked a full behind and a well-rounded thigh. Darla Corey certainly fit his definition of femininity. But something stranger, darker, and infinitely more sinister lurked behind the beautiful facade.

Sifting through a stack of pictures littering his beat-up roll-top desk, Ron decided to attack the problem again. His house was filled with a tomb-like quiet; the slick, slightly wet sound glossy pictures made as they slid against each other was the only break in the oppressive hush. Stacking every picture by date, Ron stared at them as if he could part the shroud of mystery by sheer concentration. Unfortunately, he felt as if understanding would only come if he sacrificed a goat and had their entrails deciphered by a Druid priest.

Spreading the pictures across a desktop scrimshawed with a thousand careless scratches; Ron willed an answer to come. He had no idea what he was looking for, what silken thread of truth was concealed inside the skein of Jake Russo's evil life. Stubby fingers jabbed at sore eyes. He was tired of studying these pictures--and he rubbed them with frustrated ferocity.

Ron went to the refrigerator and popped the top off a beer can, then pressed the cold, damp aluminum skin against his aching forehead.

He felt like he weighed a thousand pounds and his big frame dropped against an abused dinette chair like a wrecking ball. Its metal legs screeched a wail of protest on a sticky floor.

Okay. Start again. There had to be a common denominator. Maybe the background would provide a clue. Something he'd overlooked.

"Shit!" Ron retrieved the beer can from a wobbly television tray, which held the overflow of kitchen clutter which could no longer be contained by cupboards and turned back toward the living room. A savage electrical current crackled through his body as an idea surged to the surface. For an instant Ron thought he was going to pass out. He felt like he'd just awakened from a nightmare; experiencing those same few seconds of confusion as to what was real and what was intrinsic to the dream. Then the confusion and darkness parted.

With the thrust of a savage beast, Ron slammed the beer can on the desk. He shuffled back and forth between the pictures, seeking one of the first FBIs file photos of Jake Russo. Ransacking his desk drawers, Ron searched for the magnifying glass which was never where he thought he put it last. Finally, anger-generated motions dislodged the big round glass and it fell to the floor.

"Damn it all!" Afraid the glass might have broken in the fall, Ron was relieved to retrieve it unharmed. To find the precise distance for clarity of focus, Ron stretched his burly arm back and forth between the pictures and his examining eye several times.

There it was. No doubt about it. In several old photographs, the Feds secured from God only knew what source, a fair-haired woman stood behind Jake Russo. Although the photos were yellow and faded, the resemblance was unmistakable. A genetic thumbprint was transferred from the woman standing behind Russo to the beautiful girl in the beaded costume. The hair, the eyes, especially the eyes, body structure, even the angle of her God damned smile, for Christ sake!

The broad was younger than Jake by maybe ten or fifteen years. A looker, a real looker. Ron thumbed through the aging prints again. Something tugged at the periphery of his attention, nagging him to examine another photograph. It had been taken in a bar or restaurant. One of those expensive places where high society liked to see and be seen. Judging from the style of gowns and tuxedos, the picture was probably snapped in the early '60s. Jake was glancing over his shoulder--toward the camera. The blond was staring at Jake. Smitten, the woman was absolutely smitten with Jake Russo and Ron had to admit the not yet fading Don cut quite a

154

dashing figure in his prime.

Who was the blond in Russo's past? Like fragile strands of a spider web, Ron Mellon felt certain there was a relationship between the girl in the picture and Darla Corey although he was going on nothing but instinct. Instinct. The word reverberated through his brain like a bullet ricocheting off the metal skin of an armored car. Instinct. He'd send the picture to Catherine, thirty years meant nothing to the gifted psychic. Nothing at all. She'd pull details from the ether and provide him with a starting point. Ron began to search for his cell phone buried beneath a week's accumulation of newspaper with the energy of a charging bull elephant searching for a female in heat.

Kevin Cox pressed his back against cold tile lining the tunnel wall. Sterile, devoid of anything a human being might find comforting, the hall reminded him of a hospital. Its corridor seemed to stretch forever in either direction. With no windows, no identifying landmarks, first-time visitors wouldn't know they were over one hundred feet below the blistering surface of the Nevada desert. Down here, far into the heart of the earth, no sound or light penetrated through the solid bedrock above him. Occupants of the hallway might as well have been picked up and transported to a planet in a distant solar system.

A shiver of warning claimed Cox as he jumped away from a frantic technician running pell-mell down the hall, quickly followed by another man dressed in a white frock coat. Both technicians' eyes looked strange, as if they had seen something they didn't want to remember but would never be able to forget. He'd seen that look often enough in the jungles of Viet Nam to know something was terribly wrong in the tunnels below the Test Site. A look of desperation on the faces which continued to rush past him was far more revealing than the clang of any alarm. Hunched shoulders, sagging spines, legs flexed with tension and fatigue-etched expressions betrayed the men and women sworn to secrecy about the government's activities in Area 51. Kevin took pride in his skills as an interpreter of body language and facial nuance, but a blind man could have deciphered the wrongness in the air.

At the junction of tunnel, A and B, Kevin made a sharp left and headed toward the administrative suite of offices occupied by a phantom of a man, Colonel Sam Sampson. Kevin had no idea what awaited him, but instinct warned him he wasn't going to be happy about the upcoming assignment because he didn't trust Sampson and he *hated* subterranean corridors.

Despite miles of gleaming ceramic tile, brilliant LED lights, and antiseptically clean conditions, just knowing he was below ground caused the memory of days and nights spent pursuing Viet Cong soldiers through dismal, dank tunnels scratched into the earth by hand, leaped at him from the shadows of his subconscious. A tunnel rat never knew if each breath would be his last; if the next bend would reveal a nest of nasty yellow vipers, if a bullet or bayonet was waiting in the darkness. Kevin shuddered as he rushed down the hall, the memory of his private war propelling him forward.

There was a lot of activity outside the door next to Sampson's office. Men and women garbed in green surgical shirts and pants hustled in and out. Kevin maintained a relaxed stance, his pace casual, as if familiar with what lay beyond the mysterious door. No sentry barred admission and Kevin decided to act on the assumption rank and confidence would gain him entry.

Grabbing the handle with an assurance borne of carrying out hundreds of covert missions, Kevin shoved a thick metal door aside. He strode across the threshold with purpose, a report folder tucked beneath his arm; rows of service medals pinned to his dress uniform glistened beneath bank of lights recessed into the ceiling. Ready with a brisk salute, Kevin was astonished to find the reception area abandoned. A row of empty plastic chairs lined a blank wall. Beyond, a room filled with enough equipment to send a mission to Mars was jammed into a space not much larger than the reception area. Gesturing technicians huddled against a reinforced glass panel overlooking a cavity scooped into the base of the Sierra Nevada mountain range. Pressed against the glass by an anxious throng of advisors, Colonel Sam Sampson was the epitome of a man about to explode.

Although Sampson spent the entire war in Viet Nam and commanded a contingency of Marines in Beirut he stared into the hole in the mountain with an expression which conveyed both despair and fear. As a man accustomed to making the split-second decisions that could mean life or death, Sampson was seething because there was not a damn thing he could do to change the situation. No order, no amount of logistical planning, no reinforcements, neither forging ahead nor retreating was going to solve the present dilemma.

From the shadow-infested corner obscuring his presence, Kevin sought to translate the complex series of emotions fighting for supremacy in Sampson's face. Edging closer to the thick tempered glass panel, Kevin peered down into a crater. He expected to see the aluminum skin of a flying saucer. He expected to witness little gray men with big black, bulgy eyes marching around in circles. Kevin even entertained the notion he might have stumbled across a weird scientific experiment which defied the laws of gravity. What he saw was a tanker cask, the kind of vehicle used to haul gasoline to service stations across the country. Apparently, the oblong cylinder was being lowered into a deep hole in the center of a man-made cave when the rigging broke loose. Its metal skin ruptured, spilling what looked like tons of alfalfa pellets along a concrete floor. But the food commonly used to fatten feedlot animals would hardly give rise to the kind of panic Kevin could feel emanating from every person in the room.

It felt like an invisible liquid, with thick viscosity leaked into the atmosphere, immobilizing the occupants behind the glass, slowing activity, suspending motion. Shock. He'd seen it enough times in 'Nam to recognize glazed expressions; every person in the room couldn't think, couldn't react. That was a dangerous situation when action was called for and split seconds could mean the difference between life and death.

Kevin's gaze was attracted to a small plastic-coated square clipped to the lapel of surgical coats and to the sleeves of the collarless green shirts worn by everyone standing at the window in a state of shock. What color were they supposed to be? Black? Brown? Certainly not green, bright green, the kind of green which commanded attention. The power of observation was one of Kevin's better qualities. A natural ability to notice minute details frequently missed by others had gotten him out of more than one ugly situation. Gray, the squares were a neutral shade of gray only a moment ago. What did the badges signify and--why was everyone wearing them?

An answer shot through his brain with the fire power of a five-inch cannon on the deck of a heaving destroyer. Radiation. The small gray square was a piece of sensitive film, which could detect even a minute fluctuation of atomic isotopes. Millions of pellets, the kind of fuel used in nuclear power plants, were spilled across the floor. No longer powerful enough to turn enormous turbines, the pellets still contained a deadly radioactive half-life which would endure for thousands of years. The pane of glass provided no protection for these terrified people. Jesus Christ, they were staring at a nuclear accident more devastating than Chernobyl!

The dawn of awakening was supposed to come slowly, or so Kevin had been taught. Pieces of a puzzle normally fit together after weeks of painstaking research. Only the illuminating flash which fired across responding neurons in his brain came in an instant. Alien spacecraft were not hidden in the tunnels below the Test Site in Area 51. The underground facility was being used as a temporary nuclear waste disposal site until the Feds could get legislation passed to establish a high-level dump at Yucca Mountain one hundred miles north of Las Vegas!

God damn sons of bitches! Pilots at Nellis Air Force Base were always diverted around the air space above Area 51. Of course! *The Box*, as it was called by all the flight jockeys he knew, probably spewed so much radiation into the atmosphere it would be detected by instruments in their multi-million-dollar aircraft. Now it was Kevin's turn to be claimed by shock. The ground water from which the residents of Las Vegas drew most of their household water passed through the largest aquifer in America, which ran the length of Nevada. Holy, Jesus Christ! The Feds were probably dumping nuclear waste at the Test Site since the '50s. And they'd only been forced to stop the atom bomb detonations in the early '90s, for God's sake! Who the hell would know whether tankers were transporting jet fuel or pellets of plutonium? The Test Site was a Federal installation, anything could take place out here--and no one, absolutely no one, would ever know the difference. The boys in the brain trusts that ran Washington took advantage of people's natural tendency to give in to a superstitious fear of the unknown. The government was filled with fucking geniuses so skilled at spreading disinformation through unofficial channels it was like shooting fish in a barrel to make the overly curious and those who hoped for a better world think evidence of life on another planet was being hidden at Area 51! The masters of manipulation were busy playing God again. Rotten sons of bitches at the Pentagon! Hadn't they learned a damned thing from Viet Nam? Kevin knew the answer as soon as he formulated the question. All the thieves in Washington cared about was lining their own pockets! And every man woman and child in Nevada had a front row seat to annihilation. Unfortunately, trade winds blew from west to east and that meant every human in America was going to get their fair share of the toxic brew fomenting beneath the forlorn crust of Nevada.

"Crap!" Forbes slammed the phone into its restraining cradle.

"What's the matter, dear?" Catherine was in the kitchen preparing dinner for her two favorite men. Damascus was outside, sprawled beside the swimming pool. With a sulky gaze fixed on the cat, who relaxed in the safety of the Catherine's presence, the Rott pouted because he'd been consigned to the backyard.

"I think Mellon's gone soft on me."

"Oh? Why's that?"

"I asked him to figure out a way to get the codes the Defense Department uses for its personnel files. For obvious reasons, they're beyond the realm of a hacker. I've got to get military records for accurate information, or I'll never locate the guys who trained at the Frankford Arsenal. Danny's going to be really bummed when he finds out Dr. Worthen's friend couldn't access the files the FBI maintained on that unit's personnel either."

"And Ron hasn't been able to find out anything for you?" Catherine chopped lettuce, tomatoes, and onions with practiced ease.

"Oh, he found someone all right--but it seems he's fallen for the chick in charge of that section. Now he's wrapped up in a guilt trip." Frustrated, Forbes flopped on the couch. The cat leaped into his lap, demanding attention—which drew frustrated whines from the dog.

"Honey, will you get Ron on the phone for me? It's been ages since I talked to him."

Although surprised at the sudden request, Forbes reached for his cordless phone. "Ron, hey, Mrs. Armstrong wants to talk to you, you big ugly gorilla."

Smiling sweetly, Catherine took the handset. "Hi, sweetheart! You've been on my mind lately. What's going on? Something good, I think."

Catherine Armstrong's ways were unfathomable to Ron, but he'd known the psychic long enough not to question why she always seemed to call at just the right moment. "I'm better than I've been in a long time, Catherine--I've got a new girl."

"What's her name?" Catherine's tone was inquiring but pleasantly neutral.

"Denise. Denise Weston. She's got three little boys I'm crazy about. You told me a long time ago I'd make a good father. I never really believed you--until now."

"Well, honey, that's the funny part about seeing into the future. A psychic often provides answers to situations that haven't even come up yet! It takes patience to match events to a fragment of information which might affect a person's life years in the future. I had a feeling something romantic might be going on in your life because every time I thought about you a warm, tingly feeling passed up my arms into my heart."

"This may sound corny coming from me," the blush of delight started somewhere in the middle of Ron's big, burly chest and climbed his face to disappear in the bush of coarse black hair on the top of his head, "but I do feel tingly. I like this girl a lot. The kids seem to like me too. I guess the boys' Dad split when they were real young. They don't have many memories of him, and Denise says I'm the only positive male role model they've ever had." The statement sounded too conceited and Ron hesitated, embarrassed to go on.

"Oh, honey, I'm so happy for you. I feel as though both of you entered each other's lives at the right time. You wouldn't have been ready a year ago, and Denise has only begun to mend a broken heart. Now, tell me about the boys . . ."

Ron described their outing at the seashore and how exuberant the kids were running around the sand dunes. He talked about their personalities, and the fascinating differences in each boy. He droned on and on about Denise, happily going over every physical detail: the length of her legs, the shape of her calves and the circumference of her waist. Despite his blossoming emotions, Ron refused to indulge in a prediction about their future together. There was too much uncertainty in the world to think very far ahead. False expectations of situations, events and other people were conditions Ron tried to avoid. People didn't get hurt if they limited their expectations.

"I'm so happy to hear about your relationship with Denise and the boys, dear. That's a big step for you."

"It sure is, Catherine."

"Keep in touch, honey, and let me know how your fledgling romance is coming along."

"I don't know if I'd go so far as to call it a romance, Catherine. Not yet anyway." Ron felt the phone turn slippery in his hand. Catherine was trying to hint at what the future held in store, but she was playing her cards unusually close to her chest. He chose not to press her for more information.

"Call it whatever you like, dear. Just keep me posted." Catherine said goodbye with a cheery note in her voice, delighted by Ron's newfound interest. Returning the phone to its battery charger with exaggerated care, Catherine reached for a dish towel to wipe away the residue of moisture still on her hands.   Quietly, methodically, her motions as repetitious as an incoming tide, she finished slicing mushrooms and peeled a ripe avocado. When the last thin wedge of tomato was mixed into the lettuce, she lifted her gaze. "Forbes, write this down."

Forbes was ready. He'd been watching Catherine putter around the kitchen; her psychic abilities always seemed to work in overdrive when her body was engaged in a mindless task. "Okay, Mrs. Armstrong, I'm ready. Go."

"Denise Weston has three boys. Timothy Craven, Jeffrey Sloan and Roger Attenborough." The only analogy she could think of to describe her impression to Forbes was the ball selector in a Keno lounge. "Denise has devised a system which selects three letters of the alphabet in her sons' names at random. I think she does something like shake letters from a Scrabble game around in a shoe box. You know, like the way a blower forces a numbered Ping-Pong ball into the basket for a Keno game. A three-letter combination is the prefix." She studied the kitchen, or seemed to, as she described word pictures, impressions and feelings flooding into her mind. "The military unit comes next--like Airborne Ranger or Navy Seal, then the current date. The computer only needs two of the access codes to unravel the system. It will draw a list of possible candidates in date order for you to start on."

Catherine shifted the focus of her gaze to her hands. The veins seemed more prominent than they had only a few months ago. Because she preferred to mow the lawn and tend the flower beds by herself she kept her nails short and seldom bothered with a coat of polish. To Catherine, her hands were mechanisms for detecting secrets of the past; aids to uncover mysteries veiled by the future. She turned them over in her lap several times while searching for words to express intuitive feelings which streamed into her conscious mind like the rays of the sun after a storm. "Ron is in love with this girl. Forbes, he would never deliberately betray her."

Catherine edged onto the bar stool and gratefully accepted a glass of wine offered by Forbes. A complex array of emotions zig zagged across her expression as protective love for the abrasive detective fought with duty. "Ordinarily, I would never extract information someone wants to withhold, but so much depends on identifying Darla Corey's killer."

There was no way Forbes could contain the astonishment assaulting the fortress of logic and intellect he habitually erected every time he watched Catherine Armstrong work. "Mrs. Armstrong, I heard every word of your conversation. Mellon never offered the middle name of those boys. And in simplistic terms, you just described how a random number

161

generator works. It won't take much effort to devise a program to come up with all the possible letter combinations. Sometimes the simplest codes are the hardest to crack."

"Denise wanted to use the simplest method possible."

"How do you know?"

"I feel it."

"Mrs. Armstrong, will you excuse me? I'd like to get started."

"Go ahead, dear. I'll call you when Danny gets home. Dinner is about an hour away."

Catherine watched Forbes disappear into his office. She retrieved J.J. from the coffee table and cuddled the big orange and white tom cat close. A deafening purr came in response to the gentle caress as she leaned against the couch and stared at the horizon beyond the swimming pool. Hot desert air seemed iridescent; a violet haze shimmered over mountains at the west side of the large valley which Las Vegas continued to sprawl toward. Above the cinder block wall separating Forbes' backyard from the desert, darkness was falling with the swiftness of a descending curtain.

A superstitious feeling--a perception of an indefinable but uncanny presence crept into the periphery of her consciousness. An icy prickling began at the base of her spine, and extended up across her scalp, where it mutated from the suggestion of a feeling into a sensation of alarm. The shiver occasioned by fear gave way to the feeling something important was about to happen, that she was teetering on the brink of revelation.

The comfortable living room retreated. Catherine Armstrong found herself leaving the modern house in Las Vegas, traveling to the deep cleft of a canyon--where walls of sandstone blotted out the sun. The spirit of a man approached; an old man; a man wizened by time and experience. His gait was sluggish, as if he were weighed down by the message he bore. But come he did, like a relentless tsunami. A single feather, from the wing of an eagle, pierced the plait of graying hair above his ear.

Gooseflesh dimpled her arms. She was stricken with a sense of trepidation and fear of the unknown. The old Indian crept closer, cat-like, and cat-silent. Wind whistled down the canyon, Sycamore branches cast vague shadows along the ground. Coyotes howled in the distance and nearby, in the trees, Cicadas shrieked. Withered lips fashioned a whispered message.

When she opened her eyes, Catherine's pale gray irises, accentuated with striations of violet and blue, seemed abnormally luminous in the light reflecting off the water in the pool. J.J. swept the air with his tail, as though trying to loosen the rope of emotion which held her captive. When her gaze finally settled on the cat a chill of confirmation raised the hair on the back of her arms.

Danny had to find a way to ferret out the details of Darla Corey's childhood. The girl had done a magnificent job of dealing with the evil force which shaped her character. Darla tried to make a break with something so malignant it was beyond Catherine's ability to comprehend. A love of something wonderful came into her life and changed the way she looked at things--and that very transformation was why she had been killed.

CHAPTER NINE

The minute Harold Kennedy stepped out of his rental car; the wind sweeping down the mountains across a broad plateau pressed him backward against the sleek metal fender. Ely managed to retain its hardy, old-west flavor despite what was happening in the rest of Nevada. Cowboys still lounged at long oak bar running along one side of the Nevada Queen Casino. Basque sheep herders stared into a mirror etched with intertwining flowers suspended behind the bar, their features and dress still reminiscent of communities in the Pyrenees of Spain and France, from which their forefathers immigrated to America and ended up in Northern Nevada in the 1800s because the terrain would support large herds of sheep

Ely had been caressed by the hand of fate several times. First gold, then cattle, then copper kept the tiny city alive. The '70s brought tough times when the price of copper dropped to an all-time low. When the corporate behemoth, Kennicott Copper, closed the smelter in McGill, Ely fell on hard times once again. What few residents remained found a way to eke out a living from tourists who were brave enough to risk driving the longest, loneliest stretch of highway on the North American continent. A hamburger joint, a couple of gas stations, an antiquated grocery store, a dilapidated five and dime, two schoolteachers and the local sheriff and his deputy managed to survive the economic catastrophe dealt to Ely by the implacable hand of Lady Luck.

But Fate stepped in again--this time wearing the high heels of Kristin Hastings. She bought a sleazy gin joint and transformed it into a glamorous casino and added a hotel with an ungodly number of rooms for a place most people were anxious to drive through. She built an air strip big enough for private jet to land. And lots and lots of slot and video poker machines filled the brand-new casino. Kristin knew it was imperative to have a first-class restaurant, so she hired a chef all the way from New York who was anxious to leave the rat-race behind. The feature which had all the locals talking and shaking their heads was an enormous satellite disc. Two monitors in the Race and Sports Book broadcast nothing but the trading results on the New York and Tokyo stock exchange. She forced the boys at the phone company to lay several T-1 lines and band-width cable to accommodate an enormous flow of electronic information. She also sent fifteen local girls off to school in Salt Lake City, all expenses paid, to learn to be topflight secretaries who could take dictation and use computers to send stock reports and banking transactions around the world with no glitches.

All the old-timers said Kristin was crazier than Virginia Hill and predicted the Nevada Queen was going to end up as empty and useless as the smelter in McGill. Ranchers were astonished when crystal-clear skies over Ely were soon streaked with white contrails of some big ass corporate jets. When Kristin bulldozed forty acres of wasteland behind the new wing of the hotel and announced plans for an eighteen-hole golf course, locals knew she'd finally lost her mind. So, when planes full of Asian executives from huge corporations all over the Pacific Rim showed up in their 747s, hauled out their golf clubs and rode the links in fancy carts with Nevada Queen cell phones preprogrammed into their offices in Tokyo, Singapore, Hong Kong and Ho Chi Min City, via the satellite uplink Kristin rammed down the throats of the mayor and newly elected city council, local opinion was as shocked as if the hand of God took a forlorn backwater berg in the desert into the palm of His hand. Of course, when she revealed her plans to institute a month-long Basque festival, everyone in town knew Kristin Hastings should be committed. Who in the hell would drive to Ely, Nevada, to watch a bunch of sheep herders dance around in funny looking clothes, or buy a wine flask made from a good-for-nothing sheep? Hah! No self-respecting man or woman alive drank anything but beer from an aluminum can!

When the cash registers started ringing and you couldn't find a parking space the entire month of July in the whole God damned town-- distrust gave way to begrudging respect. Hell, Kristin was still crazy as a loon--but she was also the biggest employer in White Pine County. Local ranchers leaned on the hoods of their pick-up trucks in the casino parking lot on Saturday night, drinking beer, as amused by folks from New York, Tokyo, San Francisco, Los Angeles, and Dallas/Fort Worth as they would have been on a ride at Disneyland.

Harold watched CNN, Fox, CBS, NBC, ABC, and Turner Broadcasting corporate jets line up on the runway for takeoff. Kristin lured most of the network brass to the last real frontier in America for a conference on the influence TV played in changing the values of the upcoming generation. She organized sessions on gangs, the transformation of the family structure, women's issues, minority opportunities and the most threatened minority of them all--the white male executive. They came. They learned about the preeminent role they would play in sculpting the future of America. And they played--on the links and in the casino. Kristin hired Arnold Palmer to give private golf lessons for a couple of days. The Basques put on a performance which earned them a standing ovation and a ten-minute segment on Entertainment Tonight. Willie Nelson twanged his guts out in the lounge, much to the amusement of men who'd been whistling country tunes long before it was fashionable. For an entire week every broadcaster attending the conference did a live feed from the sound stage Kristin constructed in one of the meeting rooms. Journalists went back to their high-pressure jobs rested and refreshed--with renewed faith in their chosen career field. And every man, woman and child in America knew about Ely, Nevada, by the time Kristin stocked the last jet with chilled Taittinger and an assortment of hors d'oeuvres normally reserved for the big hotels in NYC, compliments of the Nevada Queen and the chef from the Waldorf Astoria

Kristin's impact on White Pine County was indisputable. Not only did she bring economic stability to an area raped of its minerals, abandoned by the corporate world and government agencies alike, she returned pride and dignity to its residents. Through her, outsiders formed a new opinion of the west. Once a man or woman beheld the majesty of the Ruby Mountains, watched mule deer graze at the edge of the fairway or witnessed a flock of Chukar take flight against a sunrise unclouded by a man-caused haze, they were never the same again.

Harold Kennedy realized the crazy woman in Ely bore the label because, like most geniuses, she was far ahead of her time. Ordinary folk, those who's most far-reaching thoughts revolved around how drunk they planned to get next Saturday night, found her methods and reasoning incomprehensible.

But no one in White Pine Country argued with Kristin Hastings' plans anymore. She was just too damned successful. As Harold crossed the parking lot toward a brilliantly lit entry way of the Nevada Queen, insecurity kept pace with him. How the hell was he going to laud the accomplishments of this woman? She was a human dynamo. Harold was beginning to wonder how a big part she played in getting her brother elected to the office of Senator.

By the time a chipper young secretary showed Harold inside Kristin's office, his knees were shaking. Walls were filled with one memento after another--from charities, international relief organizations, grateful victims of nature's cruelty, children smiling from hospital beds, in braces, or wheelchairs--bravely suffering the indignities of the human condition.

A woman of rare beauty came around the desk to greet him. Time left a network of fine lines around her eyes, lips and along her neck, but nothing could diminish the warmth emanating from her outstretched hand. It traveled all the way up Harold Kennedy's arm to his heart. Kristin's hair was pulled away from her oval face and clasped at the nape of her neck by a frothy bow--the only indication of a femininity Harold suspected she chose to minimize. Ostrich hide boots were topped by a pair of size eight Gloria Vanderbilt jeans and a western-cut shirt was her office attire. On Kristin, cotton and denim were as elegant as the finest watered silk.

"Mr. Kennedy. Thank you so much for coming all the way to Ely."

"Harold, please." He couldn't keep wonder from his voice. She was treating him as an equal--more than that—like someone she thought might turn out to be a friend.

"So, what do you think of our operation?"

The question was so sincere Harold found it difficult to respond. Who in the hell was he to offer an opinion? He was a washed up, two-bit broadcaster who could barely generate enough business to keep a small advertising agency afloat. He considered himself a rank amateur compared to the likes of Kristin Hastings! "I'm impressed. I guess I didn't expect to find anything quite this lavish in Ely." He stopped, afraid he might sound patronizing or condescending, because she was a woman and God knows-- the casino industry didn't expect genius to come disguised in female form. Harold was surprised when she took a seat in one of the visitor's chairs and poured them a cup of coffee like they were at an ordinary kitchen table.

"If you don't mind, I'd like to give you an overview of what I want your agency to achieve for this property. I don't pretend to understand the techniques involved, but I know you're just the man to do it."

The smile claiming her face was as bright and sunny as the morning. As if reading his thoughts, Kristin grabbed the coffee pot and headed for the walled patio on the other side of the French doors. "Let's go outside."

In the distance, purple mountains were warmed by a fast-rising sun. Shushing sounds made by Rainbird sprinklers on the eighteenth green were punctuated by the high-pitched trill of Quail bathing in the spray. Not a single full-sailed cloud whitened the sky. The only break in a field of blue was the shadow of a hawk hovering on a current of air rising above the

167

mountains. The setting was so beautiful it took Harold's breath away. "God, this is a pretty place."

"It is, isn't it?" Kristin engaged her visitor with another rapturous smile. "Some people would have you believe beauty and progress can't live side by side. Personally, I think that's a lot of bunk if progress remains responsible. Unfortunately, descendants of the hardy pioneers who settled this country are a hard-headed lot. They moan and groan about a lack of money, but you should hear them scream that everything I do will bring strangers to town. Oh, they want the tourist dollar, all right, but they refuse to realize there's a price to pay for everything. You can't get the tourist dollar without the tourist!" Dazzling white teeth flashed between sculpted lips. "People, they're so damned funny, Harold."

Harold was more than dazzled by Kristin's melodious laughter, he was mesmerized. The combination of brains and beauty was a rare, but wrapped up in one woman, who earned enough money to make the Rockefellers take notice, was overpowering. Trying not to be obvious, Harold glanced at Kristin's left hand--no wedding ring graced her finger. Maybe a woman as self-reliant as this one didn't bother with such an antiquated symbol of possession. It had been a long time since he'd entertained that kind of thought and surprise made him blush. "The Senator was rather vague about your advertising plans, Ms. Hastings. It looks as though you're doing so well up here I can't imagine why you'd need my agency."

"It's Kristin, Harold. And as to why I need you, well . . . let me tell you about my plans. They're going to take intense PR work and despite what happened to you a year ago, I know you're the man to handle the job."

So, she knew. Well, that would probably make things easier. No need to hide anything, hell--who was he kidding? Kristin Hastings was not the type to take on a new employee without investigating their background. Her ability to be methodical was undoubtedly one of the key factors in her success.

Kristin saw the former newscaster go white at the mention of his past. No wonder, he probably thought she was going to fire him before he got a chance to salvage his ailing business. "Harold, I asked Mathias to find you for me. You were set up by some treacherous snakes in government, but you know that, don't you?"

"It's nice to know someone else recognizes the fact."

"Your downfall was in thinking everyone else was as trustworthy

168

and honest as you are, Harold. You were getting too close to the truth and the snakes knew you would never accept a bribe--so they bushwhacked you. They lured you into thinking a network job was just over the horizon."

Harold felt himself turn bright red. Ordinarily, he didn't consider himself naive, but his pride, ego and arrogance had been so successfully fueled he hadn't anticipated a fall from grace.

"Harold, for heaven sake, don't feel bad! These guys have duped presidents, prime ministers, the brightest minds in the world and gotten away with it. But I think it's time for us little guys to make a stand. If all of us unite, if we stick together and refuse to give in--maybe we can accomplish something important. You're an expert in swaying public opinion, Harold. Look how you made people pay attention to what was going on at Area 51! You got global press coverage and you did it in a matter of weeks. That's what made you so dangerous Harold, and that's why the snakes had to discredit you. They didn't dare kill you, for God's sake, because your fans would have demanded an investigation. Their only recourse was to lure you away from the scent--to neutralize your growing influence. Well, people are still wondering what happened to you--where you disappeared. I think it's time for you to make a comeback, Harold, and I want you to do it by making White Pine County and Ely world-famous."

It was nearly noon by the time Harold Kennedy returned to the parking lot in front of the Nevada Queen. The tweed jacket hooked in his finger trailed along rough asphalt. All his surroundings dissolved into a niveous haze because Harold's thoughts were approaching critical mass. Kristin outlined a plan to restore Native Americans to their rightful place in society. Starting with Nevada. Starting with the Paiute tribe in Ely. She wanted to establish a game preserve--bring in antelope, deer, and a herd of big, wooly Bison which once roamed the plains by the millions. She planned to stock streams and ponds around the reserve and restore the area to its natural ecological balance with an equal number of predators-- mountain lions, wolves, coyotes, eagles, and hawks. Her plans were so sweeping Harold was staggered by the complexity of the undertaking. Original inhabitants of North America lived in harmony with nature and Kristin was anxious to prove it could still be done.

Like Williamsburg, a Paiute village was going to be recreated. Kids would hound their parents to let them spend a week, two weeks, a month in an authentic Indian camp where they would learn to ride horses, shoot bow and arrows and track wild animals through an equally wild wilderness. Women could purchase beaded moccasins, cradle boards, leather dresses fringed with long braid--all crafted by hand. She was confident tourists would come from far and wide to experience a way of life they grew up watching on movie screens and television sets. Profit would be plowed back into another Indian village somewhere else in the country. Mohawk, Sioux, Kiowa, Cherokee--it didn't matter because every tribe had a unique civilization. Pride in their heritage would be restored, and fabulous Indian cultures would flourish again.

Harold felt as though he were walking on water instead of asphalt--because the owner of the Nevada Queen also managed to restore his faith in his own ability.

Ron massaged his eyes. Spending hours at a microfiche machine was his least favorite thing about detective work but old newspapers provided a window to the past. Ordinary details faithfully recorded in daily newspapers painted in the backdrop essential to any case.

Personnel records at the Grey Group put Darla Corey's date of birth in August of 1984. Give or take a couple of months in either direction, from all the pictures he'd seen of the girl, Ron felt certain the year was right.

As the blurry copies of the Trenton Times whirled past, Ron scanned the sections dealing with local news and society pages. National headlines were ignored. He followed his feeling the information he was seeking would be obscure, buried in the irrelevant gossip it took to round out advertising space in a local paper. Ron wasn't much of a reader, which made the task even more odious. He didn't dare step outside for a breath of air for fear the machine would be claimed by some pimply faced student slaving over a research paper the teacher demanded be created without the benefit of the internet. With a deep sigh, Ron resigned himself to being stuck in the library the rest of the day.

Mesmerized, he stared at the black and white information fielded on the gray half-tones of the microfilm screen. Ron felt like he was asleep at the wheel of a speeding auto as the film whirled past sightless eyes. Then something tugged at the periphery of his consciousness.

He dialed the film back, reviewing the last page again. Society pages. Debutantes. Fashion. Teas and fund raisers. *Fund raisers.* Something on that page drew him away from the self-imposed state of mental exile.

What?

What did his subconscious react to in the brief flash across an illuminated screen? A testimonial dinner for the town's leading banker to benefit the Kidney Foundation. Nah. What about the one hundred dollar a plate fund raiser to re-elect the district's representative? No, nothing there.

There it was.

On the inside left corner.

A blurb about a group of prominent Catholics holding a bingo/raffle/dinner party to raise money for St. Anne's orphanage. A smiling nun accepted a check from a bejeweled society matron.

It finally clicked.

Ron remembered a news piece on Sister Mary Angelica on TV just the other night. The nun was New Jersey's answer to Mother Teresa. According to what he remembered, after eighty years of faithful service to the poor, the Benedictine nun was retiring because of failing health. So why had the nun's story triggered such a strong response?

Why?

Why, indeed?

Ron slid a quarter into the slot and pressed the button to generate a hard copy of the story. He could think a whole lot better on the porch with his feet on the rail overlooking the ocean while he sipped a can of cold beer. Driving home through a steadily increasing fog, Ron considered all the options. He would get a buddy at the clipping service to run a check on the nun and the Sacred Heart Convent. He could also verify a list of active parishioners.

Hell, probably half of Russo's henchmen turned up at confession, dumped some cash in the box and strolled out with a clean conscience. Who could figure where these guys got the notion it was acceptable to lie, cheat, steal, even murder--if you confessed your sins to a priest and put enough cash in the collection plate! Hah! Who said the sale of indulgences stopped with Martin Luther?

By the time he nosed his car into the ramshackle hut which served as his garage, Ron knew he was going to take the effortless way out and email the story to Danny. The kid could take it to his mother, who--in five seconds--could extract information which would take weeks to uncover by conventional means.

Ron was humming a happy but completely inharmonious tune as he dialed Danny's office. "Yo, buddy, got your computer on? I'm going to send you something right now."

Line by line, the printer received information being sent from nearly three thousand miles away. Danny extracted a single sheet of paper from the holding tray. Scanning the information the paper contained, he reached for the phone before his eyes reached the bottom of the page. "Hell, you don't need Catherine's expertise on this one."

"No?"

"No. The earliest records we have on Darla Corey indicate she was born in a home for foundlings."

"Sweet Jesus, I forgot! Sister Angelica ran an orphanage in Jersey for years!"

"I sure hope you can get some decent information out of her. She must be close to ninety by now."

"And sick. I don't know if I can even get in to see her."

"Try, Ron, try really hard. I'd sure like to be able to fill in the details of Darla's background."

"How will knowing which unwed teenager her birth mother was help you out, Danny?"

"I don't know. I'm just following a hunch."

Ron understood hunches. Not in a clinical sense, but he knew from experience his initial reaction to people, places and things was seldom wrong. "Okay, I'll bet I can get in to see her if I tell the Sisters I've been hired by a kid looking for its birth parents. Happens all the time now days."

"Let me know what you find out. Hopefully, this will give us the break we've been looking for."

Ron hung up the phone. Rain began in earnest. The moisture-silvered window overlooking his dark backyard betrayed a network of lines in his face that hadn't been there the last time he looked. Hell, when was that? A long time before he met Denise. But--it seemed as if his life before Denise and the boys hadn't really taken place. It was like he was a victim of amnesia; fragments of his past were remote and alien. After he talked to Denise a few minutes, he planned to turn in early, so he could be on the road at the crack of dawn. Ron hoped the nun had some information to disclose about the Las Vegas girl, so the case would come to an end--so he could start planning a future which included a wife and three kids.

As Catherine pulled onto the loop which headed to Red Rock Canyon, Damascus was pacing back and forth in the back of her mid-size SUV. Excited, he shot from the back of the vehicle like a miniball from a musket when Catherine opened the tailgate. The big dog sprinted over rocks, lifting his leg on every boulder, plant, or stray object--any animal who wandered within a hundred yards would recognize the scent of a dominate male. After allowing the dog's initial burst of energy to discharge, Catherine called him to her and fastened his leash. A long leather lead allowed the Rott plenty of distance to satisfy his natural curiosity, but he always returned quickly to his mistress' instruction to heel.

Few people were in the park so early in the morning. All the better because Catherine planned to find an isolated spot in which to meditate. Red Rock Canyon was known for its botanical diversity and unique scenery. Like an island rising from a vast ocean, ridges of limestone and sandstone provided a natural habitat for plants and wild life, which could not survive in the alkali soil and burning heat of the valley floor. Snow fed streams brought life-giving water to the area, while Las Vegas inhabited a plain as parched and barren as the Sinai Peninsula.

Instinct drove her to establish a connection with the land. Maybe here, in the serenity of the canyon, she'd find an answer to the identity of the fifth person in the pentagram. Beneath sheltering branches of a pine tree which probably sprouted as Christopher Columbus caught his first glimpse of the Americas, soft sand carried down mountains by centuries of spring run-off made a comfortable cushion upon which Catherine spread a worn stadium blanket.

After securing the dog's leash to a tree branch, Catherine sat cross-legged on the blanket. Happy to be outside, and winded from the sprint up the mountain, Damascus was content to lay in the shade. Only the constant twitch of his nostrils revealed the ever-present state of alert demanded by his gene pool.

Catherine admired the grandeur of scenery spread across the valley like the canvas beneath an artist's brush. Wind through Creosote bushes was the only sound to break the stillness. Serenity began to seep into her bones, breaking tension's fierce hold on her emotions. A bank of yellow wildflowers bobbed in the breeze, their tousled heads seemed to bow a gentle greeting to the stranger in their midst. As she studied the landscape filled with all the delicate pastels of a Monet watercolor, tranquility claimed her body and thoughts.

Catherine drifted like a hawk on a current of air, letting her mind wander along the surface of events surrounding Darla Corey's murder. Trying not to guide her thoughts, she allowed her subconscious to discard the irrelevant, to examine microscopic evidence overlooked by the conscious mind.

Childhood.

In Darla Corey's childhood lay an ugly, horrific secret.

Like a black-out curtain, events in the girl's life lay hidden behind an obstruction. Catherine could not penetrate the veil despite incessant probing. Frustration drew the psychic back to the periphery of consciousness, back into a world of material form and tangible substance. Hovering, not wanting to leave the comfort of the meditative state, Catherine sighed.

A harsh crack shattered nature's tranquility. Instantly alert, protective instinct made her reach for her dog to shelter him from the effect of a percussive blast, but her probing hand met nothing but sand. Panic dominated confusion as she scrambled to her feet, shouting Damascus' name. A frantic glance revealed the end of his shredded leash. One inch of leather provided no barrier to jaws which could bring three thousand pounds of force against it.

Another roar exploded; a whizzing sound passed so close to her ear the accompanying wave of air disturbed a lock of hair. The boulder against which she had been leaning fragmented into a thousand pieces. Chips of sandstone turned to sharp projectiles which drew blood on her face, neck, arms, and hands. Like events in a slow-moving dream, Catherine realized a fusillade of bullets shattered the boulder upon which she had been leaning. The instinct to survive propelled her to take shelter behind a rugged outcropping of sandstone.

A third, fourth and fifth shot echoed through the canyon. Percussive blasts were followed by an inhuman scream and the deep throated growl of a massive Rottweiler on the attack. Snarling, snapping barks and blood-curdling cries announced the dog's intention to kill. Catherine bolted for the SUV, paying no attention to the shale covered slope which gave way beneath her pounding feet.

She fumbled with the key, fear giving her hands a life of their own. When she finally jerked the door open, she lunged inside. Gunning the car to life, Catherine threw the gearshift in reverse, lowering an electric back window with a silent prayer of thanksgiving for the technology which allowed her to control all the car's functions from the door panel. Keeping her thumb depressed against the horn, she backed over cactus, lurched across rocks, thrashed across terrain which would have been a challenge to a full-size four-wheel drive vehicle--headed toward the savage sound proclaiming her dog was still alive.

Releasing the horn, she screamed. "Damascus--come!" From a thick stand of brush, the dog launched his body toward the open window. Almost the same instant the Rott cleared the tailgate, Catherine rammed the gearshift into drive. As she sailed across a trackless desert, she prayed to all the forces watching over her an errant rock would not rip off the oil pan, rendering her helpless against an unknown, unseen assailant.

Her glance flew to the rear-view mirror; blood dripped down the sides of the dog's mouth, matting the thick cape of hair around his neck. From the continued fury of his reaction as Damascus barked and snarled at the back of the car, Catherine decided if he had sustained any wounds they were superficial. Clotting blood on his coat must be that of the sniper.

When the SUV bounced onto pavement, Catherine slammed the accelerator to the floor. If Damascus was hurt, he gave no sign of it, but Catherine decided against stopping to examine him. The panic gripping her thoughts began to ebb as she reached the road leading to Las Vegas. Traffic was picking up so at least she wasn't alone anymore. From the corner of her eye, the cell phone slid into view. Initially, Catherine perceived the instrument as an invasion of privacy, but Danny insisted she carry it with her all the time after the first attack. Now, she was glad to see the silly piece of plastic.

Depressing a preprogrammed number with her thumb, the phone dialed Danny's office. "Honey? I've had a little trouble."

Danny was instantly alert. There was a quaver to his mother's voice, and he could hear Damascus panting and growling in the background. The car was still traveling at a high rate of speed and noise generated by the tires, wind and the rattle bang of a dragging muffler was all he needed to hear.

"Where are you?"

"Coming in from Red Rock. I'm about a mile out of town."

"Stop at the 7-11. There's a unit in the area. I know the owner, I'll let him know you're on the way . . . stay on the line, Mom, don't hang up. Just put the phone on the seat." Danny cupped his hand over the receiver and motioned to Sonny, who rushed from the coffee pot the minute he saw his partner's expression turn rigid. "Call Joe Mendez, at the 7-11 on the road to Red Rock. Tell him my Mom and her dog are in trouble. She should be there in about five minutes!" Danny whirled in the direction of the dispatcher, "Janet! Code Red, every available officer to the last convenience store on west Charleston. Have anyone in the area head for Red Rock--tell them to escort a white Jeep. 2015. License TAB 772." Without a backward glance, Danny hit the door on the run with Sonny in hot pursuit.

Ron parked the car beneath a canopy of branches which stretched across the entire street. The Sacred Heart Convent was surrounded by several acres of wooded hills. Children cavorted on swing sets anchored in a sandy playground, carefully supervised by several nuns. Standing on the steps leading to the entrance of the administration building, Ron decided the religious institution must be well endowed because the playground equipment was bright and shiny; buildings appeared well kept and the grounds were magnificent.

The sharp clack of wide heeled shoes announced a nun responding to the bell. Down the hardwood floor she marched, like a storm trooper charged with the responsibility of stopping an invasion. A red, rough hand, a hand which had been exposed to a lot of cleaning agents and abrasive scrub brushes but no skin softening lotions, opened the door. The wimple framed a face as harsh as the work roughened hands. "Yes?"

"I'm Ron Mellon, Detective Mellon. I called this morning about seeing Sister Angelica." Ron stopped. It wasn't exactly what he'd call a blank look in her eye; it was more an expression that managed to blot out the physical world. He started again, refusing to be intimidated by her spiritual stare. "I'm a private detective and I'm here to see if I can locate the parent of a child put up for adoption many years ago. I have a court order to go through your records." He brandished a sheaf of papers in the nun's direction.

Intimidated by something representing worldly authority, the sister stepped aside. "This way Detective Mellon. If you'll follow me I'll take you to the archives of Sacred Heart."

"I have an appointment with Sister Angelica."

Now the civilian-shy nun turned belligerent. "Mother Angelica seldom has visitors anymore. Her health is fragile."

"I have an appointment for two o'clock."

The nun checked her watch, it was fifteen minutes to two now--there would be no time to explain the archive filing system to such an aggressive man. It was probably better to take him to the Mother Superior now. "Very well, Mother is in the library at the moment."

Shock immobilized Ron Mellon on the threshold of the book-lined room. A woman encased in an old-fashion Benedictine habit which covered her body in black from head to toe was seated at a desk tucked beneath a towering stained-glass window. Her face was framed by a snowy wimple, which made her skin look so pale it seemed translucent. Time scored deep lines into her face and hands. Thick glasses perched on the bridge of her nose and watery gray eyes were glazed with vision dulling cataracts. The nun appeared as delicate and fragile as a piece of Dresden china. "Sister Angelica?"

Turning, the nun peered across the library at the man who materialized like a wraith in the hallowed halls of the convent. "Yes?" The voice was feeble and quavering.

"Sister, I'm Private Detective Ron Mellon. One of your associates said I could meet with you at two o'clock." As if on cue the tall grandfather clock in the corner boomed out two chimes.

"Oh dear, yes--I'd quite forgotten. Please, come sit by the window. You're the one whose client is looking for the mother of a child adopted out of Sacred Heart, aren't you?"

"Yes, Sister, that's me. I've got a couple of photographs here I'd like you to look at. The adoption took place years ago and I'm hoping they'll refresh your memory." Ron handed the picture of Russo and the adoring blond to the Mother Superior.

"Surely you're joking Mr. Mellon. I may be old but I'm not so senile that I wouldn't recognize Jacob Jones."

"Jacob Jones?"

"Yes, he is one of our greatest benefactors." Her mouth compressed into a taught line, and the hand holding the picture began to waver.

"What about the woman, the blond?"

Sister Angelica hadn't really noticed other people in the faded photograph until Mr. Mellon drew her attention to them--then her eyes narrowed like a night bird following prey. "You are not here seeking the identity of a birth mother, are you," she demanded.

Patiently, Ron watched the complex array of emotions undulating across the wrinkled face as the sister considered, then discarded, whatever it was she was about to say.

"This girl got in trouble a long time ago. She had a child who was placed for adoption through the convent." There was something more, far more. A sick quivering filled his stomach as the chill of intuition raising the hairs on the back of his arms warned of duplicity. The Mother Superior didn't want to talk about the girl in the picture, she forced the square of photographic paper away as if her fingers brushed against something slimy, distasteful.

"What was the girl's name, Sister?" Ron cajoled.

"I'm not sure I remember." She looked away too fast, afraid to let the detective see the alarm which had risen in her eyes.

"Sister, a young girl was murdered, brutally murdered, in Las Vegas a few weeks ago. We think people in this picture can help us find her killer."

A sharp hiss of breath preceded words spat in anger. "Mr. Jones is a saint on earth. He would never have dealings with someone who took a life." Panic pressed against the fragile cartilage of her throat as her chest tightened and her heartbeat raced, stimulated by alarm.

"Will you tell me about them? Sister, please cooperate with me. I'll do everything I can to keep the convent out of the press. But something very ugly transpired in Vegas and unless I can get to the bottom of the relationship between the people in this photograph, the newspapers might get wind of it, and you'll have reporters swarming all over Sacred Heart."

Watery gray eyes studied the detective from behind half-lowered lids. The years had marched across the Reverend Mother's face unmercifully, leaving behind scores of lines which fanned out over her skin like the many fingered branches of a desert arroyo. Defeated, the Reverend Mother launched into the story fast, "Mr. Jones arranged for Janet Barron to have her child at Sacred Heart. He thought it best to tell the girl the baby died at birth, so she could get on with her life. He didn't want her to diminish her future being consumed with guilt over a youthful transgression. Mr. Jones is a very wise man and I complied with his request."

"The girl thought the baby died?"

"Back then, a lot of anesthetic was given to the mother during birth. She wasn't awake when the baby came--a little girl." Rosary beads, always a symbol of comfort, felt cold and hard beneath her beseeching fingers. "Mr. Jones said he was sending Janet out west, where she could begin a new life. He was always very kind and extremely generous to the convent."

"What do you mean--generous?" Quickening interest plucked at Ron's adrenaline glands like a harpist selecting a high-pitched string.

"Like I said, Mr. Jones is kind. He grew quite fond of the baby and provided for her care. He gave the convent far more money than we would ever spend on one child. Margaret grew up at Sacred Heart, so we were her family."

"Where is Margaret now?"

Something shifted in the nun's eyes again. The elitist shield of being one of God's chosen dissolved; her eyes filled with sorrow and a melancholy expression took possession of the old woman's face. "I haven't heard from Margaret in several years. Margaret used to write us . . . she earned a full scholarship to college . . . then she got so busy . . ." She had folded her hands in her lap, covering her cherished rosary beads, but her fingers shook so hard it looked like she had Parkinson's disease.

"What college?" Ron pressed the advantage he sensed.

"I'm afraid I don't remember. It was a small university. I know it wasn't a Catholic school, I wanted her to continue her education at Loyola-- she had several scholarships offers. Loyola would have been best. The Jesuits are marvelous teachers, you know." The old woman seemed to slip behind the veil of time, as if she were reliving a series of painful events. "If she had to go out west I don't know why she didn't go to Santa Clara. The Jesuits in California are nearly as bright as those at Loyola."

"Try to remember the name of the school, Sister." Excitement made his heartbeat faster. It was obvious from the look of dismay on Sister Angelica's face she allowed Margaret to pursue her education at an unfamiliar school with great reluctance.

"I don't know, Mr. Mellon. I just don't know--it's been so long

179

ago."

"Do you remember where the school was located--maybe California?" Ron suggested.

"No, it was one of those God forsaken places in the desert. New Mexico, or Arizona."

Ron couldn't help it--he knew the nun was lying. He knew she remembered the name of the college; Sister Angelica knew exactly where Margaret had gone to school. "Or maybe Nevada?"

A shadow rippled across her expression, vague yet unmistakable. "I don't remember. Like I said, it was a long time ago. Hundreds of children have been at the convent since then and it's impossible to keep track of everyone after they leave Sacred Heart. We've had our successes-- and our failures. But our Lord, Jesus Christ, admonished us to leave the flock and go in search of every lost lamb. At Sacred Heart, the Benedictine sisters live that command with every fiber of their being."

"Sister, I've never been much on church, and I don't know a lot about the Bible. But I seem to remember from my Sunday school years there was more than one way to commit a sin. As I recall, there are sins of commission and sins of omission, am I right, Sister?"

There it was, the tell-tale flicker of guilt which traversed the Reverend Mother's face again, leaving an oily residue of shame in her eyes. It was all Ron Mellon needed. Jacob Jones *was* Jake Russo. The old bastard probably got the blond pregnant. The nun raised the child in exchange for Russo's financial support. And the kid--Margaret Barron, had grown up, graduated from Sacred Heart Convent, and gone to college in Nevada. Ron was willing to bet his very last dollar the school she decided to attend was the University of Nevada, Las Vegas!

"Ah, Harold! Please come in." Senator Mathias Hastings rounded his desk to greet Harold Kennedy. Pumping his hand up and down, the Senator's face was wreathed in smiles as he led Harold to a leather chair on the opposite side of his big, expensive desk. "Well, I see from the papers you've gotten Kristin's project off to a rousing start! Good press, Harold, mighty good press. I might have to hire you to run my next campaign. I knew you were good, but I didn't know you where this good! Want a cup of coffee?" Mathias buzzed his secretary before Harold had a chance to

180

respond.

"Black, please." It was impossible to keep from staring at all the pictures of Mathias Hastings with one famous person after another lining the walls of his office. Movie stars, presidents, political figures, scientists, authors, athletes. Mathias Hastings was a bedfellow to power and influence.

The secretary appeared with two cups of coffee in fancy ceramic mugs on a matching tray. Smiling politely at Harold when she handed him the coffee, the toothsome girl glided around the desk to serve the senator-- making the act of delivering coffee seem as memorable as a Japanese tea ceremony.

Mathias watched her go with an appreciative glance at the smooth contour of youthful hips, delightfully narrow waist, and the gentle billow of full breasts. Reluctantly, he dragged his attention back to Harold. "So, give me an update on Kristin's plans. She said something about wanting my help with several members of Congress?"

"The development of the Paiute reservation has gotten tremendous political support from everyone in Ely and Carson City. Of course, when you've got a private industry willing to put up the money and tax dollars that will result from the success of the venture--it's not a hardline item to sell government officials."

Hastings was a man whose looks could rival any movie star. He sipped from the cup, then sat it down with the same dramatic flurry Bogie used to grind a cigarette out in an ash tray. "You sell yourself short, my friend. If the project hadn't gotten so much good press it would have been stopped in the initial stages of development. The Indian village might have been Kristin's idea and the Hastings' family money helped, but without your talents the village project might have perished before the first herd of buffalo reached the pasture."

A vermilion flare spread across Harold's face as he blushed at the compliment from such a rich, powerful man. "Thanks Senator; that means an awful lot to me, but the validity of the project makes it an easy sell."

"So, what do you want from me?" Enough flattery, Mathias decided to get to the heart of the matter and go back to work; there were a lot of pressing matters he had to attend to during this trip to Washington.

"I want you to convince some of your colleges in the Senate to accept the concept, so it can be expanded to other Indian reservations around the country. Kristin wants to approach the most receptive political climates first. Like she says, there's no need to waste our time sowing seeds on arid ground."

"You want me to do a little investigation work?"

"If you would bring up the subject to the senators on this list," Harold handed a neatly typed piece of paper across the desk, "you'll be able to tell from their initial reaction if we should approach them about another village project."

"What about the various tribes? Will you get cooperation from them?"

"Kristin invited representatives from the Sioux in South Dakota, Nez Perce in Idaho, an Apache group from Arizona and a representative of the Oklahoma Cherokees to a conference at the site. The Paiute chief took them around. He showed them the watering ponds, elk, deer, and bison which have been reintroduced to the area. I think what got them interested was the list of people who responded to the brochure Kristin developed."

"Brochure? I don't get a chance to talk to my sister much these days. What's she doing now?"

"She's created a brochure centered on the resort features of the Paiute village. Then she mailed it to some upper-end demographic zip codes in Seattle, Portland, San Francisco, LA, San Diego and Phoenix. Paiutes haven't been able to keep up with reservation demands. Kristin got a twenty- five percent response to her mailer. That's almost unheard of. People are really interested in the culture of Native Americans and they're willing to shell out big bucks to enjoy the experience."

Mathias shook his head. "She's remarkable, isn't she?"

"Senator, Kristin is giving a whole lot of people an opportunity to take pride in themselves again. She's more than just a perceptive businesswoman who can capitalize on a current market trend." Harold bowed his head shyly; it was unlike him to have words of praise come easily to his lips. He wasn't a spontaneous talker; his medium was paper and pen. "I think your sister might well be one of the preeminent thinkers of our generation."

"Catherine, hi! What's happenin' in Hotsville?"

Pleased at the note of cheeriness in the big detective's voice, Catherine responded. "Danny's got me staying with him for a few days. Damascus is mad because I won't let him chase the cat, the cat is bent out of shape because he doesn't have the run of the house anymore and Forbes is happy because I cook and clean up the kitchen. Other than that--not a whole lot. What's going on with you?"

"I called to tell Danny about a conversation I had with the old nun who runs the Sacred Heart Convent in Jersey. She admitted the guy in the picture Danny sent was Jake Russo, only she called him Jacob Jones. Turns out, the blond girl had a kid at the convent, but she was told the baby died at birth."

"Oh?" The icy chill of alarm that claimed Catherine's spine ran up her back like the cat being pursued by a Rottweiler.

"Yeah, seems Russo thought it would relieve the mother of the burden of guilt. The sisters raised the kid and Russo became a big financial backer of the convent. The Reverend Mother plans to nominate Russo for sainthood."

"I'll bet. Where's the child now?"

"Margaret Barron graduated from high school and accepted a scholarship to a school out west--only the Reverend Mother can't remember the name of the university and she hasn't heard from Margaret for several years. Seems everyone has lost track of her."

"And you think the child was Darla Corey?"

Ron was continually unnerved by the way Catherine voiced his thoughts before they could take shape on his lips. "Yes, I do. Can't prove a damned thing yet, but if you could have seen the look on the old nun's face when I suggested Margaret might have gone to school in Nevada-- you'd know I was right."

Pacing the perimeter of the swimming pool, Damascus sniffed the air. A whole new world of scents wafted down out of the mountains and over the fence--wild burros, coyotes, quail, snakes, natives of the desert with whom the massive Rott had never come in contact. Catherine watched the dog, not really seeing him, focused instead on a scene broadcast against the inner screen of her mind. "I have the feeling you're right, dear. How involved was Russo in the child's upbringing?"

"Well, the sister said Russo gave the convent more money than they'd ever spend on one orphan, but she wouldn't volunteer any more

183

information. I've gotta real bad feeling about it though."

"If it helps any, so do I, Ron--so do I."

"You know guys like Russo can get away with anything because they have money--and money bequeaths power."

"There are laws to protect the innocent, Ron."

"Hell, I learned a long time ago the law isn't a fence which separates the good guys from the bad."

"I know, but there has to be some way to maintain social order." Catherine didn't like the feeling which kept prying the lid off her subconscious.

"Jake Russo is a man who crosses legal boundaries at will. He's impervious to moral and ethical limitations governing most of us. To him the law is just a fence that keeps the cows out of the way of the horses!"

"You're right dear, of course. It's too bad the man doesn't realize he will spend many lifetimes suffering the consequence of his actions."

Ron's voice was harsh, abrasive. "Yeah, well--he's dying from throat cancer, and I think he deserves all the pain the disease can dish out to him."

Catherine sighed, there were times the weight of the wrongs of this world were oppressive. If people only knew, if they only understood. "There is no escape from one's actions, Ron. Sooner or later, he'll have to face the consequences."

"Then it's gonna take a long time for Jake Russo to die--a real long time."

Damascus began to bark and paw at the sliding glass door as Danny entered the house through the garage.

"Oh, here's Danny now. I'll put him on the phone." Catherine still wasn't herself as she went to let in the anxious dog. It was as though she couldn't free herself of the sticky ooze of Jake Russo's illness.

Danny was forced to greet the Rottweiler, who jumped against his chest, offering an excited welcome. "Ron, what's up? Find out anything at the convent?"

It was as if the heat of the desert was pressing through the phone line, warming the instrument in his hand. Ron's palms turned sweaty, and a line of perspiration tracked its way down the side of his face. "The nun recognized Russo, only she called him Jacob Jones. *And* she said the blond was a girl by the name of Janet Barron." Ron related the information in breathless gasps as if fear and uncertainty constricted his asthmatic lungs. "I've checked a number of sources, trying to locate a Janet Barron but she seems to have vanished from the face of the earth."

"Maybe Janet Barron wasn't her real name."

"Yeah, maybe. But we're looking for a needle planted in a haystack nearly thirty years ago. I don't think I've ever had a case with so many dead ends--its frustrating."

"Tell you what, FedEx the pictures back to me. With what you've discovered, maybe Catherine can come up with something else. Just keep tabs on Russo."

"Okay, I got the telelogic chip installed in his phone line. If it picks up anything interesting, I'll send a tape right away." Ron put his free hand on the porch railing to steady himself. Superstition was at the core of human nature. And a superstitious feeling shouted something awful was about to happen. Even as the feeling began to pass, Ron was filled with a sudden terror stranger than superstition--it was darker and infinitely more terrifying.

Danny hung up, shouted at Damascus to settle down, then glanced at his mother. She was staring at the mountain range beyond the wall, so still it looked as though she had become a part of the mountain itself. Danny hooked his finger through the Rott's choke chain to make sure the dog's never-ending enthusiasm didn't intrude upon his mother's reverie. Finally, Catherine turned away from the window which framed the spectacular view. She was quiet, unnaturally quiet--from the expression on her face, Danny knew he wasn't going to like what was coming.

The sound of car tires drew Ron's attention. He wasn't expecting Denise for several hours and few of his business acquaintances knew where he lived. Footsteps on the wooden porch preceded a lively knock on the door. Caution was an innate part of Ron Mellon's character. Edging cautiously toward the window overlooking the porch, he pulled the curtain back just far enough to look at the stranger, who had his back to the door, he looked like an ordinary enough guy; maybe a salesman; or an insurance agent. Or someone with car trouble, who spotted his house from the hill and wanted to use his phone. A man of habit, Ron slipped a Colt into the waistband of his shorts and pulled his shirt over the butt of the gun. The leather sheath strapped to his ankle contained the razor-sharp stiletto he was prone to sleep with most of the time.

Ron let the stranger knock again, watching the way he reached for the door, making sure the guy didn't reach inside his coat. Finally, he pulled the door open with a fearsome yank. "Yeah?" The bark was acerbic, demanding.

"Mr. Mellon, Ron Mellon?" The stranger's tone of voice was calm, neutral.

"Yeah, who are you and what do you want?"

"I have a subpoena which requires your signature." Handing over a packet of papers, the stranger handed Ron a pen.

The thought that flashed through his mind concerned how glad he was he'd gotten all his affairs in order last week. Denise and the boys were now listed as his benefactors and a Quit Claim Deed to the house with her name on it was on file with his attorney. He had enough money set aside to see the boys' comfortably through college and by that time, although the house wasn't much, the shoreline property would probably be worth a small fortune. If she was careful, and Ron knew Denise could make one dollar do the work of five, she'd have enough money to live out her life with a degree of ease.

When the pen exploded, ripping the juggler vein and carotid artery from the right side of his neck, Ron collapsed. The bull of a man fell without a roar of protest. An ocean of crimson spread across the porch; the splatter of blood created an abstract pattern on time-grayed siding as wide rivulets began to slide down weathered walls toward the floor. Fleshy tissue was smeared against the door frame leaving a trail of red slime which hung in great droplets. Sightless eyes stared at the stranger and the scream of horror which peeled his lips back from the gaping, disbelieving look of shock was forever frozen on Ron Mellon's face. Only the soft hiss of air escaping from the huge hole in his throat denoted life.

The stranger stepped across the still shuddering body and entered the house. He knew exactly what he was looking for and conducted a rapid search.

Just as predicted, a storm broke; waves whipped high pounded the beach and rain came down in a deluge. Tracks in the sand left by his tires would be obliterated long before anyone else reached the cottage. With the way it was coming down, the porch might even be scrubbed free of blood. It took a full ten minutes to locate the Federal Express envelope because of the accumulation of clutter. The stranger hurried to his car, anxious to be out of the pounding rain. He drove up the hill with caution because sand on the unpaved road had turned slippery.

On the porch, Ron Mellon's life ebbed away. It took him more time to die than the stranger expected because he was built like a Grizzly bear and his hold on life was just as tenacious. With every ounce of his being, Ron Mellon directed his last thoughts at Catherine Armstrong, praying she would receive his message--and understand.

Terror welled in Catherine's throat; her hand flew to her larynx; the sudden pain was staggering. She tried to reach the couch but felt as though her mind disassociated from her body and all motor functions suddenly ceased. Glassy eyed, she collapsed in a heap on the floor, an awful gurgle the only sound to escape lips turned gray and bloodless.

On the patio tending to the grill, Danny heard a faint thud. Damascus began pawing at the sliding glass door with fury. "What is it?" The dog wouldn't stop, he threw himself at the glass as Danny hurried to open the door before it shattered. The Rott cleared the back of the sofa with one powerful lunge, upending the coffee table when he lifted off. "Ma, your dog has gone nuts all of a sudden." Danny looked around, wondering where Catherine had gone.

On the other side of the couch, Damascus whined--a plaintive, mournful sound. "Ma?"

The Rott hadn't moved, his head came up, his eyes accusing-- demanding Danny come around the high-back sectional.

Danny dropped the tongs when he saw his mother's crumpled body. "Oh, Jesus. Damascus get out of the way! Forbes! Come here, now!"

Scooping his mother into his arms, Danny lifted her onto the couch. The dog backed away, sensing his size and girth would interfere. "Forbes," Danny shouted again.

"Yeah, yeah. I've got a report coming in from Washington . . ." He stopped, the sentence left dangling as he caught sight of Catherine's unconscious form. "What's the matter? Has she fainted? Do you want me to call an ambulance?"

Forbes checked her pulse, which was weak and thready, but she was still breathing. A blotchy purple bruise began to seep beneath the skin on her neck. "What the hell happened?" He looked around the room, searching for something, anything, to reveal the cause of her physical condition. Danny searched her hands, lifted her arms, examined her legs for other signs of bruising. "Forbes, go look in the kitchen. She was in there fixing a salad just a few minutes ago. Do you see blood anywhere? I can't find any cuts."

Forbes sprinted around the island topped with expensive granite. Remnants of potatoes, eggs, dill pickles and onions were strewn along the top and a glass bowl filled to over-flowing with the makings of a potato salad rested on the polished surface. There was nothing on the floor, no knife, no blood, no evidence of struggle. "Jesus, Danny, there's nothing here! What the hell's wrong with her?" Forbes grabbed the phone, but he was so nervous he couldn't hit the keypad to dial 9-1-1.

Carrington LeMoye reached for the doorbell, he was looking forward to dinner. He waited a moment and when no one responded, he poked his head cautiously inside. "Catherine?" A single bark rang from the family room at the end of the hall. "Catherine!" The judge's voice demanded a reply. When the Rottweiler didn't thunder down the hall to meet him, Carrington knew something was wrong--terribly wrong. The judge rushed into the house, slamming the door behind him.

Danny was softly calling his mother's name. Her blood pressure had dropped so low she was as pale as a newly risen moon. The dog was preternaturally still, as though he sensed movement might sever the tenuous cord binding his mistress to the present.

"What happened?" His voice boomed with stentorian authority, but Carrington couldn't help it. Every nerve in his body demanded action, an answer as to why Catherine was not responding to her son's anxiety-laden voice. A primordial instinct drove him to grasp her limp hand, to draw it to his lips, to bequeath energy into the lifeless body. The prickling which began at the base of his spine and scalded a path to his scalp intensified. Atavistic fear, and reliance on the instinct it invoked, caused him to slap Catherine's face several times, to shout her name over and over, until only the dead would not have responded.

Danny and Forbes were immobilized by shock. The house became so still it was as if the flow of time was suspended. Only the wind, scouring the dry desert floor outside the house retained a voice. The sun had gone down, and darkness seemed to unlock a subterranean door, which allowed something evil to creep into the world. Outside, shadows draped the yard and spiky black patterns from the palm tree at the edge of the pool danced eerily along the wall, edged by a sulfurous yellow glow coming from the Malibu lights near the house.

"Catherine! God damn it, answer me! You will not leave, do you hear me, you will not leave!" In a voice thickened by frustration, the judge commanded, "Danny, speak to her--keep talking. Yours may be the only voice she'll respond to right now. Forbes get me a towel and some ice. I want to put a pack on her neck. We've got to keep the swelling down so her esophagus doesn't close."

Forbes galvanized himself into action, tearing open the freezer door, yanking out the bin of ice cubes, searching the well-ordered kitchen drawers for a towel in which to wrap the ice. He felt as though he were caught up in a nightmare. No matter how fast he tried to move, his body responded so slowly he was afraid Catherine might die before he could return with the ice. "Mom? Mom?" Danny couldn't control the tremor which took possession of his voice. A firm hand descended on his shoulder and the pressure of strong fingers digging into his shoulder demanded control. "Danny, stay calm. Just keep talking and for God's sake don't let your voice register fear. Wherever she's at now, you're her lifeline and damn it son, you may be the only one she's got."

Forcing back the bile threatening to burn a hole in his throat, Danny coughed, then began again. "Mom, it's Danny. Judge LeMoye is here and so is Forbes. And this big stupid dog." As though summoned by an unseen, unheard command, the Rottweiler moved close and laid his massive head on her arm. "Mom, you've got to find your way back because no one in their right mind is going to take care of Damascus. And although I've been reluctant to talk about it, for fear I'd jinx the relationship, I think I might end up asking Elaine to marry me. She's a great girl and I know she'd be a real good mother. Three or four grandkids would be great, don't you think? If we have a girl, I'd like to name her Catherine. I haven't had time to think about names for boys yet, maybe Sonny, nor Jeff--anything but Forbes, don't you think, Mom?"

Carrington patted the boy's shoulder, encouraging Danny to continue in the same vein. Forbes handed the judge the towel filled with ice cubes. Gently pressing them against the bruised flesh on her neck,

Carrington nodded at Danny to keep talking.

"Damascus, you'd better get in here, buddy. Tell her not to leave. Tell her you'd miss her chocolate chip cookies--a lot." Danny couldn't keep up the irrelevant dialogue, his throat constricted, cutting off his voice. The dam of resistance was weakening fast, and he wasn't sure he could hold back the tears any longer.

As if on cue, the Rott nudged Catherine's elbow with his cold, wet nose. When she didn't respond, he grew more insistent--shoving his floppy muzzle against her ear, muttering a low, lonesome whine that demanded attention, a response to his emotional needs.

The first to notice a pale pink tinge had returned to her cheeks, Carrington began to speak softly, soothingly, stroking the back of her arm with one hand, the side of her face with the other. "Catherine, can you hear me? Come on sweetheart, snap out of it. You've got a lot of people here who love you. Come on back now."

He'd seen Catherine induce a hypnotic trance on clients a dozen times. Now he was angry with himself that he hadn't thought of it sooner. In a commanding tone, he ordered. "Catherine, I'm going to count backward from five to one. On the count of one, you will open your eyes. On the count of one, you will be back in the present."

Danny nodded approvingly, certain Catherine would respond to a demand she'd issued to hundreds of life-battered clients.

"Five." Carrington struggled to remember the tone of voice Catherine used on people in a trance. "Four." Slow, he remembered she kept her voice slow, deliberate, keeping the pace with the boom of the human heart. "Three." There was still no response. No fluttering of her eyelids, no lifting of her chest with a deep intake of air. "Two." She always said something else about now. What was it? Suddenly, the memory of her technique exploded across his fear-locked mind. "You will listen to my voice and follow my command. On the count of one, you will open your eyes. You will be back in the present. On the count of one. One! Now, open your eyes, Catherine. Open your eyes and sit up!"

Carrington could hardly believe the woman he loved with all his heart obeyed his command. Opening eyes as blue as a nugget of turquoise, she slid her legs off the couch and sat straight up. The rush of blood made her faint and she wobbled forward. Three sets of hands and the Rottweiler's head rushed to stop her from falling.

Weak, her eyes refusing to focus, Catherine suddenly became aware of the pain in her throat. Brushing her fingertips against the bluish-black flesh, she croaked a hoarse whisper. "What happened?"

"Jesus, Mrs. Armstrong, we were hoping you'd be able to tell us!" Forbes flopped on the end of the couch, relief robbed his body of the strength required to stand.

Danny studied his mother, monitoring the rate of her breathing, the color starting to return to her face and the tone of voice still thickened by terror. "I was out on the patio at the BBQ. Suddenly Damascus started to claw the sliding glass door. When I let him in, he bounded over the couch and started barking. I couldn't see you at first, but he was acting so weird I came inside. You were lying on the floor, unconscious."

"My throat hurts. Could I have a glass of water?"

"Sure." Carrington ran to the kitchen.

"Mom, do you remember what happened at all?"

Still rubbing her neck, Catherine tried to recall what she'd been doing before the curtain of darkness descended. "I was fixing the potato salad. An impression of Ron Mellon came to mind and then everything went black. The next thing I remember was Damascus whining in my ear."

"What about Ron?" Fear gripped Danny's stomach, hard.

Catherine closed her eyes and leaned her head on the back of the couch. "Pain. I remember a lot of pain--in my throat." Her hands gingerly probed the tender area. "Then darkness descended. And. . . ." She stopped, licked her lips, forcing back the awful impression. "Danny, Ron is dead. Something happened to his throat. A shot--no, an explosion. He was trying to send me a mental message as he died . . . only I don't know what it was."

CHAPTER TEN

A bleak, gray, ugly haze, fed by a chilling drizzle, hung over a forest of black umbrellas. Long dark limousines, attended by damp chauffeurs, stood at the periphery of the cemetery, where last rites were spoken over the pale pink roses blanketing an oak coffin. Floral displays sent by friends and business associates created a vibrant backdrop, a rainbow of color cruelly out of place in the dismal setting.

Mourners listened to the eulogy with stoic control, haunted by the tears coursing down Denise Weston's hollow cheeks. In deference to the man Ron Mellon had been, she struggled to maintain her grasp on composure. How could Ron have been swept from her life just when she thought they might have a future? Her hand tightened on Jeffrey's shoulder, the other gripped a giant umbrella so hard all the color bleached from her knuckles. Denise decided the steady drizzle was a suitably desolate epitaph because the final curtain just rang down upon the only ray of hope ever to brighten her miserable world.

As the priest concluded last rites with a sweep of the cross over Ron's casket, a towering wave of grief could no longer be held in check. It simply claimed her. The umbrella drooped allowing rain to spatter the boys. Anger, terror, helplessness, constant waves battered her emotions until Denise no longer cared where she was or what she was doing. A firm, care-giving arm slid around her slender waist and turned Denise away before the coffin was lowered into the sodden ground.

Catherine herded reluctant boys into the back of the limousine, assuring them everything was going to be all right. Danny held the umbrella over Denise's head as Catherine sought to offer comfort. "Come on Denise, it's over now. Ron wouldn't want you to stand around in the rain. Let's go back to the hotel and feed the boys, then we'll decide what to do next."

Denise stared out the tinted window, too numb to carry on conversation. Danny kept the boys engaged in lively banter about school, friends, sports, anything, and everything to keep their attention diverted from their grief shattered mother. To impress the kids, Danny called Room Service from the limo phone. They squealed with delight after placing an order for ice cream, hot dogs, French fries, and Cokes. Catherine kept patting Denise's hand, as if she could transmit comfort through the young woman's skin.

When Danny opened the door to the suite, all three boys rushed forward, anxious to see if the phone call was real. In the middle of the parlor a cart was piled high with every delightful item on the menu. Suitably impressed, the babble of excited voices expressed wonder as the boys helped themselves to high-priced condiments.

With the jerky, disconnected movements of a sleepwalker, Denise allowed Catherine to remove her damp coat. Every time she thought the well of tears empty, Denise was surprised by a renewed supply which sprang up the moment her thoughts turned back to Ron. Life was so damned ugly; hope leeched from her soul as despair took up residency in her heart. It wasn't fair, it just wasn't fair. Tears began again.

As the boys constructed a mountainous ice cream sundae, Danny decided there was no point in delaying any longer. "Denise, we've got things to talk about."

Incapable of comprehending, Denise stared at the two people who were possibly the kindest people she ever met. "Oh?"

Responsibility for Denise and her family made him feel inadequate. Danny stammered, uncomfortable, "Ron made me the executor of his will. There are some things we need to go over and tomorrow you'll have a lot of papers to sign at his attorney's office."

"What papers? What do I have to sign?" Denise's voice slid up and down the scale as though she had lost control of her vocal cords.

"Ron put his money into a trust for the kids and he deeded the house at the shore over to you. The attorney wants you to decide how much money you'll need every month. I know the house isn't fancy, but it's paid for and with some diligent cleaning it will be a good place for the boys to grow up." Danny swallowed hard; he just couldn't believe he was never going to hear Ron Mellon's gruff voice on the phone again.

"Money--what money? I don't know what you're talking about." Denise felt like she was going crazy. Nothing made any sense. How could a backyard mechanic leave any money?

193

"Darling," Catherine spoke soothingly, trying to keep her own sense of loss from taking over, "Ron was a very successful private investigator. He had quite a large portfolio of investments and he left it to you and the boys because he had no other family--at least no one he cared about as much as you and the children. There's enough in the trust to see to your needs until the boys graduate from college. The will is very explicit, Ron wanted you to live in his house and raise the boys at the shore."

Sobs overpowered Denise's resolve and she lowered her face into her hands. Roger came to stand by his mother as Timothy struggled into her lap. Only Jeff, who was old enough to bear the burden of his own grief, remained at the serving cart.

Catherine sensed the best thing to do was let Denise cry it out. She went to the room service cart and began to create a sundae with chocolate syrup and a generous helping of sprinkles. "I like ice cream, don't you?"

Jeff regarded the woman, the stranger, with overt disdain. "Yeah, I guess so."

"Ron liked chocolate ice cream best. He used to bring some over to my house and we'd sit outside after the sun went down. Only--we had a severe problem because I've got a real big dog and he likes chocolate ice cream too. Damascus is my dog's name. Ron used to end up feeding his ice cream to my dog on a spoon."

"Dogs can't eat ice cream from a spoon," Jeff responded with sarcasm; he was certainly old enough to know better than that!

"No, really, I can prove it! I've got a picture right here." Catherine fished an envelope out of her purse. "Look."

A brown packet contained several pictures of Ron. Water skiing on Lake Mead. Snow skiing on Mt. Charleston. On a picnic with Danny, Sonny, Catherine, and Judge LeMoye at Valley of Fire. With patience, Catherine explained each situation to Jeff. He laughed at the pictures of Ron feeding Damascus and before long all three boys were engrossed by the unexpected side of the rough-hewn man they had grown to love. Delighted laughter filled the suite when they discovered the picture of the Rottweiler tugging a baggy pair of shorts from Ron's generous behind. Roger rushed over to his mother, demanding she look at the preposterous pose. Denise thumbed through the rest of the stack, smiling, even laughing occasionally as the pictures evoked one memory after another of the wooly mammoth of a man. Finally, she smiled at Catherine and handed the pictures back.

"They are for you and the boys to remember Ron. Maybe you can all come out to Las Vegas next summer and we can do all the things Danny and I used to do with Ron."

A chorus of excited shrieks assailed Denise and for the first time in several days she felt a faint ray of hope penetrate her despairing mood. Such an idea would have been completely impossible but now--now there just might be enough money to manage it. Thanks to Ron. Tears welled again, but this time they didn't seem to scald so deeply--instead they cleansed. This time, they were healing tears.

"Denise, do you think you'll feel up to going out to the house tomorrow? I really need to look around." Danny couldn't help the catch in his voice which made the last words squeak like a boy entering puberty.

Catherine regarded her son with renewed interest. "I thought the attorney had all the papers?"

"I've had a funny feeling nagging at me all morning and I think I finally realized what it is."

Catherine waited. From the expression on Danny's face, it was clear her son knew what he wanted.

"I never got the pictures Ron said he was going to Fed Ex to Las Vegas. When Ron Mellon said he was going to do something--he damned well did it. I think whoever killed him took the pictures."

"I'm pretty confused by all this," Denise whispered, puzzlement dominating her worn-out expression, "I didn't even know Ron was a private detective--but if you think the killer has the pictures, what do you hope to gain by searching Ron's house?"

"Ron might have been a messy guy in his personal life, but professionally he was one of the most methodical detectives I ever ran across. I think he stashed a back-up set somewhere in the house."

Denise blanched. "My God, that could be like looking for a needle in a haystack. It could take weeks to go through the stuff he has scattered everywhere."

Danny smiled reassuringly. "It will probably take my Mom ten or fifteen minutes to find them."

"Gee, Danny, I don't know. His place is such a mess. Your Mom is wonderful, but ..."

195

"Did Ron ever mention Catherine to you?"

"He talked about the two of you all the time."

"I mean, did he ever tell you what she does for a living?"

Catherine returned from the bathroom, where she tried to get a ketchup stain out of Timmy's brand-new white shirt.

Denise cocked her head, thinking back. "No, I guess he never did."

"She's a psychic."

The group of Benedictine nuns hovering around the Reverend Mother's bed were shocked into complete silence. Although frail and old, Sister Angelica appeared in good health when she retired last night after evening prayers. Death was something everyone at the convent expected sooner or later, but the frozen expression on the woman's face was unnerving. Wide eyes stared in terror and her mouth forever framed an eternally silent scream. Had the Devil come to haunt her in the last, precious moments of her life?

When the sisters entered the Mother Superior's bedroom they were stunned to find the windowpane glass shattered; the curtain shredded from blowing against the sharp edges all night. Beneath the dormitory window, the bushes were trampled, and soft soil recorded a few large footprints. It seemed like the footprints were left behind as a warning the intruder had the power and cunning to strike again--at will.

The police shipped Reverend Mother's sheets, pillowcases, curtains, and altar stole she tended with such loving care to their forensic lab. Despite the protest of her fellow Benedictines, Reverend Mother Angelica's body was bundled onto a gurney for transport to the coroner's office. The thought of such a saintly woman being carved to pieces in search of the cause of death was more than some of the more sheltered sisters could stand. They retreated to the chapel to pray for the Reverend Mother's immortal soul.

Terror reigned supreme when word leaked out the Reverend Mother had been smothered. Father Augustus was called from a neighboring abbey to restore a sense of calm among the frightened nuns. He was finally forced to hire a couple of retired policemen to stand guard so the sisters, who had been sheltered from a multitude of suffering which hounded other human beings, could sleep at night.

When Danny opened the door to Ron's beach house, a feeling of familiarity stopped Catherine in her tracks. It was as though the big guy was waiting for them on the porch, beckoning them inside. A quick sigh caught in her throat, but she forced herself over the threshold. Finding Ron's murderer might depend on impressions she could pick up in the house and she could not--would not--allow emotion to interfere.

Denise gave her boys permission to head for the water, confident Ron taught them how far out they could go safely. It was hard walking into such a messy room, probably the hardest thing she'd ever done. Stacks of newspapers, magazines, piles of clothing scattered everywhere she looked made her heart ache. Picking up a worn sweatshirt, she pressed it against her face, using it as a blotter to absorb a seemingly endless supply of tears.

Putting her arm around Denise's shoulder, Catherine hugged the trembling girl. It wasn't a good idea to bring her here so soon after the funeral. Catherine knew her feelings would still be strong, but Denise insisted on coming. Wandering around the room, Catherine allowed her glance to roam over a battered couch, the abused desk, an Early American coffee table which looked like it might have survived Valley Forge, a cheap press-board bookcase filled to overflowing with manuals, papers and manila file folder stuffed with notes on various cases. A braided rug beneath the coffee table in front of the couch was littered with cookie crumbs; an empty sack which once held those cookies lay crumpled in front of a wicker wastebasket in the corner. Several beer cans rested on the table in a ring of sticky residue and three cheap plastic trays were the cast-off detritus of Ron Mellon's last microwaved meal. Blood stains were still evident, and Catherine was drawn to what remained of his life force like a homing beacon. She bent down, stroking the stain with her fingertips.

Denise tried to strangle the sigh which caught halfway up her throat when she realized what Catherine was studying. She needed to do something, anything, so she began gathering up old newspapers.

"Denise, we might need to look through all of those," Danny said as gently as he could.

"Why?" She regarded Danny with curiosity.

"Ron hid the photos we need somewhere--we've just got to find them."

"The police said he was killed when he answered the door. Ron didn't have time to put anything away because the coroner said he died instantly." Those words faded on her lips with the same suddenness that life was taken from a man she loved.

"Ron knew he was dealing with Jake Russo, and he would have taken every precaution."

"Dear Lord," Denise surveyed the chaos, "it could take us days to sort through the newspapers alone."

"It's not in the newspapers, Danny. Let Denise start cleaning up." Catherine's eyes surveyed the ceilings, drapes, cupboards, all the doors, as she rubbed her fingertips against the rough denim fabric of her jeans.

"Are you getting something, Mom?"

"Yes . . . I am." Catherine closed her eyes, trying to give form and substance to the etheric mist of feeling. "There's a packet in the dark. A closet. No, something smaller. A very dark place. It's tucked away somewhere obscure."

It was Danny's turn to search the room. He moved furniture around, looking for a secret cache, a safe, a hole in the wall behind a picture. Finally locating a screwdriver, Danny set about taking the covers off the light switches, searching for a hidden receptacle in which photographs could have been placed. He dismantled a ceiling light fixture in the front room and was about to try the bedroom when Catherine stopped him.

"No, Danny, the pictures are here--in this room." She walked around the couch, her fingers spread, sweeping her arms through the air like a blind man. "Somewhere small, somewhere dark. About the size of a desk drawer," Catherine paused, trying to make sense of an image in her mind's eye.

Danny began to examine the roll top desk, tugging out drawers, feeling for a hidden catch, a false bottom.

"Hand me that screwdriver, Denise." Catherine knelt before a heater vent and pressed her fingertips against the grillwork. "I need to take this cover off."

Danny claimed the screwdriver, but his fingers trembled so much he could hardly keep the head in the screw slot. With a clatter, the metal grill fell to the floor. Danny reached into the vent and grimaced when he encountered spider webs and other forms of life he didn't care to identify. Nothing. His searching hand probed deeper into the vent. Lying flat on his stomach, Danny reached as far as he could, but the vent took a sudden turn, and he couldn't get his wrist around the bend in the duct. "Damn." Danny sat up and looked around. Without a word, Catherine handed him the coat hanger she'd already stretched into a hook. "Thanks."

Like a fisherman angling his line, Danny probed the vent. Something scraped along the metal tube as soon as he maneuvered the hook around the corner. "There's something in here, I can feel it." With caution and patience, Danny worked the object around the corner, close enough to grasp. When he finally determined his fingers were grasping a large envelope, a ring of bright smiles wreathed his face. "We've got them! I knew he'd do something like this, damn it, I knew it!"

Catherine reached for the dust cloaked envelope, turning it over in her hands several times. "There's more, Danny. Ron hid another packet. He knew Russo's henchmen would search the place--and he took extraordinary precautions."

Putting the envelope aside, Catherine surveyed the room. She began to wander, her hand extended like a dowser in search of water. Eyes glued to the floor, she inched forward, then back again, testing the air, seeking a sensation which registered on an inner plane of consciousness completely foreign to others. "Here." Sweeping her hand up and down the bathroom door, she motioned Danny to bring the screwdriver. "Take the door off its hinges."

Danny knew better than to question Catherine's feelings, but for the life of him, he couldn't figure out what an ordinary door might be hiding. Maybe Ron drilled a hole into the wall behind the hinges. He went to work on the metal screws with vigor. As soon as he had the door off, he laid it against the wall and began to unscrew the hinge plate in the doorjamb. "No, Danny--the door is hollow. Search the edge for a seam. I think there's something inside the door."

With a glance conveying doubt, Danny turned away from the frame. Running his fingers along the side which would have pressed against the doorjamb, he let out an excited yelp. "It's rougher here. Like another kind of wood was inserted in the middle of the raised panel." One sharp rap with the point of the screwdriver was all it took--a thin sheath of paint-coated balsa wood gave way. Danny extracted another envelope filled with micro-tapes--the kind of equipment used by surveillance experts. Ron must have recorded some incriminating conversations during his stake-out of Jake Russo's house.

For the first time since the phone call from the police in Penns Grove, Danny allowed tears to come. They left a searing trail down his sun-browned face, but he made no effort to stop them. He was going to miss Ron Mellon.

Terribly.

Horribly.

Savagely.

He would miss his very good friend.

Catherine sat at Forbes' kitchen table, silently studying the photographs. Danny insisted she stop doing readings until Darla Corey's killer was behind bars. It was far less stressful to remain inside the walls of an exclusive gated community than to argue with her son and the Judge. Although she no longer felt threatened, it proved impossible to calm their fears after two attempts on her life.

With her fingers resting lightly against the picture of Jake Russo in his younger years, Catherine slipped into a light trance--allowing impressions to filter into her conscious mind from a connection with the mobster.

Feelings so strong they descended with the power of a clenched fist hammered at Catherine. Jake Russo was a man who believed in his own worth so completely he scoffed at the moral code by which most people tried to live. He considered himself above the law--with good reason, he owned policemen, generals, senators, even presidents. Whatever Jake Russo wanted, he got--without regard for any consequences.

A sharp stab of pain in her throat conveyed Russo's disease was rapidly advancing through his body. For the first time he was living with something over which he had no control. His rage and frustration boiled like a fast-moving storm. Despite the harm Russo had done to countless others, Catherine felt sorry for him. Pity--remorse and pity welled up from somewhere deep inside; pity because Russo didn't realize he had consigned himself to a thousand painful deaths in future lifetimes; remorse because he would never repent for his actions.

"Danny! Get in here! On the double!" Forbes was so excited he rubbed his glasses hard enough to push the lens out of the plastic frame. "Shit."

"Hey, what's the matter? You're yelling loud enough to wake the dead. It's two o'clock in the morning! Some of us keep regular hours, you know."

"Wait until you get a load of this, buddy! You won't be able to go back to sleep anyway." Forbes snatched the paper from the printer churning out a ream of documentation. "Look!"

Danny took the paper thrust at him with a marked lack of enthusiasm. He scanned what appeared to be an ordinary 1040 tax report. Upon closer inspection, he realized it belonged to Jake Russo. Flipping to the next sheet, he noticed the form was filed in 1964. "So?"

"Look at Russo's deductions." Forbes was grinning like the Cheshire Cat from Alice in Wonderland.

Running his finger down the page until he came to the line item for charitable deductions, Danny glanced back at Forbes. "Where did you get this?"

"Right out of the IRS computer files."

"I'm not going to ask how." Danny felt his temperature begin to rise as adrenaline surged through his veins.

"Thanks, you don't really want to know anyway. If subpoenaed, tax records are admissible in court."

"And we can make financial records for the Sacred Heart Convent a matter of record."

Forbes flopped down in the big leather recliner, swinging his leg over the padded arm. "You know, Danny, it's always the details that snare even the smartest bastard."

"Funny, isn't it?"

Forbes was so pleased with himself he just couldn't control the grin dominating his face. "Now you have a concrete link connecting Russo to the Convent the year Darla Corey, or Janet Barron, was born. Who would have thought Russo would claim the money he gave to the Sacred Heart Convent on his taxes?"

"Maybe it was part of the veneer of respectability he chose to maintain."

"Maybe, and maybe he was just thumbing his nose at the Feds."

"You find anything yet?" Danny rubbed his eyes; they were tired, sore, and aching.

"Nah, you ready to quit?" Sonny was so sick of cross-checking microfiche dates of birth with dates of death he thought he might puke if he looked at one more record.

"I've got to hand it to whoever found the death certificate for Darla Corey. They apparently knew Mercer County, New Jersey, didn't cross reference its vital statistics until recently." Maybe a cup of coffee would provide the energy to continue. Danny slapped Sonny on the back. "Come on. Let's grab a bite to eat." Sonny reached for his dark glasses as they headed for the taco stand which fed hundreds of county and federal employees.

"There don't seem to be any flaws in the paper trail. At eighteen, Darla Corey applied for a driver's license and Social Security card in Nevada. All she needed for either one of them was a registered certificate of live birth, which she could obtain by lying to a bored, underpaid bureaucrat or purchasing a forgery," Danny fumed.

"A decent forgery is pretty easy to come by. With a bribe to a clerk or the right amount of money you can obtain an official document with a raised seal." Sonny stared at Danny as he ordered a tray of nachos swimming in a cheese sauce flavored with a healthy dose of jalapeno.

"How can you eat that stuff?" Even the smell of the fiery peppers made Sonny's stomach boil.

"Pure luck, I guess." Lifting a corn tortilla strip loaded with melted cheese, Danny watched other people waiting for food, his mind beginning to clear after the intake of food and a few deep breaths of fresh air.

Sonny flopped against the metal bench and began to unwrap his plain cheese enchilada with painstaking care. Lifting the edge of the flour tortilla, he doctored it with a thin layer of sour cream--visibly disdaining the spicy sauce supplied by the smiling girl at the counter. After a sip of Coke, he tasted the enchilada tentatively. "Forbes can't match the death certificate with a record of live birth either?"

"No." Danny felt his gray mood turn darker.

"Man, I love it here." Ogling attractive women was one of Sonny's passions and the popular taco stand gave him ample opportunity to indulge in his favorite past-time. Good looking girls seemed to be everywhere-- dressed in brief, casual clothing because of the heat. "What does Catherine say?"

"Funny you should mention that. When I called to check on her this afternoon, she suggested finding someone at the convent who might remember Janet Barron."

"How will that help? I thought Darla, or Janet, didn't keep in contact with anyone back there." The bouncing buns, tanned thighs, flowing hair of every color made Sonny's head spin.

"I have no idea why she suggested it but that's what she felt we needed to do." Traffic was mesmerizing. The sound of tires humming along hot asphalt, the tangy smell of the jalapeno dip, the heat of the day, the whirl of passing cars, all blended like a watercolor wash, forming a soft background for the panorama of thought racing across Danny's mind. "I assumed she meant a child who grew up with Janet Barron, but now I'm not sure that's what Catherine is picking up on."

Danny's words hung in the air, suspended between the two detectives like a visual message both read at the same time. Sonny wadded up the empty wrappers and jammed them into the paper bag so fast it ripped. "Let's go."

"Catherine, this is Rita Brown." Sonny escorted Rita into Forbes' big family room.

"Rita, I'm so glad you could come to dinner. Sonny's told us a lot about you. Could I get you something to drink?"

The smile lighting the other woman's face was so genuine Rita found herself feeling at home in the luxurious atmosphere she would normally find intimidating. "Sure, whatever you've got will be fine."

"Here you are." Handing the circumstance-hardened woman a tall, frosty glass of wine, Catherine glanced at Sonny. "Danny and Forbes are huddling over the computer. Would you like some wine too, Sonny?"

"Sure, Mrs. Armstrong. I guess I'll have to entertain two beautiful women all by myself while those dopes stare at a screen full of weird symbols." Sonny winked lasciviously at Rita and hugged her impulsively. "Besides, Rita and I are hitting it off pretty good, aren't we?"

Despite the impertinence of the remark and the boy's tender age, Rita was flattered. Over the rim of the wine glass her cheeks took on a rosy flush. "Sure--Sonny's always been attracted to older women, especially one his grandmother's age!"

Impulse forced Catherine to reach for a stack of photographs on the table in front of the sofa. "Rita, while we're waiting for dinner to finish cooking, would you mind looking at these pictures?"

Recognition was instant, and it showed in her expression. "It's been a long time since I've thought about Candy."

"Candy?" The wine glass went down on the coffee table with a thud as Sonny reached for the picture in Rita's hand. Danny returned just in time to join the conversation.

"Yeah, Candy something. I don't think I ever heard her last name. She and Russo were quite an item back in the old days. I'm surprised you found a picture with both of them in it. Jake kept the girl under wraps. A real society broad. Last I knew, he'd gotten her pregnant. Russo's wife pitched a fit to the local priest about how it was a sin to commit adultery and have a child out of wedlock. I guess the priest went to Don Scavantoni, Russo's boss back in the early days. Candy disappeared after that, I don't think anybody knew what happened to her for sure."

In the doorway, Danny waited for Rita to finish speaking. "Do you think you'd recognize her now, Rita?"

"Probably not. Time changes everything. Hell, I used to be quite a looker when I was young." She sighed and stared into the bottom of the empty wine glass as though it were a revealing mirror.

In a voice strained with anxiety, Catherine spoke with such a somber air it seemed like she might never smile or laugh again. "This girl went through a lot of changes for Jake Russo."

Recognizing the distant expression in his mother's eyes, Danny moved closer. "Can you explain, Mom?"

204

Catherine concentrated on the ever-changing image of a woman's face. "She might have had plastic surgery to throw Maria Russo off the trail because her tie to Russo was never broken." Catherine's voice trailed away as she tried to sift the rapid profusion of information coming at her from every direction. A map of the United States appeared on the inner screen of her mind. Like a camera lens, her thoughts zoomed in on the states bordering California. "She came out west--to run one of his casinos."

"Mom, that's hardly possible. The mob is a men-only club." Danny couldn't imagine a woman having a hand in running any facet of Russo's syndicate.

"I know, Danny, I know. Only . . . things are not what they seem."

"Hot enough for you, bro?" Sonny wiped the sweat from his forehead as he slammed the unmarked patrol car door shut. Turning the air conditioning vent in his face, he breathed a sigh of relief.

"Summer's almost over. Another month and you'll be moaning about the cold." It was a real pleasure to find something to needle his partner about because Danny was usually on the receiving end of Sonny's well-honed barbs.

"I just don't feel right unless I'm complaining."

"I've known that since we were kids!"

"Did Forbes track down any information on disenchanted priests or nuns?" Drawing his arm back with a jerk, Sunny rubbed the burned spot on his elbow when he encountered a strip of hot metal along the window sill.

"I guess I forgot to show it to you." Danny pointed at the paper pinned to the clipboard on the seat. "I'm afraid it's not very conclusive." The temperature gauge was rising, right along with his personal thermostat. Deciding he'd better head back to the station to let the car cool off, Danny hit the blinker, intending to turn left.

"Holy shit!"

"Burn yourself again?"

"No! Turn the car around!"

The light was green, and traffic was stacking up behind him. "I'm heading back to the station, the car's about to overheat."

"Let it! Head for the Shelter!"

Exasperation filled Danny's voice. "Sonny, look at the temperature gauge. We've got to get back to the station!"

Sonny thrust the sheet of paper between the steering wheel and his irritated partner's face. "See that name?" He pointed to the bottom of the list. "If I'm right, this woman is in Las Vegas!"

"What?" Horns began to blare as Danny continued to block the intersection.

"I'll bet my last tortilla chip this is the woman who helps Sam out at the shelter."

"Hit the lights." Danny spun a one hundred and eighty degree turn in the middle of Main Street and raced toward North Las Vegas, lights whirling and siren screaming.

Danny burst through the shelter doors with Sonny close on his heels. Exploding into Sam Levenkowski's office, the two detectives waved the computer sheet in the Salvation Army manager's face.

"Where's Elena Mendoza? Is she here, Sam?" Sonny shouted, so excited his voice boomed off the walls of the tiny office.

"Settle down, boys, settle down. You'll make my guests think you plan to haul them in! Sure, Elena's here. She's with a gal over in the women's section. A battery case--getting the poor woman cleaned up a bit. Sit down and cool off while I get her."

"Man, if this isn't the same woman, I'm going to be so disappointed I'll need a vacation." Sonny rubbed his hands against his tee-shirt to absorb the sweat which his body seemed to manufacture in buckets.

"I sure hope it's not too good to be true. Catherine says things always turn up when you least expect them." Regardless, Danny kept hope in a tight noose.

Sam returned to his office with a petite woman trailing close behind. Huge, dark eyes seemed strangely out of proportion in the tiny bird- like face. Sad and soulful, as if the woman had seen too much of life's misery to ever be at peace again, she perched on the edge of a folding chair beside Sam's desk, a wary sparrow about to take flight.

"Elena, this is Homicide Detective Danny Armstrong and his partner, Sonny Yi."

"Pleased to meet you." Her voice was melodious, haunting, with an airy, flute-like quality strangers never forgot.

"Miss Mendoza, I'd like to show you a picture and ask you to identify this girl--if you can." Sonny handed the woman the photo of the girl Rita Brown called Candy.

A hiss escaped her lips and wide eyes assumed the glint of a hawk that had just sighted prey. "I haven't seen her for years."

"We're investigating a murder, Miss Mendoza, were you Benedictine nun at the Sacred Heart Convent in New Jersey back in the '80s?" The words came out in one elongated rush of breath, as though Danny were afraid he might not be able to finish the sentence if he stopped.

Sorrow and disappointment dissipated as anger claimed the woman's incredible eyes. She glanced at Sam, who nodded, encouraging her to speak her mind. "That was a long time ago."

"Sister, what can you tell me about the blonde?" Sonny's heart began to bang like a trip hammer.

Glancing in the Korean's direction, she spoke in a forceful voice which belied her size. "I am not a nun anymore. Please don't ever call me *Sister* again."

"I'm sorry--Elena. Like my partner said, you might be able to help us solve a murder." He was trying to be objective, trying not to let his excitement show, but Sonny felt like jumping up and down, like whooping and hollering--he knew--knew with a surety that could not be explained by logic, this lady held the key to Darla Corey's past. "Please, tell us what you know about the woman in the picture."

Elena tried hard to forget, tried to erase the child from her memory, only to have the pain and guilt surface after years of repentance in a place as forsaken as the desert in which the Savior had been tempted by the Devil. God was punishing her, not allowing her to forget her sin. Maybe God would forgive her if she told the detectives what she knew; maybe it was her only chance for salvation. "It's an ugly story and I'm ashamed of the part I played in it." Bowing her head to hide the anguish which refused to remain bottled up any longer, Elena Mendoza fought for composure. Remorse was still overpowering--after all these years.

Sam handed the woman a box of tissues, a lump rising in his

throat. He sensed her acute vulnerability from the moment she walked in the door and applied for a job. Poor, sad, creature. Maybe confession would be good for her soul.

"A man, a very wealthy man, gave our convent a great deal of money. He brought a pregnant girl to Reverend Mother and told her when the time came she was to be told the baby died at birth. Mr. Jones thought the girl would have an easier time starting over if she did not feel guilty about giving the child up for adoption, or so Mother Angelica told us. The convent was never the same after the birth of the little girl."

He couldn't help himself, Sonny was compelled to interrupt. "Do you remember the child's name, Elena?"

"Clearly. She was at the convent for many years. Her name was Janet, Janet Barron."

Danny felt like a deep-sea diver who rose to the surface too fast. It took all the emotional restraint at his disposal to keep his expression neutral, his demeanor calm--allowing the woman to continue at her own pace, in her own fashion.

Clearing her throat, Elena went on, halting, struggling against the memory. "Mr. Jones was generous. We never worried about money after the baby was born. The convent was even able to expand its facilities. When Janet was about four, Mr. Jones started taking her with him one Sunday every month. When they returned, his limousine was filled with presents Janet shared with all the other children. It was perpetual Christmas. Most of our children were abused, abandoned, poverty stricken--so Mr. Jones' visits were looked forward to with great anticipation."

Guilt pressed on Elena's chest with the weight of a blacksmith's anvil. Her chin began to quiver, and she had to stop talking, she needed time to get a grip on her emotions. "Janet was such a wonderful little girl. So beautiful, curly blond hair, great blue eyes. You see, she knew she was the reason for Mr. Jones' visits to the orphanage. Even at such a tender age she realized how unhappy it would make the other children if he never came again."

The torture in the child's eyes sprang up to haunt Elena even though she'd tried everything to forget. "I brought Reverend Mother's attention to how withdrawn Janet was after every trip with Mr. Jones. Mother brushed it off, saying the girl was tired after all the shopping. I tried, I really tried, but Mother wouldn't listen."

Sam prodded softly, encouraging the woman to continue. "Why did you leave the convent, Elena? That must have been a difficult choice."

"When Janet was about ten, I found her in the chapel, sobbing over her rosary beads. After pleading with her to tell me what was wrong, she finally confessed she was sinning with Mr. Jones. Janet thought she was going to burn in eternal hell, but she felt responsible for the welfare of the nuns and all the other children. Mr. Jones told her he would quit giving money to Reverend Mother and buying presents for all the children if she didn't accompany him. Imagine! At ten, the child had already taken on the role of a martyr! I went to Mother Angelica again. I demanded she have Janet examined and confront Mr. Jones."

Elena couldn't continue. It was like opening the door to a room that had been shut and locked for many years, only to find nothing had changed, everything was exactly the way you left it. Ugly and brutal and painful. A beseeching glance flitted to the face of each man in the small office. "I couldn't stand it any longer. I had to leave the convent. We were not doing God's work anymore."

Pushing away from his desk, Sam offered consolation with a tender pat on Elena's shoulder. "I think we could all use a break. Why don't I get us a cup of coffee? Hey, maybe I'll even bring back some of the cheesecake the fellows at the Wynn sent over." Sam beckoned to Danny and Sonny to follow him. "Guys, I could use some help."

Sonny attacked the dessert with a big knife, hacking away the slices like he wished they were Jake Russo's balls. "Jesus H. Christ! A child molester--the bastard should be shot! No wonder Darla Corey tried to obliterate everything about her past. Who the hell would blame her?"

"Nothin' I hate worse." Sam stared at the coffee cups with dismay. It was a story he'd heard a million times--child abuse was at the root of what landed over half the troubled people in his shelter.

"Russo made the natural mother think the kid died, then used the child for his own twisted amusement. I thought I'd heard it all." Danny spoke with an anger in his voice that surprised him. His anger was as hard as steel and twice as cold as ice. Until now he never realized he had the capacity for blind rage. But it was a controlled, quiet rage--profound and frightening. "I'm going to nail that bastard if it's the last thing I ever do."

Twilight painted the mountains in hues of orchid melting into purple at the bottom of deep ravines. Swimming pool lights were on, casting pale circles of color along its gently rippling water surface. Danny swam twenty laps, enough to relieve some stress. Winded, he paddled to the shallow end and pulled himself up on the steps. Wiping water from his eyes, he leaned against the deck. A breeze wafted down from the mountains, cooling searing temperatures.

"A penny for your thoughts, Detective Armstrong."

Danny looked up into Elaine's soft brown eyes. She handed him a glass of wine.

"You look like you need to relax."

"That obvious?"

"A blind man might not notice, but he could probably sense your troubles a block away." Slipping off her sandals and terry cloth robe, Elaine sat on the steps beside him. She sipped her wine thoughtfully. "Feel like talking about the case? I'm trustworthy."

"That's about the only thing I have faith in anymore." Danny reached for her hand and brought it to his lips. "The day I lose my faith in you is the day I'll pack it in."

"Then you're assured of a long life, Detective." Her fingers lingered against his cheek and the trail of warmth made him feel better than he had in days. "There's a merry-go-round spinning in my head, and I can't seem to grab the brass ring."

"Tell me about it. Maybe you'll come to some new conclusion." Elaine inched closer, lifting water in the palm of her hand, allowing the trail of moisture to run down his back.

"Suppose Darla Corey *was* the daughter of the woman in the picture. And let's further suppose she was sexually molested as a child by Jake Russo. Sister Angelica said Russo sent the woman out west after the baby was born. And--she also said Darla decided to attend a university in the west. Suppose they both came to Nevada? Could they have known about each other? Was Darla trying to find her birth mother?"

"That's not uncommon among children given up for adoption. But one thing has always bothered me about this case." A frown creased her tanned forehead.

"What's that?" For someone with no police training, Elaine had a

210

knack for slicing to the heart of matters Danny was learning to respect.

"According to Forbes, it would take some pretty sophisticated knowledge to create a new identity. You know, like how to obtain the birth certificate of a dead child which couldn't be cross-checked. Darla was only eighteen when she left the convent and I can't imagine anyone that young, who lived her entire life in such a sheltered environment, figuring out what it would take to assume a new identity. I've got a feeling it was done for her."

Danny's admiration for Elaine grew by leaps and bounds. "Someone who was accustomed to trafficking in illegal documents. Someone like Jake Russo?"

"Suppose it was?" Elaine studied the wine glass, a rainbow of color refracted back lights from the pool. "Why would Russo go to the trouble of creating a new identity for a girl he was molesting?"

New thoughts chugged through his brain like the connected cars in a freight train. "Unless he had a specific reason for doing so. I have a hunch Darla was also sexually intimate with Jordan Gray and Robby Russo. Quite possibly, even Senator Hastings. The senator doesn't strike me as the philanthropic type, regardless of his noble rhetoric about helping a worthy student."

"Do you think it's possible Russo was using Darla to gather information?" Elaine stood up, water dripping from her swimming suit, trickling down shapely thighs to her slender ankles. "Want more wine?"

"Thanks," he handed her the empty glass without thinking about it. Danny watched Elaine saunter to the patio table, fill their glasses and return the bottle to the ice bucket, her movements fluid and graceful. Although it was difficult to keep his mind on the problem at hand, he searched for a common thread between the three men. "Maybe it was all just a game to Russo."

Elaine returned to the pool and handed Danny his wine glass. Goose flesh dimpled her arms; the temperature was dropping as the desert cooled, but she refused to suggest going inside for fear it would ruin the fragile connecting links in Danny's train of thought. "What kind of a game?"

"Men like Russo love power more than anything. To them, it's the ultimate turn on . . . and Russo is master manipulator. But his empire is firmly in place, and he doesn't need money. What purpose could Darla have served?"

Reaching for the terry cloth robe at the pool's edge, Elaine drew it across her shoulders. "What would a man like that do for enjoyment? I mean, he has everything a person could possibly want from life. What would he do for fun?"

Perplexed, Danny turned to study the girl whose porcelain skin disguised a quick and clever mind. "I don't follow your line of reasoning."

"Well, I'm certainly no expert in psychology . . ."

Her smile was so sincere, so sweet, it made Danny's breath catch half- way up his throat.

"Maybe he was just interested in achieving something impossible, for the hell of it . . . to see if it could be done."

"Like what?"

"I don't know. Manipulate government officials? Influence people through the media? Look how cleverly President Roosevelt drew us into World War II. Or Lyndon Johnson, for God's sake. He had everyone believing the Gulf of Tonkin incident justified going to war with Viet Nam!"

"That could happen, certainly. But is power his primary motivation?" Danny stared into his glass as he pondered the question.

Catherine's words came rolling through his memory like a bowling ball in search of a pin. *"Nothing is what it seems."* His mother was right, if he was going to solve this case he had to look beyond the facade of politics, beyond the obvious, through a tangled web of deceit. The plaintive howl of a lone coyote seemed to pick up the thread of Danny's thoughts and its eerie, yipping bark represented everything he loved about the desert.

Harsh.

Desolate.

Unforgiving.

Danny's whisper was so soft it was as though he only thought the words . . . *"Nothing is what it seems."*

Placing padded mitts on top of the stove, Catherine closed the oven door. The chicken enchiladas would take about an hour to finish cooking. She had already grated the cheese, the chili peppers were roasted and peeled, so there was virtually nothing left to do. With a sigh, she flopped onto the couch and reached for the channel changer.

National news was too dismal to watch, it left her feeling moody and upset for days. Jerry Springer was discussing the worst of society's problems, so she flipped to another channel. The screen filled with a panoramic vista. Rolling hills stretched across the horizon. In the background shaggy, hump-backed Bison munched on tufts of grass sprouting from the soil. Interest peaked, Catherine turned up the volume.

A reporter dressed in a suit and tie looked out of place in a setting clustered with tepees, campfires, animal hides drying on willow frames, and warm-skinned children running about in leather breeches. Turning the microphone toward a man wearing an elaborate headdress with dangling feathers and ornate beadwork, the reporter interviewed a Paiute chief.

The television camera panned across the village as the chief explained how ecological balance was restored in this protected reserve. To the curious reporter, the middle-aged Native American explained the inner workings of the encampment. Women taught young girls how to grind corn between stones. They scraped deer, buffalo, and elk hides, preparing them for a variety of uses. Men schooled boys in the art of the hunt, teaching them the proper use of bows and arrows, tomahawks, and spears. Great whoops filled the air as young men learned to ride stout Indian ponies, guiding them with their knee pressure. Baskets woven from grasses, clothing made from skins tanned to supple softness, cradle boards, beaded head bands, bracelets, and beautiful moccasins could not be produced fast enough to satisfy the tourist demand for authentic souvenirs.

Turning back to the camera, the reporter faced an unseen audience. With the microphone pressed against his chin to overcome the hollow sound created by the wind as it whistled across the camp, he withdrew a notebook from his jacket pocket. "I'd like to read the speech Chief Seattle made just before soldiers forced his people onto a reservation far from their natural hunting grounds, back in 1851. In part, the Chief admonished the white man. . . .'*The President in Washington sends word that he wishes to buy our land. But how can you buy or sell the sky? The land? The idea was strange to us. If we do not own the freshness of the air and the sparkle of the water, how can you buy them?*

'*Every part of this earth is sacred to my people. Every shining pine needle, every sandy shore, every mist in the dark woods, every meadow, every humming insect. All are holy in the memory and experience of my people.*

'The rivers are our brothers. They quench our thirst. They carry our canoes and supply us with food for our children. So, you must give to the rivers the kindness you would give any brother.

'If we sell you our land, remember that the air is precious to us, that the air shares its spirit with all the life it supports. The wind that gave our grandfather his first breath also receives his last sigh.

'Will you teach **your** *children what we have taught* **our** *children? That the earth is our mother? What befalls the earth befalls all the sons of the earth.*

'This we know: The earth does not belong to man, man belongs to the earth. All things are connected like the blood that unites us all. Man did not weave the web of life, he is merely a strand in it. Whatever he does to the web, he does to himself.

'When the last Red Man has vanished with his wilderness and his memory is only the shadow of a cloud moving across the prairie, will these shores and forests still be here? Will there be any of the spirit of my people left?

'We love this earth as a newborn loves its mother's heartbeat. So, if we sell you our land, love it as we have loved it. Care for it as we have cared for it. Hold in your mind the memory of the land as it is when you receive it. Preserve the land for all children, and love it, as God loves us all'."

Harold scuffed at a clump of grass with the toe of his shoe. The sheaf of notes rattled in the wind. When he returned his gaze to the camera, his tone was filled with sorrow. "Nearly one hundred and fifty years ago, Chief Seattle spoke with great vision. The white man, the barbaric invader, lived up to his prophecy. We plundered the land and squandered its resources. What surprises me is the Chief's words survived for they stand as a testament to our folly. This is Harold Kennedy, reporting from a Paiute Indian village in Ely, Nevada."

Catherine stared at the television set for a long, long time. The picture dissolved into an image of molten iron, white hot, burning, crusted with fiery ingots of scarlet. Shapes, skeletal shapes of men with no flesh, leered from the screen. The gaping bones of denuded skulls flashed in and out of the frothing magma. Bones turned to ash, reduced to powder before her eyes. Ash was swallowed by the vortex--swirling, whirling, spinning in a hypnotic circle.

Finally, the vision melted. Harold Kennedy's smiling face returned to the screen. He turned his back to the camera and was watching the sun go down. A blazing, blood-red sun frosted the shaggy hides of the buffalo with a crust of sparkling gold. The creek running through the village was spangled like a golden jewel. A veil of amber hung in the air, softening the features of the women, gilding the children with an etheric halo.

A voice whispered in her ear.

Nothing is what it seems.

Kevin Cox sat staring out the big sliding glass door toward the setting sun, slowly lowering behind Mt. Charleston. The beer can wobbled when he sat it down, spilling some of the liquid on a laminated, wood-like coffee table. He was about twenty minutes past sober and knew it. Hell, he planned to get so drunk he *couldn't* remember the incident at the Test Site. He was surprised they let him go, but after all, they owned him, didn't they? They owned him lock, stock and barrel.

Or so they thought. Kevin hated the tight-assed generals who predicted the next world war was near; the sons-of-bitches with 'pass the beer, screw the broads and salute the good old American flag mentality'; the bastards who reduced everything to black and white. Good here. Bad there. An invisible wall separating the desirable from undesirable. And all the snotty-nosed upper crust goody-goodies who kept him from entering the ranks of the elite bastards running the military.

And why? Why? Because he crossed an imaginary boundary somewhere early on in his career? Well, he wasn't sure he knew right from wrong, good from bad, righteousness from evil anymore. It all seemed to depend on your point of view. To the Vietnamese, the French, and Americans were the Devil incarnate. They just wanted to be left alone, to run their country as they saw fit--rather than kowtow to arrogant bastards with round eyes and yellow hair, who didn't understand the Oriental culture.

Kevin missed the beer when he reached for it, spilling more than half the contents on the table before he could upend the shiny silver container. He hadn't been this God damned drunk for ages. But then, he'd never had to confront the fact he was already a dead man, just waiting for the flesh to rot from his bones.

Stumbling into the bedroom, Kevin struggled to withdraw a sturdy wooden box, the kind of box rounds of ammunition were shipped in, from beneath the bed. He withdrew his Koch and Heckler and finally managed to shove a loaded clip up the butt; then he staggered back into the front room of the shabby apartment on Karen, a block off Paradise Road! He wasn't going to wait around, to die in the throes of agony as cancer conquered his body inch by inch, like Patton's Fifth Army took back Europe.

No, by God! He'd live life on his own terms; he wasn't about to die a victim! But now--all was lost. It was time to admit defeat. Time to cut his losses. Kevin put the gun barrel in his mouth and put his finger on the trigger.

Outside, smoky-red light seeped through the window, for day was being fast swallowed by nightfall. High, thin clouds strafed the sky, painted in every hue from scarlet to indigo. As the sun rolled down the western sky, the desert assumed a hush demanded by the heat. Nothing moved, less movement meant less energy expended, and less energy expended meant moisture was conserved. And moisture was salvation in the desert. In the lengthening shadows, in the last orange and purple light of day, Kevin let out a thin, bird-like cry, full of dread and anguish. The sound was eerie, chilling; he came face to face with the invisible boundary which separated man from animal. Suddenly, he knew what was right and what was wrong.

A few greed-filled men were going to send the entire world down the stinking toilet. He yanked the gun barrel from his mouth and laid the Koch and Heckler on the table. The sunset was magnificent. It always was in the desert. Dust particles in the air had a sorceress' way of bending light, breaking down the spectrum into colors so spectacular they couldn't be duplicated by mortals.

Kevin burst from the cheap Naugahyde recliner in which he had intended to end his life. The world wasn't going to end if he could fucking help it!

CHAPTER ELEVEN

Spiny Cypress trees bordering the cemetery were preternaturally still. Trees stood motionless under a low sky of dust-choked clouds. To Danny, it seemed as if the air turned colder than was possible on a sizzling summer day. Evergreens began to sway, and there was something ominous about the way single fingered trees scratched at the sky. An oily nausea rippled through Danny's stomach, as he stood over Darla Corey's grave, staring at a flat square of marble inscribed with a single word, "Glitter". Glitter. A beautiful word. A fitting description for such an effervescent woman. But . . . all that glitters is not gold. Catherine and Broken Blue Feather were right, *nothing was what it seemed.*

He wasn't really looking at the headstone, nor its inscription, instead, he peered into a dark, bleak interior of his own--filled with the importance of his responsibility to stand watch over others. Those who were helpless against those who held power in their hands. Innocent victims of poverty, government, indifference. Those too weak to defend themselves. Darla Corey gave her life to protect the innocent from the menace of nuclear waste in the backyard of every man, woman, and child in not only Nevada, but the rest of America too.

Danny knew Jared Pierce was a scapegoat. Although he set the blaze, Pierce had accomplices who were just as guilty as far as Danny was concerned. Pierce served the same purpose as a cheap Bic lighter-- something you used and threw away. A disposable pawn. The poor, sick bastard. Too much destructive potential locked inside a befuddled brain. A brain, clouded by the effects of Agent Orange, was manipulated by the real perpetrators of Glitter's death: Jake Russo, Robbie Russo, Senator Mathias Hastings, and Jordan Grey. It would be easy to close the case; easy to crucify Jared Pierce. He even had a motive, Pierce was in love with the gorgeous blonde. Darla's summer internship at the Nevada Queen brought their lives together--and put them on a collision course with destruction. She was the darling university student. Beautiful, brainy, a personal protégé of Senator Mathias Hastings--far beyond his reach. Unrequited love sent

217

more than one man to the gas chamber. Every citizen in Las Vegas would be happy to drive the nails into Jared Pierce's flesh. But what about the true murderers? The greedy men who used public office for personal gain. Robber barons running Nevada's casinos—taking advantage of people anxious to throw money on the tables or down the slots in hopes of scoring a big win. Mob warlords, who sent men to their death, then went home to sleep at night, satisfied results justified their bloody, vainglorious means. And what about the guy who brought her to the Rainman suite in the first place? A man who filled her with enough alcohol to make her pass out, then either administered a nearly lethal dose of cocaine or let someone else into the suite to do his dirty work. For Danny, his money was on Robbie Russo. He would have the connections to pump her full of junk until she was unconscious. As far as Danny was concerned, Mathias Hastings was just as guilty as Jared Pierce. A good cop's sixth sense demanded Hastings was in the Rainman suite for a sexual assignation with the showgirl. Danny *knew* it but didn't know if he could *prove* it enough to hold up in court. Hastings was a politically powerful man who could come up with any number of concrete alibis from a dozen upstanding Las Vegas citizens--all willing to lie, cheat and steal to protect the senior Senator from Nevada.

A rising wind huffed at his back. Its hot breath sharpened his rage. He didn't know why all of this was happening--yet he did. On a deep subconscious level, he *did* know what was happening, what strange force was swiftly destroying the world around him, and he knew if he didn't act now-- more innocent people would perish.

His cell phone split the graveyard hush with a shrill, abrasive blast. Danny grabbed it, silencing the sound reverberating through the cemetery like a harlot's laughter defiling the stillness of a chapel. In a voice thickened by anger, he barked into the phone, "Armstrong!"

Danny listened hard, pressing the phone against his ear as if pressure alone had the power to transmute evil. Like sand pouring through a cosmic tunnel, Danny knew time just ran out.

Danny stormed through the garage door, which led to the family room of Forbes' spacious home. His mother sat on the couch next to a woman he didn't recognize. Sonny was on the floor sharing cookies with her dog and Forbes perched on the barstool, overseeing the gathering like a patriarch.

"Hi." Forbes handed Danny a can of beer as he rushed past. His friend was going to want to consume a quart by the end of the evening.

"Mom, I can't believe you left the house!"

Her son's tone was so acerbic Catherine blanched. "There was no other way, Danny."

His glance swung to the stranger--probing, then turned back to his mother, accusing and angry. "That's *no* excuse."

"Kristin, this is my son--Detective Danny Armstrong." Hoping to defuse some of his hostility, Catherine kept her voice neutral. "Danny, this is Kristin Hastings--the fifth person in the pentagram."

Danny felt as though he just entered a fun house hall of mirrors at a cheap, road-weary carnival. Everything was distorted. Why was his mother sitting there so calmly? If this woman *was* the object of their desperate search, why was she sipping wine like a welcome dinner guest? And damn it, why was Sonny feeding the monstrous dog like it was any other Saturday night? The group was so casual they might as well have rented a movie! Where the hell was the popcorn?

"Honey, come sit down. I can explain everything." Catherine patted the couch cushion like she'd done a million times throughout her son's childhood.

"You're gonna love this." Sonny released the cookie a split second before the Rott's jaws snapped shut.

With deliberate calm and patience, Catherine explained why she had to rescue Kristin before Russo's henchmen got to her here in Las Vegas. She touched the other woman's arm repeatedly, conveying compassion, understanding and the loyalty which came from sharing emotions unique to women. "Kristin, why don't you tell Danny your story from the beginning."

Kristin realized Catherine was trying to sooth her. And Kristin knew she *needed* to be soothed, she was going to require a lot of soothing in the months to come. If there was any future ahead for all of them. "I met Jake Russo when I was seventeen years old. My family sent me back east to college--to absorb some culture and acquire refinement. Jake Russo was one of my father's business associates and my Dad asked him to look after me. He was the most exciting man I'd ever met."

Taking a sip of wine, Kristin wrestled with the past. She was being forced to relive the pain and humiliation she'd been running away from for almost thirty years. "It took me about a week to fall head over heels in love with such a sophisticated, cosmopolitan man. When you grow up in a little jerkwater town like Reno and a smooth-talking guy takes you to an opera, swanky dinners at exclusive night clubs, opening night on Broadway--well, it was pretty overwhelming because I was so young and inexperienced."

She moved through the door of memory, recalling her youth like a poignant movie. "Being a naïve kid, I was certain when Jake found out I was pregnant he would divorce his wife and marry me. When he locked me up in a cottage on the Jersey shore I was so shocked I couldn't think of anything to do. I was guarded day and night throughout my pregnancy. Jake said it would be better to give the baby up for adoption, so it could live a decent life. Looking back, I don't think it ever occurred to him to divorce Maria. He always had a million reasons for his actions. No matter what argument I raised he could always best me with his unique brand of logic. The nuns at Sacred Heart were very sympathetic when the baby died . . ."

Her voice trailed away. The shock of discovering her daughter lived for twenty-eight years brought anguish to her eyes. Grief overwhelmed her because she never knew her; never celebrated a birthday or Christmas; never helped with homework or nursed her through measles. The experience of motherhood was whisked away before it had a chance to blossom. Kristin felt her heart swell in her breast; it stuttered, then found a new and faster beat as the penultimate moment, when she confronted how Jake Russo used her, came to claim her.

"Jake told my Dad I had a mind like a steel trap and recommended I take over the family business because Mathias was being groomed for politics by the mob. My father said we were like sunlight and shadow. Mathias thrived in the limelight . . . he always knew the right thing to say, a born politician. Me, on the other hand, I was better at moving behind the scenes. I seemed to have a natural ability to organize and plan--to carry things out. Jake and I remained lovers over the years. Lord," she put her hand over her eyes, a shield against the pain, suffering, and heartache which seemed to stake a permanent claim on her psyche, "How could I have been so blind for *thirty* years?"

Now it was Danny's turn to offer comfort to a woman whose grief was as raw as freshly butchered beef. "Kristin, Jake Russo is a master of manipulation. He controls people at every level--presidents, senators, policemen, bankers, lawyers. You were no exception—and you loved him."

Forbes considered himself the epitome of logic. Emotion was something he held at arm's length while he analyzed, searched for solutions, planned outcomes. In his world, "A" always preceded "B" and "C" *always* came after "B". The woman's anguish made him uncomfortable because there was no way to dispense with her turbulent feelings--to consign them to a computer file, where they could be abandoned and forgotten, or at the very least analyzed later. He couldn't think of anything to say.

Catherine signed deeply. "That's probably not much comfort to Kristin right now, Danny."

Accepting a fresh supply of tissues from Catherine, Kristin blew her nose, dabbed at her eyes, and plumbed the depths of her emotional reserve. "Danny, I know the information I'm about to give you is self-incriminating, but I don't care anymore! I'll sign anything you want, make any kind of statement--I just want to hang the bastard out to dry before he dies. I want him to know I'm the one responsible for blasting his world apart."

"I'll worry about that later, Kristin, right now I want to hear the rest of your story." Danny felt the spark of hope for the first time in many days. Maybe there was a way to ring the curtain down on Russo's operation after all.

"I parlayed my father's small Carson street joint into several casinos spread across Northern Nevada. I used the mob's money to expand. They were quick to seize upon an opportunity to launder money through the Nevada Queen and all its satellite operations. Danny, I can provide you with a list of assemblymen, congressmen and senators who receive money directly, or indirectly, from Jake Russo--up to and including my brother. I'll even tell you how we subverted the slot machine computer system to skim millions of dollars a year off the drop. The Gaming Control Board will be forced to shut down my family's casinos."

Forbes almost fell off the bar stool. He considered his program infallible. "That's impossible!"

"Forbes, nothing is impossible. One of my own computer mavens discovered a way to reconfigure the number of handle pulls. The program changes manipulated information on how many coins entered the machine. I'm not saying it didn't take some doing, especially recalibrating the scales in the coin room just hours before a GCB agent appeared, but I had an excellent network of co-conspirators. Forbes, anything built by a human being can be taken apart by another one. We were looking forward to the day your pit program came out on the market."

Forbes went pale. All the warming color was forced from the surface of his skin as blood rushed to his brain--making him feel so dizzy he thought he might faint. "No one knows anything about that program."

"I knew about every move you made, Forbes. None of my computer boys were half as creative as you, so I had to wait for you to complete the program. I had plans in place to modify the pit system to suit my own ends." Kristin's face was puffy and red, her eyes ringed with dark circles; her lips suddenly peeled back in a feral snarl, every feature contorted with animal rage, "I know all the connections, all the drops, all the kingpins in the chain. I can blow Jake's entire organization to smithereens, and I don't give a damn if I have to die to do it."

Danny related his conversation with Kevin Cox--how the security guard sought Danny out--hoping to find a way to reveal the government's activities to unsuspecting residents of Nevada. "I've been wracking my brain for a way to bring this out in the open but Russo's henchmen in the legislature and reporters on his payroll would soon make me the laughingstock of Las Vegas if I said plutonium was being stored in the tunnels beneath Yucca Mountain at the Test Site. We've got to find a method so compelling, so believable, the public will be up in arms before a cover up can be put in place."

Sonny couldn't keep dismay from his voice. "This may seem like small potatoes, especially when we've been talking about something on the same magnitude as Chernobyl. To say nothing of mob activities at the highest level of government--but what's going to happen to Jared Pierce? I feel sorry for the guy--does he have to be a sacrificial lamb? Something else has been bothering me for a long time too. I never figured out why Russo needed to have Darla eliminated."

"I know." Danny was breathing hard. He sucked air through clenched teeth with a cold, hissing sound. "The chairman of UNLV's hotel administration school, Professor Jenkins, said Darla was one of the brightest students he'd ever run across. She was on intimate terms with all the major players in Russo's operation. I think she pieced something together something Russo never expected her to discover. I figure she was going to topple Russo's house of cards and he had her killed--plain and simple."

A new fit of weeping overtook Kristin at the mention of her daughter's death. To have passed through life so quickly, to end so violently, and to never have had a chance to touch her only child served to strengthen her determination to ruin Jake Russo.

Sonny stood to stretch, muscles in the back of his legs were beginning to cramp. Damascus jumped up with him, thinking his newfound friend was headed to the kitchen for more cookies. Sonny scrambled to keep his footing as the dog sprinted between his legs, so he was the first to arrive at the cookie jar. "Damascus, settle down." The dog looked disappointed as Sonny headed for the kitchen, calling back over his shoulder, "What do you think she discovered that got her killed?"

Only Kristin's eyes were visible above the wilted tissue she held against her nose. A fevered expression in the deep blue eyes reflected suffering and hate--and it ignited Catherine's anxiety. Silence seeped across the room like a bilious fog as the boys became aware of the interplay of emotion passing between two women. Catherine nodded her head, encouraging her to speak. When Kristin finally found the words, her voice was thin, raspy, chilling. The cadence of her question was that of a madman, like a crack addict in search of a fix. "Jake also had my daughter sleeping with my brother?"

"I'm afraid so." Danny felt rotten, utterly slimy, and rotten. Nothing in his psychological make-up prepared him to be the deliverer of such soul-searing news.

"Jake must have gotten a real kick out of putting my daughter under my nose for several summers. He probably did it just to see if I'd have the good sense to recognize her." Reaching for the picture of Darla Corey in a showgirl's costume, Kristin's voice broke, "I can't believe I never noticed the resemblance."

"Kristin," Catherine thought the sympathy she felt for the other woman was going to tear her own heart in two, "you thought your baby was dead. You accepted her death as an absolute fact. I don't think you would have seen the resemblance if Darla was your complete twin--your conscious mind wouldn't allow it. We are all blind to what *we don't want to see*."

When Kristin spoke again, her words came in fragments between sobs. "No matter what it takes, I'm going to put that bastard through hell."

Insensitiveness to the suffering of others was part of Forbes' character. His friends didn't fault him, it was just the way he was. When he spoke, it sounded as though he were caught up in an exciting movie and he was anxious to know how it turned out. "Okay, Detective Armstrong, what was Darla into?"

Danny sensed Kristin's need to turn inward, she would require months to come to terms with emotions storming the walls of her psychological defenses. "Several things about Darla never made any sense to me."

Sonny's curiosity ignited. Normally, he and Danny spent hours batting the details of a case around--but his friend had been unusually reticent about discussing the showgirl's death. "Like what? I've read the reports. Nothing seemed out of order."

"Remember when we checked out her house?"

"Yeah, we didn't find anything significant."

"You're right. It wasn't what we found--it was what we *didn't find* that kept nagging at me." Danny reached for his briefcase which was always at the end of the island bar in the kitchen, much to Forbes' distress. Opening the scuffed leather case, Danny rummaged through the contents for several minutes. "Remember all the designer clothing in Darla's closet?"

"Sure do, big name stuff. Saks and Neiman-Marcus kind of labels. Why?" For the life of him, Sonny couldn't figure out where Danny was going.

"But not a single fur coat, remember?"

"Yeah--well, this *is* the desert. Most women don't wear furs here."

"You could write it off like that--but look at these." Danny handed Sonny some canceled checks.

Rifling through them, Sonny didn't make any connections, so he handed them to Catherine in the hope she might dredge up some information.

"Danny, these are all made out to the Sierra Club." Catherine studied the handwriting, searching the swirls and flourishes for some clue to the girl's inner character.

"The Sierra Club is one of the most militant environmental groups in the country." Danny rubbed his eyes; the trail of logic was so faint he wasn't sure he should grasp it. "I noticed some impressive black and white photographs on Darla's living room wall. She was damn near as good a photographer as Ansel Adams. Darla had a natural ability to capture the wild, primitive aspect of the Nevada landscape. After my talk with Kevin Cox, I decided to take the pictures to a geology professor at UNLV. He identified them as photographs of a remote section of the Test Site--Area 51. Now that we know the Test Site is being used as a storage dump for nuclear fuel, I think Darla pieced together a scenario implicating Russo."

"Darla knew the kind of man she was dealing with." A misty-eyed gaze claimed Catherine as she slid into another dimension while rubbing her fingertips over the signature at the bottom of the check. "She left the pictures behind in the hope the person investigating her murder would realize they were an arrow--pointing the way to what is happening at the Test Site." Catherine shook her head, as though trying to clear away a mental haze. "Danny, I don't understand how Russo could be involved with a nuclear dump."

Kristin knew the signs of Russo's insatiable thirst for power, omens which foretold of his ultimate triumph in any project he undertook, but she had refused to acknowledge his potential for evil. She managed to rationalize his behavior, watering down his actions with the ocean of her love. Suddenly, a restraining bond snapped. Russo's voice slithered through her head, serpent like, deep inside her skull, curling and sliding through her brain as the memory of his lies tortured her. Like a magnetic current, pieces of overheard conversations, random phone calls in the middle of the night, casual remarks, came together with the force of an atomic bomb detonation. Kristin maintained eye contact with Danny. Squaring her shoulders, body language underscored the truth of her statement. "I know exactly what he was doing! Jake was the brains and power behind the Teamsters Union--he has been ever since I met him in the late '60s. He has controlling interest in a major truck line and used to brag about how easy it was to dupe the Department of Commerce. Jake said dealing with them was like shooting fish in a barrel because to a bureaucrat a job is somewhere they go--not something they do, let alone take pride in. I thought he was running guns or drugs across the state line-- maybe I wanted to believe it was only drugs. I'd be willing to bet my life Jake was responsible for transporting plutonium pellets across the country for years."

An avalanche of thunder rumbled down out of the evening sky, the crack which followed shook the house; a flash of lightning burned through the approach of night and blazed across the sliding glass door. Rain suddenly came down in torrents, beating on the window, drumming on the roof, splashing into the swimming pool.

A portent of things to come. Catherine gazed at the chimera of reflected light as another streak of lightning capered across a wide pane of glass. She paid little or no attention to the argument going on around her as Danny and the others tried to decide how to lay waste to Russo's diabolic empire.

Even if Kristin lived to testify against him, barriers protecting Russo from the law were as thick and inviolate as the Great Wall of China. Too many people in important positions owed Jake Russo. He'd done a magnificent job of insulating himself from the law's reach.

Even though rain scoured the desert, scrubbing the area clean as it passed, Danny couldn't rid himself of the stench of corruption. As the storm deteriorated, the element's hostility seemed to underscore his impotence. An interview between Larry King and the Russian writer, Andrei Sakharov, suddenly popped into his head. Danny empathized with the guilt which plagued him as he pleaded for understanding. "I could not stop something I knew was wrong and terrible. I had an awful sense of powerlessness." God, how powerless he felt now--horribly, terribly powerless. It wasn't right for a man like Jake Russo to run roughshod over decent men and women.

Sonny shook his head, despair robbing him of wit and smothering his energy. "Danny, I don't think there's any way around it. Russo is too cunning. Jared Pierce will hang for Darla Corey's murder and Russo will eventually succumb to cancer. But his legacy will go right on churning out an endless cycle of misery and corruption."

Las Vegas was dressed in a thin veneer of culture beneath which something savage--even primal--watched and waited. Catherine knew if the membrane of civilization ruptured and primordial terror burst through, no one would be safe anywhere else in the world. The black, blank glass of the patio door returned her unblinking stare. "No, you're wrong, Danny. There's one way we can stop him."

Harold Kennedy faced into the wind. His voice seemed driven back into his throat before he could give sound to words he'd rehearsed a hundred times. If he turned away his message would be shredded like a piece of paper, scattered meaninglessly across the desolate landscape before anyone had a chance to hear them. He cupped his hand over the foam shrouded head of the microphone as his soundman did one last equipment check before going live in fifteen seconds.

The Paiute village stretched along the horizon in the background. He'd chosen to stand amid a herd of buffalo because the shaggy brutes were once hunted to the brink of extinction to facilitate the genocide of America's native peoples. They represented what human greed can do.

These magnificent animals were butchered for their hides and tongues, their bodies left to rot on the plains they'd roamed for generations. The loss of the buffalo meant the loss of Native American cultures; a travesty which could not, *would not* be repeated.

Signaling with his fingers, the soundman cued Harold it was almost time. Kristin provided a state-of-the-art equipment van, from which technicians would patch in a live feed to an electronically hijacked satellite hovering somewhere in the atmosphere high above the Nevada desert.

A fierce wind howled and raged like it possessed a wild, demonic voice. And for one heart stopping moment, to Harold, it seemed a reminder of the malignant forces conspiring to turn Nevada into a barren wasteland, unfit for habitation. Beginning the final countdown, the soundman cued him they were live.

In that conclusive fraction of a second, an obsessive compulsion seemed to come from somewhere outside him. A motivating urge recharged his sense of dedication and a feeling the hand of God had been pushing him along, that he was guided by a single-minded compulsion to right an incredible wrong. Harold Kennedy squared his shoulders and faced the camera.

Kristin Hastings was a woman who understood technology was a two-edged sword. It could be the salvation of mankind--or the unleasher of an Apocalypse. Technology was impersonal, and it cut both ways. With Forbes' genius, access to unlimited amounts of mob money and the wizardry of modern electronics, she put together a semi-truck trailer full of enough sophisticated equipment to pirate CNN's global telecast from Atlanta.

Interviews with her and Kevin Cox were already videotaped. As Harold Kennedy took to the air to reveal the nuclear holocaust taking place in Nevada internet sites all over the world simultaneously received press releases documenting facts about the toxic spill at the Test Site. Enough evidence to neutralize Russo's organization was being sent around the world with the same blinding speed as the history changing events in Tiananmen Square. Catherine Armstrong was cut from the same cloth as the lone young man who stopped a tank. His courage and determination forced the rest of the world to acknowledge China's heroic student rebellion. Catherine convinced Kristin *change could begin with just one person.*

Behind Catherine stood Kristin and Danny. Behind them, Sonny, Forbes and Elaine, Jeff Cloudwalker and Dr. Worthen. Behind them, residents of Nevada. Behind them, friends and relatives spread across the globe!

Like a stone tossed in a pond, Harold prayed the effect of the television broadcast would ripple outward to save Nevada. Who knew? In time, maybe the rest of the world would find the courage to put a stop to the endless cycle of suffering.

Catherine Armstrong was right.

Nothing was what it seemed.

One person, just one dedicated person, had the power to initiate change.

www.ingramcontent.com/pod-product-compliance
Lightning Source LLC
Chambersburg PA
CBHW060155180626
46813CB00007B/2756